PENGUIN BOOKS

A Family for Christmas

A Family for Christmas

LINDA FINLAY

PENGUIN BOOKS

PENGUIN BOOKS

UK | USA | Canada | Ireland | Australia
India | New Zealand | South Africa

Penguin Books is part of the Penguin Random House group of companies
whose addresses can be found at global.penguinrandomhouse.com.

Published in Penguin Books 2015
001

Copyright © Linda Finlay, 2015

The moral right of the author has been asserted

Set in 13.75/16.25 pt Garamond Mt Std by Palimpsest Book Production Ltd, Falkirk, Stirlingshire
Printed in Great Britain by Clays Ltd, St Ives plc

A CIP catalogue record for this book is available from the British Library

ISBN: 978–1–405–92204–3

www.greenpenguin.co.uk

MIX
Paper from
responsible sources
FSC® C018179

Penguin Random House is committed to a
sustainable future for our business, our readers
and our planet. This book is made from Forest
Stewardship Council® certified paper.

For My Family – I love each
and every one of you

I

There had been no joy this day. It had in fact been the most miserable Christmas she could remember, Eliza thought, shivering beneath her thin cover.

The time had dragged with no cheer, no presents or special meal. Her father had been in a foul mood, and her two younger brothers so fractious it had taken all her energy keeping them out of his way. Even her mother had taken to her bed, saying she felt poorly. If only her two elder sisters had come home for the holiday things might have been better.

At nearly fifteen years old, Eliza was too grown up to be sharing a room with her parents, even with the dividing curtain supposedly affording her privacy, but their moorland cottage was so tiny she had little choice. Drawing up her knees for warmth, she closed her eyes and dreamed of happier times.

Suddenly she was jolted awake by her parents' violent arguing.

'But how could it have happened, woman?' her father roared.

Her mother gave a harsh laugh. 'If you don't know by now, Fred, then I'm not going to be the one to tell you. You've only yourself to blame. Since being on short time at the mine, you've thought of nothing else but your carn . . .'

'It's not my fault the copper's running out,' he cut in. 'If rumours are true, I'll be out of a job come the New Year, and let me tell you this, I'll not be sitting here listening to another blubbering brat bawling its eyes out. Anyhow, we'll probably be out on the streets by then. No job, no pay; no rent money, no home.'

As her mother's sobs filled the room, Eliza's heart turned over but it was her father's next words that turned her already chilled body to ice.

'And as for that good-for-nothing feeble filly through there, she's naught but a burden. Why, she can't even get a job. And as for marriage prospects, let's face it, no decent man will want a wife who's clumsy and looks like a . . .'

'Hush, Fred, she'll hear you,' her mother whispered. But her father was in his stride.

'She puts a drain on our meagre budget and what for? So she can spend her time picking flaming flowers to put in that blooming box of hers.'

'That's not fair, Fred. Eliza helps me with the little uns. Besides, it wasn't her fault she was born frail and with that twisted foot.'

'Pah, cloven hoof, you mean,' he snorted. 'She's a devil child, the curse of our lives. If I had my way . . .'

Hearing the crack of his belt, Eliza cowered further down the straw-filled mattress, her heart beating faster than the pistons on the mine steam train. She hardly dare breathe in case he heard and tore back the curtain, as he had before. The creaking of the old bedstead as he slumped on his mattress signalled the end of their discussion and she let out a sigh of relief. Safe for another night she might be, but she couldn't carry on like this.

As her father's guttural snores filled the room she planned her escape. She knew she couldn't steal away before dawn, for it was true her movements were clumsy and would be certain to wake the household.

With the first streaks of grey stealing through the window, Eliza heard her parents rise. Still bickering, they clattered noisily down the stairs. There was the slamming of the door as her father went out to the privy and the banging of pots as her mother prepared breakfast. Having quickly dressed in her warmest clothes, Eliza gathered together her few remaining garments and carefully wrapped them around the precious box her grandfather had carved for her. She waited until she heard her father stamping his way down the road towards the mine, then, knowing her mother would be busy feeding her brothers, she stole out of the cottage.

The biting wind took her breath away and she almost changed her mind. But with her father's words still ringing in her ears, she snatched up a piece of sacking hanging by the door and threw it round her shoulders, securing it with a knot. Then, with a stick to help her, she headed west, away from the Mole Valley Mine. She hoped there'd be work that day, because all the families for miles around relied on the mine for their survival. Of course, there'd been rumours that the copper seam was running out, but it was still a shock to hear the mine could soon close for good. Now her poor mother was pregnant again. No wonder she'd taken to her bed yesterday; she must have been worried sick. There was no way Eliza could stay and add to her burden, but now she'd made her escape, where should she go?

Drawing the sacking tighter round her, she doggedly picked her way over the frosted grasses of Grampy Ridge. It wasn't really called that, of course but, playing there as children, she and her sisters decided it looked like an old man and the name had stuck. Of course, that was years ago, when her own beloved grandfather had been alive. Oh, Grampy, she thought, if only you were here to guide me and tell me what to do. As the terrain became steeper, she began to stumble and knew if she was to put any real distance between her and the cottage, she needed to head for flatter ground.

Realizing the sounds of the mine had faded into the distance, Eliza leaned on her stick and peered around to get her bearings. A watery sun was bravely breaking the clouds, and far below she could make out a line of hedging, which surely meant there was a lane beyond. With her foot dragging, progress was slow, but finally she reached a stile and laboriously clambered over it. Once in the lane, she slumped against a mile stone while she regained her breath. She idly traced the letters before they registered. It was only four miles to Buckland. Her spirits lifted. Of course! Her sisters, Hester and Izzie, worked at the manor there and would be sure to help her. She continued her journey with renewed vigour and a definite purpose.

Although the ground was flatter now, the track was deeply rutted and strewn with dislodged stones. Hefting her bundle higher onto her shoulder, she picked her way carefully round them, trying to ignore her rumbling stomach. She should have grabbed some breakfast before slipping away, but then her mother would have returned to bed, expecting Eliza to look after the little ones. Recalling the scene from the previous night, she shivered. Of course, she'd known her father had taken against her but when she'd asked her mother why she'd said it was because, having two daughters already, he'd been hoping for a son. Yet, even when her mother had given birth to two boys in later years, Father's feelings towards Eliza hadn't changed. Her mother did her best to stand up for her but she was weak, always backing down when his temper was roused.

Lost in thought, she didn't hear the horse and cart until it pulled up alongside her.

'Need a lift?' a cheery voice called out. She looked up to see a young man grinning at her. Instinctively, she smiled back.

'I'm heading for Buckland Manor.'

'Well, isn't that a coincidence, that's where I'm taking this lot,' he said, nodding to the load piled up behind him. 'Jump up.'

Gratefully, she tossed her bundle onto the seat and began clambering up after it. Seeing her awkward movements, he leaned over to help, but she shot him such a defiant look he busied himself with the reins instead. Patiently he waited until she was settled, then called to the horse to move on.

'You visiting someone, then?' he said, jerking his head towards her bundle.

'My sisters, Hester and Izzie Watts, work at the manor. I'm Eliza,' she added with a smile in case her rebuttal had offended him.

He nodded and grinned back. 'Pleased to make your acquaintance, Eliza. Carrot Top at your service.'

'That's never your real name,' she exclaimed.

Winking, he lifted his cap and tufts of ginger hair sprang to attention. "Fraid so, but you can call me Carrots,' he said. Then his manner became serious.

'You'll not be catching Hester at the manor. Her ladyship's gone to Barnstaple for the festivities and Hester, being her personal maid, has gone with her. Izzie will be there, though, helping in the kitchens.' He turned to look at her. 'She's a bonny maid and I can certainly see the resemblance.'

'Oh, Izzie always had the looks,' Eliza answered, looking down at her feet as she recalled her father's words.

'And she's not the only one, if you don't mind my saying. Mind you, I've seen more meat on a sparrow.' Despite the chill wind, Eliza felt her cheeks grow warm. He must be jesting for, with her hazel eyes and straight brown hair, she was really quite plain. Izzie, on the other hand, had eyes the colour of a summer sky and hair like sun-ripened corn. Sighing, she changed the subject.

'Do you work at the manor?'

'I help out in the grounds, for my sins, although Bert, the head gardener, says I'm more hindrance than help. Of course, my mistaking his prize leeks for weeds didn't help.'

'You never did!' Eliza exclaimed, then saw his lips twitch and knew he was teasing. A bitter gust of wind caught them full in the face and she shivered.

"Tis a right lazy wind today and no mistake,' Carrots said with a shake of his head.

'Pardon?' she asked.

Laughing at her puzzled look, he explained, 'Goes right through you instead of round you.' He reached behind and grabbed a blanket. 'Here, put this over you before you catch your death.'

Gratefully, she draped the warm cover around her shoulders, snuggling into the soft, fleecy material. As the warmth penetrated her chilled body, she stared around at the passing landscape with interest. She'd never been this far west before. Here, where the protective beech hedges neatly lined both sides of the track and the chequered pattern of green fields rolled gently into the distance, was completely different from the harsh, windswept uplands she'd just left.

'Where does this lane lead?' she asked.

'Town of Barnstaple eventually. 'Tis a fair hike but that's where you'd end up. Anyhow, this is where we leave it,' Carrots said, as the horse automatically turned left and slowed by a gatehouse.

Carrots tipped his cap and was waved on through the archway. The driveway beyond was flanked with tall trees which stood proud like sentinels, in front of which wobbly hedges lined the gravelled sweep.

'Why are all those hedges leaning over like that?' Eliza asked. 'They seem at odds with everything else being so tidy.'

He laughed. 'Something to do with his lordship's ancestors, I think. Apparently it denotes a significant happening, though don't ask me what. They just look to me like they've had one too many,' he added with a grin.

Eliza shook her head, then gasped as she caught her first sight of the manor. It was a magnificent pink stone building sporting a castellated roof from which tall chimneys soared skywards. The formal lawns were dotted with ornate little pavilions and she was just thinking how marvellous it would be to work in such a grand place when the cart tilted as it veered left onto a narrower path that led round to the back of the building and she had to hang on to the side of the seat.

'Do you want me to tell Izzie you're here?' Carrots asked, jumping down and helping her from the cart.

Before she could reply a gruff voice shouted, 'There you are, Topper. Get a move on with them supplies, will you?'

'Coming, guv,' Carrots shouted, then turned to Eliza. 'Best do as I'm bid. The servants' entrance is over there.' He pointed to an annexe on the side of the building.

'Thanks for the lift,' she said, taking her bundle and stick, then heading for the door he'd indicated.

'Take care of yourself, Eliza. Tell Izzie I'll see her in the usual place, usual time,' he called after her.

Although she rang the bell nobody answered. As she dithered, wondering what to do, another gust caught her sideways, nearly blowing her off her feet. Tentatively she turned the knob and to her surprise the door opened. Anxious to be out of the gale, she stepped inside and stood looking around. Compared to the cottage, even here in the servants' quarters the furnishings seemed quite grand and she was just admiring the artistically arranged holly and ivy when a strident voice made her jump. Looking up, she saw a stern-faced woman, dressed in black, glaring at her over the polished balustrade.

'Be off with you. We don't want any beggars here.' Eliza looked down at her mud-spattered skirts and worn boots, and grimaced. She should have thought to tidy herself up.

'I'm not a beggar,' she said, ignoring the woman's terse manner. 'I've come to see Izzie, she's . . .'

But the woman was having none of it. 'Out I said and out I meant,' she shouted, pointing to the door Eliza had entered by.

'But . . .'

'Now, or I'll have Bert set the dogs on you,' she snarled, looking so fierce Eliza couldn't help thinking that with a face like that, they surely didn't need to keep dogs. Knowing it would serve no purpose to protest further, she squared her shoulders and retraced her steps.

2

As soon as she was safely outside, Eliza collapsed against the wall, fighting back her tears. What was she to do now? Suddenly a window nearby was flung open, and she was engulfed her in a balloon of steam. Once it had cleared, she saw a jolly-faced woman beckoning. Eliza moved closer.

'Come to see Izzie, did I hear you say?'

Eliza nodded, glancing apprehensively back at the door. She didn't want to get her sister into trouble.

'Don't mind the housekeeper, dearie. She's had her nose put out 'cos her ladyship left her behind. My, you look perishing. Take yourself down to the summerhouse and wait in there.' She indicated the direction. 'Izzie's due a break. I'll send her down. You hungry?' she asked. Then when Eliza nodded again: 'Off you go then and I'll see what I can rustle up.'

The window snapped shut and, feeling more cheerful, Eliza hurried down the path with its neatened borders. The red sandstone outbuilding with its ornate portico was bigger than the family cottage and she couldn't believe how luxuriously furnished it was inside. Thankful to be out of the biting wind she sat on one of the seats, sinking right into the plush crimson cushions, and closed her eyes.

'Eliza, I couldn't believe it when Cook said you were here.'

Eliza started as the door opened and Izzie was blown in on yet another gust. Jumping up, she waited while her sister carefully set a tray down on the wooden table, then threw her arms around her.

'Oh, Izzie, it is good to see you. You're looking well and so smart,' she exclaimed, noticing how grown up her sister looked in her smart pale blue and white pinafore.

'Afraid I can't say the same about you, sis. You always were like a string bean but now you look positively starved. Here, have some of Cook's stew.' She handed Eliza a steaming bowl. It smelled delicious and she tucked in ravenously. Izzie looked on indulgently. 'It's chicken,' she informed her. 'And I helped make it. Well, I chopped up the vegetables, anyway. Cook baked fresh bread this morning, too.'

Whilst Eliza ate, her sister told her about the Christmas party the staff had held, and how Hester was now her ladyship's maid. Then, when Eliza had mopped the last vestiges of gravy with the generous crust that accompanied it, she turned and took her hand.

'What's up, Eliza? Why have you come all this way? There's nothing wrong with Mother, is there?' she asked, her eyes clouding with concern.

Eliza shook her head. 'Mother's expecting again, but she's all right. It's Father . . .'

'He hasn't hurt you, has he?' Izzie asked, perceptive as ever.

'Oh, Izzie, it was terrible. He called me a devil child and said no man would ever want me. The mine's closing, you see, and he said I was a burden on the household budget so I decided to leave.' The words tumbled out in a rush and she took a deep breath. 'Do you think I could come and work here?' she asked.

'I wish you could, but it seems his lordship lost a fortune at the betting tables so they'll not be hiring anyone. Oh, Eliza, you didn't really think you'd get a job here? I mean, your . . .' Izzie's voice tailed off as she stared at Eliza's foot.

'That doesn't stop me working,' Eliza pointed out. 'I already tend the cot . . .'

A bell chiming in the distance interrupted their conversation and Izzie jumped to her feet.

'I hate to leave you, Eliza, but I daren't risk losing my job. You do understand, don't you?' she asked. Swallowing her disappointment, Eliza nodded. Izzie kissed her cheek. 'Go home, Eliza,' she pleaded. 'Father will have calmed down by now; you know how he blows hot and cold. Please?'

Bravely, Eliza forced a smile. Izzie didn't know the half of it, for she'd always been their father's favourite. Sadly she watched as Izzie picked up the tray and hurried back up the path, taking her hopes for the future with her.

Dashing away the tears that were now running freely down her cheeks, Eliza clambered to her feet and prepared to brace the elements once more. She'd only just stepped outside when she heard her sister shout. Her heart soared. Could there be a job for her after all? But as Izzie ran towards her, Eliza noticed she was holding out a shawl.

'Here, take this. It's perishing out here.'

'Thank you,' she whispered, her heart plummeting. 'But won't you be needing it?'

Izzie shook her head. 'I've got a fine fellow to keep me warm,' she giggled, draping the woollen garment around Eliza's shoulders. 'Anyhow, it'll soon be spring and I'll be coming home for Mothering Sunday. You can give it me back then.' A gong sounded from inside the house and, with a quick peck on Eliza's cheek, Izzie disappeared.

Wending her way back along the path the cart had taken, Eliza looked around, disappointed to see no sign of Carrots. She trudged on and, fortified by her stew, made good progress. Even the wind had dropped and before long she reached the lane. Knowing the right turn would take her back towards South Wood and the Mole Valley Mine, she resolutely turned left. Barnstaple was a big town and she'd surely be able to find work there.

Hefting her bundle, Eliza continued her journey, hoping a passing carter would stop and offer her a lift. It had been good to see Izzie but was it so far-fetched to think she could have found her some work at the manor? She was her sister, after all. Her foot began to throb, but thoughts of how intolerable life would be at home if her father lost his job spurred her on. Devil child indeed! How dare he? She was no longer a child and knew no man would want to marry her but she was prepared to work hard, get a job, become independent and show them all.

Thick cloud was building and lowering over the moor. It was growing darker by the minute and as a biting wind cut right through her, she sighed and pulled the shawl tighter round her. More bad weather was on the way. Despite her foot, she quickened her pace. Surely Barnstaple couldn't be far?

Then she heard the approaching sound of hooves and

the rumbling of carriage wheels. Her spirits rose and, hopeful of a lift, she turned and waved. To her horror, instead of slowing, the driver whipped the horses, urging them on faster. Momentarily, Eliza was frozen to the spot. Then reason returned and she threw herself into the ditch as the carriage wheels missed her by inches. Shaken, she lay there gasping for breath as the thundering and rattling receded into the distance. Only when the lane was silent once more did she reach for her stick and scramble back up onto the lane. Bending to retrieve her bundle she saw her skirt and stockings were torn, revealing scraped knees. Although they stung, they weren't bleeding, and apart from being mud-spattered, her sister's shawl hadn't suffered any damage. Brushing herself down as best she could, she continued her journey.

Anger at the driver's behaviour fuelled her steps, but she knew it would be foolish to stay on the highway. Hitching up her skirts, she clambered awkwardly over the next stile and began making her way along the edge of the moor. If she kept to the line of the fence, she would surely be following the lane to Barnstaple, she reasoned. But the ground was uneven, with bushes and boulders impeding her progress. Then the dimpsy light began playing tricks on her orientation and she lost her way. When she'd passed the same gnarled tree with its spreading roots for the third time, she knew she had strayed up onto the moor itself.

Exhaustion and the rougher terrain made her limp more pronounced. Knowing she couldn't walk much further, she peered around, hoping to see the flickering light from a homestead or farm. In every direction the barren landscape brooded under the prospect of bad weather and dark, sinister shapes loomed out of the darkness. Recalling tales she'd heard of people blundering into bogs and being sucked to their deaths, she shivered. Then the clouds parted and she saw one single star shining brightly out of the inky sky. If she used that as a guide, it would surely save her from going round in circles again.

With renewed hope, she trudged on, but had only gone a short way when large white flakes of snow began to fall, quickly covering her hair and the ground before her. The howling wind soon whipped the snow into a blizzard and before long she couldn't tell where sky met ground. There was no way she could continue walking, yet to stay in the open would mean certain death.

She squinted into the darkness and her heart leaped. Surely that was a tumbledown shed? Summoning the last of her energy, she made her way towards it and stumbled inside. Exhausted, she sank down onto soft dry hay, hardly noticing the ponies eyeing her curiously. As if sensing her distress, they moved closer and before long the heat from their bodies began to thaw her icy bones. Their snuffling and shuffling was comforting and she snuggled further into the hay. With the warmth from their breath wafting over her, she was asleep in moments.

Eliza came to with a start, almost blinded by dazzling brightness. The ponies, with their long shaggy coats, stood munching contentedly and through the doorway beyond, all she could see was shimmering whiteness. Struggling to her feet, she stretched her cramped body and pulled the shawl tighter around her. Her stomach growled, reminding her she'd had nothing to eat since noon the previous day. Picking up a mangold from the heap in the corner of the shed, she bit into it and grimaced. A pony lifted his head and whinnied as if he was laughing at her reaction and, despite her hunger, she couldn't help smiling.

'It's all right for you,' she whispered, picking out burrs and gorse from his grubby grey coat and patting his head. 'Well, boy, it's been lovely sharing your shed but I must be making tracks,' she added, more to convince herself than her companions.

Stepping out into the glistening wonderland, she shook her head. Talking to animals indeed! Carefully picking her way across the snow-covered ground, for the first time in her life she was glad for the protection her thick, ugly boots afforded. The sparse vegetation was bent away from the wind, rimed with frost and capped with snow. It looked so pretty, and despite the cold air that almost took her breath away, she felt her spirits lifting. If she kept going in the same direction, she'd surely come to a farm or dwelling before long.

She plodded on but as the terrain rose higher the drifts became deeper impeding her progress. All she could see was an endless expanse of white as sky merged with ground. The crunch of her footsteps was accompanied by the lone call of the stormcock, the only bird brave enough to sing in this wild weather.

Then the singing stopped, the sky darkened and out of the east came more snow, blotting out the moor ahead. Tears rolled down Eliza's cheeks and she felt as if they were frozen to her skin. Stopping to pull the shawl further over her head, she caught a whiff of smoke. She sniffed again, her spirits rising. Was civilization close after all? Hope lending her strength, she followed the scent until she found herself at a rickety fence. Beyond, a low building, its sloping turf and gorse roof powdered with snow, huddled into the side of the moor.

Unlatching the gate, Eliza limped up the white-blanketed path. As she stood there plucking up courage to seek refuge, the door burst open and a strange-looking woman appeared, shot-gun in hand.

'Who's there?' she demanded. Then, spotting Eliza, she lifted it to her shoulder and aimed directly at her head. Eliza slumped to the ground, her clothes and her precious box spilling out over the snow.

Red eyes grinned. 'We've come to get you,' the goblins hissed, long arms reaching out to snake around her body.

'No!'

'Drink this,' a voice urged. Liquid wetted her lips. They were poisoning her. No goblin was going to get her. She tried to spit it out but her head was heavy and wouldn't move. Darkness closed over her.

Green lips grinned. 'Devil child . . .' the dragons hissed, breathing red flames over her face.

'On fire,' she mumbled, her throat burning. Damp material smothered her. It smelled vile. She couldn't breathe. Darkness descended.

Icy laughter crackled. 'Turn hideous child to toad,' the witch cackled, rubbing her long fingers together with glee.

'No!' she croaked.

Something washed over her face, damp, harsh-smelling. More liquid was poured down her throat. Cold, it was so cold. White powder drifted down, enfolding her in its soft cloud.

Through the fog, came voices. Cackling and croaking; spitting and smoking. She tried to open her eyes but couldn't. Cotton wool engulfed her, thick, warm and so snug.

Slowly, the veil inched upwards. A witch's face stared down at her.

'Decided to join us, have you?' she cackled.

'Don't put a spell on me,' Eliza whispered.

The crone gave a harsh laugh and, cloth in hand, leaned closer. Eliza's eyes widened in terror, she opened her mouth to scream, but no sound came.

3

Eliza tried to open her eyes but they were too heavy. She tried again, shocked to see a giant hovering high above her. As she opened her mouth to scream, he grinned and patted her hand. Through her wooziness, fragments of nightmare returned.

'The witch?' she muttered, trying to sit up. He frowned, gently pushing her back down again.

'Lie still or you'll get dizzy. High temperature has made you delirious. Even the storm raging outside's no match for your moaning and thrashing.' Leaning forward, he moistened her lips with a cloth.

'No more poison,' she protested. But the effort was too much and the last thing that registered was the giant shaking his head, a halo swirling around him.

When she next surfaced, the first thing she heard was that crackling sound. This time, piercing green eyes stared down at her, seemingly seeing right into her soul. Long bony fingers clutching a cloth reached out to cover her face. She gasped.

'Go away, you witch.'

'You'll do,' the woman chortled. 'You had us worried for a while, child.'

'Fever's broken. Give her some cooled water and let her sleep.' As the giant's voice came out of the shadows, she felt the damp cloth on her forehead, then more liquid spooned into her mouth. She tried to speak but the effort was too much. Her head swirled and whirled then darkness descended, claiming her once more.

Next time Eliza opened her eyes no one was peering down at her, and to her relief, the room wasn't moving. She struggled to sit up.

'Welcome back to the world, little one.' The giant, seemingly appearing from nowhere, grinned down at her, his voice soft and reassuring. Then she heard the crackling.

'The witch,' she croaked.

'Hush, there's no witch here. Fever probably gave you strange dreams.'

'I think she means me,' the woman grunted, bending over her again. 'Here, have a drink.' She held a mug to Eliza's lips, snorting when she recoiled. 'It's only boiled water.' Tentatively Eliza took a sip then, realizing how thirsty she was, gulped greedily.

'Gently does it, little un,' the giant urged. 'You'll be sick if you drink too much.'

Hearing another crackle, Eliza looked round and saw she was lying in front of a roaring fire. For a few moments, she lay watching the flames shooting up the chimney like orange rockets. Then the wood spat, giving a loud crack that made her jump. Another memory surfaced and she turned back to face the woman.

'You shot me,' she exclaimed.

The giant laughed. 'Believe you me, if Fay had, you'd be dead meat. She's a crack shot; never missed a rabbit or pigeon in her life.'

'But you pointed your gun at me,' she insisted.

'Indeed I did,' the woman nodded. 'I thought you were an intruder, prowling around my homestead like that. I didn't need to shoot; you fainted clean away in the snow.'

'Oh,' Eliza muttered, sinking weakly back onto the mattress.

'Oh? Is that all you can say after I let you sleep in my bed?' the woman retorted.

'Now then, Fay, don't torment the girl. She's frail as a feather. Give her some of your beef tea. I'll be back to see how you are tomorrow, little un,' the giant said, leaning closer. Eliza noticed he had kind eyes, the colour of ripe chestnuts, and realized the halo she had seen was the riot of dark curls tumbling around his head. Reassured, she smiled back at him, but even that effort was too much and her eyelids fluttered closed. She barely registered the door shutting or the woman moving around before sleep claimed her once more.

Next time Eliza woke, her head felt clearer. She tried to sit up, only to collapse again.

'Steady, child, you're feebler than a runt. Hold onto me,' the woman urged, helping her into a sitting position then propping her up with soft sheepskins. 'What's your name?'

'Eliza.'

'Well, Eliza, people around these parts call me Fay. Now we've been properly introduced, let's see about getting you something to eat.' She lifted a blackened iron pot from the crook over the fire and deftly poured liquid into a mug. As a savoury aroma wafted Eliza's way, her stomach growled with hunger.

'Drink this,' the woman ordered before settling herself

onto the chair beside the hearth. Eliza did as she'd been bid and before long she felt her strength returning.

'I'm sorry for turning up like that yesterday,' she said, thinking an apology was in order.

To her surprise Fay gave a harsh laugh. 'Yesterday? Ten days ago, more like.'

'Ten days!' Eliza spluttered.

'You've been really poorly, my girl. In fact, on a couple of occasions, you very nearly went to join your Maker. The fever was so high, even my curatives couldn't contain it. Thank heaven for Duncan the Druid and his greater knowledge or you wouldn't be here.'

'Duncan the Druid – he's the giant?' Eliza asked.

'He is tall, I grant you, but I can't say I've ever thought of him as a giant. Anyhow, you've much to thank him for, my girl. He refused to leave your side until that fever finally broke. Satisfied you're on the mend, he's finally gone to get some rest.' Fay stifled a yawn and Eliza guessed Duncan wasn't the only one who'd gone without sleep.

'I'm truly grateful for everything you've done.'

'Couldn't leave you outside to perish, could we?' she said brusquely. 'Now, if you've finished that broth, I'll take the mug and have some myself. Lie down and get some more sleep. It's the most restorative thing for you now.'

'I can't spend all my time sleeping,' Eliza protested. 'I need to find somewhere to shelter, get a job and . . .' She slumped back against the sheepskins, drained of energy. In truth she had no idea where she could go.

'You must rest. It's Mother Nature's way of helping you recover. Besides, the sooner you're better the sooner you can be on your way to wherever it was you were going.'

Sensing Fay's animosity, Eliza turned over and eased herself further down the cover. The woman obviously resented her presence so the best thing she could do was get well and leave. Although where she was going to, goodness only knew.

She must have drifted off again for it was dark when she woke. The only light was coming from the fire, which cast flickering shadows across the walls, scenting the room with the sweet smell of applewood. She heard soft snoring and saw Fay asleep in the chair, covered by an old greatcoat. Despite her gruff manner, the woman was still keeping a watch over her and Eliza felt guilty for putting her to so much trouble. Even thinking made her head hurt. She closed her eyes and it wasn't long before sleep claimed her once more.

When next she woke, soft grey light of morning was filtering through the window. The room was quiet and she saw the chair was empty. Feeling stronger, she eased herself into a sitting position. Holding the cover around her, she struggled to her feet but the room started spinning. Eliza reached for the chair, collapsing onto it just as the door clattered open. Fay stood there, wearing the greatcoat that had been keeping her warm the night before, a length of string tied around her middle. She was laden with sticks and logs, but as soon as she saw Eliza she tossed them in the direction of the fireplace where they landed on the stone hearth with a clatter. Clicking her tongue in annoyance, she eased Eliza back down onto the mattress.

'You're going to have to take it easy, my girl,' she chided, piling the fleecy sheepskins over Eliza's shivering body.

'But I felt so much better,' Eliza protested weakly.

'No arguing. That fever's knocked the stuffing out of you and it's going to take time to regain your strength. Now, for heaven's sake do as you're told and rest. I'll bank up the fire and make breakfast. Nourishing food and rest, that's what you need, my girl.'

Weakly, Eliza nodded then watched through half-closed eyes as the woman threw off her coat and kneeled beside the fire. Once she'd riddled the embers, she added sticks and logs until the grate was a fiery blaze. Then she poured water from a hide pitcher into an old kettle and stood it on the fender to boil. With the dripping in a battered old pan sizzling, she tossed in huge lumps of black-red meat. Hearing Eliza gasp, Fay turned and stared down at her.

'Breakfast's the most important meal of the day, girl. Nobody can function on an empty stomach,' she said, deftly flipping the steaks onto a plate and setting them on the hearth to keep warm. Finally she chucked vegetables into a pot, then sat back in the chair. 'Of course, your weak system won't be able to digest a rich venison steak, so I'll cut yours up finely and add it to the broth.'

So that's what the dark meat was. Eliza had never even seen deer flesh, let alone tasted it. She stared around the room, taking in the blackened timbers of the low roof, the inglenook fireplace and a mounted antlered head on the wall. Animal skins covered the floor, sheathed knives hung from hooks, and a gun was slung on the back of the door. She shuddered. Had Fay shot the deer, then? And if she had, was it safe to remain here? She only had the woman's word that she'd fainted, hadn't she? Feeling queasy, she swallowed hard and closed her eyes.

A sudden knocking made her jump, then a gust of wind tore through the room, sending smoke from the fire swirling and billowing around.

'For heaven's sake shut that door, Duncan, before we turn into ice angels,' Fay barked as Duncan stood on the step stamping the snow from his boots.

'Morning, Fay, and a beautiful angel you'd make too. Something smells good,' he said, sniffing the air appreciatively.

'I swear you hear me set the pan to the fire from those woods you choose to inhabit,' Fay replied, shaking the spoon at him.

'Reckoned I might be too late today, though. Ben asked me to call by the farm. He thought Rose had gone into labour. False alarm, but I gave her some raspberry leaf to help her relax and ease the cramps. He was fussing like a mother hen. You'd think having dealt with lambing he'd take it all in his stride,' he muttered.

Fay shook her head. 'A baby's a bit different, Duncan, and it is their first.'

'True. Rose's mother was coming over to help, but she's snowed in down at Beechcombe. Ben insisted I take some fresh food for my trouble,' he said, placing a covered jug of milk on the table then carefully taking four speckled brown eggs from each pocket. 'Think one of these will be more nourishing for our little guest than your bloody red meat. Talking of which, how is the patient today?' he asked, hunkering down beside Eliza. Immediately his expression changed to one of concern. 'You're whiter than the snow outside.'

'Just feeling a bit sick,' Eliza muttered.

'Probably from the frying. It does smell a bit rich this time of a morning. I'll mix something to settle your system. All right to use the mug, Fay?' he asked, pointing to the hearth.

'Of course, but you'd best make me another. It's a bind having to use the same one all the time.'

Duncan lowered his voice. 'Poor Fay, it's a shock having to share your home, isn't it? I'd have the little un but don't think she'd appreciate my tree dwelling. Besides, it's too cold for her out there.'

'Well, I can hardly throw her out in the snow so she'll just have to stay until she's recovered. She said she'd been seeking work so I'm sure someone round these parts will be glad of help. It's inconvenient, though, for I've little space to spare and I don't know anything about children. Still, if the meat's too strong for her, I'll coddle one of those eggs when she's feeling better. With stocks running low, those provisions are most welcome, thank you. Did you ask Ben if he'd heard anything . . .?' Fay's voice became softer and although Eliza couldn't make out what she was saying she knew they were still talking about her.

Eliza stared into the flames and sighed. No matter where she went, she was in the way. As soon as she was strong enough to leave, she would.

'Here, drink this.' She jumped as the gentle giant crouched beside her, holding the mug to her lips.

'What is it?' she asked suspiciously.

'Never fear, 'tis only a bit of betony. Cure anything and everything, that will,' he assured her.

'Now, Duncan, you and I both know it's those herbs

you add that makes the difference. You're lucky, girl, this boy's a wizard,' Fay said with a sniff.

His big belly laugh filled the room and Eliza felt her spirits rise again. She felt more comfortable when the giant was around.

'I got some sacking off Ben. When we've eaten, I'll go out to the barn and stuff up a mattress for you. You can't carry on sleeping on that chair and there's room enough for you both alongside the fire.'

Fay grunted, but Eliza could see she was pleased.

As the drink had settled her stomach, Eliza found herself relaxing. She must have drifted to sleep because the next thing she knew, Fay was shaking her awake.

'I promise to cook you breakfast and then you sleep until noon.' Eliza opened her eyes to find Fay frowning down at her. 'Let's sit you up so you can eat. You need to build your strength,' said the woman, tucking skins behind her.

To her surprise, Eliza found she was ravenous and tucked into the coddled egg. Fay sat in her chair on the other side of the fire stitching away at a length of material that looked familiar. Surely that was her dress, Eliza thought, but the woman was concentrating so fiercely, she didn't like to interrupt. She ate her meal, then sighed contentedly.

'That was delicious, thank you.'

Fay grunted, put down her sewing and took away the platter.

'Now you're feeling stronger, we need to talk,' she said, returning to her chair.

Eliza looked at the woman's serious expression and swallowed hard. Was she going to turn her out so soon?

'You gave me a real scare collapsing outside like that. Only a fool would wander around in that atrocious weather so I'm guessing you must have run away from home.' Eliza looked down at the floor and Fay nodded. 'I thought as much. I don't know what caused you to take such drastic action but I'm sure your parents will be worried sick.'

Eliza shook her head. 'Father will be pleased I've gone. He said I was naught but a burden,' she burst out.

'Sometimes things are said in the heat of the moment. I'm sure he will now be regretting his harsh words.'

'You don't understand. He called me useless, saying no man will want to marry me.'

Fay gave a harsh laugh. 'Marry you? Why, you have years yet before you need think of such a thing. How old are you – eleven?' Eliza shook her head. 'Well, twelve at the most then?'

'I shall be fifteen on the 19th of February,' Eliza burst out indignantly.

Fay narrowed her eyes. 'I warn you, I have no time for liars, girl. Deceit is the work of the devil,' she spat.

'But that's what I am. A child of the devil,' Eliza muttered.

4

Fay stared at Eliza in horror, the crackling of the logs in the hearth sounded unnaturally loud in the long silence.

'Why would you think such a preposterous thing?' Fay asked eventually.

'Father called me that. I was born with a twisted foot, you see.'

'I have seen your foot, Eliza, a tragic birthing accident certainly, but no work of the devil. I thought that kind of fallacy lost in the mists of time. Surely your mother under-stands that?'

'Mother tries to stand up to Father, but as head of the household what he says goes, doesn't it?'

Fay pursed her lips but said nothing.

Eliza stared dismally into the fire, recalling her father's harsh words, the crack of his belt . . . 'He's always taken against me and I am not going back, ever,' she cried.

'Calm down, Eliza. I take it your name really is Eliza?' Fay asked, shooting her a penetrating look.

Eliza nodded.

'You claim to be nearly fifteen . . .'

'Yes, I am. Whatever you may think, I am no liar,' Eliza protested.

'I can't help unless I know the facts. You have been very ill and are little more than skin and bones, although it is my guess you were malnourished to begin with. As it's going to take a while for you to regain enough strength to go anywhere, I was trying to establish if we need to inform anyone of your whereabouts.'

Eliza shook her head.

'Your family will be worrying, surely?' Fay persisted.

'No! They'll be glad to be rid of me, as will you,' Eliza shouted. Silence descended like a fog and, ashamed of her outburst, she stared miserably into the fire.

'I can't deny I prefer my solitude,' Fay finally admitted. 'However, I believe in the moorland ways, which would not permit me to let you leave before you've regained your strength. Any caring human would surely think the same. That's why I can't believe your parents won't be worrying about you and wishing you safely back with them.'

Eliza gave a harsh laugh. 'Believe you me, that'll be the last thing they're wishing. They think I'm worthless, totally and utterly useless.'

'Rubbish. Can you cook? Clean a house? Sew?'

'Of course. I've been doing all of those things at home for years,' Eliza retorted, indignant at being questioned about such minor tasks.

'Well, there you are then; hardly useless, are you?' Fay commented.

'But it wasn't enough for them,' Eliza cried. 'You wouldn't understand what it's like to feel lonely.'

'Is that so?' Fay sighed, staring into the fire. Then her manner became brisk again. 'Now, having been confined to barracks, which I detest, I've used the time to mend your clothes. You were so drenched I literally had to peel all your things from you. They were torn and covered in mud, beggar's buttons and all kinds of animal waste,' she said with a grimace. 'Why, I even had to cut burrs out of your hair, it was that matted.'

Remembering the leap she'd had to make into the ditch and her night spent in the animal byre, Eliza shuddered. Then the implication of what Fay had said sunk in. Gingerly she peered under the cover. Sure enough she was wearing only a chemise, and her legs and feet were quite bare. Quickly she covered herself up again. Then a thought struck.

'Duncan – did he help . . . you know, undress me?' she whispered in horror.

To her surprise, Fay chuckled. 'Don't look so worried. You were decently bedded down long before he appeared. And now I've washed your dress, you can be respectably attired when he next appears. I've added a flounce to hide the worst of the damage.' She passed the garment to Eliza, who stared at her old dress in amazement. The varying shades of green sewn onto her homespun made it look like a patchwork of fields in summertime.

'That's beautiful,' she gasped. 'Thank you.'

Fay shrugged. 'Like I said, it was a good way of passing the time. I'm not one to be idle, or indoors, come to that. Besides, it was just some spare cloth I had.' That the woman should have material of such fine quality lying around amazed Eliza, but she wasn't going to question her good fortune.

'I collected up the things you dropped in the snow when you fell.'

Eliza's eyes lit up. 'You found my box then?'

'Your box?'

'Yes, my treasure box. Grampy made it for me and I keep my flowers in it. I wrapped it in my bundle,' Eliza cried.

'There wasn't any box amongst your things,' Fay said.

'Are you sure?' Eliza asked, her heart sinking.

The woman frowned. 'I know a box when I see one.'

Feeling tears well, Eliza quickly turned her head away so the woman wouldn't see.

'I'll take another look around when I go out for more wood,' Fay said brusquely. 'Now, you've had quite enough excitement for one day. Lie down and get some rest.'

Eliza did as she was told, not thinking for one moment she'd be able to sleep, but when she opened her eyes again bright sunshine was streaming through the window from the east.

'So, Sleeping Beauty wakes at last,' Fay said as she struggled to sit up. 'How are you feeling today?'

'Much better, thank you,' Eliza answered as her stomach gave a loud rumble.

Fay grunted. 'I'll pour you some broth and when you've eaten, we'll get you cleaned up. A wash and change of clothes will make you feel and smell better.'

Eliza spent the next few days sitting in the chair beside the fire. To her chagrin, Fay refused to let her help with the household chores, insisting she rest. Although the woman was civil, Eliza still felt uncomfortable in her presence and hoped Duncan would soon reappear.

Fay could not stay still, though, and whilst she bustled around tidying the room Eliza took in her surroundings, noticing for the first time how spartan they were. A table tucked under the small window was scattered with papers and books, the two mattresses were propped against the wall on one side of the fireplace, and there was a heavy dresser stacked with odd dishes. The various knives in their leather sheaves still hung from their hooks, and the gun was on the back of the door. Further along, an old satchel was slung over a hook and in the corner stood a pail of water. Then she spied the tiny jar of snowdrops on the sill of the window and felt a pang. Her mother would have a fit if she saw those, believing the old superstition that white, shroud-like flowers were redolent of death and should never be brought indoors.

'Surprised to see the Fair Maids of February blooming so early, eh?' Fay said, breaking into her thoughts. 'Got a sheltered spot beyond the vegetable patch where, with a little attention, they thrive and arrive a month earlier than the rest up here, just for old Fay,' she chuckled.

As the woman opened the door to sweep out the dust, all Eliza could see was the snow-clad moorland spreading endlessly before her. A sudden gust of wind made her shiver and, pulling the sheepskin cover round her, she watched as Fay viciously stabbed the ice on top of a pail with the broom handle. With a shock, she realized the woman was much older than she'd first thought. Her dark hair was streaked with silver threads and she had reddened cheeks and roughened hands. Despite the cold, she was dressed only in an old woollen shirt and baggy trousers; as she disappeared outside Eliza saw that from behind she had the athletic appearance of a man.

'I've had another look around but couldn't see any sign of your box, Eliza,' she said, reappearing moments later.

Eliza's heart sank. Her last link with Grampy and the happy times she'd spent with him at home was gone. How could she have been so careless as to lose her most treasured possession? Blinking back the tears, she watched as the woman haphazardly threw the animal skins back down onto the earth floor.

'There, that's better, all clean,' Fay announced, hands on hips, staring around the room. Eliza didn't like to point out the cobwebs festooning the fireplace and corners, or the dust that covered every surface.

'I don't know how much longer you'll have to stay here, Eliza, but . . .' Fay was interrupted by a sharp rap on the door. 'This place is busier than a blessed hunt meeting,' she grunted, flinging open the door. 'Oh, it's you again. Haven't you got your own home to go to?'

'Thought you'd like to know Rose had her baby in the early hours. Little boy they've named Joshua. Mother and baby doing well, Father exhausted, but I guess that's the way of things,' Duncan said with a chuckle.

'From what I can make out, you men just get the fun bit of things, as you call it,' Fay said, wagging her finger at him. 'Still, it is good news the baby's delivered safely. Right, you can make yourself useful and entertain our guest. It'll give me a chance to get out of this place before I go barmy as a Bath bun.' Having thrown on her coat, she grabbed the satchel and was gone.

Eliza's eyes widened in shock but Duncan grinned, seemingly unperturbed by the woman's abrupt manner.

'It's good to see you up and dressed. Are you feeling better, little un?' he asked, lowering himself down on the rug beside her.

'Yes, but I really feel I'm in Fay's way here. I wish I was stronger so I could get up and go,' she said miserably.

'You mustn't mind her. She's used to being by herself. I expect she's finding company claustrophobic, especially only having the one room.'

'I intend leaving as soon as I can,' Eliza assured him. 'I shall seek work and board in the nearest town.'

Duncan shook his head. 'Take one day at a time,' he advised. 'You certainly look different in that pretty dress,' he added, trying to calm her by changing the subject.

'Fay added this flounce to my old homespun,' she said, holding out her skirt. 'Why would she do that, if she hates me so much?'

'Look, Fay doesn't hate you. In fact she was out of her mind with worry when her own remedy failed to bring down your temperature. That's why she sent her precious Woody to get me.'

'Woody? Is he a dog?' Eliza said, looking around as if one might materialize out of the shadows.

Duncan laughed. 'Woody is her pet pigeon.'

'But I thought she shot pigeons.'

Duncan's deep belly laugh rumbled around the room. 'She does if they eat her precious vegetables, but then she does have to live,' he said, shrugging philosophically. 'Woody's different, though. Fay tended his broken wing and they seem to have formed a bond. He's stayed with her ever since. Follows her around all day, then roosts on the wood pile in the shed outside. When you failed to respond to her ministering she tied a message to his leg telling me to come quickly as there was a child in need of strong curatives to bring down the fever.'

'She never said. But then she never says much at all.'

'She can appear aloof, a bit eccentric even, but we're all different. I'm hoping this should make things a bit easier,' he said, taking a wooden mug from his pocket and placing it on the hearth.

'Why, that's beautiful,' Eliza exclaimed, marvelling at the way the handle seemed to flow seamlessly from the body of the mug. Then she noticed the E carved on the front. 'It's for me?'

'Of course. Fay can have her own back,' he said with a wink. 'I've also made an elixir to purify your blood and stimulate your appetite.' He got up, poured some dark liquid into the mug and handed it to Eliza. She took a sip then grimaced at the bitter taste.

'What's in this?' she asked warily.

'Nature's bounty, now drink it up,' he said, watching until she'd finished every last drop.

'That's better. Both Fay and I agree that nature will provide, always supposing you know where to look for it, of course.'

'She said you were a druid – what does that mean?'

'Druids believe in spiritual powers, that all nature is part of the great web of life.'

'Like a spider's web?' she asked curiously.

'Exactly,' he agreed. 'We worship the land, the earth, the trees, the stars and the universe. We encourage love and peace and believe no animal has supremacy over another.'

Hearing the sincerity in his words, Eliza remembered the gentleness of his hands as he sponged the fever away.

'But Fay kills animals for their meat, doesn't she?'

'Indeed, for man must eat. However, she firmly believes that if an animal needs to be killed it should be done humanely and every last scrap used out of respect. And, of course, animals themselves kill to live. 'Tis the cycle of things. But that's quite enough for now, my little dryad.' Eliza looked askance at him. 'It means female spirit of the tree. With your elfin features, you remind me of one.'

'Dryad – I like that. Soon I shall leave here and will be known as Eliza Dryad,' she declared.

'Don't be hasty, little un. We are still in the deadness of January and haven't reached the moorland turn of the year yet. Up here in the hills 'tis only at Candlemas next month we mark our midwinter. Hence the old saying, till Candlemas Day keep half your hay.'

Eliza looked at him in horror. 'But that's ages yet.'

He chuckled. 'Miss Impatience. When the thaw comes, I'll show you the woods where I live and tell you more about our way of life. That'll be a treat for you to look forward to,' he winked. 'Now, though, you need to rest and I must chop some wood for Fay. She's an independent old thing and more than capable, but I like to help, especially when she's out of the way,' he said, grinning as he got to his feet.

Eliza closed her eyes and dreamed she was a dryad soaring over trees and lush green meadows. The sun was blazing from an azure sky and she felt alive with happiness. She was rudely awakened by a sharp rap on the door. Thinking Duncan would answer, she remained where she was but the knocking persisted. Groggily she got to her feet and tugged at the rickety wood. A man of middle years stood there. He was shabbily, if cleanly, dressed and grinning inanely.

'Afternoon, maid. It's perishing out here, can I come in?'

'No. It's not my home, you see.'

'So I gathered. I been told you're seeking a live-in position so happen this could be your lucky day. I farm lower down the moor. Wife died before Christmas and I need someone to keep house. You're not as scrawny as I feared so if you play your cards right happen you could be the next missus. A fellow needs someone to warm his bed of a night,' he said, giving a raucous guffaw. His suggestive remarks made her feel sick. Where was Duncan? Surely he hadn't left whilst she was asleep?

'I think you must have heard wrong,' she ventured.

'Don't think so, maid. The old woman was quite certain, though I have to say her description didn't do you justice,' he said, eyeing her up and down. Then he caught sight of the ugly black boot under her skirt and his expression changed. 'Seems like old Jed here will be doing you a favour, maid. Told the woman I'd take you so never let it be said I don't honour my word. Good job I brought the harvest cart up, though,' he said, gesturing to the gate where a grey pony was stamping the frozen ground impatiently.

Eliza looked at the long low wagon, with neatly railed sides, and shuddered. He really expected her to go with him, she thought, taking a step backwards.

'Yer, 'tis cold,' he said, mistaking her movement. 'So hurry up, get your things and we'll be on our way.'

Eliza shook her head. She'd rather live rough on the moors than go anywhere with this bumptious bumpkin.

Frantically, she pushed the door shut but his foot shot out, preventing it from closing, and he grabbed her arm.

'I haven't come all this way for nothing, maid, and you ain't in any position to be fussy, are you? Now be quick and get your things,' he hissed.

Eliza shuddered. Although she was hurt that Fay seemed so keen for her to move on, she had no intention of going anywhere with this obnoxious creep. She'd rather starve than sink that low.

5

'Take your hands off her this minute,' a voice called. Seeing Duncan striding up the path, Eliza almost fainted with relief.

'No need to take that tone, I'm sure,' the man blustered. 'The old woman told me the maid was looking for board and bed so . . .'

'I'm afraid you're mistaken. Eliza is a guest here so I'd be obliged if you would leave,' Duncan insisted firmly.

The man spat in disgust, a globule of spittle glistening on his lip.

'Go inside, Eliza,' Duncan ordered. 'I'll see our visitor safely on his way.'

As Eliza hurried back to the warmth of the fire, she could hear the sound of raised voices. Unwittingly, she'd caused trouble again, she thought, stumbling across the room, fear and nerves making her limp more pronounced. She heard the man shout to his horse as she collapsed weakly into the chair. Then Duncan appeared, pushing the door firmly shut behind him. He looked furious.

'I'm sorry . . .' she began.

'Whatever for?' he asked.

'For causing trouble. I can see you're cross with me.'

He shook his head, his expression softening. 'I am cross but not with you, little un.'

Eliza struggled to her feet. 'I must go. I won't stay

where I'm not wanted,' she muttered, but the room started spinning and she clutched at the arm of the chair for support. In an instant, Duncan was by her side, gently settling her back down again.

'You are in no fit state to go anywhere. Close your eyes and get some rest,' he ordered, drawing the cover over her.

'But . . .' she began weakly.

'Hush, no arguing now,' he soothed, reaching into his capacious pocket and drawing out a wooden flute. As a lilting melody filled the room Eliza felt her agitation easing. The mellow notes reminded her of a spring breeze rustling leaves in the trees and she closed her eyes, dreaming again that she was a spirit floating free.

'Whatever were you thinking of, Fay? She could have come to real harm.' Eliza was woken by Duncan's angry whispering.

'Seemed like the perfect solution. Jed mentioned that he was looking for help around the home and . . .'

'But she's only a child, Fay,' Duncan interrupted.

'Apparently she'll be fifteen in a few weeks. That's hardly a child, Duncan.'

'Fifteen, you say? You'd never think to look at her, she's so tiny. Still, that's hardly the point, Fay. She's malnourished, exhausted . . .'

'Stop going on, Duncan. Like I said, it would have solved all our problems. She'd have had a job and a roof over her head and I'd have got my space back.'

'But you should have seen the way he was leering at her,' he protested.

'So I'm a nursemaid now, am I?' Fay's voice became querulous and Eliza bit her lip to stop herself from crying out. Yet again people were arguing over her. Well, she wasn't going to stay where she wasn't wanted. But before she could move, the wrangling started again.

'Being by yourself has made you selfish and self-centred, Fay. If, as you maintain, you live by the moorland ways, you've certainly got a funny way of showing it.'

'How dare you? Get out, you whippersnapper!'

'Don't worry, I'm going. Think on what I said, though. You've got a heart of gold hidden beneath that prickly exterior, Fay, and that girl's crying out for a bit of love and attention. Is it too much to ask that you give her a little compassion?'

Eliza heard his footsteps crossing the room and the door closing. Then there was a thud as something hit the wood after him.

'Good riddance,' Fay muttered. Eliza heard her poking the fire vigorously. 'Can't even sit in my own chair,' she added. Feeling the woman staring at her, Eliza could stay quiet no longer. Struggling to her feet, she reached for her shawl.

'I'm sorry, Fay,' she said. 'I'll leave right away.'

'It's dark outside. Can't be responsible for you getting sucked into a bog so you'd better stay another night,' the woman grunted. Then she turned and held a spill to the flame before lighting an unused candle that was stuck in a bottle beside her. 'There, as it's been an eventful day we'll treat ourselves to a bit of comfort,' she said, snuffing out the spill between her finger and thumb. 'Bring over one of those chairs so we can both have a seat.' Eliza hesitated. 'For goodness' sake, hurry up, girl. It's not often I light a candle at suppertime, or any other time, come to that. Cost money, they do. Now, we need sustenance; can't think on an empty stomach.' She nodded towards the chairs by the table, then swung the crook from over the fire and began ladling stew into two mismatched platters.

As the savoury aroma wafted her way, Eliza was surprised to find she was hungry. They ate in silence then sat staring into the fire. Fay seemed lost in her own thoughts and Eliza didn't like to disturb her. How she wished Duncan had stayed. His calm presence gave her confidence and Fay's moods were unpredictable. At this very moment she might be hatching another plan to get rid of her. She clutched the edge of her chair, hardly daring to move in case she upset the woman.

After a while, she sensed Fay glancing at her. Fay opened her mouth as if she wanted to say something then thought better of it. Finally she looked directly at Eliza.

'Duncan says I'm prickly. Would you agree?' she asked, her voice sounding loud after the silence.

Eliza took in the woman's unkempt appearance. With her hair sticking out at odd angles, bright button eyes and the shadows cast by the candle making her nose look wrinkled she certainly didn't give the impression of being approachable. Eliza swallowed, not sure how to answer. If she said what she was thinking she would offend, yet she'd been brought up to be truthful.

'I guess if you were an animal, you'd be a hedgehog,' she finally ventured.

Fay stared at her in surprise, then burst out laughing,

the raucous sound echoing round the small room, making the dishes on the dresser rattle.

'You'll do, girl. I like someone who's not afraid to speak their mind. It was wrong of me to send Jed up here, I can see that now. When I bumped into him it seemed the perfect solution but I didn't think it through. Believe me when I say I meant no harm?' She paused, staring at Eliza intently as she waited for her to answer.

Not trusting herself to speak, Eliza merely nodded.

'Truth is, I become restless cooped up indoors,' the woman continued. 'I need to be outside, working the land, hunting meat for the pot or drawing the flora and fauna. They're my passion, you see, and the hours of daylight are short this time of year. Obviously whilst I'm doing that I can't see to things here and if you're to stay until you're fully recovered there'll be more to do. So the answer's obvious, isn't it?'

Eliza frowned. 'I'm not sure I understand,' she ventured.

'Goodness, girl, have you lost your marbles along with your mutton? You said you can cook, clean and sew?'

Eliza nodded, hardly daring to hope the woman meant what she thought she did.

'Well, then. If you keep the hovel clean and cook our meals that will leave me free to skip off and sketch.' The incongruous vision of the older woman skipping about the moors made her smile.

'Why do you call this place a hovel?' she asked, looking around the room.

Fay frowned. 'It's just one name for a tiny dwelling hereabouts. Hovel? Hobble? Does it matter?' she said eventually.

'I think hobble sounds much nicer.'

'Then by all means call it that. The place has been hobbled together anyhow. Now, do you agree to my suggestion?' Fay asked, holding out her hand. 'No doubt Duncan will make sure I'm looking after you properly.'

That clinched it. With him around she'd feel safe. She just hoped he hadn't taken offence at the woman's parting shot.

Eliza placed her hand in Fay's, trying not to flinch at her vice-like grip. She felt as if a weight had been lifted from her. Not only would she have somewhere to stay whilst she recovered, she could make herself useful. Then a thought hit her.

'I don't have any money, though,' she ventured.

Fay snorted. 'Nor do I, Eliza, nor do I. Many years ago, when I decided to come here and live the moorland way, I thought long and hard about how I would exist. In order to survive one needs running water, which the streams around here supply in abundance. One also needs access to fresh food, which I get from various means, including my vegetable plot out the back. With careful management and planning it supplies my needs year round.'

Eliza watched as the woman became quite animated. To live without money seemed a fascinating concept and she leaned forward to make sure she did not miss a word.

'Then there's a roof over one's head. You might not think this a palace,' Fay said, gesturing around the room, 'but to me it is home. It provides shelter from the elements and is a haven to return to at nightfall. A fire provides both heat and a means of cooking food. There is an abundance of wood to collect for fuel around these parts if one is prepared to expend the energy. Of course one also needs clothes on one's back but I had a good supply when I left . . .' She stuttered to a halt and her eyes glazed over as if she was thinking back to another time. Eliza stared into the fire and waited.

After a few moments, Fay shook her head. 'Anyway, as you can see, I am virtually self-sufficient and don't recall mentioning that money word along the way.' She saw Eliza staring at her in amazement and chuckled. 'Don't worry, girl, you'll not want for anything. Now it's time we bedded down for the night. I'll see if we can't rig up something to give us a bit of privacy when the weather warms up. Meantime, we'll have to carry on sleeping in front of the fire or we'll find ourselves frozen to our mattresses.'

Although Eliza resolved to be up before Fay, she woke to the smell of frying meat. The woman was in an amiable mood, though, and handed her a platter before she'd even risen.

'Here, get that down you. Remember, breakfast is the most important meal of the day. Eat well at the beginning and you'll have energy enough to cope with everything the day throws at you.' Eliza stared down at the black-red meat and shook her head. How quickly she'd become accustomed to having venison for breakfast. Whatever would her mother and father think of such luxury? Knowing it would serve no purpose pursuing that line of thought she stifled a sigh and began to eat.

'What would you like me to do today, Fay?' she asked, putting her empty platter aside. The woman stared around the room and shrugged.

'Tidy and clean up a bit. Don't overdo things, though, or I'll have Duncan to answer to. There's barley in the shed out back if you've a yen to make some bread any time. Now that would be a rare treat. I'll bring in some wood before I leave.'

'What about animals? Do you keep any?'

Fay shook her head. 'I live on very modest means, Eliza, and livestock cost money both to buy and to keep. Got some chickens initially but the foxes and pine martens soon had them. Waste of good money that was,' she snorted. 'Remember what I said last night about money? Well, that was my one and only investment. You can keep your animals.'

'Duncan mentioned your pet pigeon, Woody,' Eliza persisted.

The woman's expression softened. 'He's different. Understand each other, we do. Now, where were we?' she said brusquely. 'Ah yes, provisions. Sometimes I get milk and eggs from the farm in return for helping out, otherwise it's whatever I happen across.' She gave a broad wink. 'As I said, my garden keeps me in vegetables and herbs so stews are my mainstay. You can use whatever you fancy for our evening meals. Which reminds me: wood supplies. You'll not be doing any cooking without a good fire,' she said, getting to her feet. Eliza watched as she shrugged into the tattered greatcoat, tying it around her waist with the length of string before pulling a battered old bonnet down over her ears. The incongruous sight made her smile.

As Fay tugged open the door, a mighty gust of wind almost took it from its hinges, sending smoke from the

47

fire billowing around the already gloomy room. Eliza coughed and shivered, causing Fay to frown. 'You can't afford to get a chill after that fever, girl. Best help yourself to one of my warm shirts and a pair of serge trousers from that drawer over there,' she said, nodding towards the chest in the corner.

Trousers? Eliza had never worn such a garment in all her life.

Before she could answer, Fay had disappeared into the bright, white outside, only to reappear moments later with an armful of logs, which she threw down unceremoniously on the hearth. She tossed one onto the fire, then snatched up her satchel.

'Back before dark,' she said, disappearing outside again.

Eliza sat listening to the wind roaring around the building and the crackling coming from the grate. It was really quite cosy if you stayed by the fire and she couldn't understand why Fay would choose to venture out. She stared around the untidy room and decided that after clearing away the breakfast things she'd tackle the cobwebs. Then come midday, when it should be warmer, she'd take herself out to the garden and see what vegetables there were before making a start on the bread.

The ceilings and fireplace were festooned with huge cobwebs that must have been there for years. Nature's lace, her grampy had called them. Big black, hairy spiders, angry at being disturbed, scuttled across the ceiling and down the walls, making Eliza shudder. When she was satisfied not a web or dead fly remained, she snatched up a rag and began removing the patina of dust that covered every surface. Early snowdrops or not, she was tempted to remove the drooping flowers but by the time she'd got the room reasonably clean and tidy she was feeling weary.

Noticing her hands were covered in muck and feeling sticky after her exertions, she took herself outside. She was rinsing the worst of the grime from her face and hands when she sensed she was being watched. Afraid it was another unwanted visitor she spun round quickly and saw a dark pigeon eyeing her from the top of the shed door. It opened its beak and gave a shrill squawk, like a warning, before disappearing into the depths. Unnerved, Eliza fled inside.

6

Back indoors, Eliza began to shiver uncontrollably. The cold had penetrated her bones and she felt light-headed. Collapsing onto the chair, she huddled closer to the fire and closed her eyes.

When she opened them it was to see Fay sitting on the chair opposite, cutting vegetables into a large pot.

'So you've woken then?' the woman grunted.

Eliza's eyes widened in horror; surely she hadn't slept the whole day away?

'Sorry, I only closed my eyes for a moment but I must have dropped off,' she muttered. 'I fully intended to prepare supper after I'd rested.'

'Suppose it'll take time for you to get back on your feet. Looks like you've been busy, anyway. Room's cleaner than it's ever been. Bet those spiders weren't too pleased having to find new homes, though,' she chuckled.

'Well, at least the flies will be safe, poor things,' Eliza retorted.

'Pah, it's nature's way. Eat or be eaten. You can't afford to be sentimental up here, girl. Anyhow, it's not supper time yet. It was too cold to be sitting outside for long. Wind was savage and cut right through me so I came back for a warm. Still, I managed to sketch the outline of the icicles that were hanging from the bridge over the river. Like huge glassy daggers, they were.'

Eliza shivered.

'I see you went outside without putting on something warmer like I suggested,' said Fay, going over and rummaging in the chest. She threw Eliza a large woollen shirt and a pair of masculine-looking trousers. 'Best put them on now.' Eliza stared at the huge, rough garments and hesitated. 'We don't stand on ceremony here. Freeze to death if we did,' Fay said pointedly.

'But surely the warmer weather's on its way?' Eliza said, only to receive another look.

Realizing there was no use arguing, Eliza struggled into the heavy shirt. It reached almost to her ankles and was so baggy she could hardly see the floor, which was just as well, she thought, after she'd struggled into the ill-fitting trousers. She'd just finished buttoning them up when there was a knock on the door.

'Thought you'd be back,' Fay grunted as Duncan stepped into the room, his breath spiralling into the air as he blew on his hands. Catching sight of Eliza, he grinned broadly.

'Why, Fay, you're turning little un here into a smaller version of you,' he laughed. Then his expression turned serious. 'You're looking very pale, Eliza. I hope Fay hasn't been working you too hard.'

The woman snorted. 'Hardly. She was sound asleep when I returned.'

Eliza hung her head in shame while Duncan stared around the room.

'I'm not sure Eliza's strong enough to be doing anything strenuous yet,' he said, gently feeling her forehead with his large hand. 'And it's still cold in here, even with the fire blazing.'

'Huh, it's warmer than out on the moors,' Fay snapped.

'True,' he agreed mildly, reaching in his voluminous pocket and drawing out a bottle. 'Let's get some of this down you, little un,' he said, pouring red syrupy liquid into her mug.

'I'm sorry to be a nuisance,' she said.

He shook his head. 'You can't help being poorly. 'Tis up to us to help you get back on your feet,' he said, gazing at her warmly with his chestnut eyes. Eliza's heart jumped. No one had ever looked at her like that before. 'Now get some sleep.'

'But I've been sleeping most of the afternoon,' she protested, her eyelids fluttering closed.

Next morning, they were just finishing their breakfast when Duncan reappeared.

'Goodness, lad, don't tell me you want feeding again?' Fay joked as he perched on a rug on the floor and held his hands out to warm in front of the fire.

He shook his head. 'I had something to eat at the farm earlier. They're in a right state down there. Rose's mother slipped on the ice and is housebound so can't help them out. Ben's torn between seeing to the animals and looking after Rose, who is apparently fretting each time the baby whimpers. I mixed something to help calm her, but even so . . .' He shrugged.

'Well, it's natural for Rose to be anxious, I guess,' Fay said, putting her dish to one side. 'Anyhow, I can't sit here chatting with you two. There's a bright new morn and my sketchpad beckons. I'll replenish the wood supply and then be on my way.'

'You know I'm happy to bring in the logs for you,' Duncan said mildly, only to receive a scowl.

'Quite capable of doing it myself,' Fay grunted, shrugging into her coat and striding out of the door.

Duncan grinned at Eliza. 'Can't get used to seeing you dressed like that.'

She stared ruefully down at her weird attire. 'And I can't get used to wearing trousers. I feel all trussed up like a chicken.'

'Guess they'll keep you warm. You're looking brighter this morning so that curative must be working. Which reminds me . . .' he said, going over to the dresser and picking up the bottle. He was carefully pouring the ruby liquid into her cup when a terrible cry rent the air.

'Stay here,' Duncan ordered, rushing outside.

Eliza swallowed. What was going on? She didn't have to wait long to find out. Moments later Duncan reappeared, supporting an ashen-faced Fay.

'What's happened?' Eliza asked, helping the trembling woman into her chair.

Fay shook her head, tears coursing down her cheeks. 'It's Woody,' she whispered.

'You mean he's . . .?' Eliza asked.

Duncan nodded. 'Cold got to him. Look after Fay, I'll see to his . . .'

'No! Leave him to me. Oh, Woody, Woody,' Fay cried. As her gut-wrenching sobs filled the room Eliza stared helplessly at Duncan.

'I'll mix something to calm you, Fay,' he said.

'Just leave me alone, can't you? Go on, get out, both of you,' she ordered.

Eliza shuddered at the vehemence in her voice but Duncan nodded.

'Happen that would be best, Fay. I've got the sled outside so I'll take Eliza down to the farm for a while. It'll be warmer there and Rose will be pleased of the company. Get your things together then wrap up as warm as you can, little un, for it's still bitter out there.'

Eliza glanced over at Fay but the woman had her head in her lap and was sobbing her soul out. Catching sight of the snowdrops on the sill she felt a pang. She knew she should have got rid of them.

'Come along,' Duncan urged as she hesitated.

'Are you sure we should leave Fay by herself?'

''Tis the best thing, believe me, and keep those things on,' he added as she went to remove the baggy garments. 'They might not become thee, young un, but they'll help keep out the cold.'

Quickly she threw her sister's shawl over the shirt, then gathered her few things into a bundle. All the while her thoughts were raging and, once outside, she turned to Duncan.

'It's my fault Woody died, you know,' she burst out.

'How do you make that out?'

'I should have warned Fay about bringing snowdrops indoors. They betoken death.'

To her surprise Duncan snorted. 'Oh, little un, if we believed every false notion we heard we'd never pick a living thing. Now come along before you catch your death. Sun might be out but 'tis a lazy wind blowing from the north and there's still nothing of you.'

The sun was indeed shining brightly, making the snow-clad moor sparkle like a bejewelled wonderland. Despite her concern about Fay, Eliza felt excitement rising as Duncan helped her onto the sled, then piled her high with sheepskins until only her nose was showing.

'Can't be too careful,' he said, picking up the ropes and pulling the sled effortlessly behind him.

As they slid over the frozen ground, Eliza stared around in fascination. She hadn't realized she'd wandered this high up the moors. There were undulating hilltops as far as the eye could see, intersected by grey stone walling. The track was bordered with wind-bent beech hedge banks, and everywhere was blanketed in the silence of deep white snow.

Squinting down the valley, she could just make out the tops of trees and a scattering of buildings far below them. Overhead the sky was as bright blue as a dunnock's egg, and dark buzzards were mewling as they circled their prey. Revelling in being outdoors again, Eliza was slow to realize they'd come to a stop. Smiling down at her, Duncan gently eased her back along the sled.

''Tis all downhill from now, so hold onto my waist and we'll soar like swallows,' he said, perching himself in front of her. Taking up the ropes, he pushed off with his foot and she clung tightly onto him as they sped down the moorland, the sled picking up pace as it went.

It was exhilarating to see the scenery whooshing by. She could taste the freshness of snow on the breeze and was enjoying herself so much she felt quite disappointed when they eventually came to a halt beside a strong fence surrounding Ashcombe Farm.

'Are you sure they won't mind me coming here, what with the new baby and everything?' she asked, as Duncan helped her to her feet.

'You're used to dealing with infants, aren't you?' he asked.

'Yes, I cared for my two younger brothers from the day they were born.'

'Well then, you can teach Rose the mysterious ways of babyhood while I help Ben around the farm. And Fay needs peace and quiet to come to terms with her loss. Woody was her companion and confidant all rolled into one and she's going miss him terribly. A pigeon might seem a peculiar friend to have but Fay really loved that bird and she's not one to give her emotions lightly.' Remembering the woman's earlier resentment towards her, Eliza could only agree. 'Come along, let's get you in the warm,' Duncan said, leaning the sled against the fence and tucking the sheepskins under his arm.

Clutching her bundle, Eliza followed him round the side of the large, blue-grey stone building, where long icicles dangled from the gutters like glass daggers. She'd hardly had time to take in her surroundings before the door was thrown open by a harassed-looking young man.

'Duncan, am I glad to see you,' he cried, showing them into a homely, if somewhat untidy kitchen. As a high-pitched squeal came from above, he threw up his hands. 'As you can see, chaos reigns.'

'Ben, this is Eliza. She has experience of babies and I thought Rose might be glad of some help until her mother can get here. Not that Eliza can do anything too strenuous as she's still recovering from the fever.'

The young man grasped Eliza's hand. 'Welcome, Eliza. Any help you can give Rose with the baby will be gratefully received. He won't stop crying and she's convinced she must be doing something wrong.'

He looked so concerned her heart went out to the open-faced young farmer.

'I'll do my best, sir. It's amazing how much havoc one little baby can cause. Luckily everything usually settles down within a week or so.'

'Thank heavens for that, and please call me Ben,' he said, raking his hand through his corn-coloured hair. 'But where are my manners? You must be ready for a hot drink,' he said, lifting a kettle onto the range. 'Then I must go and milk the cows before it turns to cream in their udders.'

'I'll give you a hand,' Duncan said.

'Why don't I tidy up in here and call you when the tea's brewed?' Eliza ventured.

Ben smiled for the first time since they'd arrived. 'That would be a great help. By then, I hope Rose will be ready to join us.' He pulled on his flat cap and headed towards the door.

'Don't overdo it, little un,' Duncan warned before following after him.

Eliza looked around the farmhouse kitchen. Although the range was quite clean and burning brightly, the copper pans on the dresser would benefit from a polish. The big square deal table was littered with dirty dishes and mugs, but there was water simmering in a large pot alongside the kettle. Quickly discarding her shawl, Eliza rolled up the voluminous sleeves of the woollen shirt and set to work.

The stone sink was set beneath a window that looked out over the farmyard to rolling moors beyond.

She was pouring boiling water into the teapot when a fair-haired woman appeared, a sleeping babe in her arms. Her beautiful gentian eyes were shadowed by bruise-like smudges, and as she stood looking askance, Eliza bobbed a curtsy.

'Morning, mistress. Eliza Dryad at your service.'

'Oh, you must be Duncan's friend,' the woman said, smiling warmly. 'I'm Rose, in case you didn't realize, and this bundle of trouble is Joshua.' She stared around in amazement. 'My word, you have been busy.'

'Tea should be mashed by now. Shall I pour or would you prefer to?' Eliza asked automatically, then hesitated wondering if she'd been too forward in her dealings with this lady she'd only just met.

Rose nodded and smiled. 'Would you mind? I've only just got Joshua here quiet and am dying for a hot drink,' she said, collapsing onto one of the spindle-backed chairs. 'Are you staying then?' she asked, nodding to Eliza's bundle.

'If it's all right with you,' Eliza said. 'Woody died in the cold and Duncan says it would be better for Fay to be by herself.'

The woman's expression changed. 'Oh, no,' she said, shaking her head.

'Well, of course I don't have to,' Eliza began, snatching up her bundle. She wouldn't stay where she wasn't wanted although where she'd go she had no idea. Returning to the hobble while Fay was so distressed wasn't an option.

7

'I meant, oh, no, poor Fay. She worshipped that pigeon. You're very welcome here, Eliza.' Rose smiled.

Then the door clattered open, jolting the baby awake. As his indignant wails filled the room, the men stood shame-faced on the step.

'For heaven's sake, hurry up and put the wood in the hole before we all catch our deaths,' Rose snapped. As Joshua's lusty yells reverberated around the kitchen, sending a tabby cat, which was winding itself about Rose's chair, fleeing for cover, she got to her feet and began rocking the infant back and forth.

'He was asleep, Ben.' She glared at her husband accusingly.

'If it's any help, my mother always says you should start as you mean to go on,' Eliza said quietly, and Rose stared at her in surprise. 'By her reckoning, if a baby gets used to the usual household bustle he'll ignore it, whereas if you tiptoe around he'll wake at the slightest sound.'

'Well, it would help if people were more considerate,' Rose snorted, and stalked out of the room, the baby in her arms.

'Shall I see if I can help?' Eliza asked. Ben nodded gratefully.

Upstairs Rose was pacing the floor, tears streaming down her face while Joshua lay in a beautifully carved wooden cradle, his face bright red, little fists beating the air in anger.

'He hates me,' Rose cried.

'Of course, he doesn't,' Eliza soothed. 'He's just puzzled by his new surroundings. Don't forget he's been swimming around in a pool of warm water for nine months. Now hush, little one,' she said, lifting him into her arms. The baby's sobs quietened and he gave a little hic.

'How did you do that?' Rose asked, her mouth hanging open in surprise.

Eliza chuckled. 'Practice. If I didn't keep the babes quiet at home, Father would hit the roof – or worse.'

Rose looked at her speculatively, opened her mouth to say something but was overtaken by a huge yawn.

'Why don't you go and get some rest?' Eliza suggested.

'He'll only start up again as soon as I walk away.'

'Take off your cardigan,' Eliza suggested.

'Why?' Rose frowned.

'It'll smell of you and Joshua needs to be able to recognize your scent in order to settle.'

'Really?' Rose asked sceptically, but took it off anyway. Eliza swaddled him in the woollen, then placed him back in his cradle. Humming softly, she rocked it from side to side until his eyelids fluttered closed and the hiccups gave way to little snorts.

'Well I never,' Rose exclaimed.

'Now he's settled, take a nap,' Eliza urged.

Rose nodded gratefully and disappeared into a room on the other side of the stairs.

With a last look at the sleeping infant, Eliza made her

way back down the stairs. However, her exertions of the morning caught up with her and she caught her twisted foot on the step. Just as she began to fall, a hand reached out and pushed her back onto the landing. Shaken, she stared at the old man before her. With his whiskered chin and kind eyes he reminded her of Grampy.

'Thank you,' she whispered. He smiled and waved his clay pipe in a friendly gesture. As he placed it back in his mouth, she noticed the tops of the fingers on his right hand were missing.

'Are you all right?' Duncan's anxious face was peering up the stairs at her.

'I nearly fell but luckily he saved me,' she explained, gesturing behind her. Duncan frowned and, spinning round, Eliza saw the man had disappeared, leaving behind the faintest whiff of tobacco smoke. 'He was here a moment ago,' she added, taking Duncan's proffered hand.

'You need a rest and something to eat,' he said, helping her towards the kitchen. 'We've set out luncheon.' She saw three plates set with slices of mutton pie and pickles.

'Won't the old man be joining us?' Eliza asked Ben, who gave her a strange look. 'Only I saw him on the stairs and . . .'

A piercing wail came from upstairs but as Eliza got up, Ben shook his head.

'I'll go, you finish your meal,' he said, giving a rueful grin and striding from the room.

'I fear you've overdone things, Eliza. Ben's great-grandfather once lived here but he's been dead for years.'

'He can't be. He saved me from falling. He had the kindest eyes and was smoking a pipe. I remember clearly, for the tops of his fingers were missing.'

Duncan frowned then got to his feet. 'Come with me.'

'Where are we going?'

'To see a picture,' he said abruptly, striding out of the room.

'Yes, that was the man who saved me,' Eliza said, as they stood looking at the portrait of the man with kind eyes and whiskered face. 'Do you believe me now?'

Duncan nodded. 'I didn't disbelieve you, Eliza. You haven't had time to venture down to this old hall so you wouldn't have known about those otherwise, would you?' he said, pointing to the damaged fingers holding a clay pipe.

'That's definitely the man who saved me,' she said, shaking her head in wonder.

'Apparently, his wife hated him smoking so he used to hide himself away down here and smoke his pipe in peace.'

'Do you believe in ghosts, Duncan?' she asked after a few moments.

'That's a good question, young un. Ghosts? Spirits?' He shrugged. 'What's in a name?'

'But you do believe?'

'I believe something of us – our energy, perhaps – remains behind, otherwise what's the point of this life?'

'I'm so pleased,' she said, clapping her hands excitedly.

'It means that much to you?'

'Oh, yes. You see Grampy was the only person who ever really loved me, what with . . .' She pointed to her foot and grimaced. 'Sometimes I feel his presence and find it comforting. He made me this lovely wooden box for my flowers but I lost it in the snow and . . .' She came to a halt as they heard Ben calling them.

Back in the kitchen they found him grinning like a demented donkey.

'It seems I have the magic touch,' he announced proudly. 'Picked up the young rascal, threw him over my shoulder and told him who was boss. He did an almighty burp, then closed his eyes again. Rose never stirred. You wait until I tell her how easy this parenting thing is,' he grinned.

'I wouldn't go boasting, my friend. If you sound too capable she'll have you seeing to him every time he murmurs,' Duncan said sagely.

Ben frowned. 'Heavens, that would never do,' he said, reaching for his mug. 'Where did you two disappear to?'

'Duncan showed me the picture of your great-grandfather,' Eliza answered.

Ben smiled. 'Old Joshua, for whom our son's named, was a great chap. He built this place with his bare hands. Having been abandoned as a babe, he wanted his family to have the home he'd never had. Anyhow, he'd nearly finished when the rope on a pulley snapped, trapping his fingers under a beam, cutting off the tips. Friends and neighbours pitched in to help him finish the house. He was so grateful he opened his home to them every Christmas, then after he'd planted the orchard, again at Wassail. They were some gatherings, by all accounts. He even devised his own version of the cider cup for the toast. As the family grew so did the celebrations. Everyone was included, everyone wanted.'

'How wonderful,' Eliza murmured, remembering her recent desolate Christmas.

'The tradition has been carried on over the years, first

by Grandfather, then Father and now it's down to us. Of course, we would have opened the house this Christmas if Rose hadn't been about to give birth.'

'Did your great-grandfather have many children?' Eliza asked.

'He had five sons but apparently it was his daughter, Carole, who was the apple of his eye. He loved her so much he couldn't help giving her the best he could afford.'

'Oh, how wonderful,' Eliza exclaimed.

'She was certainly indulged.'

'No, I meant how wonderful to be loved like that. Will you carry on the tradition next year?'

'Indeed, but all this talk has made me realize we should really do something for Wassail this year,' Ben replied.

'It's only a couple of days away so you'll have to get busy organizing,' Duncan pointed out.

'Get busy organizing what?' Rose asked, coming into the kitchen. She looked brighter for her sleep and Eliza jumped up to pour more water into the teapot.

'Wassail, my dear. I was just saying, we might not have been able to open Ashcombe for Christmas but we can certainly invite everyone to celebrate Wassail now Joshua's safely here. We could make it a double celebration,' Ben said, looking pleased with his idea. 'And of course we must make the Ashcombe wassail cup to toast the trees and young Joshua.'

'What is this Wassail?' Eliza asked.

Duncan laughed. 'Anyone can tell you're not a maid of these moors, young un. Here in Somerset, Wassail is when we pay tribute to the Apple Tree Man. He is the spirit of the oldest apple tree in the orchard. In him the fertility of the orchard is said to reside. The idea is to scare away evil spirits, wake the trees, then toast them with the special Ashcombe wassail cup to provide us with a good harvest. Tradition decrees this ritual is held on old Twelfth Night.'

'But it'll mean inviting people, then preparing the food and drink. And the house will need to look presentable. When we spoke about this last year, Mother was going to be here to help. I can't possibly do it by myself, especially with young Joshua needing so much attention,' Rose moaned, slumping in her seat.

'I could help,' Eliza said, then realized she was making assumptions. 'I mean, I would be happy to assist if you don't mind my staying on till then?'

Rose brightened. 'You can stay as long as you like, Eliza. If you're sure you don't mind helping with the preparations, then we'll do it,' she declared.

'I'll break open a bottle of cider to celebrate,' Ben said, grinning.

'Ben Ashley, it's barely mid-afternoon. What kind of example would that be to set our son, and what use will you be for the rest of the day, if you're worse for wear?' Rose admonished

'I was only thinking of the one bottle, Rose.'

'You can content yourself with mixing the special Ashcombe cider cup. No doubt you will sample it sufficiently to quench your thirst. Now, we'll need to make a list,' Rose said, grabbing a pencil and frowning in concentration.

'While you girls make the arrangements, Duncan and I will take the harvest cart and spread the word,' Ben said, getting quickly to his feet.

'Make sure we have enough cider for the wassail cup,

then look out your great-grandfather's clayen to serve it in,' Rose told him.

'Yes, ma'am,' Ben said with a salute. 'Gosh, she's getting as bossy as Great-Grandmother,' he grumbled to Duncan.

'When did you say this Wassail is held?' Eliza asked.

'On the old Twelfth Night, which is the 17th of January,' Rose said. 'Why, that's in two days' time,' she squawked. Flinging open the back door she yelled, 'Ben Ashley, get yourself back in here this very minute.' But all they could hear was the sound of hooves and the clatter of the cart making its way down the icy track.

8

'Have you ever made apple cakes before?' Rose asked Eliza the next morning.

She shook her head. 'I made apple pie once for a special treat,' she replied.

'Well, I've no idea how to make them,' Rose muttered. 'Worse still, there's some special ingredient one has to use to make them the Ashcombe way. Apparently this marries with what's used in the wassail cup.'

'Is there a receipt somewhere?'

'Gosh, I am a clod. Great-Grandmother's book's kept in the old hall. Come on.'

Eliza followed Rose along the hallway until they came to a halt in front of a magnificent dresser reflecting the patina of age. Pulling down a huge tome, Rose began flicking through the pages, which gave Eliza a chance to look around.

This part of the building had a completely different feel to it. She couldn't help nodding to Great-Grandfather Joshua on the wall opposite and could have sworn his eyes twinkled back. She was convinced she could detect a whiff of tobacco smoke. How lovely it would have been to have a picture of Grampy on the wall of their cottage, she thought. Then she noticed what looked like a tiny door in the wall to the right of his picture.

'What's that?' she asked Rose.

'It's the hidy-hole where Ben's great-grandfather placed their babies' first shoes.' Seeing Eliza's puzzled look, she continued, 'According to some ancient custom, bricking up a shoe in the wall brings luck to the household. Of course, Joshua, being Joshua, insisted on placing a pair of each of his children's shoes in there. He was never one to do things by halves. The tradition has continued down the generations so I guess we'll have to do the same with Joshua's first pair.' Rose shuddered. 'This hallway gives me the creeps. It feels like a flipping mausoleum. I'm hoping that in time I'll be able to persuade Ben to rip it out. I quite fancy turning this part into a garden room.'

'Oh, you mustn't,' cried Eliza. Then, when Rose stared at her in amazement: 'You're so lucky having all this family history around you. I've never experienced that.'

'Whatever's gone on in your past can't be changed. However, the future lies ahead. When you marry and have children you'll be able to create your own memories, won't you?' Rose pointed out.

Eliza snorted and pointed down to her heavy-booted foot. 'No man's going to want me with this.'

'Whatever gave you that idea?' Rose said.

'My father told me so,' Eliza muttered.

'Well, I think he's wrong, Eliza. You're an attractive young woman, you know.'

Eliza stared down at the baggy rough shirt and ill-fitting serge trousers, and both women burst out laughing.

'Why are you wearing those dreadful clothes anyway?' Rose asked.

'Fay lent them to me. It's so cold in the hobble and I only had one thin dress with me.'

'Oh, they're Fay's clothes. I might have known. Well, just because she goes around dressed like a man doesn't mean you have to. Once we've found out how to make these hecking apple cakes, we'll sort you some decent clothes to wear. It'll be ages before I'm back into my nice things,' she said, grimacing down at her still-rounded stomach.

With a sigh, she resumed her search for the receipt and after a few moments yelled in triumph, 'Here it is!' However, her delight was cut short by the wailing baby. 'Damn,' she muttered.

'Shall I see to him or go back to the kitchen and make a start?' Eliza asked.

'Here, take this,' Rose said, thrusting the heavy book into her hands. 'Joshua will need feeding, so I'd best go. Don't know why I bother, though. No sooner do I put it in one end than it comes gushing out the other.'

Eliza chuckled, remembering how her mother had said the same thing.

Back in the kitchen, she made sure the table was clean, then carefully set down the ancient tome. She was methodically going through the list of ingredients when the door opened and Duncan appeared. He smiled warmly at her and she beamed back, realizing she'd missed him in the short time he'd been away.

'Hello, little un. How are you feeling today?' he asked, rubbing his hands and holding them to warm beside the range.

'I'm much better, thank you. And guess what? I've got a room all to myself and a real bed to sleep in,' she enthused.

'My, my, we'll have to be calling you "my lady" soon,' he

quipped. 'You know, Eliza, life here suits you. You've already got more colour in your cheeks.'

Eliza felt herself blushing at the compliment, pleased beyond words at what he'd said.

'By the way, I looked in on Fay earlier.'

'How is she?'

'Coming to terms with Woody's loss in her own time and way.'

Eliza nodded. 'It probably helps not having me around.'

Duncan smiled. 'Peace is her solace at the moment, little un. Now, Ben's sent me in to see if there's any tea in the offing.'

She gestured to the pot, then turned back to the receipt, hardly noticing when he went out again.

Cream golden butter with the richest of sugars ye possess. Raise arm and sift ye flours from yon highest place.

'Crikey, I feel like one of the blinking cows this morning,' Rose said, rubbing her chest as she came back into the kitchen.

'That'll be your milk coming in fully,' Eliza said.

'You mean he might go longer between feeds?' Eliza nodded. 'Blimey, thank heavens for that. Good job you're here; you've much more idea than me. I could never discuss such things with my mother. Oh good, you've brewed tea. I'm parched. Let's go through the ingredients whilst we have our tea.'

'This receipt looks quite straightforward,' Eliza said glancing down at the page again.

Beat in freshest eggs and apples finely smashest.

'Here, don't keep it to yourself, let me see,' Rose said, leaning across the table.

Cream golden butter with the richest of sugars ye possess.
Raise arm and sift ye flours from yon highest place.
Beat in freshest eggs and apples finely smashest.
Take crimson-coloured aril, the . . . ou . . . lace,
A pinch will be sufficient to add the secret . . .
A sprinkling of su . . .
Thus will complement the wassa . . .
Your good health . . .

'Blimey, half the words are worn away. We won't have good health if we don't discover what the secret ingredient is,' Rose moaned, putting her head in her hands. 'Maybe if we make a trial batch of apple cakes we can work out what this crimson-coloured aril thingy is.'

Eliza looked at Rose sceptically.

'Well, we've got to try something, haven't we?' Rose muttered, getting to her feet as Joshua's shrill cry rent the air.

Eliza sat staring at the ingredients. Obviously, these would make little apple sponge-like cakes but what could the special ingredient be? She was just reading through Rose's notes when the door opened and Ben put his head around it.

'I suppose you've come for more refreshments,' she said, reaching for the empty mugs he was holding.

'I see you've made a start on the apple cakes,' he said.

'Hmm, just going through the ingredients,' she said. Then she had a thought. 'When will you be making this wassail cup?'

'It will probably be tomorrow now. We've got to see to the animals first. I'm a bit behind, what with Rose and the baby. Luckily, Duncan insisted on helping and I'm mighty grateful. Don't worry,' he said, mistaking Eliza's crestfallen look. 'We won't be too busy to sample the apple cakes when they're cooked. Have to make sure they taste right, haven't we?'

'What do they taste like, Ben? I've never eaten one,' she added quickly as he gave her a strange look.

'Of course you haven't. Well, they're sweet, spicy, and of course the sugar coating makes them crunchy,' he added, disappearing outside again.

Eliza returned to the notes. *A sprinkling of su . . .* so that would be a sprinkling of sugar on the top then, she thought, carefully completing the sentence. *One step at a time, Eliza.* Unbidden, Grampy's saying popped into her head and she sighed. If only she could work out what the other missing words were. She went back over the receipt. Perhaps if she looked in the pantry she'd find some of this crimson-coloured aril. It would be better than sitting here waiting for Rose to return.

Although she searched the shelves, she could find no trace of anything called aril, or anything crimson. And as for that lace, you wouldn't put material into a cake mixture, surely? She returned to her chair and was pondering the puzzle when Duncan reappeared. Immediately the room seemed brighter and Eliza felt her spirits rise.

'Finished what I was doing so Ben thought it would be a good idea if I began gathering together the things for the wassail cup. You look pale, little un. Not been overdoing things, have you?'

'We're trying to making a start on those apple cakes but some of the words have faded. Do you know what the secret Ashcombe ingredient is?' she asked.

'Not exactly,' he said. 'You have been thrown in at the deep end, haven't you?'

9

'Without the complete receipt you won't be able to make those cakes, will you?' Eliza shook her head and he sighed. 'Can I help?'

'Do you know what crimson-coloured aril is?' she burst out.

'As it happens, I do.'

Hope flared in her heart. 'And is that what you put in the Ashcombe wassail cup?'

'Crimson aril is the lacy covering of nutmeg, young un. When it's dried it turns yellow or tan.'

'Oh, thank you,' she cried, taking the paper from him. 'But that can't be right,' she said, her heart sinking. 'Nutmeg has six letters and there's room for only four on the receipt, look,' she said, stabbing at the notes with her finger.

'Dear, dear, young un, mace is the word you need. It's what the outer covering of the nutmeg is called.'

'Oh. So you put this mace into both the apple cakes and the wassail cup?'

'No, mace, the outer covering of the nutmeg, is what the Ashleys use for their apple cakes. The nutmeg itself they put into the wassail cup. They have very similar, yet not quite the same, tastes, which complement each other perfectly. Clever, eh?'

As he smiled gently at her across the table, Eliza felt

herself going warm. He made her feel loved like Grampy used to. Yet like those two spices, mace and nutmeg, not in quite the same way. While she was musing he disappeared into the pantry, reappearing with what looked like two dark, oval conkers, which rattled together when he shook them. In his other hand he held some bark-like strips.

'I'll be back shortly to complete your spice lesson,' he said grinning. Eliza went back to Rose's notes but was none the wiser when Duncan returned holding out two jars.

'I've ground the spices and, as you can see, this nutmeg is darker than the mace here. Now what can you smell? Careful, they are quite pungent.' He held first one and then the other jar under her nose. She inhaled.

'Hmm, they are lovely. Warm and very spicy but this one is sweeter, isn't it?' she said, pointing to the nutmeg.

'Well done, little un. You have a very good nose. The mace here is more refined and slightly bitter. Hence you put mace in the cakes and save the nutmeg for the wassail cup. Well, for the Ashcombe receipts, anyway.'

As Rose came into the kitchen Duncan jumped to his feet, snatching up the jar of nutmeg.

'I'll leave you to it. I know you'll be itching to get on with your baking now,' he said, winking at Eliza.

As the door shut behind him, Rose arched an eyebrow.

'Good news,' Eliza said excitedly. 'We've found the secret ingredient.' She held up the jar of mace. Rose clapped her hands in delight. 'But that's not all. I discovered we need to sprinkle sugar on the tops to ensure a crispy coating.'

'Thank the Lord,' Rose muttered. 'Right, let's get mixing these wretched cakes.'

While Eliza peeled and smashed the apples, Rose mixed the dry ingredients together.

'Hey, go easy,' Eliza cautioned, as the other woman went to tip in the mace. 'Duncan says that's pungent and the receipt does say a pinch.'

'Surely that won't be enough,' Rose scoffed. 'There's loads of cake mixture.'

'Yes, but smell the spice. It's very strong,' Eliza pointed out. 'Look, this is a sample batch so let's use a pinch and if these aren't spicy enough we can add more when we bake tomorrow.'

Once the cakes were cooking in the range, they made tea and collapsed onto the chairs to recover. Before long, the kitchen was suffused with the aroma of spices.

'Well, they smell all right, don't they?' Rose observed, topping up their mugs.

'Yes, and they smell ready, too,' Eliza said, getting to her feet.

'But they've not been in long enough yet,' Rose said, frowning at the ormolu clock on the dresser. 'My mother gave us that expensive clock for our wedding present. It came from the very best clockmaker in London and is accurate to the second.'

'Yes, and it's quite lovely,' Eliza said, crossing her fingers beneath her apron. 'But all ranges have different temperatures. You have to trust your nose, not the time.' Privately she thought the ornate timepiece looked out of place in the cosy room.

'All right, it won't do any harm if we have a look,' agreed Rose.

Eliza bent down and opened the range door. Carefully

she took out the cakes and placed the tray onto the table. 'These are ready, see.'

'Goodness, so they are,' Rose exclaimed, looking up as she heard the latch click. Ben popped his head around the door.

'Something smells good,' he said.

'Oh, Ben,' she gushed, throwing herself into his arms, 'come in and try one of our apple cakes.'

'Is that invitation extended to me?' Duncan asked, following in behind. As they stood sampling the cakes, Rose and Eliza exchanged anxious glances.

'Delicious. The best I've ever tasted and with just the right amount of spice, too,' Ben said, putting his arm around his wife and drawing her close. 'What a clever girl you are,' he murmured. As Rose flushed with pleasure, Duncan winked at Eliza. It seemed good relations had been restored.

'By the way, Tinks called by with a message from your mother. She simply cannot wait any longer to see her grandson. The weather down the valley has cleared sufficiently for her to make the journey so she'll be arriving after luncheon tomorrow.'

'Oh, no,' Rose groaned.

'But that's good, isn't it?' Ben asked. 'She'll be able to do her first spot of babysitting whilst we host the festivities. Come on, Duncan, no peace for the wicked,' he said, kissing Rose's cheek.

As the door shut behind them, Rose grimaced.

'Now I'll have to make sure everywhere is spick and span. Mother can spot a dust mote from a hundred paces. Still, as Ben says, it does mean I can join in the wassailing.'

Eliza smiled but she was wondering what was going to happen to her. Rose's mother would expect to sleep in the room she was using, wouldn't she?

Her thoughts were interrupted by the sound of Joshua's whimpering. While Rose hurried to attend to him, Eliza set about clearing up the kitchen. At the least the apple cakes had turned out successfully. Now they knew how to make them, it wouldn't take long to knock up sufficient for the festivities.

'Come on, Eliza, let's see what we can find for you to wear for the celebrations.' She was roused from her reverie by Rose calling to her from the doorway. Eliza followed her up the stairs and into a bedroom with dainty yellow sprigged curtains at the window and a matching coverlet on the bed.

Rose rummaged in a chest, then tossed two dark red flannel petticoats onto the bed. 'Didn't you say you only had a thin dress with you?' Eliza nodded. 'Well, these should go nicely underneath and add an extra layer. I imagine it's freezing higher up the moors.'

'It is, but don't you want them?' Eliza asked, running her hand over the warm material.

'Not now I'm a married woman,' Rose giggled. 'Right then, let's see what else is in here. Ah, yes.' Rose drew out a leaf-green cape, edged with emerald velvet, followed by a gown in corded dimity. Then a cotton lawn petticoat trimmed with broderie anglaise joined the pile. Rose dangled a stomacher in front of her, grimacing. 'Mother will make me wear this, I know she will, and no doubt she'll have me tightly laced in stays, too.' She pouted down at her post-baby figure. 'One mustn't let oneself go, Rosaline,' she parroted in a hoity-toity voice.

Eliza giggled. 'I didn't know your name was Rosaline.'

Rose sighed. 'Rosaline Evangaline Josaphine Madaleine, to be precise. Mouthful or what? What's your full name?'

'I don't have any fancy middle names. Nor do my sisters Hester and Isabel,' she said.

'Oh, you have sisters?'

Eliza nodded, feeling a sudden pang. 'Don't you?' she asked.

Rose shook her head. 'No, I'm an only child. Obviously one time of "it" was enough for Mother,' she said. As Eliza eyed her curiously she giggled. 'I shall definitely be having lots more children, in case you're wondering.'

Not knowing what to say, Eliza stared down at the clothes on the bed.

'Here, Eliza Dryad, these are for you,' Rose said, scooping them up and handing them to her.

'I can't take them all,' Eliza protested.

'Well, they won't fit me for a while and if I don't have anything suitable to wear, Mother will take pity on me and insist on treating me to some new outfits,' Rose said shamelessly. 'Besides, you'll need to dress up for the Wassail tomorrow night and that cape will bring out the colour of your eyes.'

Eliza ran her fingers over the soft nap of the velvet trim. 'I've never worn anything so beautiful,' she sighed.

Next morning, the farmhouse was a frenzy of activity, but by lunchtime the cakes, wassail cup and slices of toasted bread were laid out on the scrubbed kitchen table ready for the evening's festivities. While Rose fed the baby, Eliza put clean linen on the bed. She looked around the room she'd been using and sighed. The apple-green curtains and matching coverlet gave it a cosy feel whilst the wool rug was bliss to step onto first thing in the morning. Resolutely, she tied her things into a bundle, donned the gown Rose had given her and brushed her hair until it crackled with electricity.

'Oh, you look really pretty. That dress suits you,' Rose said, appearing in the doorway. She was wearing a satin gown in soft claret, which made her gentian eyes look bluer than ever. 'You can leave your things in the cupboard by the kitchen. Are you sure you don't mind sleeping by the range tonight? I don't like asking you to move but Mother will expect to sleep in here. The rooms down the old hallway haven't been used in ages and need a good airing.'

Eliza smiled, and gave a final look around the room she'd spent the two most comfortable nights of her life in.

'It's been kind of you to let me use it,' she said, her gaze coming to rest on a miniature painting of a gentian.

'Phooey. I don't know how I'd have managed without your help, Eliza. Fay painted that for our wedding present,' Rose said, noticing her interest. 'She wouldn't come to the ceremony herself but insisted on giving us something for our home.'

'It's exquisite,' Eliza whispered.

'I think it's amazing that a woman who can heft hay bales and shear sheep should have such a delicate touch,' Rose said. She looked as though she was going to say something else but was distracted by the sound of voices.

'You can put my luggage in my room, Benjamin.'

'Certainly, Mother Evangaline,' Ben answered.

Eliza stared at Rose in surprise.

'Just Ben's little joke,' Rose whispered.

'Then I simply must see my grandson,' the strident voice rang down the hallway. 'And where is Rosaline?'

Rose stared at Eliza in dismay. 'Why do I always feel like a child as soon as I hear her?' she whispered, smoothing down her skirts. 'Please come with me for moral support.'

With a last look around the room, Eliza hurried after her. A woman of middle years, fair hair swept up in a coronet and wearing a grey day dress, stood waiting impatiently in the parlour.

'Mother, how lovely to see you,' Rose said, kissing the woman's cheek. 'May I introduce Eliza Dryad. She has been helping me until you could get here.'

The woman accepted her daughter's kiss, then lifted her lorgnette. She had eyes the same gentian as Rose but her gaze, as it swept over Eliza, was hard and assessing.

'I didn't know you'd engaged the services of a nanny?' she said finally.

Rose raised her eyebrows at Eliza behind the woman's back. 'I haven't, Mother. Eliza is a friend.'

'Dryad, you say? I can't say I've ever heard that of name. You're not from around these parts, then?'

Eliza shook her head.

'Eliza is a friend of Duncan's.'

The woman sniffed dismissively. 'Well, I'm sure you have plenty to do, Miss Dryad. Now, Rose, you must take me to the nursery. I simply cannot wait a moment longer to see my grandson.'

As Rose led her mother up the stairs, Eliza shook her head. What a pompous woman, and clearly she'd found

Eliza wanting. Ben, who had stayed out of the way until the coast was clear, suddenly appeared.

'Don't worry about Mother Evangaline. She has ideas far above her station,' he said, giving a rueful grin. They heard the woman cooing, followed by an angry wail. 'Babies are wondrous levellers, aren't they?' he grinned. 'Fancy a brew before the festivities? With any luck we've time to drink it in the kitchen before Mother E comes back. She insists we use the parlour. Only one's staff partake of refreshment in the kitchen, Benjamin,' he parroted in that hoity-toity voice Rose had affected earlier. 'Of course, that'd be fine if one had staff.'

Despite herself, Eliza burst out laughing. Retrieving her bundle and cloak, she followed Ben into the kitchen.

'Does that mean Rose's mother doesn't come in here?' she asked, thinking of the bed she intended making up beside the range.

'Only to inspect things,' Ben said. 'Luckily for me, she's an insomniac and mainly roams at night then sleeps in during the day. Though Joshua might put paid to that, of course.'

Eliza stared at the range in dismay. She wouldn't be able to sleep here now, would she?

I 0

Before she had time to say anything, the door opened and Duncan appeared. His eyes widened in surprise when he saw her.

'I was looking for the little un but it seems I'm in the wrong place. Who is this beautiful young lady, pray?' he asked, turning to Ben.

'Don't know but if I weren't a married man, I'd be begging to escort her to the festivities myself,' Ben replied, winking at her. Eliza giggled.

'Everything's prepared. Your guests are arriving so you'd better get moving,' Duncan said, becoming serious.

Ben sighed. 'No time for that cuppa, then. I'd better change into my outfit, then rescue Rose. I'm sure Mother Evangaline can't wait to have her new grandson to herself. Hopefully he'll be in fine voice,' he grinned.

'Come along, Eliza, I'll guide you down to the orchard,' Duncan said, picking up her cloak from the back of the chair. As he gallantly draped it around her shoulders, he whispered, 'You look stunning. However, no self-respecting maid would ever go to the festivities bare-headed so I've made this for you.' He held up a circle of laurel leaves and placed it gently on her hair. She blushed self-consciously.

'Well, at least I've changed,' she quipped, trying to hide her awkwardness.

'Indeed you have,' he agreed, giving her a lingering

look. 'I'll have you know, young lady, I braved a shower in the waterfall earlier and the water stung like icy needles. I also changed into a clean shirt, which I'm wearing beneath my coat.' For some reason she didn't understand, this information made her cheeks go warm again.

'Well, what are we waiting for?' he continued, opening the door and holding out his arm for her to take.

It was crisp outside, their breath spiralling before them as it rose into the night air. As Duncan helped her down the slippery path towards the festivities, Eliza saw a huge bonfire had been lit, its red and orange flames illuminating the inky darkness. As they drew nearer, she could hear the crackle of burning branches and smell the wood smoke mingling with the aroma of pungent spices. Judging by the sounds of joviality, this was an important event, she thought, pulling the cape tighter around her. Mistaking her gesture, Duncan pulled her closer and she caught the scent of pine from the soap he'd used. Feeling her cheeks growing ever hotter, she was thankful for the cover of darkness. She couldn't imagine life without him now and hoped she wouldn't ever have to.

'You'll soon get warm amongst all these people,' he said, smiling down at her. As they entered the orchard, the bare trees loomed out of the shadows like dark sentinels, their branches closing together like a great canopy.

'Goodness, just look at all those nests. They must have very big birds round here,' she exclaimed, pointing to the higher branches where little bushes hung like pendants.

Duncan chuckled. 'That is mistletoe, little un. Some think it a parasitic plant but we Druids believe it protects

the possessor from evil. It has wonderful curative properties but, of course, most people use it to decorate their
homes at Christmas when it is the tradition to steal a kiss
beneath it.'

'Steal a kiss?'

'Indeed, it is deemed permissible to kiss the object of
one's desire when he or she is standing under mistletoe,
though one must be scrupulous about removing a berry for
each kiss. When none remain, the kissing must stop. Did you
never decorate your home with mistletoe at Christmas, then?'

Eliza shook her head. Why, her parents barely acknowledged the day, let alone decorated their cottage.

He led her through the thronging crowd, calling out
greetings as he went. Finally they came to a halt in front
of a platform that had been erected from old branches.
'Now we await the arrival of our King and Queen,' he
said. 'That's Ben and Rose,' he teased, seeing her eyes
widen in amazement. 'They will lead the festivities and
when it comes to the singing and dancing I shall accompany them.' He dug in his pocket and brought out his
flute. 'Here they come,' he whispered.

The crowd gave a triumphant cheer as Ben and Rose,
dressed in their regal finery, appeared. Suddenly the air
was rent with the deafening sound of drumming as everyone banged vigorously on the pots and pans they'd
brought with them.

'This is to wake the cider apple trees and scare off the
evil spirits who inhabit the woods in the form of worms
and maggots. Once they're gone, the good spirits will be
attracted,' Duncan explained, raising his voice above the
clamour.

'Wassail,' shouted the crowd as Ben and Rose climbed onto the makeshift platform. Ben held up his mug and the orchard fell silent, the atmosphere crackling with anticipation.

'Greetings and welcome to one and all,' Ben cried. 'I shall now call upon the Spirit of the Apple Tree.'

Here's to Thee,
Spirit of the Apple Tree
Waken now and hear our plea
Upon every single apple bough
Your fertility you will bestow
To make our apples bloom and grow

As his voice died away everyone clapped and cheered. With a flourish, he took a piece of the toast they'd made earlier and dipped it into the clayen, which was now brimming with the spiced cider, rings of apple floating on the top. Handing it ceremoniously to Rose, he then lifted her up to the large old tree behind the platform, where she placed it firmly between its branches.

'This is a present to the spirit of the oldest tree where the fertility of the orchard is housed,' Duncan whispered.

That done, Ben and Rose dipped their mugs into the clayen and skipped through the orchard sprinkling cider around the roots of the trees. Finally, they climbed back onto the platform and carefully lifted the precious clayen.

'Wassail,' shouted Ben. The crowd cheered and began to sing.

Here's to the old apple tree
Hats full, caps full,
Bushel sacks full

As the song died away, Ben again shouted, 'Wassail.'

'Drink ale,' the crowd responded, surging towards the platform, holding out their mugs. As Ben ladled out the spiced cider, Duncan grabbed a brimming mug and handed it to Eliza.

'Drink and enjoy, little un. It'll warm your insides.'

'Thank you,' she whispered, cautiously taking a sip. 'That's delicious.' She took another drink.

'Take heed: it's stronger than you think,' Duncan warned, raising his voice above the noise. Reluctantly, she handed him back the mug. Then she saw Rose handing out the apple cakes to the eager revellers and she went over and helped herself from the tray.

'These are really good, aren't they?' she said, biting into one and pocketing another.

Duncan nodded. 'Hmm, just the right amount of mace, young un. Well done. Oh, look, Ben and Rose are about to start off the dancing.' He lifted his flute to his lips and began to play. As the lilting melody filled the air, everyone began to sing and dance.

Never before had she seen so many people laughing and having fun, Eliza thought, clapping and swaying in time to the music. Suddenly she felt a prickle crawl up the back of her neck. Someone was watching her. Looking up, she found herself staring into Fay's eyes. The woman was standing a little way back from the revellers and she nodded to Eliza.

'Fay,' Eliza called, hurrying over. 'How are you?'

'Just came to make sure the Spirit of the Apple Tree was invoked,' she said gruffly.

'Here, have an apple cake. I made them with Rose,' Eliza said, taking out the cake she'd pocketed earlier. 'Shall I get you some cider cup?'

'Stop fussing, child,' Fay grunted, but she bit into the cake hungrily. 'Not bad,' she pronounced, and Eliza grinned into the darkness. Obviously the woman was back to her taciturn self. 'Suppose you're finding it nice and comfortable at the farmhouse?' Fay asked, staring at the bonfire as she spoke.

'Suppose you're finding it comfortable with your own company?' Eliza countered, taking care not to look at the woman.

'Don't suppose you'd fancy coming back to the homestead, anyhow.'

'Don't suppose you'd want me cluttering up your space.'

'Honestly, you two sound just like grandmother and granddaughter,' Duncan said, appearing out of the shadows. Fay snorted. 'Good to see you again, Fay,' he added.

She let out another snort. 'You visited yesterday, whippersnapper, and don't think I didn't realize you were checking up on me.'

'As if,' he protested, grinning at Eliza. 'Doesn't little un look good in her finery?'

'Smart clothes, like fine words, don't butter no parsnips. And they won't be much good for keeping warm back at home, will they?'

Duncan and Eliza looked at one another.

'Home? You mean you want me to come back?' Eliza asked.

'Can't impose on Rose and Ben any longer, can you? I heard her mother had arrived and you'll only be in the way now. Likes to rule the roost, that one, and I'm not sure you'd measure up in her books, anyhow.'

Remembering the woman's condescending attitude towards her earlier, Eliza privately agreed. She could just imagine the fuss if she was caught sleeping by the range.

'Well, that's settled then,' Duncan said. 'It's a fair walk back, so I'll ask Ben if I can borrow his wagon.'

'Not for me you won't, boy. I made my own way down and I'll make my own way back. Don't keep Eliza out too late, though; can't do with having my sleep disturbed at my age.' She turned and began striding back towards the path.

'Shouldn't we go after her?' Eliza asked.

Duncan shook his head. 'No point in upsetting her. Still, it's obvious she's missed you.'

'Come on, Duncan, we're waiting for more music,' someone called. As others murmured in agreement, he grinned ruefully.

'Let's enjoy the rest of the festivities, then I'll take you home,' he said, picking up his flute.

Home! Home! Home! The words went round Eliza's head in time to the beating music. She watched Duncan's fingers moving gracefully up and down the wooden instrument and felt . . . she didn't know what she was feeling. Just then, he looked up and caught her watching. Passing his flute to a lad standing nearby, he held out his arms.

'May I request the honour of this dance, little un?'

Involuntarily, she glanced down at her foot.

'Come on,' he urged.

As he whirled her around in time to the music she felt as if she was floating, her feet hardly seeming to touch the ground. Before long she was caught up in the merriment. Never before had she enjoyed herself like this, she thought, smiling up at Duncan.

'Come on, little un, time we were getting back. We can't have you getting exhausted,' he said gruffly, taking her hand and leading her through the crowds until they came to the platform where Rose and Ben were presiding over the festivities. 'Just spoken to Fay and she's ready for Eliza to return so I'm taking her home. As it's been a long day for her – can I borrow the wagon?'

'Of course,' Ben agreed.

'I wish you could stay,' Rose said, turning to Eliza.

'You don't need me now your mother has arrived. She'll want you and Joshua to herself.'

'But I'll miss you. You will come and see us soon, won't you?' Eliza nodded. 'Duncan thinks the world of you,' Rose whispered, throwing her arms around her.

'And I think the world of him. He makes me feel happier than I've ever been,' she sighed. 'I've loved staying with you, Rose. Thank you for making me so welcome.' She felt a pang deep inside for she would miss her new friend. Then with another sigh, she turned and began making her way up the path towards the farmhouse.

She just had time to snatch up her precious bundle of new clothes before Duncan appeared at the door. He was holding a candle lantern and, placing it carefully on the seat, helped her into the wagon.

'Don't want you catching another chill, do we?' he murmured, covering her with a blanket. Then, with a call to the horse, they began moving.

Soon they'd left the sounds of revelry behind, and apart from the rhythmic clip-clop of the horse's hooves they were enclosed in the night's silent cloak. Cold moonlight shone from a clear sky, while hedges coated in silver frost cast eerie ebony shadows all around them.

'Look at all those stars,' she marvelled, staring up at the sky, where seemingly millions were twinkling like diamonds on a velvet cloth. 'It's been a magical evening,' she sighed. He nodded.

'Wassail is a special time.'

'I really like Ben and Rose,' she said. 'I can't believe how snooty her mother is, though.'

Duncan's laughter sounded loud in the quiet of the night. 'She does have a certain aura, I'll grant you.'

Eliza hooted in derision. 'That's not what I'd call it. What was Rose's father like?'

'Lovely chap. Too meek and mild for his own good, though. He absolutely adored his wife and strove to provide everything she wanted. Not that it was ever enough for Mother Evangaline. He worked himself into the ground, poor man. And for what? Chattels, which, however fine, were never good enough, that's what. 'Tis people that matter in this world, little un, not possessions.' He shook his head, then turned to look at her. 'Talking of auras, did you see any more of Great-Grandfather Joshua?' Although he spoke casually, Eliza sensed her answer was important to him.

'I didn't see him again but I'm sure I smelled his pipe a few times. Or do you think that's fanciful?'

Duncan shook his head. 'No, I don't. Christmas and Wassail were his favourite time of year so if his spirit were to pay a visit it would be around now.'

Suddenly the horse whinnied and came to an abrupt halt. 'Don't tell me you've seen him too, old boy,' Duncan called, leaning forward and patting him soothingly. 'Come along, walk on.' But the animal was having none of it and refused to budge. Duncan peered into the darkness.

'What the . . .?' The rest of his sentence was lost as he leaped down from the wagon. Then Eliza heard him murmuring gently and she saw he was trying to lift something into an upright position.

'What's going on?' she asked, clambering down and crouching beside him.

'It's Fay,' he said, shaking his head.

'She's not dead, is she?' Eliza whispered, staring aghast at the lifeless body

'Of course I'm not,' Fay snorted, her eyes snapping open. 'I slipped on that blooming glass frost. Well, don't just stand there, pull me up, boy,' she commanded, holding out her hand to Duncan.

'Careful does it, Fay. Let's make sure nothing's broken first,' he said, running assessing fingers over her leg. He began pulling off her boot but she slapped his hands away.

'If you think I'm lying in the perishing cold whilst you play doctors, you've got another think coming. Come on, take me home.' Duncan and Eliza exchanged glances but, knowing it would be futile to argue, they began manoeuvring Fay as gently as possible into the wagon. It was obvious she was in pain, but she stoically stared straight ahead and they knew better than to comment. Once they'd got her onto the bench, Eliza covered her with the blanket, then went round and slid awkwardly into the middle so she could support the woman. Duncan swung himself up next to her and, unbidden, the horse began to move.

Eliza couldn't believe how much the temperature had fallen. The higher they climbed the colder it got. All around, seemingly endless moorland glistened with virgin white snow, which even in the moonlight hurt her eyes. Here and there trees bent low by the harsh weather lined the path, their branches coated with thick glittering ice.

She shivered; winter certainly lasted much longer this high up on the moors.

Her thoughts were interrupted by a screech that pierced the silence of the night. It sounded like a tortured soul in pain and Eliza shuddered, feeling the hairs on her neck prickle. Hearing her sharp intake of breath, Duncan reached out and patted her hand.

'Easy, little un. That's just a vixen calling for her lover.'

'You mean that noise is normal?' she gasped. He nodded and Eliza was sure Fay gave a faint chuckle from beneath the cover.

'Listen and you'll hear him answer,' he instructed. Sure enough a moment later, she heard a sharp bark echoing across the fields. 'There, that's the dogfox. I'll show you their tracks in the snow one day, if you like. You'll be amazed how large their paw prints are.'

Eliza shivered, thinking that was one treat she could do without. Luckily she was saved from answering as they'd reached the river and all his concentration was centred on guiding the wagon over the narrow bridge.

'Nearly home, Fay,' Duncan commented, but the woman's eyes were closed and she didn't answer. However, no sooner had the wagon come to a halt than she snapped awake, cast aside the blanket and attempted to climb down. Her usually agile movements were clumsy and Eliza could see her wincing.

'Stay there, old thing,' Duncan said, jumping down and going around to her side. Making sure the blanket was tucked tightly around her, he lifted her into his arms. As Eliza went to climb down, he shook his head.

'Wait here. That ground's as slippery as the glass the

frost is named after and it will do none of us any good if you fall and hurt yourself as well. Hold out the lantern so I can see.'

She did as he asked, then watched as he slowly inched his way along the path, carefully holding Fay. The wind rose, moaning across the vast expanse of moorland and Eliza pulled the cloak tighter round her. Then Duncan was back, tossing her bundle over his shoulder and lifting her into his arms as if she weighed no more than a fistful of feathers. Gripping the lantern tightly, she held her breath as he slipped and skidded towards the hobble.

Thankfully, they made it inside without mishap. Fay, covered by the blanket, was perched awkwardly on the chair holding out her hands to the fire, which had almost died. As Duncan lit another candle from the one in the lantern, Eliza could see she was ashen, her face pinched with pain.

'You get a blaze going while I take the horse into the barn before the poor thing freezes. I'll bring in more wood when I return,' Duncan said. His calm, authoritative voice spurred Eliza into action and she bent and raked through the embers, adding twigs and the smaller pieces of chopped wood until it flared. Thankfully the pot was full of water and after hooking it onto the arm she pulled it over the fire to heat, then turned to Fay.

The woman had her eyes closed and was shivering violently. Quickly, Eliza piled the sheepskins around her shoulders and on top of the blanket, then eased the chair closer to the fire. She'd just finished when Duncan reappeared. He took one look at Fay and shook his head.

'Shock's set in,' he said, taking a bottle out of his pocket then going over to the dresser and pouring liquid into a mug. 'Right, Fay, drink this,' he urged, holding it to her lips. To Eliza's surprise she meekly did as he said. Then, exhausted, she sank back in the chair and closed her eyes. He dropped to his knees, ignoring her protests as he tugged off her boots. Gently he began feeling along her feet and ankles. 'Hmm, I think that's wrenched but not broken or sprained. Now let's have a look at your hands.' Meekly she held them up for him to examine. 'A couple of cuts and you've definitely sprained your right wrist. You must have gone down with a good wallop, old girl,' he murmured.

'Call me that again, whippersnapper, and I'll toss you out in the snow, sprain or no sprain,' she grunted weakly.

Eliza saw the colour returning to the woman's cheeks and realized Duncan had goaded her on purpose. While he gently cleaned Fay's hands then bound her wrist and ankle with strips of old sheeting, Eliza busied herself making them hot drinks.

They sat in front of the fire, sipping their tea and listening to the ferocious wind howling around the building like a wild animal. Fay had stopped shivering and was dozing quietly when Duncan, who was perched on the floor between the two chairs, leaned forward and tossed more logs onto the blaze.

'Time you got some sleep, ladies,' he said, getting to his feet and pulling down their mattresses. Eliza stifled a yawn. The day had been so eventful, she hadn't realized she was tired until now. As another strong gust of wind buffeted the hobble, Fay turned to Duncan.

'Weather's worsening. You'd best stay the night.'

'Only if you ladies promise not to fight over me,' he quipped.

Fay snorted. 'It was the horse I was concerned about,' she muttered weakly, then winced.

Instantly, he was on his feet, mixing more liquid and handing it to Fay. 'Drink this, it'll ease the pain and settle you.' While the woman drank it down, he piled her mattress with sheepskins. Then, he helped her remove the greatcoat and placed it on top.

'Look the other way, whippersnapper, whilst we get into bed,' Fay grunted. 'Got little un's reputation to think of.'

'I'll check the horse is all right and bring in more wood,' he said. 'When I return, I expect to see you both asleep.'

Eliza smiled as he disappeared. Who would ever have imagined Fay obeying him, she thought, watching as the woman sank down awkwardly onto the mattress. Knowing better than to offer to help, she took off her cloak and spread it over the sheepskins. She was just settling onto her own bed when she felt something prickle her hair. Reaching up, she smiled when her hands came into contact with the coronet of laurel leaves. Carefully removing it, she placed it on the table. She would press it to keep for ever. It was just a shame she'd lost her grampy's box, she thought, pulling the covers over her.

It had been such an exciting day. Her mind drifted back to the Wassail. Who would have thought that she, Eliza Dryad, would spend the night dancing? And in the arms of the handsome giant? She closed her eyes, reliving what it had felt like.

The next thing she knew, cold grey light of the morning was filtering through the window. Fay was still sleeping but of Duncan there was no sign. Surely he hadn't spent the night outside in the freezing weather? Quickly she removed the beautiful dress, shaking out the creases before tugging on the old warm shirt and trousers of Fay's. Then she riddled the embers until the fire blazed once more.

The door burst open and Duncan appeared, buffeted in on yet another strong gust of wind. He was carrying a pail of fresh water in one hand and had more logs under his other arm. Eliza hurried to push the door closed behind him.

'Morning, little un. Fay's still asleep, then?' Eliza nodded. 'Best thing for her. That's a fair blaze you've got going there, so let's get some water heated for a drink. I'm parched. Fay keeps a good wood store but we don't how long this weather will last so I'll bring in some peat before I leave. You can use that to keep the fire in overnight without using up her stock.'

'You're leaving?' she asked, staring at him in dismay.

He nodded, opened his mouth to say something but Fay winced and he hunkered down beside her.

'Hmm, temperature's high. How are you feeling?'

'Stiff as a board,' she moaned, trying to sit up. Duncan helped her, propping her back against the sheepskins.

'Your ankle's like a puffball so you won't be getting your boots on for a few days. In fact you are going to have to take it easy.'

'I wasn't thinking of going for a sprint over the moors,' she snapped.

'Maybe not, but you'll have to stay indoors so I'll bring in a gazunder for you to use.'

'Do that and you'll be wearing it over your head,' she grunted. 'Besides, I keep me onions in it. Haven't you anything more useful to spend your time doing, like making me a good brew?'

He grinned. 'Luckily for you, Eliza's already got the water heating. Now let's have a look at those cuts and bruises.'

'I haven't got any bruises, whippersnapper.'

'That's where you're wrong, old woman. There's one as black as the hobs of hell on your forehead. Now let me look at you whilst Eliza makes us that drink. If you're very good, she might even fry you an egg and a chop of bacon.'

The woman cackled. 'Oh, and I just happen to have luxuries like that around here, have I?'

Duncan nodded. 'Indeed you have. Ben insisted on giving me some supplies last night in appreciation for Eliza helping with young Joshua.' As Duncan pointed to the table by the window where he'd placed the food, Eliza looked up in surprise.

'Don't ever say nay to recompense for a job done, girl,' Fay told her. 'Well, come on, get cooking. My stomach thinks my throat's been cut.'

Leaving Duncan to deal with Fay, Eliza tossed fat into the large, battered pan and whilst it was melting, made their tea. Before long, the delicious aroma of frying bacon and eggs filled the room, making her stomach growl.

As she dished up their food, Duncan grinned, producing a package from his capacious pocket with a flourish.

'Bit of bread to mop up the juices,' he said, hacking at it with a knife.

'We'll have a feast,' Eliza exclaimed, adding a thick slice

to Fay's plate and passing it to her. 'Would you like me to help you?' she asked, glancing down at the woman's strapped wrist.

'You keep your hands off my food, girl. I can manage just fine,' she grunted, slipping her wrist out of the make-shift sling.

''Tis a shame you injured your right wrist, Fay,' Duncan commented.

'Why? You know full well I'm left-handed,' the woman smirked, digging into her bacon with determination. Eliza shook her head. He really did know how to pull her strings, didn't he?

'That was a good meal, young un,' he commented, tossing his plate on the hearth.

'Why do you call me "little un" and "young un" when I'm neither of those things?' Eliza asked.

He stared at her in surprise. ''Tis only names.'

'But I'll be fifteen next month,' she cried, hardly understanding why it suddenly mattered he should know she was on the threshold of womanhood.

'So I understand,' he said, frowning at her outburst.

Sighing, Eliza got to her feet. Why she was feeling restless she had no idea. And did it really matter what Duncan called her?

They were sitting in front of the fire sipping their tea when another gust blew a cloud of thick smoke back out of the hearth, making them all cough and splutter.

'Seems to be getting even worse,' muttered Duncan, inclining his head towards the back of the building where the north wind was howling.

No sooner had he finished speaking than the blast of

the storm increased to a wail, followed by a loud crack and the tearing of wood.

'My God, did you hear that?' Fay gasped.

Before they could answer, a huge crash rent the air, shaking the hobble and showering them with dust, gorse spines and fine snow. Shocked, they looked up to see the roof sagging down towards them.

I 2

As the roof slowly bounced back again, they sat in frozen silence until the building had stopped shaking. Duncan was the first to recover and he dashed out of the door, only to reappear a few moments later.

'A large bough has broken off the old beech tree,' he announced. 'Unable to stand the force of the wind, I suppose.'

'How is the roof?' asked Fay anxiously, looking as white as the snow clinging to his coat.

'It will survive,' assured Duncan. "Twas lucky we used the best timber rafters from the old barn when we strengthened it last year. The gorse and turf will need to be looked at when the thaw sets in, though.'

'But is it safe? Does anything need to be done now?' Fay asked, glaring down at her bound ankle.

'Don't worry, Fay, I'll see it's made safe. The branch has fallen onto the slope that almost reaches the ground so I can use Ben's horse to haul it off.'

'Can I help?' Eliza asked, getting to her feet and shaking the debris off her clothes.

'Best if you stay in here. No telling where the bough might land and I don't want to have to worry about it hitting anyone. I'll be ready for a brew when I'm finished, though,' he added, seeing her crestfallen look.

'And I'm to sit here like a dummy, I suppose,' Fay said glumly.

'Cheer up. At least it didn't damage the chimney, otherwise I'd be taking you down to the farm before you freeze in your bed. Then you'd have the pleasure of passing the time of day with Mother Evangaline.' Fay scowled and Eliza marvelled yet again at the way Duncan could manage her moods.

As he disappeared outside, she swung the pot back over the fire, then picked up the broom.

'What are you doing?' Fay grunted.

'I thought I'd sweep some of this dust and gorse spines outside.'

'And stir up a load more dirt besides. Best to leave that until the weather warms and you can do a thorough job. Now make yourself useful by washing some of this filth off my face and getting me up onto my chair. Can't sit in my bed all day like some sloth, can I?'

Eliza filled a bowl with warm water and gathered up a rag. As she wiped the worst of the grime from the woman's face, they heard sounds of banging and scraping coming from overhead. She was just washing her own face and hands when there was a whooshing sound followed by a thud as the bough slid down the side of the roof onto the ground. Then all went quiet. Trusting the removing of the branch was going well, Eliza set the pot to warm for their tea while Fay sat staring fixedly at the antlered head on the wall.

It was still some time before Duncan reappeared, wiping muck and sweat from his brow. Eliza held out a bowl of fresh water for him and while he cleaned himself up she poured their drinks. Duncan took his mug and gulped down the scalding liquid with little heed to his throat.

'Gosh, I needed that, little un – sorry, I mean Eliza. I've put the bough alongside the wood store,' he said, turning to Fay. 'It'll make a nice addition to your stocks when it dries out and the leaves will make a soft fragrant stuffing for your mattress come spring.'

'Talking beds, eh?'

'Talking beds?' Eliza asked, looking puzzled.

'Beech leaves whisper musically and the French call them *lits de parlement*, or talking beds,' Fay explained. 'I suppose you could say that after the cloud of dust this will be our silver lining.' She chuckled at her little joke.

'That's better, Fay. You've got some colour in your cheeks now. I've put a couple of ropes over the roof to make sure nothing moves when the thaw sets in. Then I'll go up and repair any damage. I must get going and return the horse and wagon to Ben.'

Eliza's heart dropped. 'Do you have to go?' she asked.

'Afraid so. Ben's got stock to deliver. He'll already be late so the least I can do is help. Anything else need bringing in before I leave?' he asked Fay.

She shook her head. 'We can manage now. Thanks for seeing to the roof. I'm indebted.'

'I'll be back for some of your wondrous cooking before long,' Duncan said with a grin. 'Keep those joints strapped or you'll still be hobbling come spring. I'm sure Eliza will make sure you take your curative regularly. It's been an eventful morning so I suggest both of you spend the rest of the day relaxing. See you soon,' he added, turning up the collar of his coat and striding out of the door.

'Bossy boots,' Fay muttered, but settled back in her chair anyway. Eliza began clearing away their mugs and plates but was overcome by a wave of weariness. Noticing her yawn, Fay sighed.

'Come and sit down, girl. They can wait. Happen it's taken it out of both of us.'

Exhausted, they spent the rest of the day dozing by the fire. Then, not feeling up to cooking, they had a handful of oats and a hot drink to sustain them, before turning in early. Despite the moaning of the wind and an occasional creak, the roof didn't collapse on them, as Eliza had feared, and she found herself beginning to relax for the first time since Duncan had left.

It was some days before the weather improved sufficiently for Eliza to go outside for anything other than quick visits to the earth closet or to top up their water and wood supplies. Duncan hadn't returned and she found herself staring out of the window at frequent intervals.

As Fay's injuries got better so did her temper, until one day when Eliza was limping towards the dresser Fay burst out laughing.

'What are we like, Eliza? You hobbling one way and me the other.'

Eliza smiled. 'This is what it's like for me all the time, though. That's why Father said I'll never get a job or marry.'

'Phooey!' the woman scoffed. 'You're a pretty little thing now you've filled out a bit. Not like that bag of bones I found on my doorstep. You never did say where you were headed.'

'Barnstaple,' she replied.

'Barnstaple! Why, that's miles away from here.'

'I was hoping to find work there but the weather was so bad, I lost my bearings. I had no idea I'd wandered this high up the moors.'

'Well, if it's work you want, there'll soon be plenty to do cleaning this place up. Meantime you can make yourself useful preparing vegetables for our meal. There are roots in the store shed, and a drop of stew later will do us both good. I feel like a bit of sketching so you can pass me my pad on your way out.'

It was still bitterly cold outside but the wind had dropped. Although Eliza searched all around the shed, she couldn't find any vegetables other than the onions in the gazunder. Snatching up a couple, she went back indoors.

'I think someone must have taken the other vegetables,' she said, putting the onions on the dresser.

'Don't be silly, girl. How would anyone know they were there?'

'Well, there's just a huge pile of earth along the back now.' To her surprise the woman threw down her pad and roared with laughter.

'That's where they're stored,' she spluttered. 'The soil keeps them fresh through the winter and prevents the rats and mice helping themselves to a feast.'

Eliza shuddered. 'Why don't you just keep them in the garden and dig them up when you need them?' she asked, thinking it sounded like unnecessary work.

Fay snorted. 'And you'd be able to dig them out of this frozen ground?'

'Oh . . .' she said, feeling stupid.

Sure enough the vegetables were stacked in layers beneath the earth. Having collected up carrots, turnips and potatoes in her basket, she was just replacing the soil when she felt a presence behind her. Turning slowly, she gasped. A row of eyes were glistening down at her. Then she saw they were attached to dark, furry bodies. Rats. She let out a scream.

''Tis only me, little un,' Duncan said, backing into the shed with a brace of rabbits slung over each shoulder. As the room began swaying around her, he quickly placed them on the shelf and put out his hand to steady her.

'I thought you were a rat,' she gasped.

'Well, I'd be a pretty large one,' he chuckled, then saw she was shivering. 'Come on, let's get you inside.' Taking the basket, he led her back towards the hobble where Fay was hovering in the doorway, a worried look on her face.

'What's going on? I heard a scream.'

'Eliza encountered a rat,' Duncan said with a chuckle.

'Was it big?' Fay asked.

'Huge. At least this big,' he said, putting down the vegetables and extending his hands as far as they'd reach. 'It had dark eyes and brown curly hair as well.' As Fay's eyes widened, he shook his head. 'That's how Eliza saw me, anyhow.'

'You made me jump, creeping up like that with those rabbits,' she protested, feeling stupid for the second time in as many minutes. It was bad enough Fay thinking she was a numpty but she wanted Duncan to think well of her.

'Didn't know you were scared of rabbits, and there was me thinking you'd welcome a bit of meat for your stew,' he teased.

'We certainly will,' Fay said. 'Well, come on, girl. Don't just stand there gaping like a tickled trout. Go and fetch some water. I'm parched and bet Duncan here could do with a hot drink, too. Now, there's something I want to talk to you about . . .' she said, turning back to him.

Eliza picked up the pail, glad of a few moments to compose herself. Outside, she splashed water over her flushed cheeks, almost welcoming its icy sting. She'd show Duncan she wasn't stupid, but when she returned he was deep in conversation with Fay, their heads bent close together. Seeing her, they lowered their voices but continued their discussion. Angry at being excluded, she sloshed the water into the pot, making the fire hiss and spit.

'Careful, Eliza,' Fay admonished.

'I was taught it was rude to whisper,' she answered petulantly.

'It's also rude to back answer your elders and betters.'

'Sounds like you two have been cooped up together for too long,' Duncan commented.

'Does that mean you're staying?' Eliza asked, hope flaring in her chest.

He looked at Fay then shook his head. ''Fraid not. Things to do,' he said getting to his feet.

'He didn't stay long,' she commented as soon as the door had shut behind him. 'What did he want, anyway?' she asked, feeling out of sorts.

'He brought those rabbits, for a start, and some provisions from the farm,' Fay replied.

Eliza went over to the table where Duncan had placed fresh milk and eggs but instead of picking them up she stood watching through the window as he made his way down the path. She let out a sigh.

'Duncan's a free spirit, my dear, and a busy one at that. It would be better if you read a book or found something to interest you, rather than mope around,' Fay said briskly, giving Eliza a knowing look. Picking up her pad, she resumed her sketching, leaving Eliza alone with her thoughts.

'Happy birthday,' Fay said, handing Eliza a small parcel. It had been some weeks since Duncan's last visit and as the weather had improved they'd spent the morning cleaning the hobble. Now they were relaxing with their noon-time drink.

'You remembered,' Eliza cried. Which was more than her family ever had, she thought with a pang.

'Hard not to with you keep reminding us every five minutes,' the woman grunted.

'I didn't . . .' she began, then noticed Fay was grinning and realized she was being teased. Eagerly she peeled back the wrapping, then gasped at the picture of a pretty young woman. 'Why, she's beautiful.'

'Yes, you are,' Fay replied.

'Me?'

'Yes. Look closely and you will see it's you. That's how you looked the night of the Wassail, glowing with happiness.'

'So that's what you've been doing at the table each morning. I wondered what you were painting,' she said, remembering she'd been forbidden to look.

Fay nodded. 'It worries me you have such a low opinion of yourself, Eliza. Your father's mocking has left a terrible scar, which could fester and mar the rest of your life. That would be a shame, especially as his taunts were unfounded.'

Eliza stared down at her foot.

'So you've a twisted foot. Well, according to you I have prickles and Duncan is a rat, so we each have our cross to bear.' As Eliza opened her mouth to protest, Fay held up her hand. 'Every time you look at this picture, I want you to see the lovely warm person Duncan and I perceive you to be.'

'Duncan thinks I'm lovely?' she asked, looking up. Fay frowned, about to say something but then, as if she'd conjured him up, the door opened and there he was.

'I heard there's a birthday princess here today,' he said, giving his disarming grin. 'My goodness, she's beautiful,' he said, pointing to the picture Eliza was still holding. 'Looks just like you, too. Well done, Fay, that's a true likeness if ever I saw one.' He sounded so sincere Eliza stared up at him in surprise.

'I don't really look like that, do I?' she whispered.

'Course not, little un,' he snorted. 'Let's see now, if Fay's a prickly hedgehog and I'm a dark rat, then with that keen sense of smell and reddish brown hair you must surely be a dormouse.'

Fay looked up sharply. 'Don't tease, Duncan. It's Eliza's birthday and don't you have something for her yourself?'

'Ah, yes, I do,' he said, producing a bunch of brightly coloured crocus from behind his back. 'Not a drooping pendant in sight,' he whispered. Eliza stared at the vibrant purple and golden cup-shaped flowers, touched he'd remembered their previous conversation about snow-drops. 'Rose and Ben send you birthday greetings and this,' he said handing over a square carton. Peering inside, she saw a beautiful sponge cake with 'Eliza' piped in wobbly icing on the top. 'Needless to say young Rose didn't make it. Mother Evangaline has her uses, though,' he said with a wink.

'Pah, she never made that,' Fay scoffed.

He laughed. 'Never said she did, just that she had her uses. One being her contacts at the market in Dulvester. Rose spent ages piping your name on top, little un – sorry, I mean Eliza,' he corrected, staring at her with those chestnut eyes. Suddenly the room seemed brighter and Eliza didn't care a tinker's cuss what he called her.

'Evangaline's still at the farmhouse then?' Fay asked. He nodded.

'She's that besotted with young Joshua, Ben despairs of her ever returning home. Oh, I was forgetting, I have something else for, princess. Close your eyes.' She heard him scrabble about, then felt something hard placed in her hands. 'Right you can open them now.'

She stared down, blinked and stared again. Then she shook her head in disbelief and felt the tears welling.

'It's Grampy's box,' she gasped.

'I found it when that beech bough came down. The snow hadn't done the wood any favours, but I cleaned it up, then polished it with beeswax and replaced the rusted catch. Your grampy was obviously a skilled man, Eliza, for the box is beautifully crafted. Didn't think I'd made that bad a job of restoring it, though,' he said, reaching out and gently wiping her wet cheeks.

'I don't know what to say,' she whispered.

'Well, "thank you, Duncan, for all your hard work" would do,' he teased.

Smiling through her tears, Eliza opened the lid, then ran her fingers over the emerald silk material that now lined the inside.

'It's beautiful. Thank you so much,' she said, leaning over and kissing his cheek, then blushing with embarrassment. He cleared his throat and stared awkwardly back at her.

'There now, you know she's happy with your present,' Fay said, her voice sounding loud in the ensuing silence.

13

'I'll make some tea to go with that cake,' Fay added.

Duncan nodded, then jumped to his feet. 'Water pail's almost empty. I'll go and fill it.'

Spring must be in the air for she hadn't felt this warm in ages, Eliza thought, taking her precious laurel leaves from the pages of a flower book that Fay had given her. She smiled at the pressed circlet before carefully placing it in her box.

'There, treasures in my treasure box,' she said, holding it out for Fay to see.

'Duncan's made a good job of restoring that, hasn't he?' Fay asked.

'Yes, he has, and I'm thrilled. Did you know he'd found it?'

'Yes. That's what we were discussing the afternoon you got all huffy. To do the restoration justice, he wanted to line it and wondered if I had any suitable material.'

Remembering her bad mood when she'd felt excluded, Eliza sighed. Hadn't her grampy warned her about jumping to conclusions?

'Why don't you cut your cake and we'll sit at the table and make it a real birthday party?' Fay said.

By the time Duncan reappeared Fay had made the tea and as they raised their mugs to toast her, Eliza felt a warm glow of happiness. These two, dear people had come to mean the world to her and for the first time in her life she felt a real sense of belonging. But for how long, she couldn't help wondering.

'Hmm, tasty cake,' Duncan said, brushing crumbs from his lips. 'Not as good as your apple cakes, though. Do you know Eliza can smell the subtle difference between mace and nutmeg?'

Fay stared at Eliza in amazement then turned to Duncan. 'Thus the sensitive nose you mentioned.'

He nodded and helped himself to another slice of cake.

'Apart from laurel leaves, what else do you intend to keep in your box now you've got it back, Eliza?' Fay asked.

'I used to collect wild flowers and keep a specimen of each one in it. But that was before . . .' Her voice tailed off.

'And what's to stop you from doing that again?' Duncan asked.

'Do you get many flowers this far up the moor?' she asked.

To her surprise they both chuckled.

'My dear child, I'll have you know that when the sun warms the earth, the moors become a veritable riot of colour from the creamy yellow of primroses to the brilliant blues of Germander speedwell. The acid soil is perfect for producing the deep purple erica, pink-mauves of the bog violet, blue-pink heath violets, sun-bright gorse, golden saxifrage, virginal white flowers of the wood sorrel and many others too numerous to mention,' Fay enthused, her eyes becoming animated as she spoke.

'Spoken like a true artist . . .' Duncan said, his voice trailing off as Fay shot him a warning look.

'Then, of course, there are all the flowers in my garden,' she cut in quickly.

'You grow flowers as well as vegetables?' Eliza asked.

'And herbs. They all have their uses. I cultivate as much of everything here as I can so we'll see about putting that fine nose of yours to work,' she said. As Eliza stared in surprise, Faye got to her feet and started collecting their mugs and plates. 'I'll see to these as it's your birthday. I do believe a watery sun is breaking the clouds. Why don't you two take a stroll outside? Who knows, you might even spot some early flowers.'

'Why do I get the feeling Fay wanted us out of the way?' Eliza asked, once they were outside.

Duncan shrugged. 'She needs to be on her own sometimes. Memories, you know? She'd kill me for saying it, but she's not as young as she likes to think.'

'But she was definitely hiding something,' Eliza persisted, wrapping her shawl tighter around her. Despite the sunshine, the easterly wind was distinctly cool.

'Look, any secrets she has are hers to tell,' he said enigmatically. 'Look down there, see the red deer?' He pointed towards the wood where she could just make out the shapes of animals moving gracefully between the trees. 'Come on, let's walk; it's too chilly to stand around.'

'I've never really had time to look at the outside of the hobble house,' she said, staring back at the old grey stone building with the turfed roof almost reaching the ground. Blue smoke plumed from the chimney at the far end and she could see the damaged beech leaning to one side with a white scar where the bough had broken away. Adjacent was the store where Woody had frightened her with his piercing eyes just days before the cold did for him.

'Is all this land Fay's?' Eliza asked as they strolled around the fenced enclosure screened by the hedge bank.

Duncan nodded. 'She grows herbs in the higher ground between the hobble and the barn, and her precious flowers in the sun to the front of the building. Come the spring she'll be spending much of her time here in her beloved garden.'

'It's hard to believe these high white moors will soon be covered in all those flowers she mentioned,' said Eliza in amazement. 'I can't wait.'

'Once the temperature rises and the thaw sets in properly, you will see everywhere literally blossom overnight. If you want to collect flowers for your box, you couldn't be in a better place.'

'How wonderful. I love identifying all their distinctive smells. I'm so happy to have Grampy's box back. It makes me feel close to him again. You've made it look beautiful and I really appreciate all your hard work.'

'My pleasure. A beautiful box for a beautiful young woman. Now, we'd better go inside again, little un. It's no good you getting cold,' he said, noticing Eliza's pink cheeks.

'Why do you still call me "little un", even though I'm fifteen now?' she asked, pouting up at him.

'Happen 'tis safer that way,' he muttered. 'Come on, Fay will be wondering where we've got to.' He turned and hurried back indoors, leaving her to follow.

*

In the weeks that followed, as the sun climbed higher and the temperature rose, Eliza pondered on Duncan's words. Why was it safer him calling her 'little un'? She hadn't seen him since her birthday and found herself wandering aimlessly around the hobble, unable to settle yet not sure why. Fay became impatient, urging her again to find something to occupy her time. She pored over the little book of flowers in which she'd pressed her laurel leaves but found her concentration wandering. In the end she gave up and used it to press one of the golden crocus heads Duncan had given her, lovingly placing it in her box alongside the laurel.

Then, one morning Eliza was woken by the sound of gushing water.

'What's that noise?' she asked Fay.

'Thaw's begun. Doesn't mean we're out of the woods yet but it's a sure sign spring is on its way, and to celebrate I shall take the old sketchbook out for an airing. My ankle could do with some exercise to strengthen it.'

'Shouldn't you have your wrist bound, though?' Eliza asked as the woman picked up her things.

'It doesn't hurt half as much as it did and I'm mighty relieved not to have it strapped up any more. Why don't you take yourself off and search for wild flowers? It's a bit early but there's bound to be something you can bring back for that box of yours. It'll do you good to get outside and you can walk off some of that pent-up energy.'

Eliza's heart lifted at the thought of searching for flowers. Who knew what she would find?

'I'll tidy up in here and then go out,' she replied, but Fay shook her head.

'Don't waste this good weather. Sun's fickle this time of year and could be gone by noon. Time enough for tidying up then.'

The brisk March wind tugged at Eliza's hair and stung her ears but, happy to be outside, she hardly noticed. Pausing by the vegetable plot, she saw the green tops of leeks and winter cabbages were now visible through the snow melt. Spring really was on its way at last.

Wandering out of the enclosure she felt a delicious sense of freedom. All around, the buds on trees and bushes were showing the first signs of swelling and the smell of freshly ploughed ground carried towards her on the breeze. Peering down the valley, she wondered how Rose was getting on.

But her thoughts were distracted by a swathe of daffodils in the shelter of a hedge bank. With their golden heads bobbing and swaying on slim green legs it looked as if they were dancing their way across the moorland. Laughing at her foolish thoughts, she was just about to continue her journey when a strange noise rooted her to the spot.

Seemingly out of nowhere came a tremendous thundering, shaking the ground around her. It was louder than any noise she'd ever heard at the mine and it was getting nearer. Instinctively, she took shelter behind a tree, then watched wide-eyed as a huddle of horses galloped past. There must have been sixteen or eighteen of the magnificent beasts and they were so close she could hear them panting, their breath rising from flaring nostrils like steam in the cold air. The scarlet-jacketed riders, sporting black hats above flushed faces, urged them faster, sending black mud flying in all directions. Eliza shrank further into the shadows as the cavalcade thrummed by, inches from where she was standing. Then, as quickly as they'd appeared, they were gone, the drumming of their hooves receding until all she could hear was the beating of her heart.

'Eliza? What are you doing here?' She turned to see Duncan appearing out of the trees behind, his hands full of dandelions and other plants. 'Why, you're shaking,' he said, quickly setting them down on the ground beside her. Taking her hands in his, he rubbed them briskly until she felt the warmth returning. With her heart still beating faster than Rose's little ormolu clock, she stared up at him.

'Men on horses. Dashing like the devil was after them. Thought I'd be trampled,' she gasped. A cry of hounds was followed by the sound of a horn, and Duncan smiled.

''Tis only the hunt, little un. Nothing to fret about, unless you're the fox, of course.'

She glared at him. 'That's not nice.'

'No, it isn't, but some think of it as sport. When the riders ask which way the fox was heading I send them the opposite way.'

She smiled. She should have known her gentle giant wouldn't agree with such things.

'You all right now?' he asked, giving her an assessing look.

'Yes, thank you. I'd just never seen anything like that before. Were you on your way to see us?' she asked, looking at him hopefully.

He shook his head. 'Sorry, got curatives and elixirs to make. With so many people out of sorts after the winter, my remedies are in demand.' He turned and picked up his plants. 'I dare say Fay will be busy concocting her own as well. She'll probably be glad of your help, too. Give her my love and tell her I'll be over soon to empty the earth closet onto her vegetable plot.'

Before she could answer, he was striding down the moors, his greatcoat billowing behind like a sail on a ship. With all interest in searching for flowers gone, Eliza trudged back to the hobble.

To her surprise, Fay was sitting by the fire when she walked in. She had an old book on her lap and was screwing up her eyes as she looked down at the pages.

'You're back early, Fay,' she commented, taking off her shawl and giving it a vigorous shake in the doorway.

'Could say the same for you,' the woman grunted. 'And since when did we shake out our clothes before coming indoors?'

'I got covered in clods of black mud when the hunt rode by. I've never heard or seen anything like it and was really frightened until Duncan explained what they were doing.'

Fay shrugged. 'Moorland people have their own ways. Is Duncan with you then?' she asked, looking over Eliza's shoulder as if she expected to see him standing there.

'No, he said he has to make his remedies and thought you'd be doing the same. He said you might need my help,' she said, looking hopefully at Fay.

'Can you read?'

'Yes, I went to the charity school for mine workers' children – when Mum could spare me, that is.'

'Well, I do need your help, as it happens. Truth is, I've been seeing things a bit skewed since that fall.'

Eliza stared at Fay in alarm. 'Have you told anyone?'

'Stop fussing, child. In order to supplement my larder, I must make my usual seasonal curatives and need you to read out the receipts. They're all written up but it's essential to get the proportions right otherwise folk will be feeling down when they should be up and hurting when they should be healing.'

'Shall I get us some luncheon first?' Eliza asked.

Getting no answer, she turned round to find Fay slumped in the chair, her eyes firmly closed.

14

Worried that Fay was ill or worse, Eliza hurried across the room. Then, seeing the rhythmic rise and fall of her chest and hearing her gentle snores, she let out a sigh of relief. Really, she could do without any more shocks today, she thought, gently removing the book from the woman's lap and replacing it with a sheepskin. Catching sight of the illustration on the cover of the book she began flicking through the pages. On the left-hand side of each was a delicate watercolour of a plant or herb with a short description written underneath. Then on the right was a list of ingredients followed by the receipt. Imagine being able to use plants and herbs for curing or easing all these ailments, she thought, placing it on the table and carefully running her finger down the index at the back.

It was fascinating and she was so absorbed, it took her a few moments to realize Fay had woken and was staring across the room at her.

'Interesting, isn't it?' the woman asked.

'Yes. I had no idea you could do all this,' Eliza answered. Then a thought struck her. 'I hope you don't think me rude for reading your receipt book?'

Fay smiled and shook her head. 'I've been watching you for some time and it made my heart glad to see you so animated. Judging by the way the fire's gone down, you must have been studying it ever since I fell asleep.'

Eliza glanced over at the hearth in dismay. 'Goodness, Fay, I'm sorry. I had no idea the day had got so late,' she said, jumping up guiltily. She raked the embers until they blazed red, tossed on a couple of logs then set the pot of water over the fire to heat. 'I'll go and bring in some vegetables for our meal.'

'Calm down, Eliza, we're not in any hurry. I collected a couple of potatoes from the store when I came back and even managed to prise a couple of leeks out of the ground as well. We could fry them up with that bit of rabbit that's left. I was intending to do so much today and yet there I go sleeping the afternoon away,' she said, clicking her tongue in disgust. Putting a spill into the fire, she watched as it flared, then she turned and lit the candle beside her. 'To chase away the gloom,' she muttered when she saw Eliza's surprised expression. 'We'll need the wax for our elder salve anyway. Nothing's ever wasted here, girl. After supper we'll look through the book and decide what receipt to use first.'

'Can we make some of those flower essences?' Eliza asked excitedly.

Fay shook her head. 'It's the wrong time of year. There's a season for everything, Eliza, remember that. You said the hunt was out so this then is the season for curatives.'

'Do you get paid much for them?' Eliza asked curiously.

'Generally, we people of the moors are cash poor so we exchange our produce and labour. I thought you realized that. Living in these wonderful surroundings brings greater satisfaction than any material goods. Thus I make my special flower essences during the right season and add these to the curatives and remedies. Then I bestow them upon the folk who have given to me over the past months.'

'So you exist totally without money?' Eliza stared at Fay in amazement.

'I didn't say that. A person still needs some income to buy commodities. It's just recognizing who has the readies to buy. Like I said, the hunt's been out so there are sure to be sore muscles come the morrow. They'll be staying at the hostelry in Dulvester and no doubt making merry far into the night. Those men will pay well for salves and plaisters to ease their painful limbs along with tinctures for tomorrow's tender heads. If fools and their money are easily parted, who are we to stand in their way?' Fay rubbed her hands together in glee.

Eliza stared into the fire, mulling over what the woman had said. It was such a different concept from the way her parents had lived. Everyone's very existence at South Wood relied upon wages from working in the mine, pitiful though they were.

'Well, I don't have a farthing to my name but if what you say is true, then by helping with the receipts I'll be repaying you for taking me in?' she asked.

'Indeed, and thus you can hold your head up high. Of course, by helping with the chores you've already been paying your way.'

The woman slapped down the old frying pan on the hearth and tossed in a lump of fat. As it began to sizzle, she threw in the rabbit and prodded it around. Before long the smell of frying filled the room, making Eliza's stomach growl. Having become so engrossed in the book, she'd quite forgotten to have any luncheon.

'Duncan said he'd be over soon to empty the earth closet,' she said as they settled down to their meal.

'Fine choice of subject when we're about to eat, child,' Fay snapped, but Eliza was used to her moods by now and kept quiet.

That evening as they pored over the receipts by candle-light, Eliza felt excitement stir inside her.

'There are so many, how do you know which to choose?'

'By checking what ingredients you have available. Then you need to consider the time of year and what ails folk. The cold and wet weather causes pain in joints and so we'll need plaisters, remedies for fevers, salves for sores and infusions for general health.'

'It all sounds fascinating. Will you teach me how to make them?' Eliza asked, excitement rising in her chest.

'Certainly. You can read out the receipts, then watch what I do. I have some elder buds stored and rosemary and sage oils made so we'll make a start first thing in the morning,' Fay said, stifling a yawn.

'We need to get an early night then,' Eliza said, antici-pating the woman as she dragged on her greatcoat.

Whilst she paid her visit outside, Eliza stacked their dishes ready to wash in the morning, then covered the fire with blocks of peat so that it would stay in all night. She'd just set out their mattresses when Fay returned. Before long, the room was rocked by the sound of the woman's snores but Eliza hardly noticed. With the musky, sweet smell of burning peat scenting the room, her senses reeled with excitement at the prospect of the day to come.

They began at first light. Fay's spirits had definitely revived and she eagerly showed Eliza where her supplies were stored. Then, with equipment and ingredients set out, Fay donned an enormous apron and set to work. Anxious to help, Eliza read the receipts and watched carefully as Fay mixed and blended.

'Can I help?' she asked after a while.

'You are. The best way to learn is by watching,' the woman grunted.

Eliza read out the quantities and duly watched as Fay melted pig fat and candle wax, then stirred in elder buds.

'Right, now we need to stir this well,' Fay instructed. Eliza looked at the gloopy, lumpy mixture and grimaced. 'That's next month's bread and butter, girl, so it's no use you looking like that. Make yourself useful and line up those jars ready for me to spoon this in . . . Right, now for the rosemary,' Fay said, picking up a flagon from the table. As she went to pour it, Eliza wrinkled her nose.

'That smell's too strong for rosemary,' she said.

Fay frowned then inhaled. 'You must have put the wrong flagon out,' she growled, but her hand was trembling and Eliza could tell she was worried.

'Make a start on those labels,' Fay barked when she saw Eliza watching her.

'Can't I help with the mixing and making?' Eliza asked.

'Not today. Time is of the essence,' she said, then chuckled. 'Sorry, my little jest. Haven't you learned anything this morning? Essence is what I've just used.' Yes, and nearly the wrong one, Eliza wanted to say but bit her tongue. She'd expected to be more involved in the making of these magical lotions and potions but knew it would be stupid to annoy the woman.

Seeing her discontent, Fay shrugged.

'When we have more time, I'll show you how everything's done. Come summer there'll be so many flowers and herbs around, you'll be sick of the sight of them. Now, have you finished labelling those bottles?'

'Almost.' She sighed, wondering how anyone could be sick of the sight of flowers. She wanted to know what they all were and how to use them. Sensing Fay's glare, she returned to her task and was just pressing on the last label when there was a knock on the door.

As Duncan strode into the room with his disarming grin, her mood lifted.

'Ah, the very person,' Fay said.

'I thought you might have some remedies for selling at the Dulvester market. I'm taking some produce of Ben's so he's lent me the wagon.'

'Indeed I have,' Fay said, gesturing to the table, which was lined with the result of their morning's labours.

'You have been busy,' he said, turning to Eliza.

'Fay made them all. I just read out the receipts and wrote the labels,' she muttered.

'And beautifully labelled they are too,' he said, picking up a little bottle and studying it. 'She's got much neater writing than you, Fay.'

'No need to be cheeky, whippersnapper. I suppose you want a brew and something to eat?'

'No time, I'm afraid. I'll pack up your wares then head straight down to Dulvester. I've people to see as well as going to market so I'll be staying down there a few days.'

'I hear the hunt's been out. They'll be putting up at the Horn and Stirrup Cup as usual so presumably I can leave you to do the necessary?'

'Of course, Fay.'

'And no taking less than top whack. Some of those ingredients are costly.'

Duncan laughed. 'Wouldn't dare bring anything back other than your fortune, Fay, you know that. Any provisions you need?'

'Honey, if it's a fair price. I used the last for the mustard and honey plaisters.'

'Can I come with you?' Eliza asked, suddenly feeling the need to get away from this bossy woman.

Duncan looked at Fay who clucked her tongue. 'And set tongues wagging, young missy. I think not.'

Eliza glared at the woman.

'Perhaps you could help me load the remedies onto the wagon?' Duncan suggested, gathering up the bottles and jars.

'What's wrong?' he asked, as they walked towards the fence, where the horse was tethered.

'It's so unfair. I wanted to help but all she let me do was read the receipts and write out the labels. Then she nearly used the wrong essence . . .' Eliza burst out.

'What! That's not like her. And she let you read her precious receipts?'

'She said the words have gone all skewed since her fall but I think that was an excuse not to let me help make them.' As Duncan's frown deepened Eliza felt her anger evaporate.

'It's not like Fay to admit something's wrong either. I'll check her out when I get back. It will have to be done subtly, though, so don't mention you've said anything. See you in a few days, little un,' he said, retrieving the last of the jars from his capacious pocket and jumping into the seat.

Watching him ride away, Eliza felt a prickle of unease. Could there really be something wrong with Fay? She'd been so bound up in her own sense of injustice, she'd paid little heed, but from now on she'd watch her like a hawk.

Fay was dozing in her chair and Eliza set about tidying the room after their morning's work. Glancing over at the sleeping woman, Eliza felt another pang for she looked really quite old and frail. She'd just have to curb her impatience until Fay was ready to show her how to make the receipts.

'Another day, another duty,' Fay said, a few days later. Eliza smiled, pleased to see the woman had recovered her strength. The strained atmosphere that had persisted since Duncan's departure evaporated like mist on the moor.

'Now the weather's warming nicely we need to start digging over the vegetable plot ready for Duncan to empty the earth closet when he returns. Lots of good fertilizer there, and once the chimney's been swept we can add the soot to the saved ashes and spread those. I love this time of year: it's like a new start.'

Eliza was pleased harmony had been restored but thought the proposed digging of the plot sounded boring.

'Wouldn't you prefer me to make a start on the spring cleaning?'

Fay chuckled. 'That can wait. We must get the ground ready for planting. You can't eat a clean floor, now, can you?' Eliza shook her head. 'I know you're impatient to start making those receipts but you only get out of the ground what you put in.'

'Well, that's obvious,' Eliza giggled. 'If you put in a leek you won't dig up a potato, will you?'

Fay gave her a long-suffering look. 'I was referring to the compost heap. You need to nourish the soil in order for it to produce vegetables, herbs and flowers of the highest quality. That's the only way you can ensure the excellence of the receipts you make.'

Feeling stupid, Eliza grabbed her shawl and followed Fay outside. Digging the heavy earth was hard going and before long, she noticed Fay was struggling. Her wrist and ankle were obviously still weak, despite what she'd professed. Then Eliza saw her wince and the blood drain from her face and knew she had to say something before the woman did herself a further mischief.

'Phew, I'm not used to this hard work,' Eliza said, rubbing the small of her back.

Fay grunted but put her fork to one side. 'I suppose it wouldn't hurt to take a break. What do you know about herbs?' she asked, as they put down their tools.

'Not much really,' Eliza admitted.

'Well, that bush over there is the rosemary and it produces blue flowers,' Fay explained, going over and breaking off a stem. Rubbing it between her fingers, she held her hand out to Eliza. 'What does it smell like?'

Eliza sniffed. 'It's sort of sweet yet slightly pungent at the same time.' She was going to say, a bit like the essence Fay had nearly got wrong, but thought better of it.

'It's extremely versatile. Mix it with other herbs, pour on boiling water, inhale the vapour and you have a remedy for colds, but mixed with vervain and taken as an infusion it will help headaches. Rosemary oil is good for rheumatism but can be used to lift fatigue and boost memory.' Eliza blinked in amazement then watched as Fay picked another herb.

'This is thyme,' Fay said, holding out a leaf. 'Mixed with aniseed it makes a good cough suppressant, with lavender it can help insomnia, yet with this sage,' she said, snapping off another specimen, 'it makes a good gargle for sore throats. It's the synergy between them that's powerful.'

'The what?'

'Synergy means the way they work together. It's all about balance and harmony, and that's why it's important to get the quantities exactly right, especially when it comes to essential oils.'

'There's so much to learn,' Eliza groaned, but her eyes were alight with interest. Fay chuckled.

'People have been distilling plant materials to extract their powerful healing essences as far back as the shamans.'

'The shamans?'

'They were wise men from early civilization and they had the ability to heal using natural plants. Their knowledge has been passed down through the centuries.'

'So how do you do this distilling then?'

'First things first, girl. You need to learn about the plants themselves because oils are distilled from specific parts of them. In lavender the oils come from the flowers. Vascular plants such as flowering species and conifers contain special tissues for the circulation of fluids. Oh, forgive me, that's way too much for you to take in at this stage,' Fay muttered, as Eliza frowned.

'It's much more complicated than I realized.'

'It is the complexity that makes it interesting. However, it's the nose that's most important. This earth is made up of all manner of aromas and it's a matter of discerning what they are. It will be high summer before I can distil any plant material so the best thing you can do is spend your time exploring the garden and moorland, smell everything and anything to really get that nose of yours tuned in . . .'

Fay was interrupted by the sound of the gate opening and Eliza's heart flipped as she saw Duncan loping up the path.

'Come to empty the earth closet for you, Fay,' he announced and couldn't understand why they dissolved into hysterics.

15

As the tears ran down their cheeks, Duncan stared from one to the other.

'Pleased to see I have such an uplifting effect on you, ladies. A chap likes to spread happiness wherever he goes,' he said, shaking his head.

'Sorry, Duncan, it's just that we were talking about . . .' Eliza began, but Fay cut in.

'Never mind that now. How did you get on in Dulvester?'

'Sold all your remedies and here's your money,' he said, drawing out a bulging purse from his pocket. 'As you rightly guessed, the riders at the Horn and Stirrup Cup were suffering from sore muscles along with the excess from the night before. They eagerly snapped up everything they could get their hands on. The promise of something to ease their throbbing heads made them generous with their payments, too.'

'See, Eliza, horses for courses,' Fay chuckled.

'I sold the rest in the market,' Duncan continued. 'That idea you had of giving a discount to people returning their empty bottles and jars is proving popular. You have quite a following, Fay, and I was asked when you'll have more supplies available.'

'I suppose I could make some more now I have a helper,' Fay said, taking the purse and weighing it in her hand with a delighted grin. 'You were certainly right about Eliza's olfactory senses.'

'Talking of which, I brought some pies back with me. The smell of mutton's been teasing my nose all the way back.' Fay and Eliza exchanged glances and burst out laughing again. 'While it's good to see you getting on so well, can we please go inside and eat?' he pleaded.

The fresh air and exercise had made Eliza hungry as a horse and she finished before the others.

'Goodness, little un, 'twas only a few weeks back you barely had the appetite of a sparrow,' Duncan teased, but she could tell he was pleased.

While Duncan and Fay discussed the latest happenings in Dulvester, Eliza pored over the receipt book. She found the pages relating to rosemary and thyme and studied them with renewed interest. Fay was obviously a clever woman, she thought, seeing all the different remedies for those two herbs alone. Suddenly she was filled with a longing to learn more but before she could say anything, Duncan got to his feet.

'Right, I'll get on and empty the closet.'

'And Eliza can finish preparing the ground ready to dig in all that nutrient-rich excreta to make the plants grow,' Fay said.

Eliza wrinkled her nose and reluctantly set the book aside.

'Don't worry, little un, there'll be wet days when you can stay indoors and try out those receipts,' Duncan assured her.

'Not if we haven't anything grown to use, we won't,' Fay grunted. 'It's a means to an end, child. Sooner it's done the sooner we'll have something to distil.'

Eliza nodded; after all, she wanted to learn how to make curatives and essences, didn't she?

The weather stayed dry for the rest of March and well into April. While Duncan carried out the necessary repairs to the roof, then ensured the enclosure was secure from wild animals, Eliza dug and Fay planted, making the most of the lengthening daylight hours. Each evening Fay carefully covered the ground with hessian to protect the new plants from frost and Eliza couldn't help likening it to the woman tucking her babies up for the night.

Although she'd much rather be exploring the moors and finding specimens for her box than planting potatoes, Eliza worked hard. Then they moved onto the herb and flower gardens, and as Fay began pointing out their various properties, Eliza's excitement mounted.

'You mean you can use flowers as well?' she asked in amazement.

Fay clicked her tongue. 'Don't you remember me showing you that lavender?'

'Yes, of course, but it looked more like that herb bush,' Eliza said, pointing to the rosemary. 'And there aren't any other flowers here that I can see.'

'Only a few survive the winter this high up the moors where the climate is so harsh. That's why at the end of each summer I harvest the seeds to plant out in spring. You just wait, Eliza. Come summer when they blossom and bloom you will have so many to choose from, you'll be spoiled for choice,' Fay announced.

'I can't wait,' Eliza said, clapping her hands in delight.

'Calm down, girl. Once this little lot's planted, there's the spring cleaning to be tackled and new mattresses to be stuffed. Don't look like that,' she berated as Eliza pouted. 'Now it's warmer and we won't have to sleep virtually on top of the fire each night, Duncan's promised to rig up a curtain that will give us both a bit of privacy.'

Eliza's heart soared. That must mean the woman wanted her to stay.

'But what about the plants?' she pointed out.

Fay laughed. 'They'll still be busy growing while we're working. On the moors, spring cleaning's a celebration of winter passing as well as a necessary chore.'

Duncan duly arrived early and began clearing the room of furniture. Eliza watched in fascination as he clipped the top off a nearby holly bush, climbed up onto the roof and dropped a rope down the chimney. Heedless of his warning, Eliza ran inside to find the holly disappearing upwards and soot cascading down onto the hearth, sending clouds of inky dust billowing around the room. As the thick smog engulfed her, she ran coughing and spluttering out into the fresh air where Duncan and Fay started laughing.

'Why 'tis the wee black bogey boy from down the pit,' Duncan shouted from above. Stung by his words, she hurried back indoors, followed by Fay.

'I'll sweep and you wipe,' the woman said, holding out a damp cloth.

Methodically, they worked their way around the hobble. When that was done, Fay handed Eliza an enormous white feather.

'Here, you can use this for dusting the cobwebs and top of the dresser.'

'Surely it's too beautiful to use,' she commented, running her fingers along the plume.

'It's from the goose we had on Christmas Eve. I saved it specially,' Fay explained with a shrug.

'You had a whole goose?' Eliza cried, thinking of the frugal meal she'd shared with her parents and siblings.

'Well, I didn't eat it by myself. Duncan had his fair share. You did as well, come to that,' Fay said, making a start on the window.

'Me?'

'Oh, yes. I smeared so much of the grease on your front, Duncan thought I was basting you for another meal,' she chuckled. As Eliza stared at her in horror Fay's roar of laughter rocked the room. 'Blimey, girl, he never saw you, if that is what's worrying you. Now start high and work down. My poor stag looks like a new species with those black-tipped antlers.'

Eliza grimaced at the head. Why on earth would Fay have such a monstrosity on her wall, she wondered, standing on a chair to reach it.

'Don't you glare at my pet, young lady, he safeguards all my secrets,' Fay admonished.

There was no accounting for taste, Eliza thought, as Duncan came in, dragging a mattress under each arm.

'Just stuffed you a new one each. You'll sleep like babies tonight with these singing lullabies beneath you,' he said, throwing them down onto the swept floor.

Finally, order was restored and they collapsed thankfully onto the chairs.

'I reckon my little room has never looked so clean,' Fay announced, staring around in satisfaction.

Eliza smiled delightedly, then noticed Duncan watching her, a grin tugging his lips.

'You look like you've been scoffing whortleberries, little un,' he chortled.

Still smarting from his earlier jibe, she ran her fingers over her mouth, then grimaced at the purple-black smears on them. After all the quips he'd made about her appearance, she wanted him to see her looking her best and without saying anything, ran outside to wash.

As she stood sponging herself down with the icy water, she wondered why it mattered that Duncan should approve of how she looked. His teasing had never bothered her before but now it rankled. In the privacy of the shed, she brushed out her hair then changed into her spare clothes. Satisfied, she made her way inside, only to hear the sound of angry voices.

'I insist on paying my way, Duncan, you know that,' she heard Fay say as she hovered on the doorstep.

'If I can't help a friend without taking their money then it's a pretty poor show,' Duncan muttered.

'But you got me a good price in Dulvester,' Fay insisted.

'Aye, and you'll be needing the money, what with little un to look after. Put your purse away, Fay. You'll not be able to do as much now and . . .' His voice trailed off as he spotted Eliza.

'Well, that looks better,' Fay said, and Eliza could have sworn the woman looked relieved to see her.

Duncan, however, was shrugging into his coat. 'I'll be helping out with the lambing so it'll be a while till I next see you,' he muttered, and with a tight grin he was gone.

Why, he hadn't even noticed she'd changed, she thought, staring after him.

Fay looked quizzically at her. 'I told you before, Eliza,

Duncan's a free spirit. While you were outside, he rigged up that curtain so at least we can each have some privacy now, eh?'

As spring turned to summer and the flowers began to blossom and bloom so did Eliza. One morning she was tending the garden when she heard Fay call from where she sat sketching under the shade of the gorse. Going over, she noticed that, seemingly overnight, the bare bushes had burst into a riot of flowers, enclosing the garden in a fragrant gold curtain. In spite of their beauty, she knew that, underneath, the thorny needles were like steel giving protection against the rabbits and other wild creatures intent on raiding the vegetable plot.

'Tell me what you smell, Eliza?' Fay asked, crushing one of the yellow blossoms and holding it out.

Eliza inhaled then wrinkled her nose. 'Sort of sweet,' she said.

'And?' the woman persisted.

Eliza held the flower to her nose. 'Spicy?'

'I would go further and say it smells like sweet peas with the pungent tinge, befitting a wild flower. If you want to learn how to distil essence then you must always go deeper, Eliza. Get your nose right in, for there's more to perfume than the first scent you encounter.' She winced and put her hand to her head.

'Are you all right, Fay?' Eliza asked, noting the woman's pallor.

'Feel a bit hot and my eyes are playing up,' she commented, throwing down her pad in disgust. 'Why don't you take yourself off over the moors and see what you can find for that box of yours?' Then when Eliza hesitated: 'Go on, away with you and leave me to rest.'

Happy to be free from the seemingly endless gardening and weeding, she changed into her cotton skirt, snatched up her basket and took herself onto the moor. The black thorn trees were now smothered in creamy white May blossom, their heavy sweet scent hanging in the air. A swathe of bluebells spread out like a carpet beneath her feet as she bent and inhaled their sweet, dusky fragrance.

Enjoying her freedom and the feel of the warm sun on her bare arms, she wandered on. The cries of cuckoo and blackbird mingling with the bleating of sheep reminded her of Duncan. She wondered how he was getting on with the lambing. She missed his gentle presence and it was only now she was stronger that she realized how much he had done for her and Fay.

Ahead the river shimmered under the hot May sun and she could see a blaze of yellow-gold kingcups on the bank. Remembering she'd seen a receipt for them, she decided to pick some but as she drew nearer, she heard the sound of splashing. Her eyes widened in amazement for there was Duncan in all his glory diving and swimming like a fish in the crystal-clear waters.

Seeing her approach, he waved.

'Come on in, little un,' he called but she shook her head and, kingcups forgotten, scuttled away.

16

Moments later, Eliza heard his footsteps pounding behind her but she didn't turn round.

'What's up?' he asked, catching up with her. Then he saw her crimson face and grinned.

'Not used to skinny dipping, eh?'

She shook her head. 'Where I come from the rivers run red and orange from the copper mines,' she muttered. 'That water was so clear I could see, I mean I saw . . .'

'We're all the same – well, more or less,' he conceded. 'When I said come in for a dip, I only meant for you to refresh yourself. Still, I'm fully dressed, if a bit wet, so you can look at me without blushing.'

She smiled feeling silly now that she'd run away.

He returned her smile, saying, 'I want to show you something interesting, little un. Although, you don't look so little today, I must say,' he said, standing back and appraising her. 'Fay's food must be doing you good for you've filled out nicely since I last saw you and you seem to be walking easier as well.'

He'd noticed her at last, she thought, her heart singing. Then she realized he was speaking again.

'Down there is the marsh where you'll find meadow-sweet and all manner of other flowers you've probably never seen before. Come on,' he said, taking her hand and leading her towards the scrub.

She could smell the heady meadowsweet before they even reached the marsh. The soggy ground was clothed in the white flowers and under the withies she saw a profusion of flowers she certainly couldn't identify.

'These here are gold ragwort, those silvery-mauve ones are water valerian, the purple, horehound, and pink brambles,' Duncan said, pointing to each species in turn.

'They're beautiful,' she gasped, her awkwardness forgotten. Reaching out she gathered up a bunch of the meadowsweet, then eagerly picked a specimen of each of the other brightly coloured flowers and placed them in her basket.

'Careful now or you'll take a tumble. Fay won't thank me if you go back home smelling like a bog. How is she, by the way?'

Eliza sighed and shook her head. 'She was complaining about being hot and said her eyes hurt. I left her resting in the garden under the gorse bush.' Conscious he'd referred to the hobble as her home, she grinned but Duncan was frowning.

'Has she been out and about recently?' he asked.

'No, she's been pottering about her garden. Why?'

'Just checking. Has she made any more of her remedies or distilled any essences?'

'No. I've been badgering her to, but she said it's not the right time of year yet. As soon as I get back, I intend making her an infusion with these,' she said, holding up the meadowsweet. 'That should help, shouldn't it?'

He nodded and the look of admiration in his eyes made her heart flip.

'So our little un's growing up and thinking of others.

Make sure she drinks it and I'll be over to see her as soon as I can.'

Disappointed that he wasn't returning to the hobble with her, she nodded.

'Come on, I'll carry your basket until we reach the track,' he said, taking it from her.

Fay was asleep in the garden when Eliza returned. Her battered bonnet had slipped over her face and was rising and falling as she gently snored. However, as Eliza made her way up the path, she woke with a start.

'Had a good day?' she asked.

'Yes, I bumped into Duncan. He was swimming in the river and . . .' she flushed. 'Well, anyway, he showed me where to find the prettiest marsh flowers. They smell wonderful.'

Fay stared at her knowingly. 'And how is Duncan?'

'He's busy at the moment but said he'd call by to see you soon. He wanted to know if you'd distilled any essences or anything yet,' she told Fay, looking at her hopefully.

'Busybodying whippersnapper,' the woman muttered, rising stiffly to her feet. 'Can't sit here all afternoon. I've got my plants to see to.'

Eliza sighed and took herself indoors. She'd have liked to ask Fay what she could use her flowers for. Carefully she placed her specimens between the pages of the flower book, then set about making an infusion with the meadow-sweet. At least she knew how to do that.

'Here you are, Fay,' she said, when the woman came indoors.

'What's this?' she asked, eyeing the steaming mug suspiciously.

'It's to help you feel better,' Eliza explained.

The woman snorted but inhaled the liquid. 'Meadow-sweet, eh?' she commented, looking at Eliza knowingly.

Eliza nodded then smiled as Fay took a sip.

'You made this without a receipt?'

'Yes. Why, is something wrong with it?'

'It's as I thought, you've got the nose,' Fay grudgingly admitted. 'Not that I needed any fancy drink, mind. Early night's what's called for, I think.'

Although she was far from sleepy, Eliza saw how weary the woman looked and didn't argue.

Next morning, Eliza woke to the sound of pots and pans being banged about. Quickly dressing, she pulled back the dividing curtain to find Fay had lit the fire and was busy placing something inside a big pan.

'Morning, Fay,' she said. 'You're up early.'

'Well, seeing how you now think yourself competent in the use of flowers, I thought I'd better demonstrate the distillation process.'

Eliza's spirits soared. 'So the meadowsweet worked, then?'

'It did, as it happens. But don't get cocky,' she warned as Eliza grinned. 'You've got much to learn so watch and observe.' She put a heavy flat stone into the bottom of the pan, then placed a mug on top. 'This is to collect the distillate. Pass me that pail of water.'

Eliza did as she'd been asked and watched as Fay carefully poured in the liquid until it reached the bottom of the mug. Then she tore up a handful of rosemary, placed it in the water and covered the pan with the lid upside down.

'Oh,' Eliza exclaimed. 'You've put the lid on the wrong way up – shall I turn it over?'

Fay clicked her tongue. 'I'm not stupid, girl.'

'Sorry, I was only trying to help.'

'If that's the extent of your helping then you can go back to bed,' the woman admonished. 'Now, are you going to watch and learn or interrupt me with inane comments?'

'I'll be quiet as a mouse,' Eliza promised.

'Mice twitch and I can't abide that.'

Eliza bit her lip. Really, the woman was in a contrary mood this morning.

'Now that lid's upside down for a reason,' Fay continued. 'The handle in the middle is going to act as a collector, which will drip condensed steam into the mug.'

'Will it take long?' Eliza asked as the woman carefully placed the pan on a stand to the side of the fire.

'It'll take as long as it needs,' Fay muttered, giving her a sharp look. 'We'll leave this now until the steam rises and the condensate drips into the cold mug.'

'What's condensate?'

'It's the substance resulting from condensation, in this case the liquid that comes from the vapour. I'm starving, so let's eat while this does its job,' Fay said, taking out her frying pan and throwing fat and thick bacon rashers into it.

As they sat eating their breakfast, Eliza kept her eye on the pan at the side of the fire.

'It's going to take a little time,' Fay pointed out.

'What will you use this condensate for?'

'As I've told you before, rosemary is versatile and can be used to treat many ailments. It can counteract exhaustion, fatigue, help rheumatism, lift mood,' Fay muttered.

Eliza smiled inwardly. Perhaps Fay could use it to help her bad temper.

'But how does it work?'

'You need to start with the basics, Eliza. Essential oils are produced by chlorophyll-bearing plants that absorb the sun's rays and synthesize or produce organic or natural compounds.'

Eliza smiled and nodded as if she understood. Goodness, this was far more complicated than she'd thought. Fay wasn't fooled, though.

'Don't worry if you can't remember everything. The more you practise the better you understand. Now, I think it's time to change the mug over otherwise it will overheat and redistil.'

As the heady aroma filled the room, Eliza began to see how the process worked.

Later, when Eliza had cleared away their things, Fay pulled the pan from the fire and lifted the inverted lid. Again the pungent aroma filled the room and Eliza watched as Fay carefully lifted out the mug and put it on the table.

'There's not much, is there?' Eliza ventured, peering at the liquid.

'Ah, but that liquid's very potent and to be used sparingly. Later we'll need to separate the oil from the distilled water, for both have their uses. Now stop standing there with arms both the same length and find something useful to occupy your time. I noticed weeds in the vegetable plot when I went out earlier. By the time you've done that this will have cooled and we can siphon off the oil.'

Eliza grimaced but seeing the doughty look on Fay's face, she snatched up the receipt book and went outside.

Ignoring the weeds, she threw herself down on the grass and thumbed through the pages to see what she could use her flowers for. As the sun rose higher so did her spirits. There were so many different receipts she couldn't wait to start. She stared around the garden, wondering what else she could use and then saw the dreaded weeds.

It didn't take long to tidy the plot for her movements were easier now that the weather was warm and dry. Not having to wear the flannel petticoat under her cotton skirt made her feel liberated and she enjoyed the feel of fresh air on her bare arms. If only she didn't have to wear those ugly black boots, she thought, scowling down at them.

Her musing was interrupted by Fay's cry of dismay. Hurrying indoors, she found the woman staring at the spilled mug in disbelief while the liquid spread out over the table in ever increasing circles.

'How could I have been so careless?' she moaned. 'I didn't even see the damn mug.'

'Shall I scoop up as much as I can and put it back?'

Fay sighed and shook her head. 'The oil and water have all mixed now.'

'I'll wipe up the mess then.'

'I'll see to it,' Fay snapped.

'Well, let me make you some tea,' Eliza suggested, seeing how ashen the woman looked. 'It's not the end of the world. We can make some more for there's plenty more of that rosema—'

'It's not that simple,' Fay cut in. 'Oh for Heaven's sake, leave me alone. I've got much to think about.'

Eliza collected her basket and went back outside, hoping Fay would feel better once she'd had some time to herself. She couldn't shake off the feeling of despondency that had descended like a cloak of doom.

As if echoing her mood, clouds covered the sun and she shivered. She wondered if she should return for her shawl but didn't want to disturb Fay. Knowing it would be warmer in the woods, she made her way there hoping to find new flowers she could look up in the receipt book.

She found some exquisite plants nestling in the shade and was breathing in their sweet fragrance when, seemingly out of nowhere, a thick hill fog descended. It wrapped around her in strange dirty white swirls. Everywhere was still and quiet, everything cloaked in damp, desolate greyness. Strange shapes loomed, then disappeared like phantoms into the night. Shivering, she turned back and was trying to locate the path she'd taken earlier when a huge shadowy figure rose up before her, stopping her in her tracks.

'Who are you?' she shrieked, but there was no answer. She called out again, her voice quavering as she stared hard into the mist. 'Who's there?' But the only sound was the echo of her own voice coming back to her in the eerie silence.

Hampered by her dragging foot, which felt leaden in the cold and damp, she made her way back to where she hoped the hobble was. Cursing as she stumbled on unseen roots and rocks, she urged herself on. Then she saw it, the glimmer of candlelight flickering out of the murk. Almost crying with relief, she limped up the path and threw open the door.

'Goodness, where's the fire?' Fay asked, looking up from the table where she was studying her receipt book by the light from the candle.

'A monster, huge,' Eliza gasped, holding out her hands as far as they'd reach, then collapsing on the chair opposite. 'It rose right up in front of me then disappeared in the mist.'

'And did this monster say anything?' Fay asked.

'I called out but nobody answered. There was only the echo of my voice.'

'Happen it was the Brocken, then.'

'Who is this Brocken?'

'Why, you, of course,' Fay chuckled. Then seeing Eliza's frown she explained, 'That's what they call the figure of your own self when it's projected into the mist. There must have been some sort of light behind you for that to have happened.'

'Oh and I'd just found some beautiful mauve flowers, too,' Eliza muttered, feeling stupid and exhausted at the same time. She huddled nearer to the fire, wondering if she'd ever feel warm again.

'Well, they'll still be there tomorrow. Go and put on some dry clothes while I heat something to nourish you.'

By the time she'd dried herself and changed into the thick shirt and serge trousers, Fay had warmed some soup. As she passed over her mug, Eliza wondered what had happened to the essence they'd made earlier but knew better than to mention it. Instead she cupped her hands gratefully around the mug and sipped the tasty liquid, savouring the warmth as it thawed her both inside and out.

'That was lovely,' she said as she placed the empty mug on the hearth. 'It's so nice to be home again.' As she gave a sigh of contentment, Fay shot her a searching look.

'You like it here, then?'

'Oh, yes, I love it. As I said to Duncan the other day, I'm so grateful to you for taking me in. I'd hate to live anywhere else now.'

Fay stared intently into the fire but didn't answer.

17

It was some weeks before Duncan called on them again and, to Eliza's surprise, no sooner had he sat down than Fay sent her outside.

'We need vegetables for supper, Eliza, and when you've dug some please tidy the herb garden.'

'Can't I do that later? Duncan's only just got here and I've so much to tell him.'

'Now, please, Eliza. I have something important I need to discuss. You can chat with him later.'

'But I . . .'

'Now, if you would be so kind,' Fay insisted firmly, and Eliza knew it would be useless to argue.

'I'll be out for a chat soon,' Duncan assured her.

It seemed ages before he appeared and then he was looking grave.

'Is everything all right?' she asked.

'I'm sorry but I can't stop now. There's an errand Fay's asked me to do.'

'Oh, Duncan, I haven't seen you for weeks. Can't you stay for just a little while?'

'Sorry, little un. This is important.'

She opened her mouth to ask what could be more important than spending time sharing their news but he was already striding down the path. Picking up her fork, she stabbed it into the ground with frustration.

'Don't blame Duncan. He's running an errand for me,' Fay said, coming out to join her. 'Now, I've something to show you.'

Eliza followed her over to the flower garden and gasped in surprise. The rose bush, which had been showing tight buds the previous day, was now a mass of red blooms. Bending her head, Eliza inhaled the intoxicating fragrance.

'Don't you just wish you could bottle this wonderful smell?' she cried in delight.

Fay smiled. 'You can, Eliza.'

Eliza stared at the woman, her thoughts running as fast as the stream. 'You mean we can use flowers in the same way as the rosemary?'

'With luck, without spilling it everywhere,' Fay grinned.

'Can we do it now?' Eliza asked, hopping up and down excitedly.

Fay smiled indulgently. 'You can, certainly'

'Me?'

'Yes, Eliza. I'd like to see how you get on. Collect the petals while I prepare the equipment. The fire should be just about right for heating the pan.'

Eliza ran inside to collect her basket and by the time she'd picked the flowers the woman had laid out everything ready.

'The first thing you need to do is tear the petals into strips,' Fay told her. Eliza carefully followed the woman's instructions but her insides were bubbling with excitement. When at last the pan was heating gently over the fire she stood watching it, impatient to see the steam gently rising.

'A watched pot never works, Eliza,' Fay chuckled.

'Instead of just standing there, why don't you get the bottles out ready? Don't forget you'll need to change the mug to avoid it overheating,' she reminded her, then sat promptly in her chair and fell asleep.

Having set the bottles on the table and swapped the mug, Eliza looked at the sleeping figure and frowned. Why, she hadn't even consulted the receipt. Quickly she thumbed through the book until she came to the page on roses.

'Know that one by heart,' Fay muttered, opening one eye. 'Smells like it's ready now anyway,' she added, rising to her feet and lifting the lid.

Eliza hurried over to the fire and gasped at the fragrant aroma rising from the pot. Carefully she took the drying cloth and lifted the mug over to the table.

Later, she sat staring in wonderment at the little row of bottles she'd filled and neatly labelled, hardly daring to believe she'd made the perfume herself. Then she unscrewed one, inhaled the heady aroma and gave a sigh of pleasure.

'Well done, Eliza. Did you enjoy that?' Fay asked.

'Oh, yes,' Eliza exclaimed. 'It's a wonderful feeling to have created something so fragrant and uplifting.'

'It will certainly be a testament to what you can achieve,' Fay agreed, but Eliza was too preoccupied to take in her words.

When Duncan popped his head around the door a week or so later, Eliza could hardly contain her excitement. 'Duncan, I've made my very own rose scent,' she burst out, snatching up a bottle to show him. To her surprise, though, he frowned and turned to Fay.

'You didn't waste any time, then?' he said, his voice tight as he handed her a letter.

'What do you mean?' Eliza asked, staring from one to the other but neither answered.

While Fay hurriedly tore at the seal, Duncan stared down at the floor. Then as she scrutinized the sheet of paper, a heavy hush descended.

'Farrant's agreed,' she finally announced.

Duncan's head snapped up and he turned to Eliza. When she saw the look in his eyes, she felt fear flame in her breast yet didn't understand why.

'Who's agreed to what?' she asked. 'Will someone please tell me what's going on?'

'Sit down, Eliza. We have something to discuss,' Fay ordered. Eliza glanced at Duncan, who nodded. Fay waited until she'd perched on the edge of her chair. 'Eliza, you have a talent for aromas that I feel should be encouraged. The son of an old friend of mine is a Master Perfumer in Devonshire and he has agreed to train you in the business. Now, is that not a wonderful opportunity?'

'Devonshire? But that's miles away from here. I couldn't possibly travel there and back each day,' she exclaimed. Then she saw the look on the woman's face. 'You want to get rid of me, don't you?'

'No, I don't, as it happens. However, circumstances change, and this is a wonderful opportunity for you to make something of your life.'

'Circumstances? What do you mean?' she asked.

'Eliza, Mr Farrant is one of the most respected names in the business. To be trained by him would be . . .'

'I'm not going,' she insisted, jumping to her feet.

'Why don't you tell her everything, Fay?' Duncan said.

'Remember what we agreed, whippersnapper,' Fay said, her tight voice brooking any argument.

'What are you keeping from me?' Eliza cried. 'You are the dearest people in my world and I thought you cared about me too.' Fay and Duncan exchanged meaningful looks but didn't answer. Unable to bear the tense atmosphere any longer, Eliza ran outside.

Throwing herself down on the little patch of grass, she stared up at the hobble and tried to make sense of what she'd been told. She was happy here and didn't want to go away. This funny little place had become her home, Fay and Duncan her dearest friends. She loved this way of life. Why, she'd even got used to digging those perishing vegetables.

Suddenly she became aware of Duncan hunkering down beside her.

'Don't cry, little un. Happen it's for the best. You've got your whole life ahead of you.'

'But I don't want to leave you both,' she sobbed. 'Promise you won't let her send me away?'

'Fay's become really fond of you, Eliza, and she wants to make sure you're looked after.'

'But I love it here and I love you, too,' she whispered.

He gave a lopsided grin, leaned over so that she caught the fresh smell of the woods that was him and gently kissed her cheek.

'Love you too, Eliza Dryad. Be happy.' Then with a tight smile, he jumped to his feet and strode purposefully down the path.

'You will be back soon, won't you?' she called. When he

didn't answer, she ran after him but by the time she'd got to the gate he was disappearing into the trees.

Fay was still sitting in her chair clutching the letter when Eliza went back indoors.

'I'm not going to Devonshire,' she announced stubbornly.

'Why ever not?' the woman asked.

'It's too far away, for one thing.'

'Why, child, it's merely a cat's jump,' Fay scoffed, clicking her fingers. 'There is a huge wide world out there and you're afraid of travelling as far as the next county? Pff. Now, Mr Farrant is calling for you on . . .' She stopped and squinted down at the letter. 'Well, shortly,' she amended, 'and you will be ready to accompany him back to his premises in Follytown.'

Eliza glared at her. Next time she saw Duncan she'd enlist his help, she vowed. Between them, she was certain they could get the woman to change her mind. After all, Duncan had told her he loved her. He'd even kissed her, she thought, reaching up and touching her cheek. He wouldn't have done that if he wanted her to go, would he?

Over the next few days, while Fay cleaned and tidied the hobble, she insisted Eliza launder all her clothes. More to humour her than anything, Eliza took her things down to the river and vented her frustration and hurt bashing them with the largest stone she could find. All the while she waited for Duncan to call. As time passed and he didn't appear, she began to worry. Surely he would come before this Mr Farrant arrived. He wouldn't let her go, she just knew it.

To her surprise, when she returned Fay had the flat iron

heating beside the fire. Never before had she seen the woman press her clothes.

'Come along, you can't take wrinkled clothes with you,' Fay admonished.

'Look, Fay, I appreciate you trying to secure my future but I really love it here with you. When Duncan comes, he'll make you see sense.' Fay smiled sadly. 'Duncan will be here soon, you'll see. He loves me, even if you don't. Why, at this very moment he's probably arranging for me to stay with Rose,' Eliza insisted.

'Not with Mother Evangaline there.'

'What's she got to do with anything?'

'Look, Eliza, there is no way to dress this up. Rose's mother is an out-and-out snob. She expects her daughter to mix with people of a certain class. Unfortunately, she considers you a country bumpkin.'

'Oh,' Eliza said, collapsing onto the chair.

'Why do you think Duncan's never taken you back to the farm?' Fay continued. 'Now, if you go with Mr Farrant and train as a perfumer you will be able to hold your head up high in society. Then you can come back and show Mother Evangaline how well you've done. This truly is a wonderful opportunity for you. I know you think I'm trying to get rid of you but that is not the case. If things were different . . .' She shrugged. 'Now when we've sorted your clothes there's something I wish to discuss with you.'

Early next morning, dressed in the corded dimity gown and cotton lawn petticoat trimmed with broderie anglaise that Rose had given her, Eliza nervously waited for Mr Farrant to arrive. Fay had also donned a dress for the occasion and Eliza was surprised to see how elegant, yet frail, the woman looked. Although they'd been expecting it, the sharp ratatat made them both jump. Fay gave Eliza a reassuring smile before hurrying to open the door.

'Bonjour, Madame Beaumont.'

Eliza stared in surprise as the dapper gentleman, dressed in a smart frock coat, took Fay's hand and kissed it gallantly. Was he foreign?

'Mr Farrant, how kind of you to call,' Fay said. 'Won't you come in?' Deftly, he removed his top hat and stepped inside the hobble. As he stared around the little room, Eliza saw the lift of his brows before he turned to face Fay.

'The pleasure, it is mine, Madame, and this charming mademoiselle is your daughter, Eliza, yes?'

'Flatterer, you know full well if she were related, she'd be my granddaughter,' Fay laughed. 'Let me introduce you to Eliza.'

'Enchanté, Mademoiselle Eliza,' the man said, smiling and giving a slight bow. Eliza stifled a giggle. With his shock of fair, almost yellow hair and moustache shiny with pomade, he was unlike any male she had ever encountered before. She wrinkled her nose. He had a most curious smell about him too.

'Please take a seat, Mr Farrant,' Fay invited. 'May we offer you some refreshment?'

'Charles, please, Madame. That is très kind but I stayed in Dulvester and only recently partook of le petit déjeuner,' he said, smiling politely. 'Now, to business, oui?'

'It's funny, Charles, but I don't remember you having a French accent before,' Fay said.

'Ah, business it has taken me to Grasse, and when in

France . . .' he shrugged. Now you have those receipts for me, oui?'

'All in good time. First, I want you to assure me Eliza will receive the finest training in the art of perfumery.'

'But of course, Madame. Mademoiselle Eliza, she will become the finest perfumer in the land – after me, of course,' he laughed.

'And you have a housekeeper, staff?'

'Indeed. I will put my housekeeper at Eliza's disposal. She will be looked after as if she were my own. The cook provides meals par excellence. As for my business, Eliza will train alongside my other apprentice, Amos. He is in his second year and très promising. I trust the terms I set out in my letter proved satisfactory?'

Fay nodded. 'And you engaged the services of a chaperone?'

'Oui, at extra cost, you understand? Madame Simmons is waiting outside in my carriage.'

'Chaperone?' Eliza gasped.

'Oui, Mademoiselle. Our journey to Follytown is long, necessitating an overnight stop at the hostelry in Tiffeton. It would be inappropriate for us to travel alone, n'est-ce pas? Now tell me, have you made any perfume before?'

'Oh, yes, I have made rosewater and other infusions, of course,' Eliza said, producing a bottle.

He inhaled and smiled. 'Bon, you have used the roses well. With a little training in the blending you have the potential to be très bon. Now, Madame, I do not wish to hurry our discussion but we need to embark upon our journey. You have your receipt book?'

'Indeed, Charles. Here is my part of the bargain,' Fay

said, handing over the book along with a sealed envelope.

His green eyes glittered with greed as he jumped up and took them with almost indecent haste. But the look was so quickly replaced with that charming smile, Eliza wondered if she'd imagined it.

Pocketing the envelope, he then began flicking through the pages. 'Excellent.' Then he frowned. 'I had thought there to be more, however . . .' he commented, raising an immaculately arched eyebrow.

Fay shrugged but said nothing.

'Well, if you are ready, Mademoiselle?' he said, turning to Eliza and smiling graciously.

'I would just like to say farewell to Eliza in private, if you could spare us a few moments, Charles?' Fay asked.

'Of course, Madame. I will wait outside in my carriage. It has been a pleasure doing business with you,' he said, bending and kissing Fay's hand.

'And you will send me regular news of Eliza's progress?'

'Mais oui, of course,' he confirmed.

As soon as the door had closed behind him, Fay turned to Eliza.

'Remember what I said?' she asked, inclining her head towards Eliza's bundle that lay waiting on the dresser. 'On no account is Charles to know you have my other book of receipts. It is my present to you and insurance for your future. Promise me?'

Eliza could only nod as the prospect of leaving made her too choked to speak.

'I also want you to take this black scent bottle,' Fay said, drawing a small parcel wrapped in velvet from her pocket. 'When you are alone, inhale the aroma that still lingers inside and commit it to your memory. Once you are trained, see if you can find the flower to recreate it. Do that, Eliza, and you will become a woman of standing in your own right. I began once myself, but circumstances . . .' She swallowed, then shrugged. 'Well, let's just say, sketching the flora became the focus of my life. This is also to be your secret. I'll hide the bottle in your bundle whilst you put on your cape.'

'Do I really have to go?' Eliza asked, staring sadly around the hobble that had been her home these past months.

'Yes, and you'd better not keep Charles waiting,' Fay urged, gently smoothing down Eliza's cape then all but pushing her out of the door.

Making her way down the path, Eliza swallowed hard, determined not to disgrace herself by crying. At the gate, she turned back to give a final wave and was dismayed to see tears glistening on the woman's cheeks. She hesitated and was about to go back, but Fay pushed the door closed and Eliza knew her old life was over.

She sighed. Nobody truly wanted or loved her. Even Duncan hadn't found the time to come and say goodbye. Well, she could stand on her own two feet. She would go with this Monsieur Farrant, learn what she could, then make her own way in life.

18

Eliza took a deep breath and hurried towards the waiting carriage. The driver jumped down and took her bundle. Then, as Charles Farrant put out his hand to help her up the step, he noticed her ugly boots and frowned.

'Oh, I hadn't realized,' he muttered, looking quickly away.

'It doesn't affect my sense of smell,' she advised him pointedly. As she took her seat opposite she caught a whiff of his peculiar aroma and wished it did.

There was no time to dwell on it, though, for no sooner had she settled herself onto the plush leather squabs than the carriage began moving. Eliza glanced back at the hobble for the last time but could see no sign of Fay.

'This is Madame Simmons, who will be chaperoning you until we reach Follytown,' Charles Farrant said, gesturing towards the woman sitting in the corner. She was smartly dressed and wearing the most enormous hat Eliza had ever seen. Smiling and thinking it would be nice to have some cheerful company on the journey, she moved closer, but Madame Simmons merely nodded and turned quickly away.

Charming, Eliza thought, staring out at the scenery as the carriage lurched and rocked its way down the steep incline of the moors. Ponies and sheep grazed contentedly on the heather and she wished she was out there with them. As the driver carefully negotiated his way over the stone bridge spanning the river, Eliza thought of Duncan and the night they'd found Fay by the side of the road. Then they were passing the hills they'd sledged down to reach the farm, and with every turn of the wheels taking her away from all that was familiar her heart grew heavier.

Fay didn't want her and she hadn't seen Duncan since that day in the garden. Involuntarily her hand went to her cheek and she sighed. She'd thought he cared for her as much as she did him but as he hadn't even called to say goodbye, obviously he didn't.

Now they were passing his beloved woods and she angrily dashed away a tear. If that was what they wanted, so be it. She would concentrate all her energy on becoming a perfumer. No, not just a perfumer, a master one – or should that be mistress one? She was pondering the conundrum when the hairs on her neck prickled and for one mad moment she thought she saw Duncan's chestnut eyes peering out from the dense foliage. Hoping for a better look, she leaned against the window, but the carriage had already passed by.

'You have travelled to Devonshire before, Miss Eliza?' Madame Simmons asked, her West Country burr breaking the silence. Surprised but welcoming the diversion, Eliza looked up to find the woman smiling at her. Well, she assumed the woman was smiling but that outrageous hat obscured nearly all of her face.

'No, I've lived in Somerset all my life,' she answered.

'And a beautiful place it is, too,' the woman said.

'Remember your status, please, Madame,' Charles Farrant rebuked, looking up from the book to give her a warning glare. The woman flushed and Eliza caught the faintest whiff of violet before she stared down at the floor.

Charming again, Eliza thought, turning her attention back to the passing scenery. Far below she saw Ben and Rose's fields, brown speckled with gold now their harvest was gathered. What happy days she'd spent there, helping with Joshua, preparing for the Wassail celebrations and dancing with Duncan. It had been such a contrast to her unhappy life back home and for the first time ever in her life she'd felt wanted. Then she recalled what Mother Evangaline had purportedly said about her and sighed. Seemingly she wasn't deemed good enough to mix with anyone, even this Madame Simmons. Well, whatever life had in store for her, she was determined to make something of herself. She'd show them all.

The sun was high in the sky now, its rays almost burning Eliza's cheek through the glass, the glare making her squint.

'You wish some shade, Mademoiselle?' Charles Farrant asked, reaching up and pulling on the cord to lower the blind. She smiled her thanks, relaxed back in her seat and closed her eyes.

'Dulvester,' the driver shouted, jerking her awake. No sooner had the carriage ground to a halt in the hostelry yard than it became a hive of activity with ostlers running out to see to the horses. As the driver threw open the door and let down the steps, Charles Farrant carefully alighted, smoothing the creases from his trousers. Then he helped them down the steps and ushered them into the taproom, which was gloomy after the brilliant sunshine outside. The buxom barmaid was clearly bowled over by his charm, fluttering her eyelashes and leaning lower over the bar to reveal her magnificent bosom. Eliza stared around the dingy room, grimacing at the smell of ale, tobacco and sawdust.

Then the landlord appeared and the woman reluctantly left Charles to show Eliza and Madame Simmons where they could refresh themselves before luncheon. A little table had been set for two in the corner of a private room and platters of ham, pickles and bread were placed in front of them. Madame Simmons gasped in delight and immediately tucked in with relish, but the colossal hat kept coming between her mouth and the food. Finally, with a cry of exasperation she pushed it to the back of her head and Eliza was able to see her velvety brown eyes for the first time. The woman would have been quite attractive if she hadn't been shovelling great handfuls of fare into her mouth as if she'd never been fed before. Well, Eliza thought, status or not, she at least had better table manners. They were just finishing when Monsieur Farrant appeared and glared at Madame Simmons, who hastily pulled her bonnet down over her face again.

The tension in the carriage was palpable, nobody spoke and Eliza found the rest of the journey tedious. Tree followed tree, and fields stretched out as far as the eye could see as the carriage continued its seemingly endless descent. By the time they pulled up at the hostelry in Tiffeton where they were to spend the night, the shadows were gathering and Eliza couldn't help yawning.

'Show Mademoiselle to her room,' Charles Farrant ordered as soon as the landlady appeared. The woman nodded and led the way up a steep flight of stairs and along a narrow corridor. Eliza tried to keep up but her legs were wobbling like jelly after being in the coach for so long and her foot throbbed, making her limp more pronounced. When she was eventually shown into the small but comfortable room, she sank thankfully onto the one single bed. She was surprised Madame Simmons wasn't to share with her then remembered Monsieur Farrant's earlier comment about status. Obviously, Eliza wasn't deemed of the right class to associate with even the chaperone.

Too exhausted to remove her clothes, she closed her eyes but it seemed like she was still moving. Although the bed was comfortable, she tossed and turned, wild thoughts going round and round her head. Unused to noise, she was kept awake by the loud voices and bawdy laughter rising up from the taproom. Grey dawn was lightening the sky before all went quiet and she fell into a dreamless sleep.

When she woke the sun had already risen and she could hear men shouting and the sound of hooves on the cobbles outside. Quickly splashing her face with water from the ewer, she ran her fingers through her hair, smoothed down her crumpled clothes and hurried down the stairs.

Charles Farrant glanced impatiently at his fob watch as she reached the hallway. 'Bonjour, Mademoiselle Eliza, I trust you slept well? You are requiring le petit déjeuner, non?' From the way he emphasized the non, Eliza took this as a signal she was to refuse. Ignoring her rumbling stomach, she shook her head then followed him out to the carriage where Madame Simmons was already seated.

As the carriage moved away, Eliza leaned back against the leather squabs and promptly fell asleep.

When she woke some time later, they were travelling alongside a river. Nearby was a huddle of buildings from which the most noxious stench emanated. She wrinkled her nose.

'Ah, you have woken, Mademoiselle,' Charles Farrant commented. 'That delightful smell it comes from the tanyard, but luckily for us the prevailing winds blow from the south-west. It is fortunate my premises are situated on the far side of town, for perfume and tanned hides are not usually renowned for mixing,' he said, rocking with mirth so that his shiny moustache quivered. Eliza stared at it in fascination wondering what could have amused him so much.

Fearful of being thought rude, she turned to look back out of the window and her eyes widened in amazement. She blinked and looked again but there it was, a monster cockerel rising up from behind the trees. Why, it must surely be as tall as me, she thought.

'That's the octagonal lantern of St Andrew's church,' Charles Farrant said, serious once more. 'It is beautiful, non? Truly a sign of money and worth,' he added, puffing out his chest as if he was personally responsible for building it.

After that, Eliza didn't like to admit she'd been looking at the church's weathercock, which she could now see was perched magnificently atop the tower.

'My perfumery is but a few moments' ride from here.'

They were passing through the town square now. How busy everywhere seemed and how smartly dressed the people were. The men wore toppers, frock coats edged with braid down the front and brightly coloured cravats showing at the neck, while the women were attired in tailored dresses, matching waisted jackets and high plumed hats. Eliza gazed down at her crumpled gown and worn, down-at-heel boots and wondered how she'd ever fit in.

The carriage duly slowed outside an imposing grey limestone and flint house, with so many chimneys on the roof that Eliza could only wonder how many rooms were inside. It was surrounded by a weathered stone wall with a bolted arched gate at the front and a wide-open gate to the side. The coachman turned into this gate and onto the drive, coming to a halt by the front door. It was opened by a butler wearing a white shirt, long black coat and grey striped trousers, who greeted Charles Farrant as if he were gentry.

Monsieur Farrant nodded and turned to the little maid who was standing behind him. 'Mimi will show you to your room where a light lunch should be ready and waiting.' Turning, he quirked an eyebrow at the little maid, who nodded vigorously.

'Bon. Now Eliza, do you have any formal attire with you?'

'Formal?' she asked.

'Oui. I noticed that what you wear is past its best and many seasons out of mode. As for your bundle, it is well . . .' he grimaced and shook his head, '. . . hardly worth bringing inside.'

'But it contains some precious personal belongings,' she said quickly, thinking of her treasured box and the things Fay had given her.

'Then I will order it to be sent to your room. When you have decided what you really must keep, perhaps you would be good enough to get the housekeeper to dispose of the rest. Ask Mrs Symms to arrange for the dressmaker to call at her earliest convenience,' he said, turning to the maid, who nodded and bobbed a curtsy.

'But that will cost money and . . .' Eliza began.

'Your guardian, she has provided.'

'My guardian?' Eliza muttered, shaking her head in bewilderment.

'Oui. I explained in my letter to Madame Beaumont that your attire will need to befit a perfumer's apprentice, and perhaps a linen cap would also be in order,' he said, frowning at Eliza's head.

'A cap?' she gasped.

'At the very least you must wear your hair Cadogan manner. It would be unseemly for you to be seen around my premises with it dangling, how you say, like drowned rat's-tails. I shall expect you to look smart and dignified at all times. Remember you represent moi, Monsieur Charles Farrant, Master Perfumer. I am very well known around these parts,' he said, puffing up his chest in the way Eliza had come to recognize. Hearing a titter from behind, he spun round.

'And servants are easy to replace,' he added, frowning at the little maid who stared nervously down at the floor. 'Now Mimi can show you to your room and I will see you later, Mademoiselle Eliza.'

He hurried away leaving Eliza to follow the maid along a light airy vestibule, its walls hung with ornate pictures of amber-coloured amphorae and amber-coloured scent bottles similar to the ones she'd seen in Fay's book. Then the maid threw open a door and led her across a little courtyard and into another, more modest building.

'This be where you sleep, miss,' the maid said, opening yet another door. 'Monsieur likes his staff to be housed here in the west wing,' she lowered her voice, 'out of the way.' Before Eliza could say anything, she gave a quick bob and left.

Relieved to be alone, Eliza stared around the modest room, which was furnished with a bed, closet and washstand. The rose coverlet matched the curtains, which gave the room a cheery look. A tray was set on the little table by the window and as she lifted the cloth a rich aroma assailed her nostrils, making her stomach rumble hungrily. The platter of thinly sliced meat was arranged in semicircles around dainty triangles of bread. She'd never tasted anything like it before and soon the plate was empty. Replete, she sat back sipping the elderflower cordial that had also been left for her, and looking out over the courtyard to the field beyond. How different it was to the doorsteps of bread and mugs of tea she'd shared with Fay in the hobble.

That the woman had deemed herself to be Eliza's guardian as well as handing over her precious receipts and paying for her apprenticeship had come as a shock. As she'd never appeared to have any money Eliza couldn't understand how she had managed to do this. Yet it would appear she had made provision for Eliza's future. Perhaps it had been to assuage her guilt for wanting Eliza gone. Had Duncan known, she wondered. If he had, why hadn't he told her instead of disappearing like that? It was all very confusing, but at least she should write a letter to Fay thanking her for her generosity.

She might be housed in this prison-like wing but she would work hard and successfully complete her training. Then as a fine perfumer she, Eliza Dryad, would return to the moors and repay Fay's kindness. She would also show Mother Evangaline that she was indeed good enough to mix with her daughter.

19

A knock at the door interrupted Eliza's musing.

'Mrs Buttons is here, miss,' the maid announced. A cheery woman, tape measure round her neck, roll of material tucked under one arm and a sewing basket in her hand, bustled into the room. 'I'll take these back to the kitchen,' Mimi added, picking up the tray.

'That was quick, Mrs Buttons,' Eliza said.

'Don't do to keep Monsieur waiting if you want his custom, ducks,' the woman said briskly. 'Now, he's ordered you be fitted for two day dresses and one jacket . . . oh, and a matching apron. He was most insistent it be matching, too.'

Eliza grimaced as the woman unrolled the mustard-coloured material across the bed.

'All in this brownish-yellow?'

Mrs Buttons nodded. 'Yes, he's adamant your clothes match his amber scent bottles. Still, the colour will set off that pretty hair of yours.'

Pretty? Since when had her mousy colouring been pretty, Eliza thought. Then she remembered what else her new boss had said.

'Monsieur said I had to wear my hair in a Cadogan manner,' she said, trying to remember his exact words.

'Smarter than wearing a cap, eh?' Then she saw Eliza's expression and chuckled. 'Want me to show you how it's done?'

'Please.'

'I'll do the fitting first and then we'll get you put in the net,' Mrs Buttons said, taking her tape from around her neck. Put her in a net? She wasn't a fish. But the woman was too busy measuring and jotting down numbers with a stubby pencil to notice her puzzled expression.

'If you don't mind me saying, I'm surprised Monsieur allowed you onto his premises dressed liked that,' she murmured through a mouth full of pins, as she held the material up against Eliza. 'Most particular, he is, especially since he came back from France. Still, I guess he could see you'd look elegant once you was properly attired.'

'How much will all this cost, Mrs Buttons?' Eliza asked, worried about Fay receiving a huge bill.

'Don't ask me, ducks. I just does the sewing. 'Tis the master who sees to the finances. This material don't come cheap, though, that I do know. Now, I'm done with your measurements so let's see about this hair,' the woman said, throwing her tape onto the bed and rummaging in her box. 'Ah, yes, thought I had one.' She held up some brown mesh. 'You'll need to sit down so I can get at you.'

Eliza perched on the chair while Mrs Buttons twisted her hair into some kind of knot at the back of her head, then placed the net over it. So it was her hair that went into the net, she thought, relieved that it wasn't to be all of her. This was turning out to be such a weird place that nothing would surprise her.

'Now I think this is how Monsieur would like you to look for work. In the evenings you can tease out some ringlets and let them hang down the back of your neck.

You looks a picture, ducks,' the dressmaker pronounced, standing back and admiring her handiwork.

Eliza jumped up and stood in front of the mirror on the closet door. Was that really her? Why she looked so smart and grown up.

'Thank you, Mrs Buttons. Do you think I'll be able to do the knot myself?'

'Course you will. Everyone can fix a bun, and that net will hide any stragglers. Don't worry, you'll look right dandy,' she chuckled.

Eliza stared down at her ugly boots.

'Want me to make them dresses longer to cover them?'

'Could you?' Eliza asked, brightening again.

'You leave it to Mrs Buttons, ducks,' the woman said, winking and gathering up her things. 'I'll see you in a couple of days or so.'

'That soon?' Eliza gasped in surprise.

'When Monsieur Charles wants something, he wants it yesterday,' she said, shaking her head. 'Course, he was always Thomas before he went to France. Tommy two-ways, he was called, and it suit . . .' She was interrupted by another knock on the door. Eliza hurried to answer it and found the maid standing there, a white-haired man hovering behind.

'Mr Leatherjacket's here to see about your new boots,' Mimi said, bobbing a curtsy.

'Well, I'll be on my way then,' Mrs Buttons said, hurrying out.

As Eliza stood back to let the woman pass, Mimi hesitated, looking unsure.

'Is something wrong, Mimi?'

'I've been told to stay here while he measures you as it

would be inap . . . inappro . . . wrong to have a man in your room with you being by yourself.' The words burst out in a rush and the man laughed.

'Begging your pardon, miss, but with me rheumatics and everything, I hardly think you're in any danger – pretty lass though you be,' he added quickly, doffing his cap.

'Come in, both of you,' Eliza invited. 'We don't want to go upsetting anyone.'

Hastily stuffing his cap in his pocket, the man picked up his workbox and followed the maid into the room.

'See, I'm in the nick of time,' Mr Leatherjacket commented, pointing to Eliza's boots. 'Them soles is more off than on. No good for that 'ere foot of yers, either. Let's take 'em off and get you properly sized. Blimey, girl, bet you been limping like a good un,' he whistled. 'Them's at least three sizes too small. It'd be better to walk around barefoot till your new ones is ready.'

Eliza flexed her feet and had to admit they did indeed feel better without the confines of the ill-fitting boots. Finally, the man was satisfied and Eliza showed both him and the little maid out. She was just about to close the door when she saw the driver of the carriage hurrying across the courtyard, her bundle over his shoulder.

'Oh thank you,' she cried in delight.

'My pleasure, miss, shall I carry it inside?'

'I can manage,' she said, taking it from him.

Placing it down on the bed, she perched beside it and eagerly pulled at the knot. Carefully she pulled back the clothes that were wrapped around her box, the black scent bottle and Fay's receipt book. She sighed with pleasure at the sight of her treasures, running her fingers along the polished surface of the box and was just about to pull out the stopper on the little bottle when there was yet another knock on the door. Almost immediately came another more insistent knocking. Quickly she covered her things and hurried to answer it.

'Ah, Mademoiselle, I came to make sure that you have settled in,' Monsieur Farrant said, glancing past her to the things strewn across her bed.

'Thank you, Monsieur,' she said.

'I happened to see Dawkins carrying your bundle and wondered if you had perchance found something for me, like more receipts?' he said, eyeing her closely.

Eliza shook her head. 'I don't understand. Why should I have more?'

'That book your guardian gave me is not as thick as I was led to believe. I have waited years to get my hands on her receipts and frankly I was expecting more in exchange for your training,' he said, frowning.

'I have just this minute unpacked everything. They are mainly my undergarments and old clothes, but if you wish you can go through them to check,' she offered, praying he'd decline.

'Non, that is all right,' he said, holding his hands up in horror. Then he spotted her bare feet and glowered. 'I will see you after petit déjeuner tomorrow morning and we will discuss your training.' He hurried away, almost tripping over the rug in his haste. Eliza stifled a giggle. If he was so appalled by the thought of seeing her underthings she knew the very place to conceal the receipt book and scent bottle. And hide them she must, for hadn't Fay said they were her insurance? She took out the little bottle and studied it carefully for the first time. Its sleek black lines screamed elegance and the blue stopper twinkled like a jewel. Carefully, she pulled it out and inhaled the last traces of the lingering fragrance. It was unlike anything she had ever smelled before and she vowed to find the source. Then she'd return to Fay and tell her.

The next morning, Eliza donned her clean skirt and blouse, then spent ages trying to recreate the way Mrs Buttons had put up her hair. She'd just managed a passable effort when there was a knock on her door. Honestly, this place was as busy as one of those new-fangled railway stations she'd heard about.

'I've come to show you to the dining room for breakfast,' Mimi announced.

'Thanks heavens for that. I thought I was going to be confined to my room for all meals, Mimi,' Eliza said. 'That's a lovely name, by the way. Are your family French?'

The girl laughed and shook her head. 'Monsieur called me that when I first came here 'cos he said everything I said started with me this or me that. Oh, I'm meant to take your supper things back to the kitchen,' she added, spotting the tray on the table. 'You can have supper in the dining room tonight, miss. I heard Monsieur tell Cook he'll be out this evening.'

'Does he usually eat with everyone then?'

The maid dissolved into peals of laughter. 'Hardly, miss, but I also heard him say you was a ragamuffin and not fit to grace his house until you was suitably atti . . . dressed, but if he's out he won't know, will he?'

Charming, Eliza thought as she followed the maid through the courtyard and into the main house.

'This door is always locked at 8 p.m. sharp, so make sure you're in your room by then,' Mimi advised.

'But why should the door to the main house be locked so early, if at all?' Eliza asked, but they'd reached the dining room and Mimi was showing her to the table. She was seated next to Dawkins, the driver of the carriage, who explained that he was also the handyman.

'And that's Mrs Symms, the housekeeper,' he said, gesturing to the woman sitting at the far end of the table. 'Though why she's keeping her distance this morning, goodness only knows. Anyhow, help yourself.'

Eliza served herself a portion of the stewed fruit and what looked like cream from the dishes set down the middle of the table. Cream at breakfast? She helped herself to a generous portion then grimaced at the sour taste.

'Whatever is this?'

''Tis called yogurt, apparently. We've had to suffer it since his lordship came back from France,' Dawkins said mournfully. 'Afore that we always had a good healthy fried breakfast.'

Eliza ate her fruit then spread the ghastly yogurt stuff around her dish before putting down her spoon. She hoped she didn't have to eat this every morning. Remembering how she'd moaned about Fay's venison, she sighed. What she wouldn't give to have a dish of red meat now. She jumped as Dawkins patted her arm.

'I think young Amos is trying to attract your attention,' he whispered, nodding his head towards the door. She looked up to see a young man with a flop of sandy hair smiling at her.

'Who is he?'

'The other apprentice. He's a good un, is Amos. Stick by him an' you'll be all right,' the man advised.

Eliza smiled her thanks. Getting to her feet, she noticed the housekeeper was watching her. Although the woman looked quickly away, Eliza couldn't help thinking she'd seen her somewhere before.

'Hello, you must be Eliza,' the young man said, giving her another warm smile. 'I'm Amos, Monsieur Farrant's apprentice. Regrettably, he has been delayed and asked me to show you where you will be working.' Eliza smiled back, taking to the man immediately. She saw that he was wearing a short tabard over his shirt and trousers, all of which were in the same mustard-coloured material Mrs Buttons had measured her for the previous day. Obviously, it was some kind of uniform.

'Ghastly colour, isn't it?' he said, giving a rueful grin. 'First thing I do when I get back to my lodgings of an evening is change my clothes. My landlady thinks it's a hoot.'

'You don't stay here, then?' Eliza asked as he led her along another corridor hung with pictures of perfume amphorae, atomizers and cut-glass bottles all in amber.

'Not likely.' He grimaced and threw open a door. 'Here we are, the workhouse,' he announced. This room was cooler than the rest of the house and she peered around, taking in the copper stills, various tubes and jars on the worktops, the rows of amber-coloured perfume bottles lining the shelves that ran the length of the walls. Amos walked around, pointing out what all the various equipment was and its uses.

'I thought it would smell of perfume,' Eliza said.

'It does when we're making it. Monsieur has just per-fected his special Christmas ones and it will be our job to bottle and label them ready to be sold to his special clients.'

'But it's only autumn,' she said.

'The very time he begins his little "spreading the word" campaign. It's his busiest and most profitable time of year. The more we help him sell, the larger our Christmas box will be.'

'What is this Christmas box?' Eliza asked.

'You really are green, aren't you?' Amos chuckled, not unkindly. 'It's money we're given in the spirit of the season of goodwill. Now do you have an apron or something to protect your frock?'

She shook her head. 'Mrs Buttons is making me one in that colour,' she said, pointing to his clothes.

'Mais naturellement,' Amos intoned, throwing up his arms in a fair imitation of their boss.

'I am glad to find my two apprentices getting on so well,' Monsieur Farrant declared, making them jump as he strode into the room. 'It would be even better to find them working, non?'

'Sorry, Monsieur, I was just helping Eliza settle in. Alas she has no apron at the moment and I would not like her to spill anything on her frock,' Amos answered so inno-cently, that Monsieur Farrant smiled.

'That is très considerate, Amos. If you will continue with what you were doing yesterday, I shall begin by tak-ing Mademoiselle through some theory.'

'Of course, Monsieur,' Amos said, hurrying over to a workbench at the far side of the room.

'Now, Eliza,' Monsieur Farrant said, nodding at her hair with approval, 'we shall start at the very beginning with smell, for it is the most important of our senses and we need to learn how to use it properly for getting the best effect, oui?' Monsieur Farrant picked up one of his amber bottles. He unscrewed it, dipped in a thin strip of blotting-like paper and swung it around in a wide circle under Eliza's nose. Immediately the pleasant smell of rose assailed her senses, reminding her of Fay's garden.

'We do this to excite the aroma molecules. By creating a vortex these will be more easily detectable. Now sniff with your right nostril,' he said, handing her the paper. She inhaled. 'Now do the same with the left. Good, good, and now with both. Breathe in until you feel it right at the top; like so,' he said, pointing to the bridge of his nose. 'Concentrate really hard. You feel the smell now?' She nodded, trying hard not to sneeze. How could you feel a smell? 'Now we have a little rest or we will overload the olfactory.'

'That would be terrible,' she agreed.

'Indeed, for in the art of the perfume making one must be able to detect one's smell clearly, non?' he said, leaning towards her.

Catching a whiff of his peculiar odour, Eliza wondered if he knew how bad his own smell was.

20

'Now, Eliza, we shall return to the olfactory,' Monsieur Farrant continued, oblivious to her thoughts. 'The olfaction bulbs are housed high up in your nose and the bigger they are, the better you can smell.'

'Yes, I know. Fay told me,' she said.

Monsieur Farrant frowned but ignored her. 'We humans can only detect vapour, yet dogs have noses that stream when they smell something interesting. Do you know why that is?'

Eliza shook her head. What had dogs got to do with making perfume?

'It is because they still have the verminasory canal, referred to as v.c. by perfumers, which runs down the bridge of the nose. You see, smell used to be our prime sense and it is thought we lost this v.c. around the time man got colour vision or c.v. Can you imagine us as dogs, getting a whiff of something so exciting it sends us running around with our noses streaming?'

Eliza stared at the sleek-haired perfumer. With his glittering eyes, shiny moustache and amber cravat he reminded her of the King Charles spaniel the mine owner's wife had carried the day she'd graced their charity school with her presence. He'd slipped his lead, then ran around sniffing everything in sight. As a picture of Charles Farrant doing the same popped into her mind she had to bite her lip to stop herself from laughing out loud. Glancing over the man's shoulder, she saw Amos's lips twitching and knew he was thinking along similar lines.

Engrossed in his subject and completely oblivious to their amusement, Monsieur Farrant continued, 'Now, Eliza, what do you know of the notes, eh?'

Notes? She was here to make perfume, not music.

'By your bemused expression, I can see you have no concept of the way a perfume is structured. Perfumes have three sets of notes that make the scent harmonious, yes?'

'I see,' Eliza said, trying to sound as if she understood.

'These unfold over time. The top note it is revealed first, then the deeper middle note with the base appearing last. Think of it like a triangle, non? Top notes or head notes are what you smell initially. They are made of small, light molecules that evaporate quickly. Middle notes emerge just as the top notes dissipate and are known as the heart or main body of the perfume. Finally, the base notes materialize as the middle notes disappear, bringing depth to the perfume. These are the deep, rich compounds that take up to thirty minutes to emerge. Then we have the whole symphony, non?'

Eliza nodded vigorously, hoping they could now move on to actually making some perfume. However, Monsieur Farrant was reaching over to pick up the bottle of rose scent she'd made with Fay. He placed it alongside the one he had used earlier and undid the lid.

'First smell this,' he said, dipping a pointed stick of paper into her bottle and waving it under her left nostril.

'Now we do the same with the other scent.' He dipped another stick in the other bottle and flamboyantly waved it under her other one. 'What do they smell like?'

'Very similar,' she answered.

'Now try the sticks again,' he said, repeating the process. 'And what do you find?'

'That one seems stronger?' she said, pointing to the sample from his bottle.

'Non, Mademoiselle, not stronger, deeper. Now why do we leave them for thirty minutes or so before smelling again?'

'To let the base notes emerge,' she said.

'Bon. That is correct,' he said, beaming with pleasure.

'Well, I'm parched after all that smelling so shall I make us a brew while we're waiting?' she asked.

'A brew?' he asked, his smile vanishing. 'What is this *brew*?'

'A pot of tea,' Eliza explained.

He shook his head in amazement, his shiny moustache quivering.

Just then a little bell on the wall jangled, interrupting the awkward silence. Monsieur Farrant jumped to his feet.

'Ah, a client has arrived. Excusez-moi, my presence, it is required in the perfumery.'

'I'll come with you, shall I?' Eliza asked, eagerly. He looked her up and down then held up his hands in horror.

'When you are more suitably attired, Mademoiselle. My clients, they expect . . .' He shrugged, put his nose in the air and strutted from the room, leaving the rest of the sentence hanging in the air.

'I seem to have put my foot in it,' she said, walking over

to Amos. 'Oh, are you all right?' she asked, noticing his shoulders were shaking and that tears streamed down his cheeks.

'Oh, Eliza, you're so amusing,' he answered, wiping his face with his kerchief. 'You've really brightened my morning with your funny questions.'

'I was only trying to be helpful.'

'And I must admit a brew would go down a treat,' he admitted.

'Monsieur looked at me as though I was mad when I suggested it,' she sighed.

'I don't think he's ever heard that expression before. Besides, he only drinks Earl Grey.'

'What's that?' she asked.

'It's flavoured with bergamot. I suppose you could call it perfumed tea,' he laughed.

'Yuk,' she grimaced. 'Well, I hope he's going to show me how to make perfume when he comes back. I wasn't expecting a morning full of that theory stuff.'

'There is a lot to learn, Eliza. Making perfume is an art that requires you to know all about chemistry and composition. Then there's formula and mixing, as well as the blending and bottling. For all his flamboyant ways, Monsieur Farrant is the best in the business and we really are fortunate to have the opportunity to be trained by him.'

'Yes, I realize that. It's just that he's so pompous.'

'He is egotistical, I'll grant you. When he returns and asks you which rose sample is the better one, you will know to say his,' Amos said, giving her a broad wink. 'Even if you think otherwise, it is always best to stay on the right side of him.'

'Thanks, I'll remember that. So what have you been doing then?' she asked, staring at the array of little bottles and dropper things in front of him.

'I've just finished blending these together, which is the satisfying part of the process. Now, though, I have to clear away,' he said, grimacing.

'Non, Eliza will do that,' Monsieur Farrant said, coming back into the room. 'I need you to assist in the perfumery, Amos, as I have to leave to attend an important client in the town.'

'Yes, Monsieur.'

'From now on, Eliza, it will be your job to clean all the equipment and worktops. Then you will polish the floor until you can see your face clearly in the tiles. When you have finished doing that, you may begin studying these notes I have prepared for you,' he said, sliding a notepad towards her. 'The quicker you learn the theory, the faster you make the perfume, oui?'

Before she could answer, he'd gone. Amos grinned apologetically then took off his tabard. As he shrugged into the jacket that matched his trousers, Eliza giggled.

'I know, I look like a golden eagle,' he grinned, puffing out his chest. She stared at his lean frame.

'You're joking. I've seen more meat on a sparrow.'

'At least spare my pride and make it a sparrowhawk,' he begged, placing a hand to his chest as if wounded.

'Wrong colour, Amos,' she chuckled.

'Well, I'd better not keep Monsieur waiting. I shall be in the perfumery for the rest of the day so I'll see you tomorrow.' And with a last cheeky wink, he hurried out of the door.

Eliza shook her head. Everyone seemed to move so quickly here. She stared around the room and saw the sample sticks on the work counter. Picking them up, she carefully inhaled each one. Monsieur Farrant's was undoubtedly stronger and more complex and she could detect a hint of something else as well as the rose. Hers was softer and more natural, somehow, reminding her of Fay's garden on the moors. She must remember to ask Monsieur what his was, she thought, placing them in her pocket. Then she put the bottles back on the shelves and began the task of clearing away and cleaning up.

Determined to do a good job, she scrubbed and polished the tiles on the floor until she could see her reflection. Satisfied, she snatched up the notes and hurried back to her room. She was just making her way out of the main house when she saw Mrs Symms coming towards her. Giving her a bright smile, Eliza was puzzled when the woman averted her gaze and barely nodded. As she hurried past, Eliza caught a whiff of violet and couldn't help wondering why the smell seemed familiar.

There was a convivial atmosphere in the dining room that evening. All the staff were seated around the long table and as soon as Cook had placed a huge tureen in the middle, with the order to help themselves, everyone tucked in. The woman then took her seat at the end of the table next to Eliza, who was sat opposite Dawkins with Mimi to her right. The butler was next to Dawkins with Mrs Symms at the far end as usual. Something about the way she was gobbling her food tugged at Eliza's memory but she soon forgot about the woman as she tucked into the tasty chicken casserole.

'This is delicious,' she said to Cook, who beamed with pleasure.

'Thanks, dearie. It's a pleasure to be able to prepare a good English dish instead of that foreign stuff his lordship insists on these days. Why, I can't even make faggots no more. It has to be a hazelette, if you please. It's still pork, just with all manner of spices and herbs added,' she sighed.

'He says food has to have alco . . . alki . . . all go together,' Mimi chirped.

'If you don't know the proper word, you'd be better off not saying anything at all,' Bertram the butler sniffed.

'At least I know what me hands is meant for,' Mimi muttered. 'You don't want to get too close to him. He ain't known as dirty Bertie for nothing,' she muttered to Eliza.

'It's rude to whisper, child,' Bertram chided.

'And it's rude to . . .'

'Well, that were a most tasty drop of stew, Cook,' Dawkins intervened quickly.

'I believe the correct term for the meal we have just eaten is casserole,' announced Bertram, but everyone ignored him.

'Glad you enjoyed it,' Cook said. 'Pass down your dishes and I'll bring in pudding. Seeing as we're by ourselves tonight, I've made Devonshire cider cake to celebrate and there's clotted cream too. None of that, er, yogurt stuff.'

Thank heavens, thought Eliza, feeling relaxed for the first time since she'd arrived.

They were enjoying a cup of tea at the end of their meal when a bell on the wall jangled. Sighing heavily,

Bertram got to his feet and marched stiff-backed out of the room.

'Glad he's gone,' Mimi muttered. 'Gives me goose bumps, he does. He acts all prim and proper in front of his lordship when all the time he's a dirty old man. Mind what I said and watch his hands.'

'Perhaps it's the way you wiggle that behind of yours when you walk past him,' Mrs Symms said. Hearing the woman speak for the first time, Eliza looked up in surprise and found herself staring straight into velvet brown eyes.

'It's you, Madame Simmons,' she gasped. 'You pretended to be the chaperone my guardian paid for when really you're Monsieur Farrant's housekeeper.'

'Don't know about any payment, I'm sure,' the woman sniffed. 'I was told to sit in the carriage, keep me face covered and me mouth shut. Got a right telling off for pushing me hat back but, as I said to his lordship, how else could I have eaten me meal? That food was the only thing worth doing all that travelling for. And I had to catch up on me chores when we got back as well,' she said in martyred tones. 'Still, now you know who I am I'll be able to talk at the table again. It's been a right pain having to keep me mouth shut, I can tell you.'

'And there'll be pain aplenty if we don't get to our rooms before Bertram locks the door.'

'Why . . .?' Eliza began, but everyone was too busy clearing the table to take any notice of her. Seeing someone had already taken her dish away, she made her way to her room.

Eliza lay in bed, thoughts going round her head faster than the wheels on a carriage. Had Monsieur really taken money from Fay under false pretences? Perhaps she should ask him. But then if she did, and Mrs Symms had got it wrong, he might send Eliza home. The housekeeper might be in trouble for letting out his secret. And why did everyone have to be in their rooms by eight o'clock? Stranger still, why was the door to the main house locked at night? This was certainly a weird place.

'You've made a splendid job of that floor, Eliza,' Amos greeted her cheerily the next morning.

She grinned, pleased to see his friendly face. 'Monsieur Farrant not here yet?' she asked, peering around as though the man might be hiding under one of the counters.

'To be honest, he rarely appears until late morning.'

'Ah, but this morning he appears like the lark, non?' Monsieur Farrant said, standing in the doorway and wagging his finger at Amos, who quickly turned his attention to his work. 'Now Eliza, did you remember to smell those samples yesterday?'

'Indeed I did, Monsieur.'

'And did you detect any difference between them?'

'Oh yes, yours was definitely more sophisticated,' she enthused.

'Bon,' he said, his delighted smile shinier than her floor. 'It is about the alchemy, non? The marrying of the constituents.' Eliza smiled, realizing that 'alchemy' was the word Mimi had been trying to remember at supper the previous evening. 'You think that is funny?' Monsieur Farrant frowned.

'No, Monsieur, I was just thinking that it's like preparing a good meal. All the ingredients need to go together.'

'That is a good analogy, Eliza. Well done. Now we shall step outside to the perfume garden.'

'You have a garden that grows perfume?' she asked, her eyes widening. As a vision of rows of little amber bottles sprouting up out of the soil flashed in front of her, she had to stop herself from laughing.

'In a way, yes,' he agreed. 'We have to grow the ingredients for the perfume as we do our meals.'

Proudly he strutted around the garden, pointing out the names of flowers that were planted in neat rows and swaying in the early autumn breeze like colourful ribbons. Their heady bouquet was intoxicating. Never before had Eliza seen so many different flowers and herbs growing in one place. She must be sure to bring Fay's little black bottle out here one day. Surely one of their scents would match?

'It is beautiful, so vibrant, so fragrant, Monsieur,' she enthused. 'Oh, bunny rabbits' ears,' she cried, seeing the brightly coloured flowers they'd had fun popping as children.

'Non.' He shook his head emphatically. 'We have no rabbits here. It would spoil the garden, non?' He shuddered and Eliza knew it would be useless to try to explain. Then she spotted a glasshouse nearby. 'What is that?'

'That is our hothouse. In there, we cultivate plants for use when the frosts kill off those out here.' Never having heard of such a thing, Eliza was amazed.

'Oh, and what's in that building there?' she asked, pointing down to the far end of the long garden. His eyes darkened.

'That is forbidden territory, Eliza. You are never, ever to venture in there. Understand?'

21

'Of course, Monsieur,' Eliza answered quickly, puzzled by his sharp tone. Then he was smiling again.

'Now, you walk around by yourself and really smell the flowers. Take the aroma right up each nostril, oui? Then, I want you to select six that you think will work together in harmony. Can you manage to do that?'

'Of course,' she said, delighted at the prospect of spending time alone in this wondrous garden.

'When you have made your selection, bring them to me and I will see what your nose has told you, oui?'

She nodded and watched as he strode back to the house. This was certainly much better than being cooped up indoors, she thought as she wandered from flower to flower, sniffing their bouquet.

The fragrance and peacefulness of the garden lifted her spirits. For the first time since she'd arrived, she felt happy and could have lingered all morning, but mindful of her instructions, she carefully made her choices. Then, as she was strolling back towards the house, she noticed the lavender bushes lining the path and plucked a stem to add to her posy.

Back inside, she placed her specimens on the worktop then held out the rose and lavender.

'That is a curious mix, Mademoiselle,' Monsieur Farrant said. 'And before we start assessing them, I will show you something interesting, non?' He reached up and selected two little amber bottles from the shelves.

'Now we dip a tester strip in each, hold them up together and what do we find? That they do not blend harmoniously, non?' He waved both samples in front of her nose before handing them to her.

Eliza inhaled deeply. 'They don't go well together like that,' she agreed.

Monsieur's eyes glittered. 'So you think we cannot make a perfume with the lavender and rose?' he asked.

Eliza frowned, remembering what she'd read in Fay's book and also something the woman had told her.

'Yes, actually, I believe you can,' she informed him. But she was talking to his retreating back. Astounded by Monsieur's abrupt departure, Eliza stared after him. Then she heard Amos chuckling.

'What did I say?' she asked, turning to face him.

'Dear Eliza, you were not meant to tell him that they actually can work together. You were supposed to smell the lavender and rose and agree that they did not marry, then let him have the pleasure of magnanimously enlightening you. Remember what I said about his ego? Don't worry, he'll be back in a moment and will carry on as though nothing has happened. Of course, he'll go off on a completely different tack.'

'But I am right, they can be used together?' she asked, anxious to get things right.

'Indeed, but it all depends on the amounts involved. If you are adding only a tenth of one per cent to a complex mixture, you can use a huge range of materials that, in higher proportions, would not harmonize.'

'You sound very knowledgeable, Amos,' she said, not liking to admit she'd only understood half of what he'd explained.

'As I've mentioned before, Monsieur Farrant is a highly skilled perfumer. He loves to impart what he knows and as long as you let him think he is brilliant, you can learn a lot.'

'Don't you find it annoying having to pander to him?' she asked.

Amos shrugged. 'I keep my head down and get on with things, but perhaps I'm not as inquisitive as you, little Eliza,' he grinned, then quickly turned back to his work as Monsieur reappeared.

'Now, Mademoiselle, I believe you were wanting to know about the different emotions that lavender and rose invoke?'

'I was?' she began, then saw Amos nodding. 'I mean, that's right, I was.'

'Bon. Perfume affects the emotions so it is vital you understand how these things work. Lavender, it has the calming properties, while rose invokes happiness and positivity. All this the perfumer takes into account when he is creating his masterpiece. It is essential to know the effect each fragrance has on a person. If you can tune into their feelings and emotions, you will be able to sell to them. Which, of course, is the whole point, is it not?'

'It is?'

'But of course, it is no good spending time and money creating the finest fragrance if you do not have the client to sell it to. When a client asks me to create a perfume especially for them, I spend time finding out the smells they like, what time of day they wish to wear it, etcetera,

etcetera,' he said, waving his hands flamboyantly in the air.

'I see,' Eliza said, thinking that the one smell she did not like was his. 'So you are saying that you need to really find out what a person is feeling, what they like and when they are going to wear it, then match the fragrance accordingly.'

There was a moment's silence and Eliza wondered if she'd got it horribly wrong but he clapped his hands delightedly.

'That is exactly right, Mademoiselle. It is most interesting, non? Of course, you have much to learn but it is good to see you grasping the principles.'

There was a timid tapping on the door and Monsieur Farrant's mood changed instantly.

'Amos, find out who dares disturb my work,' he snapped.

'Yes, Monsieur,' Amos answered, only to return a moment later. 'Mrs Buttons apologizes for intruding but she has finished the first of Eliza's dresses and wonders if this would be a convenient time for her to try it on. She knows how eager you are to have Eliza suitably attired for her position.'

'Indeed I am. Fortunately, I have a client due at any moment so, Eliza, you may attend to your fitting. As I shall be busy for the rest of the day, when Mrs Buttons has finished you may remain in your room and study the notes I gave you. We will be sitting a little test soon, non?'

Eliza nodded, then quickly made her escape.

Mrs Buttons was hovering nervously in the hallway, her tape around her neck and sewing basket in her hand as usual.

'Hope it was all right coming now, only as I've finished

the first dress and apron I thought it would be sensible to make sure they fit before I start on the others. Course, the master was keen for me to bring his payment demand as well, only Bertram wasn't keen to take it,' she chuckled.

'I can't believe you've managed to sew them already,' Eliza said, leading the way to her room.

'Oh, yes, fingers like lightning, I have. I see you managed to put your hair up, ducks. It looks lovely and makes your neck look all long and ladylike. You're going to look a right stunner in your new things.'

'Thank you, Mrs Buttons.' The woman must need a lorgnette, she thought, remembering she'd been called the mousy maid of the moor as a child, and she hadn't changed since then, had she? 'Shall I slip into that dress?' she said, as soon as she'd closed the door behind her.

'Not so fast, ducks. We got to make sure your corset fits first.'

Eliza looked at her in horror. 'Corsets? But I don't wear corsets.'

'Well, ducks, you do now. Got to have the right shape under your dress, haven't you? Now slip out of your things. Don't worry, you ain't got nothing I haven't seen before. Course, if you have then we'll make history together,' she chortled, shaking out a dress in that mustard-coloured material that was now familiar to Eliza. She was relieved to see that the corset was more of a buff tone and not nearly as bright. Mrs Buttons helped fit her into the flared garment that had spiral stays and ended several inches below her waist. Feeling decidedly restricted, she wrinkled her nose.

'You're lucky to have one made by hand to your own

measurements. Some poor girls are having to make do with cheaper mass-produced ones. Goodness only knows what sizes they're trying to squeeze their bodies into.'

'I can hardly move,' Eliza moaned.

'Gawd, ducks. I can remember when we had tight-lacing and believe you me you could hardly breathe, let alone move. Had to have everything pulled in, we did. Not that you've anything that needs holding in, of course, you being young and of firm flesh. I see your buds are blossoming nicely,' she said, glancing at her chest. Automatically, Eliza covered it with her hands and Mrs Buttons clucked her tongue like a mother hen.

'Like I say, nothing I haven't seen before, ducks. You not got a mother nearby?'

Talk of her mother gave Eliza a momentary pang but she couldn't imagine in her wildest dreams ever being able to talk about personal matters like this with her. And as for Fay, well, Eliza bet she'd never even seen a corset in her life, let alone worn one. She shook her head, hoping the woman wouldn't ask about her family but Mrs Buttons had turned her attentions to the dress.

'Now let's see how this fits,' she said, holding it out for Eliza to step into, then doing up the little bone buttons. 'Course, it's an important time in a girl's life. Got three girls of me own so if there's anything womanly you want to ask, anything at all, then ask away, girl. Mrs Buttons know how to button it,' she said, staring at Eliza with shrewd eyes.

'Well, actually . . . no, it's all right,' Eliza said, quickly looking away.

'Well, ducks, like I said, I'm a mother meself so if you

got anything worrying you . . .' She let the rest of her sentence hang in the air and busied herself tying the matching apron in a bow behind Eliza's back.

'Well, there is something,' Eliza whispered, and proceeded to tell the woman what had been bothering her. When she'd finished, Mrs Buttons patted her shoulder.

''Tis what happens when you grow up, ducks. Yous probably a bit later 'cos of your circumstances but now your body's ripening ready for having children. I'll come back, bring you some rags and things to help, and explain it all then. Just make sure you have them ready every month and you'll save yourself a lot of laundry. Now let's have a look at you,' she said, spinning Eliza round and casting a critical look over her outfit. 'That longer length covers those boots nicely but you'll have to remember to lift your skirts when you go outside.'

Relieved she wasn't suffering from some terrible ailment, Eliza smiled. Then, unable to contain her curiosity any longer, she ran over to the mirror and twirled around.

'Is that really me?' she exclaimed, gazing at her reflection in amazement. She swished the material from side to side, thinking how lucky she was and how different it felt from her simple cotton skirt.

'You look just like a young lady, ducks. You'll have all the lads of Follytown beating a path to your door.'

Eliza frowned. 'Not much chance of that, Mrs Buttons. The door to the main house is locked at eight o'clock each evening. I really don't know why, though.'

The woman grunted. 'There's talk in the town about the funny goings-on upstairs here.'

'What kind of things?'

'Don't ask me,' Mrs Buttons said, packing her pins back into her sewing box. ''Tis just gossip.'

'But that's Monsieur Farrant's private quarters. Mimi says he has the whole of the upstairs to himself.'

'He might have the upper floor, but to himself? Well, that's debatable. Now, I'll be off to get on with your other dress and the jacket. I'll drop those other bits and pieces by in the meantime.'

'Thank you, Mrs Buttons,' Eliza said, impulsively pecking her on the cheek.

'Why, 'tis just me job, ducks,' she said, indicating the dress, clearly pleased. 'Course, if you have any other questions, well, you knows who to ask.' She gave Eliza a broad wink.

As the woman hurried away, Eliza saw Mimi walking towards her.

'Cook thought you might like something to eat as you missed luncheon,' the little maid said. 'As it's the evening she visits her sister, she's made enough for your supper, as well.'

'That's kind of her,' Eliza said.

'It's that hazelette stuff again. She can't get rid of it. Bertram says it repeats on him and Dawkins prefers cheese,' she confided, putting the tray on the table.

'Well, I quite like it so please thank Cook, won't you?'

Mimi nodded then stood staring at Eliza.

'Is something wrong, Mimi?' she asked.

'It's just that you look different. Sort of like a lady, I suppose.'

Eliza laughed. 'This is my new work outfit.'

'Well, I like that lovely skirt,' Mimi said, pointing to

Eliza's old cotton garment on the bed. 'All those green pieces of material make it look really pretty. I'd love to have something like that to wear when Toby calls on me half day. He'd really take notice then.'

'Is he your follower?' Eliza asked.

The little maid blushed as red as the rose she'd picked that morning. 'He's a friend of me brother's, miss, but I catch him staring at me when he thinks I'm not looking. My brother says he only visits when I'm home and . . . well, he is very nice,' she said, the last bit coming out in a rush.

'Then why don't you borrow it on your next half day?' Eliza suggested.

'Oh, I couldn't,' Mimi protested, staring at her in surprise.

'Why ever not? We're about the same size so it should fit. Mind you, it needs laundering first.'

The girl's face lit up. 'I'll wash it for you right now,' she said, snatching up the skirt and hurrying away before Eliza could change her mind.

What a busy morning it had been, Eliza thought as she settled in the chair to enjoy her late meal. She'd only just taken the first bite when there was another knock at the door. This time it was Mr Leatherjacket with Mimi dutifully hovering behind, still hugging Eliza's skirt.

'Begging your pardon, miss, only Monsieur said yous needed these as soon as I could have them ready,' he said, holding out a shiny pair of brown leather boots.

'They look lovely. Do come in,' she said to them both, opening the door wide.

As she eased off her scuffed ones, Mimi perched on the bed, lovingly fingering the different materials on the skirt.

'Oh, you look so smart,' she exclaimed, as Eliza walked across the room in her new footwear. 'And you're hardly limping either,' she said. Then, worried she'd spoken out of turn her hand flew to her mouth.

'I must agree, they make walking much easier,' Eliza said.

'Well, them old things were much too small and you was literally on your uppers, so you should find these are better,' Mr Leatherjacket pointed out. He bent down and felt along Eliza's feet, pressing down on the toes, before straightening and giving a grunt of satisfaction.

'Are they comfortable, miss?' he asked.

'Indeed they are,' she assured him. 'Thank you so much, Mr Leatherjacket.'

'My pleasure, I'm sure,' he said, pulling his old cap out of his pocket and heading for the door. Mimi hurried after him, clutching the skirt as if her life depended upon it.

Eliza took a last look in the mirror before returning to her meal and the notes Monsieur Farrant have given her. Never before had she worn such fine clothes and she hoped he would approve of her attire. She would write to Fay and thank her. It would be nice to tell her what she had learned so far, except that didn't seem to be much. She didn't want to upset the woman so perhaps she'd wait until she actually had something to tell her. Eliza couldn't help wondering if she'd have learned more if she'd stayed with Fay. But that hadn't been an option, had it?

As she glanced down at her new clothes, excitement bubbled up inside her. She couldn't wait for breakfast time when she'd be able to show her friends in the dining room her new things.

22

Eliza felt as if she was walking on air as she made her way to breakfast the next morning. However, her appearance was met with stunned silence.

'I think you'll find this is the staff dining room, my lady,' Bertram sniffed.

Eliza giggled, thinking he was joking. As she took her usual seat, the housekeeper stared at her and frowned.

'My, aren't we all dressed up like a dog's dinner?' she commented, looking so surly Eliza felt obliged to respond.

'I was not aware dogs wore their dinners, Mrs Symms. Still, at least I don't feel the need to hide behind a big hat.' The housekeeper sniffed and turned her attention back to her food.

'Well, you looks right dandy to me,' Dawkins said, winking at Eliza across the table. 'Now let's finish our meal before Monsieur comes in and finds us gossiping.'

'In that case, we've got all morning,' Mrs Symms muttered, eyeing Eliza's outfit with what could only have been a covetous look.

Eliza helped herself to stewed fruit and bread and butter, and while she ignored the sour yogurt stuff, she couldn't help comparing it to the housekeeper's demeanour. The atmosphere round the table was frosty and Eliza ate as quickly as she could. Then, excusing herself, she hurried out of the room.

Making her way to the laboratory, as Monsieur Farrant

had told her to call it, she couldn't help wondering why her new clothes should have caused that much of a stir. As she opened the door, Amos looked up and whistled.

'Well, that's a sight for sore eyes. You look absolutely stunning, Eliza.'

'Thank you, Amos,' she said, her confidence restored. Then she noticed he was wiping the floor and her hand flew to her mouth. 'Oh, no, in all the excitement of being fitted for my new things I forgot to come back and do the cleaning. I'm really sorry.'

'Don't worry. Grab that cloth and wipe the counter tops while I finish this. I've used a dry one, in case Monsieur arrives. Luckily, it's brought up the shine, for you know what a stickler he is for appearances.'

'It's kind of you to do this, Amos. I would have been in real trouble if Monsieur had seen the place dirty. You'll have to let me know what I can do to repay you.'

'With you looking like that, my working days will be much brighter,' he said, eyeing her appreciatively. For a moment their gaze held and something sparked between them. Then he turned his attention back to the floor, muttering, 'Better get this cleared up.'

Eliza noticed the red flush creeping up his cheek and she began polishing the worktops furiously.

Soon the room was spotless and Amos, having recovered his composure, put the cleaning cloths away, then perched on his stool.

'So have you been studying the notes ready for Monsieur's exam?' he asked.

Eliza stared at him in dismay. 'You mean he'll expect me to know the answers already?'

'Most of them. He's quite a stickler. Want me to test you?'

Eliza gulped. 'I suppose so, but I've only had the notes a couple of days.'

'That won't worry him,' he said, raising his eyebrows in the way Monsieur did. 'Now, he usually begins with chemistry, so do you know where does the word come from?'

'It's from the Greek word *chemia*, meaning plant juice,' she answered.

'Good. And where is the best place to harvest the plants for making perfume?'

She closed her eyes, trying to remember what was on the notes. 'Where they grow best,' she said.

'Correct. What used to be our prime sense?'

'Smell, until the time we got colour vision.'

'There, not so difficult, is it?' he asked, grinning. 'Now I'd better get on with this blending before Monsieur arrives. Want to watch?'

'Yes, please. What are you doing exactly?' she asked as he took a pipette and began counting out drops from the array of bottles in front of him.

'Making up a perfume for one of his clients,' Amos said, furrowing his brow in concentration. As he began stirring the concoction in the glass beaker before him, she bent over and inhaled deeply.

'That smells pungent,' she cried, wrinkling her nose. 'Almost sort of animally, if that makes sense.'

'Très bon, Eliza, you are quite right. Amongst the ingredients in here, we have the musk, but where does it come from, eh?' he asked, waving his hands around theatrically like Monsieur Farrant did when he was in full flow. She giggled. 'You don't know, hmm? Well, I will tell you, Mademoiselle, it is from the civet.'

'You are only partly right, Amos. What you are using comes from the male musk deer,' Monsieur Farrant announced, having crept into the room without them hearing. 'Before you presume to elevate your status to that of tutor, Amos, kindly make sure your facts are right. Now, if you have time for the chatting then I assume you have finished making up the perfume for my client's mistr— er, lady,' he asked, green eyes glittering.

'Bonjour, Monsieur,' Eliza greeted him, jumping to her feet and smiling sweetly. 'I'm afraid I'm to blame for keeping Amos from his work. Being anxious to please, I asked him to test me on my notes.'

'Ah, bon,' he said, his eyes sweeping over her. 'Mademoiselle, may I say how delightful it is to see you suitably attired. It is a great improvement, non? The length of the skirt, it hides a multitude of sins, yes? You also have the jacket to match?'

'Mrs Buttons has nearly finished it,' she answered, crossing her fingers and hoping it was true. The last thing she wanted was to get the helpful woman into trouble.

'Once it is made, then you may assist me in the perfumery. So Amos has been testing you, has he? Well, Mademoiselle, you will probably find my way more difficult, for I like to start at the beginning with chemistry. Tell me, where does the word come from?' he asked, arching his eyebrow.

'From the Greek word *chemia*, meaning plant juice,' she repeated.

'Bon, I am teaching you well, oui?'

Eliza could see Amos grinning behind his back and

tried to keep her face deadpan as she answered. 'Indeed, Monsieur, you are the finest teacher.'

He nodded and preened his moustache with a manicured hand.

'That is true. Now to business. We are heading towards Christmas, which is one of our busiest times of the year. From now on it is all hands to the perfume bottles,' he said, grinning at his perceived joke. 'Until you have your jacket, you must remain working in here, Mademoiselle. Now, this is your writing, non?' he asked, holding up her bottle of rose perfume and pointing to the label.

'Yes, I wrote out all the labels for Fay's . . .' she began, but he cut her off.

'Yes, yes. Now, the man who usually pens for me has gone and died, which is most inconvenient,' he said, throwing up his hands as though the unfortunate being had done it on purpose. 'As you have elegant script, I wish for you to write out the ones for my festive fragrances,' he said, placing a pile of labels, ink and a quill in front of her.

She stared at them in dismay. When was she going to start making perfume?

'Here are the names for you to copy. Underneath each title you write "Fine Fragrance by Monsieur Farrant".' Eliza gulped, wondering how on earth she would manage to get all that written in such a small space, but already he had turned his attention to Amos. 'You will have to work in the perfumery with me today.'

'Of course, Monsieur,' he answered, starting to take off his tabard though by the time he had shrugged on his jacket, the man had disappeared.

Seeing Eliza grimacing at the labels, Amos placed a hand

sympathetically on her shoulder. 'You practise on some scrap paper first, eh, Mademoiselle?' he suggested, waving his hands in the air.

She laughed at his imitation and immediately the task seemed less daunting.

'Good idea,' she agreed, picking up the quill. It was long and white, reminding her of the goose feather Fay had given her to clean the hobble. How she missed the woman, and Duncan too, although she was still cross with him. Sighing, she dipped the plume into the ink and began practising the names Monsieur had written out for her.

Gold Etoile, Frankinscent and *Myrrh Maid*. Oh, please! When she had her own perfumery she would certainly think up more imaginative names than that. She shook her head, wondering where that ambition had sprung from. Forcing herself to concentrate, she mastered the words and painstakingly set about her task.

A fortnight later and her matching jacket was ready. Proudly, Eliza made her way towards the laboratory. Mindful of the way the staff had treated her the morning she'd appeared in her new dress, she decided to give the dining room a miss for that day. Although they'd resumed their friendly manner, she wasn't taking any chances. Besides, Amos had taken to sharing his noon piece with her and she enjoyed the easy friendship that had developed between them. He was happy to teach her what he knew and in Monsieur Farrant's frequent absences, she'd learned a lot from him.

'Excuse me, your highness, you surely have strayed into the wrong place, for this is the workhouse, you know,' Amos joked when she appeared beside him. She thumped him playfully on the arm, then sighed when she saw the stack of labels still waiting to be written.

'I swear blind Monsieur adds more to that pile each evening.'

'Well, it's your fault for having such elegant script. One of his clients was admiring it the other day and Monsieur told him he prided himself on training us in calligraphy as well.'

'Calli what?' she asked. 'I tell you, Amos, I've never heard so many fancy words in my life. What magic potion are you brewing today?' She pointed to the bottles in front of him, which were of far more interest.

'This is a blend of patchouli, bergamot and rose,' he explained.

She leaned forward and inhaled deeply. 'It's quite nice but too overpowering for me,' she said, wrinkling her nose.

'So what perfume does my lady desire? What are your favourite smells?' he asked, watching her keenly.

'I'd like to smell light and fresh, like the heather on the moors, the moss in the woods, the sweat peas in Fay's garden,' she enthused, hugging her arms around her.

'A blend like that could work,' he agreed, jotting down a few notes.

'Bonjour, mes enfants. With all the tasks I have set you, I am surprised you have time to think, let alone chat,' announced Monsieur Farrant, his green eyes glittering with something Eliza hadn't seen before. It was gone in a flash and he was all smiles again. 'I see Mrs Buttons has at last finished your jacket, Mademoiselle, so today you may work alongside me in the perfumery.'

'If you really think I will be of help, Monsieur,' she cried, her heart skipping a beat.

'Indeed. All the scent bottles need dusting and the shelves restocking from the storeroom, ready for our Christmas rush,' he said, rubbing his hands together. 'Amos, when you have finished what you are doing, here is another receipt for you to make up. I need it for this evening, so none of your dallying and dillying,' he said, reminding Eliza of the song her mother used to sing about lavender.

'Of course, Monsieur Farrant,' he answered seriously, giving Eliza an outrageous wink behind the man's back.

Stifling a giggle, she followed Monsieur from the laboratory and down a passageway until they came to the hallway beside the front door. She stared in wonder at the crystal chandelier twinkling above the grand staircase that led to the upper floor.

'They're your quarters up there, aren't they?' she asked.

Immediately, his back stiffened and, as he turned to face her, she saw he was glowering.

'The rooms upstairs are private. You are never, ever to go up there, understand?' he snapped, for a moment forgetting his French accent.

'Of course, Monsieur,' she said, smiling sweetly at him.

'Now we find the perfumery,' he said, tugging down his jacket and leading the way along another passage. This one was thickly carpeted and although the walls were hung with yet more pictures of perfume bottles and amphorae, these were more elaborately adorned than the ones she'd seen before. Then they came to a painted wall and she gasped.

'It is magnifique, n'est-ce pas?' Monsieur asked, stopping to admire the nubile maiden being anointed with oil by the handsome youth. At least she assumed it was the maiden's glistening body he was admiring. From the way he was staring, she couldn't be sure.

Taking a key from his pocket with a flourish, Monsieur Farrant unlocked the door. At once Eliza's senses were assailed by the intoxicating scent of roses.

'It is wonderfully aromatic, yes?' Monsieur beamed. 'The fragrance of the Bulgarian rose is second to none. Now your rose from the moors pales into insignificance, yes?'

'Actually, I like the freshness that rose invokes, Monsieur. It is like . . . oh, I don't know, the smell of innocence,' she said, remembering the look of wonder on her young brothers' faces when she'd taken them out to smell the wild flowers. To her chagrin, he roared with laughter.

'Oh, Mademoiselle, you have much to learn. Do you really think the rich men who grace my establishment wish to pay for the smell of innocence? Non, they want the exotic, the exciting aroma of experience. Now, you will begin your duties by polishing those scent bottles until you see your face in the amber crystals, oui?'

Hurt by his dismissive attitude, she snatched up a cloth and walked over to the glass cabinet where all the bottles were displayed. To her eye, they already gleamed like gold, but not wishing to be taken for a fool again she duly began to polish them. They were quite exquisite, all in differing shapes and sizes. As her fingers traced their elegant lines, she found herself imagining them filled with different coloured perfumes.

'Why are they all in this dark colour, Monsieur?' she couldn't help asking.

'What colour would you suggest, hmm?' he asked, looking up from the ledger he was studying.

'Well, if the glass was clear, people would be able to see the exciting liquids inside,' she said, her voice rising with enthusiasm.

Monsieur Farrant winced. 'We do not speak loudly in here, Mademoiselle. The perfumery, it is a sanctuary, an oasis of calm with fragrance carried on the air.'

The bouquet in the room was indeed wonderful but as he stood there waving his arms around, Eliza sincerely hoped his own peculiar scent wouldn't be wafted her way.

'And as for clear bottles? Non, non, non,' he continued, wagging his finger at her. 'We use the dark glass for a very good reason, Mademoiselle. It is so that the fragrance lasts. In the clear bottle it would evaporate, non?'

'Oh,' she said, feeling stupid. Vowing not to ask any more questions, she turned back to the bottles, imagining how her labels would look on them. Suddenly she had an idea.

'Monsieur?'

'Oui, Mademoiselle?' he sighed, barely able to conceal his exasperation.

'Wouldn't the labels for the Christmas perfumes look more festive if the script was in colour rather than black?'

He gave a loud sigh. 'Please do not concern yourself with such detail, Mademoiselle. It takes years of expertise to understand what the client wants. Perhaps you could concentrate on the job you are suited to, like the dusting, non?' he snapped.

But as she picked up her cloth, she saw him frowning at the amber bottles.

23

'I shall be but a moment, Mademoiselle,' Monsieur Farrant said a few seconds later. She nodded and watched as he hurried from the room, shiny shoes squeaking on the polished tiles.

Eliza made sure the bottles were polished to perfection, then took advantage of being alone to explore. The perfumery was a delightful place designed to tempt the buyer with its attractive array of merchandise. In fact it had all sorts of things you wouldn't know you wanted until you saw them. She took great delight in investigating the contents of all the bottles, sniffing the flagons of tester perfumes and squeezing the tops of the atomizing sprays, laughing when they squirted little puffs of air in her face. Compared to the sterile laboratory, this was a paradise of fragrance and she hoped to spend more of her time working in here. She might even secrete Fay's little black bottle into her apron pocket and compare the faint aroma that still lingered.

When Monsieur Farrant returned he showed Eliza round the stockroom and directed her where he wanted the new bottles to be displayed. She became so entranced with arranging everything, she hardly noticed his presence. It was only when he told her it was time for her to leave that she realized the working day was over.

'I will escort you to the main hall. I suggest you go straight to your room and study your notes,' he said. 'Cook has been asked to leave a light supper in your room so you will not have to interrupt your studying to go to the staff dining room. Tomorrow, I shall not be in the laboratory until late morning, so you can ensure it is cleaned then, non?'

'Thank you, Monsieur. I have really enjoyed being in the perfumery today. Please can I work here again soon?'

He raised his eyebrows but didn't answer. Instead, he led the way back down the hallway, past the erotic mural and into the hall. 'I will see you tomorrow, Mademoiselle, and trust you have your answers ready for my questions,' he instructed. He smiled but she could feel his eyes boring into her back as she made her way along the corridor. Probably worried I was going to take a sneaky peek upstairs, she thought.

In her room the tray was set on the little table and even before lifting the cloth, she knew what she would find. She spread the bread with the spicy hazelette then settled down to read the notes, determined to be ready for Monsieur's test the next day. They made fascinating reading and soon she was lost in the world of perfume and its origins. It was only when the shadows were gathering and she could no longer make out the words that she set them aside. Deciding a stroll across the yard to get some fresh air and visit the privy would be a good idea, she took herself outside.

It was a cool night and myriad stars were sparkling in the heavens, like the crystals of the huge chandelier in the hall of the main house. A night for frost, her grampy would have said. She sighed, still missing him after all this time, then impulsively plucked a late bloom from the border, vowing to place it in her box. Pulling her jacket

tighter round her, she hurried back towards the staff wing
before the door was locked at curfew. Suddenly, the sound
of merrymaking drifted her way and, looking up, she saw
the silhouettes of three young men outlined in the flickering gaslight. A burst of raucous laughter followed, then
Monsieur Farrant snapped the window shut, drew the
curtains and all went quiet.

Next morning Eliza was busy putting up her hair when
there was an urgent rapping on her door.

'Come in,' she called, recognizing Mimi's knock.

'Monsieur Farrant says you're to go straight to the laboratory,' the little maid panted in the doorway. Eliza was
about to ask why, when she saw the girl was agitated.

'Is something wrong, Mimi?'

'He said you was to hurry,' she answered, ignoring her
question.

'Tell him I'm on my way.'

The girl nodded and scuttled off, leaving Eliza wondering what Monsieur Farrant could want of her at this early
hour. Hadn't he said he wouldn't be in the laboratory until
later?

Quickly fixing the net over her bun, she turned to check
her reflection, then made her way into the main house. As
she passed the dining room, the smell of toasting bread
made her stomach rumble and she hoped Monsieur
wouldn't take long.

However, when she opened the door to the laboratory
it was an entirely different aroma that assailed her nostrils.

'Goodness, something smells strong,' she said,
wrinkling her nose. Then she noticed the man in uniform
standing beside Monsieur Farrant.

'Oh, have I interrupted something?' she asked, looking from one to the other.

Monsieur Farrant shook his head. 'Indeed you have not.'

'Yes, I'm afraid you have,' the constable responded at the same time. Bewildered, Eliza stared from one to the other.

'That was a very good observation, Mademoiselle,' Monsieur Farrant continued. 'You are absolutely right, for compared to the delicate fragrances we inhaled in the perfumery yesterday, this is indeed pungent. You see, Constable,' he said, turning to the police officer, 'Mademoiselle here is one of my best pupils and I like to set the little tests for her. When I call, she jumps, is that not right, Eliza?'

'Er, yes,' she answered. What was going on?

'Monsieur Farrant, I really must ask you some questions,' the constable insisted, but again Monsieur ignored him.

'Today I have lit the incense for Mademoiselle to identify. Now why is incense significant, Eliza?' His eyes seemed to bore right into her as he waited for her answer.

Eliza gulped and thought back to the notes she'd been reading the previous evening. 'Because it was the original perfume,' she said.

He clapped his hands. 'See, Constable, she is clever, non? Now we will move on to the attarwalla.'

Eliza gulped. Attar what? But Monsieur Farrant was in his stride.

'The attarwalla was the perfume seller. He would visit the grand palaces of India and . . .' He was interrupted by the constable coughing.

'This is all very interesting, Monsieur Farrant, but if you insist on ignoring my question, I shall have to report back to my superior. In the meantime, I must caution you that your activities are being watched.'

Again Monsieur Farrant ignored him. 'It is a shame you cannot stay for more of our lesson, Constable. Another time, perhaps?' Monsieur Farrant invited.

'Be sure I shall return with some questions of my own,' the man said, placing his helmet firmly on his balding head as he strode away. Eliza got the feeling he had every intention of coming back but not for a lesson on the attar whatsit. She wondered what questions he wanted to ask Monsieur Farrant and what activities of his were being watched. He'd been determined to ignore the constable.

'That showed him, did it not?' Monsieur Farrant said, butting into her thoughts and giving a supercilious grin. 'It is always good to show who is master in his own castle. You answered the questions well, Eliza. It is good you read my notes, non?'

'I don't remember anything about the attar . . .'

'Not to worry,' he interrupted, waving his hands in the air. 'Interesting though it is, attarwalla is not really part of the course and the incense was just a smoke screen anyway,' he chuckled as he looked at the little burning cones.

'I wasn't expecting you to be up so early, Monsieur, especially after your party last night.'

Monsieur Farrant's eyes narrowed to green slits and his moustache bristled.

'And what party might that be?' he hissed.

'The one upstairs. I heard laughter, saw those young men and . . .'

'You saw and heard nothing, Mademoiselle Eliza. Absolutely nothing, understand?' He leaned towards her and she smelled his own particular smell. It really was peculiar and she much preferred the incense. But Monsieur was still glowering. 'Clean this place up immediately; it is like a piggery,' he snapped.

He stormed from the room, leaving her alone with her thoughts. She knew what she'd seen, all right. Had the constable's visit had anything to do with the revelry of the previous night?

'Someone's up bright and early,' Amos chirped, breezing into the room. Then he saw the burning incense and looked at Eliza in surprise.

'Oh, no, this has nothing to do with me,' she declared, shaking her head then explaining about the constable's visit.

'I think it might have something to do with the party Monsieur had last night, although when I mentioned I'd seen young men upstairs, he denied it. Anyway, the constable said he'd be back,' she said, shrugging.

'Eliza, there are rumours about . . . happenings here. Things you're better off not knowing. Be very careful what you say to Monsieur, and for heaven's sake never venture upstairs,' Amos advised.

'That sounds sinister.'

'Forewarned is forearmed, isn't that what they say?'

'Never could understand why having four arms would help anything,' she quipped.

'You are impossible,' he grinned. 'Now, Mademoiselle,

this place it is a disgrace. We should clean up immediately, non?' he said, throwing his hands up in the air.

Eliza grinned, pleased they were back to their usual friendly banter.

As she set about disposing of the incense, she spotted a fresh pile of labels along with three pots of different coloured ink. 'Oh, no, me and my big mouth,' she cried.

'What have you put in it this time?' joked Amos.

'I suggested to Monsieur the labels on the Christmas perfumes would look more celebratory if they were scripted in colour,' she cried, pointing to the counter.

'Well, at least you'll be too busy to go sleuthing,' he grinned, then ducked as she threw the cleaning cloth at him.

Knowing she had no choice, Eliza settled down to her task. However, as she pictured the respective titles scripted in gold, green or red she nodded her head in satisfaction. Her idea might mean extra work but she could imagine how festive the little bottles would look, especially if they were grouped in their various colours on the shelves. She picked up her pens and by the time Amos invited her to share his noon piece, the little pile of labels had grown.

'You'd better be careful,' he quipped, admiring her handiwork as they munched on the bread his landlady had baked. 'If you continue having these bright ideas, Monsieur will think you're making a takeover bid.'

They didn't see Monsieur for the rest of the day and when the little bell rang, signalling the arrival of a client, it was Amos who went to the perfumery to deal with them. That evening, when Eliza joined the staff in the dining room for supper, they were agog to find out the details of the constable's visit, which they had all heard about.

'I don't really know why he was here,' Eliza said carefully. 'He did say he'd be back, though.' That was enough to set the tongues wagging and speculation was rife for the rest of the meal.

Afterwards, as they sat relaxing over their cups of tea, Mimi turned to Eliza.

'When I went home on Sunday, Toby asked Father's permission to become my follower. We're walking out on my next day off, so if it's all right with you I'm going to wear your lovely skirt. It washed up a treat,' she said, hardly able to contain her excitement.

Cook looked up and frowned. 'I'm sorry, dearie, that's the last Sunday before Advent, Stir-up Sunday. We'll be too busy making the Christmas cakes and puddings for you to take that day off,' she said.

Mimi's face fell. 'But I can't cook so why do you need me?' she wailed.

'To stone the fruit, grease and line the tins, then wash up all the pots and pans.'

'But . . .' the little maid spluttered.

'Perhaps it would be possible for Mimi to take her day off a little earlier?' suggested Eliza, feeling sorry for the little maid.

'Well, I don't see why not. What do you think, Mrs Symms?' Cook asked, deferring to the housekeeper.

'Wouldn't do no harm to take the Saturday, I suppose,' the woman sniffed.

Mimi brightened. 'I'll ask Amos to pop a note through me mum's door on his way home tomorrow.'

'Will you be spending Christmas here with us, Eliza?' Dawkins asked.

Eliza stared at him in surprise. 'I hadn't given it any thought but I don't have anywhere else to go . . .' Her voice trailed off as she remembered the terrible events of the previous year.

'We have a lovely time, don't we, Mrs Symms?'

The housekeeper nodded, becoming quite animated for once. 'We do indeed. Cook always does us proud and we even have a glass or two of elderflower bubbly.'

'Of course, some imbibe more than others,' Bertram commented, staring pointedly at the housekeeper.

'Do join us, Eliza. Monsieur Farrant takes himself away for the festivities so we are able to eat what we want,' Cook intervened.

'It sounds fun. You must let me know what I can do to help,' Eliza offered, happy to be accepted again. Of course she'd rather be celebrating with Fay and Duncan but this was her new life now and she had to move on, didn't she?

Bertram got to his feet and stared pointedly at his pocket watch. Immediately the conversation ceased and everyone began tidying away. Then, calling goodnight to the butler, they scurried to their rooms before he locked the main door.

As Eliza lay in her bed reflecting on the events of the day, her thoughts turned to Fay. She wondered how the woman was. Now she'd begun learning she would send her that letter. After all, she wanted to thank her for her amazing generosity and let her know how she was getting on with her apprenticeship. Monsieur Farrant would have her address, wouldn't he?

Eliza arrived in the laboratory the next morning to find Monsieur inspecting the bottles Amos was filling. She was relieved to see he was back to his charming self and when he complimented her on the good job she'd made of the labels, she took the opportunity of asking for Fay's address.

'Why would you want that?' he asked, peering at her suspiciously.

'I thought I'd let her know about things here?' she said.

'What things here exactly?' he asked, his voice ominously quiet.

'How I'm getting on with my apprenticeship, what it's like in the perfumery, that kind of thing.'

'Ah, yes, I see.' He stood there stroking his moustache for a moment. 'However, would it not be better to wait until you've have made some perfume? Now that would be exciting to tell her, non?'

She nodded. 'But when will that be, Monsieur? I'm really disappointed not to have begun making some by now. Why, I haven't even seen anything made in those,' she cried, pointing to the stills.

'Patience, Mademoiselle. Have I not told you it is the lead-in to Christmas? We have to have everything prepared for our clients so the perfume, it is already made. When Amos here has finished decanting it into the bottles, you, my dear Eliza, are to be given the prestigious job of placing the festive labels on the bottles. It was a good idea I had to use the colourful inks, non?' As she stared at him in astonishment, she heard Amos snort, then quickly turn it into a cough when Monsieur turned his way.

'Except it was my . . .' Eliza began, but Monsieur Farrant cut her short.

'Amos, I am out to see a client. Please show Eliza how I like my labels to be placed on the bottles. Remember, they are to be dead centre or . . .?'

'I'm dead,' he answered.

'Oui, precisely, Amos,' the man chortled.

'Well!' Eliza exploded, as soon as the door had closed behind him.

'It's no good getting upset, Eliza, Monsieur's ways are simple. Come up with a good idea and he takes the credit. Come up with a bad one, you get the blame. Stop frowning and I'll show you how to place your beautiful labels dead in the centre so that you are not . . .' He pretended to cut his throat, looking so comical with his tongue lolling and eyes popping out, she couldn't help but laugh.

But each time she slapped on a label she imagined it was Monsieur Farrant's supercilious grin she was smacking.

24

The following weeks passed in a frenzy of activity as they dealt with the ever-growing number of clients to the perfumery. The staff was busy preparing the Christmas fare as well as carrying out their normal duties.

In the perfumery Eliza was tasked with wrapping the purchases and scripting personal greetings if the clients desired. Monsieur was emphatic she keep both the shop and stockroom clean and tidy at all times. It was also her job to replenish the shelves, and with the seemingly endless demand, Amos was back and forth to the laboratory on the other side of the house, filling little amber bottles from the flagons.

'I'll be needing new boots if I carry on like this,' he muttered, placing yet another full box on the stockroom table.

'Never mind, Monsieur has locked the shop and gone out for an hour so we can have a rest.' Eliza gave a sigh of relief and collapsed onto a chair. Her hands were sore from spending the morning cutting paper and tying ribbons, while all the traipsing from the perfumery to the stockroom and back had made her limp more pronounced.

'Thank heavens for that; I'm starving,' he said, pulling out the tin his landlady packed his lunchtime piece in. 'Oh good, cheese,' he observed gleefully, proffering a sandwich.

'Thanks, Amos. I shouldn't keep taking your food but I can't bear the thought of walking all the way to the staff dining room,' she muttered, rubbing her aching foot. He smiled sympathetically, but didn't pass comment, for which she was grateful.

'It's just as well you do. Mrs Barker packs enough to feed a horse. Says she enjoys having a lad to fuss over again. Apparently she's missing her son since he married and moved out.'

'Will you be staying with her for Christmas or going home?' she asked.

He pulled a face. 'Got to see the folks, be mothered and smothered. Still, with any luck the old man will slip me a little something to add to my allowance and Mother will fill my bag with goodies to bring back.' He grinned and shrugged but Eliza could tell he was fond of them. 'What about you?'

'I'll be celebrating with the staff in the dining room. Apparently Cook prepares a feast and . . .'

'This is very cosy, is it not, mes enfants?' Monsieur Farrant said, appearing in the doorway.

'We were just having our luncheon,' Eliza commented, hating the way he always sneaked up on them.

'And a rest from all that back and forth from the laboratory,' Amos said.

'You dare to complain?' Monsieur Farrant asked.

'Actually, Monsieur, whilst we were taking our break we were also debating,' Eliza said quickly.

'Eating and debating, Eliza? Perhaps you would care to explain just what it was you were discussing?'

'Well, I suppose it was me, really, Monsieur. You see I

was thinking about how much time we waste every day. Time that could be better spent helping you sell more perfume.'

'Indeed?' he answered. 'Perhaps you, as my newest, not to mention youngest, employee would enlighten me.'

'If you were to set up a table in the corner, Amos could fill the bottles in here. Then I would be able to replenish the shelves as and when required instead of having to wait while he traipses back to the laboratory each time.'

'So now you presume to tell me how to run my business, non?' He shook his head and went to unlock the perfumery.

'That makes sound sense, Eliza,' Amos said. 'It would also save my poor feet.'

'Amos, Eliza, come here immediately, there is work to be done,' Monsieur Farrant called.

Raising their eyebrows, they did as they'd been bid.

For the next hour or so the perfumery was busy with a stream of clients. With both men serving, Eliza could hardly keep up with all the wrapping and entering of purchases in the ledger. It never ceased to amaze her how the customers made their purchases without enquiring about cost, merely trusting Monsieur Farrant to bill them at the end of the month. She could only think they had more money than sense, for she could never consider buying something without knowing how much it was.

'I have something to attend to, Amos, so please serve any clients who appear in my absence. Eliza, the counter needs polishing and the shelves replenishing. I'll be back shortly,' Monsieur Farrant announced, breaking into her thoughts. They watched as he strode out of the perfumery and down towards the main hall, then Amos grinned and went to stand behind the counter.

'May I help you choose something to delight your young lady, sir?' he asked, mimicking his boss.

'Do you only have men buying perfume here?' she asked.

He laughed. 'At this time of year, yes. When they suddenly remember, or have been prompted, that a present will be expected on Christmas Day.'

'I'd only want a present if someone really wanted to give me one,' she said with feeling. 'Don't suppose I'll get anything, anyway.'

'Well, apart from sharing my luncheon, Eliza, I'm afraid, being a poor apprentice who has spent his allowance, I have nothing to give you. Unless Monsieur's generous with his Christmas box, of course. When is your birthday?' he asked suddenly.

'February the 19th. Why? When's yours?'

'May the 21st. We might be impoverished apprentices but I shall make sure we celebrate your birthday, Eliza,' he said solemnly.

'And I yours, Amos,' she replied, thinking she'd ask Cook if she could bake a cake.

'Amos, I have had the most marvellous idea,' Monsieur Farrant said, striding back into the room. Eliza and Amos looked at each other and grinned.

'You have, Monsieur?' Amos asked, regaining his composure as he turned to face the man.

'Indeed. It occurred to me you are wasting valuable selling time with all the toing and froing you do. I have instructed Dawkins to place a table in the stockroom so that you can fill the bottles in there. Is that not a splendid idea?'

'It is indeed, Monsieur,' he said, winking at Eliza behind his back.

'Do you not wish you had the genius of your boss, Eliza?' Monsieur Farrant asked, turning to her.

'I wish I had your intelligence, Monsieur,' she responded, 'for then I would surely set up another table alongside so that the bottles, when filled, could be wrapped ready to give the client. If they only had to wait whilst the personal label was scripted for them, they would think your service was par excellence, Monsieur.' She saw Amos's astounded look and wondered if she'd gone too far. Monsieur Farrant, however, stared at her with that supercilious look she'd come to recognize.

'Ah, but Monsieur would never come up with a plan that is flawed. For if the bottles were already wrapped, how would you know you were giving them the correct perfume?'

'As you say, Monsieur, you are a genius and, as such, wouldn't.' As he stood there smirking, she added, 'Of course, if the bottles were to have ribbons that matched the labels, there would be no confusion. I mean, it would be obvious that a parcel tied with yellow ribbon would denote the yellow label of Gold Etoile inside, would it not?'

Leaving him to ponder her words, she turned and began tidying the counter. Sure enough, moments later Monsieur Farrant disappeared. Amos burst out laughing.

'You are priceless, Eliza. My mother always says women are wilier than wolves and now I see why.'

With the two tables duly set up in the stockroom, Amos was able to spend the time between attending to clients and filling the bottles, while Eliza labelled, wrapped and tied them with the appropriate ribbons. Monsieur Farrant, pleased that 'his' ideas were working so well, strutted around like the proverbial peacock. They didn't mind, though. It meant they could spend more time together in the stockroom sharing their easy banter. Amos made the working day fun.

Excitement was building in the staff dining room and each evening Eliza was regaled with news of the latest preparation for the festivities. It was so infectious, she found herself looking forward to sharing the day with them. Apparently they all wore their Sunday best for the occasion, so she decided she'd wear the green dress that Rose had given her.

First thing on Christmas Eve Amos packed his bag with the last of the deliveries. Having been told that once he'd dropped off the last parcel, he could go straight to the railway station, he was in good spirits. As she watched him preparing to leave, Eliza felt a momentary pang that she had no caring family waiting for her to visit. Although she'd got on well with her sisters, she'd been a burden to her parents, and Fay had wanted her gone from her hobble. Even now the letter she'd started writing lay abandoned alongside her box. She'd thought of adding Christmas greetings but couldn't shake off the feeling of rejection that threatened to overwhelm her at times. Amos broke into her thoughts.

'Season's greetings, Eliza. If I had a Wishing Ball, well, you know what I'd be doing now, don't you?' he said, giving her a last cheeky grin before he left. Having no idea what he meant, she shook her head. Then the little bell tinkled and his words went out of her head as she hurried through to the perfumery.

To her surprise, Monsieur Farrant was nowhere to be seen. Fixing on her brightest smile, she turned to attend to the well-dressed gentleman.

'Good morning. I am looking to purchase two bottles of perfume, Miss . . . er . . .?'

'Eliza, sir,'

'Well, Eliza, as I said, I require two bottles of perfume.'

'Would that be two of the same perfume, sir?'

'Why not – and if they could be wrapped . . .?'

Eliza nodded, trying hard to remember what she'd been taught about attending to the client's needs. 'May I ask what the lady in question is like, sir?'

'I beg your pardon?'

'Well, sir, if you could tell me something about the lady and what her tastes are, I'll be able to recommend something suitable.'

'Oh, yes, I see. Well, sort of charming, womanly, spirited,' he said, a gleam sparking in his eyes.

'Your wife sounds lovely, sir,' Eliza said.

'My wife?' he spluttered, looking shocked.

'Sorry, sir, you don't require perfume for your wife?'

'Well, yes, of course I do. That is why I wish to purchase two bottles. Not that my wife ever touches the one I give her.'

'Then why . . .' Eliza began, but he leaned across the counter.

'One is for my wife, the other for my special lady,' he whispered.

'Oh, I see, sir,' she said. 'You say your wife never uses the bottle you give her?'

'No, it's a ridiculous waste of money, but I have to treat them both the same, don't I?'

'May I ask if these women are alike? Do they have the same tastes?'

'Hardly. Well, apart from their very good choice in men, of course,' he chuckled. 'No, my wife is gentle, sweet and very biddable, whilst my mist— er, other lady is, as I have said, seductive and spirited . . .' His voice trailed off as if he was worried he'd said too much.

Determined to appear a woman who knew about such matters, Eliza turned and selected two tester bottles.

'Well then, sir, if they are not alike, does it not follow they will not share the same taste in fragrance? Perfume is such a personal thing and really needs to reflect the wearer. From what you've told me, your wife would perhaps like this light, floral fragrance,' she suggested, holding out the glass tester wand. Hesitantly he gave a sniff, then inhaled more deeply.

'By Jove, that's Felicity down to the ground,' he enthused. 'Do you know, I think she might even wear that?' Eliza nodded, pleased that she'd got something right. Then she held up the wand from the other bottle and waved it in front of him. As the aromatic scent of patchouli and spice wafted around, his face lit up. 'Perfect. I can just imagine . . .'

'I am so sorry to have kept you waiting, sir,' Monsieur Farrant said, bustling round to where Eliza was standing behind the counter. 'I hope Mademoiselle has been keeping you amused in my absence.'

'More than that, Monsieur, Eliza here has been enlightening me in the ways of women and their perfume,' he announced.

'Really? Well, I am pleased she has been of some help. Now, I expect you would like Monsieur's expertise in recommending a fragrance?'

'You misunderstand, Monsieur. Eliza here has solved my dilemma and I wish to purchase three bottles of each of these wonderful perfumes.' Monsieur Farrant gasped, but whether it was surprise at the size of the order or the sudden appearance of the constable who was watching intently, Eliza wasn't sure.

'You did say three bottles of each perfume, sir?'

'I did indeed. This remarkable assistant of yours has been most helpful and I am truly grateful. She is a wonderful woman, Monsieur.'

Monsieur Farrant turned to Eliza, a smile curling his lips. 'She is indeed, sir, and that is why I am hoping one day she will do me the honour of becoming my wife.' Monsieur Farrant turned and smiled at the constable.

Eliza heard a gasp and couldn't be sure if it came from her or the constable, who was edging towards them. Even the client was looking shocked.

'Oh, but I thought you . . . well, never mind. That's wonderful news. I hope you will be very happy,' the gentleman said quickly. 'Now, would cash be all right?'

'Indeed, indeed.' Monsieur was beside himself as he made out the gentleman's bill. 'Eliza will wrap and write any cards you require.'

'Monsieur Farrant, I need to ask you some questions, please,' the constable interrupted.

'Ah, Constable, I expect you'll be requiring assistance choosing a special fragrance for that lovely wife of yours,' Monsieur said, turning to the policeman. The constable shook his head and made for the door, an incredulous look on his face. 'I will return when you are less busy, Farrant, and then you will answer my questions.'

Too stunned to speak and wondering what game Monsieur Farrant was playing, Eliza wrapped the perfume and penned the requisite words. Marry Monsieur! What an absurd notion. She had as much intention of marrying him as flying to the moon, and something told her that wasn't really his objective either.

'You have my undying gratitude,' the gentleman said, breaking into her thoughts. 'Season's greetings to you both,' he added, clutching his parcels and hurrying towards the door.

'Goodbye, sir,' Eliza called, then noticed the perfumery was empty of customers. 'Oh, the constable didn't wait,' she stammered in surprise.

Monsieur Farrant laughed. 'I think when he heard you were to become my wife he got the shock of his life.'

'But . . .' she protested, but he held up his hand.

'Don't worry, Eliza, you and I are going to get along famously.'

Not sure what he meant, and not sure she wanted to find out, she smiled nervously. Thank goodness tomorrow was Christmas Day and she'd be able to spend the day away from him.

'Now that is all for today. Do not worry, though. Monsieur Farrant, he will be making the formal proposal for he likes to do things properly, non?'

'But . . .' she began again.

'None of these buts. We will lock up early and prepare for the festivities. I am sure you will want time to beautify yourself, oui?' he declared, giving her a wink.

Not sure if this was an insult or compliment, but relieved to be able to leave, Eliza hurried out of the perfumery before Monsieur could change his mind. Thankfully, for once he didn't follow her. He really did come out with the most preposterous things at times. Lost in thought she'd just reached the dining hall when Mimi stopped her.

'Cook's in a right state. She's got so much to do, she said to tell you supper will have to be early tonight. She'll be serving up pot luck or lump it at five o'clock,' the maid stammered before dashing back to the kitchen.

25

Eliza sympathized, guessing Cook was overtired. As for herself, after monsieur's preposterous declaration, she'd welcome the company of the other staff and their excitement about the coming festivities.

Back in her room, the half-finished letter to Fay seemed to mock her. Tears welled and she wished she was back in the safety of the hobble. *But Fay didn't want you there*, a voice inside her head reminded her. Snatching up the paper, she tore it to shreds.

Wiping her face, she changed into her cotton clothes and made her way to the dining room. However, instead of the usual convivial atmosphere she was met with mayhem.

'I've never heard the like before,' Mrs Symms cried.

'And where he expected me to get a goose from at such a late hour, I don't know,' Cook wailed.

'You didn't; it were me who had to plead with the butcher,' Dawkins protested. 'Mind you, when he heard who it were for, he suddenly remembered he had a spare one. At twice the price, I might add.'

'Well, it's me who's got to cook the blooming thing,' Cook moaned.

'I told him the staff would never eat goose,' Mrs Symms continued. 'But all he said was, "Then let them eat beef."'

'So I have to cook beef as well as goose,' Cook spluttered. 'Then he wants asparagus soup to start. Where the heck am I expected to get asparagus from at this time of year? He'll have to make do with green vegetables. And does he want Christmas pudding like the rest of us? Does he heck; he wants a soufflé, if you please!'

When the moaning and groaning finally ground to a halt, Eliza asked what was wrong.

'His lordship's decided he's staying home for Christmas. Apparently he intends entertaining a friend and would like the table set for two in his downstairs parlour, no less,' Mrs Symms informed her.

'So much for our staff Christmas luncheon,' wailed Cook. 'By the time we've served him and his so-called friend, we'll be too knackered to enjoy ourselves.'

'And we won't be able to have a snifter until he's finished either,' moaned Mrs Symms.

'Can I help?' Eliza asked.

'You can't work with us,' Mimi exclaimed.

'Why ever not? I'm one of the staff too, aren't I?'

'But yous works in the perfumery, that's different,' Mimi stated.

'You could help decorate the room. I've been that busy making the parlour look festive I haven't had time to do anything in here,' Mrs Symms suggested.

Glad to be able to help, and remembering she'd seen holly and ivy in the garden, Eliza said, 'Leave it to me, Mrs Symms. I'll make this room look cheerful and celebratory. Anything else?' She turned to Cook. 'Can I help in the kitchen?'

'Don't like people under me feet. Ta for the offer, though.'

'Better get eating,' Bertram ordered. 'His lordship's decreed it's to be early doors tonight.'

As Eliza frowned, Mimi whispered, 'It means we got to be in our rooms by seven 'cos the door's going to be locked then. See you're wearing your skirt. Toby thought I looked lovely in it,' she sighed.

'I'll make sure it's laundered and you can borrow it again next time you see him,' Eliza promised.

'I told me mum you're a good un,' Mimi smiled.

Next morning, Eliza woke early, determined to make the dining room look as festive as possible, then enjoy the day with these people who had become her friends. Humming under her breath, she was about to make her way to the garden when there was a sharp rap on the door. To her surprise, the butler was standing there looking even more officious than usual.

'Merry Christmas, Bertram,' she smiled.

'Indeed,' he said gravely, handing her an enormous box tied with a gold bow. 'Monsieur Farrant sends his greetings and requests you join him in the parlour at noon for pre-luncheon drinkies.'

'What?' she asked, wide-eyed.

'I believe you heard, miss. I shall return at 11.55a.m. precisely to escort you. He wishes you to wear . . .' He sniffed and pointed to the box.

'But you know I promised to collect greenery to decorate the dining room,' she explained.

'I think not, miss. His lordship is most emphatic you do not mingle with the domestic staff. You are to stay here and prepare yourself for festive celebrations in the parlour. As I said, I shall return.' Then he gave a formal bow and marched away, leaving Eliza staring at him open-mouthed.

What was going on? She threw the box down on the bed. Why would Monsieur send her a present? Surely this didn't have anything to do with his preposterous suggestion in the perfumery? He wasn't about to propose officially, was he? Perhaps she could stay here, ignore him and his present.

But the box was too tempting to resist and, tearing open the wrapping, she gasped in amazement. Nestling in the softest tissue, was a shimmering swathe of gold silk and lying alongside, a little amber bottle of Gold Etoile. Remembering its pungent smell, she wrinkled her nose. No way was she wearing that.

She shook out the dress and held it up in front of her. It was absolutely gorgeous. Unable to resist, she tore off her clothes and stepped into it. As the silky folds slithered over her body like a second skin, she shivered in delight, then ran over to the mirror. Was that woman with sparkling eyes and radiant skin really her? She swished this way and that, quite overcome with delight. Realizing her hair spoiled the effect, she coiled it into its customary Cadogan, covered it with the little net and stood back to admire the effect: much better.

Then, as if someone had thrown a large snowball at her, she shivered and slumped down on the chair. Why would Monsieur give her an expensive new dress and perfume? And why had he invited her to luncheon in his parlour? Did this really have anything to do with his outrageous suggestion the previous day? She sat for an age, staring out of the window, trying to make sense of it all.

A sharp knock on the door rudely roused her from her reverie. It couldn't be that time already, surely? Opening the door, she saw Bertram striding back towards the main house and had no option but to follow. As they passed the staff dining room, she wondered if she should explain why she wouldn't be joining them but, as if her thoughts had been transmitted, Bertram turned and frowned.

'May I wish you the season's greetings, Mademoiselle?' Monsieur Farrant said, rising to his feet as she was shown into the parlour.

'Thank you,' she stammered, staring at the most enormous fir tree that graced the window. It was lit by myriad candles and she couldn't help exclaiming, 'Why, that's beautiful!'

'Mais oui, but not as beautiful as you, Mademoiselle. I must say, you look enchanting, non?' he said, gazing at her so intently, she felt uncomfortable and had to look away.

'Thank you for this dress but I don't understand why you've given it to me.'

'You don't like it?' He frowned.

'It's gorgeous but . . .' Her voice trailed off.

'It is my Christmas box to you. I believe it is the custom for an employer to give a token of his appreciation, non?' He sniffed the air and frowned. 'But you are not wearing the perfume?'

'I'm sorry, I was so surprised by your invitation I forgot to put any on,' she stuttered, not wishing to admit she hated its potent smell.

'Never mind, you can wear it when we dine together

again, non?' She stared at him in horror. This was going to be repeated? 'You see, Mademoiselle Eliza, I chose that fragrance because I think it the very epitome of you. It captures your very being, non?'

She shuddered, hoping the overpowering pong was nothing like her.

'You are cold? Come and sit down nearer the warmth,' he said, taking her hand and leading her towards the enormous fireplace where logs crackled and snapped. She was just comparing it to the tiny grate and twigs Fay used at the hobble when Bertram appeared offering refreshment.

'A glass of lemonade would be nice,' she said, smiling at the butler, who sniffed and turned away.

'You would perhaps prefer a glass of champagne instead?' Monsieur Farrant asked.

Eliza shook her head and he sighed, then took a sip of his own. The bubbles fizzing in his glass seemed extraordinarily loud but his next words took all thought of their drinks from her mind.

'I expect you are deliriously delighted I have invited you to join me today but you would not be a woman if you were not wondering why, eh?'

Not sure what to say she merely nodded.

'It is simple, dear Eliza. I thought after my proposal in the perfumery yesterday we should get to know each other better,' he said, placing his glass on the table beside him.

'But surely you weren't serious?' she stuttered, her stomach churning.

'You were surprised, non? Mais, you are a beautiful woman and I'm a handsome man so . . .' he shrugged, leaning forward so the smell of him wafted her way. *NO!*

she wanted to shout, instinctively pulling away. 'Now, before we eat, I think we should get one thing straight, yes?' He paused and her stomach tied itself in knots as she wondered what was coming next.

'When we are alone, I shall call you Eliza and you may call me Charles,' he said, smiling as though he were bestowing a great honour. She was saved from answering by the dinner gong.

'Luncheon is served,' Bertram intoned, appearing in the doorway.

Monsieur Farrant rose to his feet and held out his hand.

'Allow me to escort you to the table, Eliza,' he said, taking her arm and leading her all of eight paces to the table that was set on the other side of the room.

'May I sit beside the tree?' she asked, thinking the smell of pine might mask the smell of him, though how she was going to eat she couldn't think. She gazed at the ornate, and no doubt expensive, decorations smothering every branch of the tree and couldn't help thinking less would be more tasteful. In her mind, Christmas should be about family, sharing and warmth, not possessions and shows of ostentation.

'Ah, you like it, oui?' he smiled, mistaking her look. Bertram hurried over and pulled out her chair, then shook out a snowy white serviette and placed it over her lap. She just had time to take in the flickering candles in the silver candelabra and the holly adorning the picture rails, when a dish was slapped down in front of her. Startled, she looked up only to be met with the glacial look of the housekeeper.

'Hope it chokes you, I'm sure,' the woman hissed.

'Oh, Mrs Symms, I was going to help but . . .' Eliza gasped, hurt that the woman had misunderstood her reasons for dining here rather than with the people she would prefer to be with, but the woman stuck her nose in the air and hurried away. Eliza stared down at the green gloop and gulped. Oblivious, Charles began to eat, making little slurping noises that, had she been hungry, would quite have put her off. Luckily he was so engrossed he failed to notice Eliza surreptitiously spooning her soup into the poinsettia. When the empty bowls had been cleared, he turned to her and smiled.

'Tell me, Eliza, I have been perusing Fay's receipts. They are most interesting. Did you perchance find any more?' he asked, staring at her intently.

'I'm afraid not,' she said quickly. Then anxious to change the subject, added. 'You have a delightful garden, Monsieur. I was hoping to take another walk around it later.'

He sighed. 'Alas, by the time we have finished the meal today, it will be dark, non?' Eliza's eyes widened in amazement; how long could it take to eat Christmas luncheon?

'Ah,' he said, looking up as Mrs Symms reappeared. She was carrying an enormous salver on which lay the cooked goose, an apple adorning its neck end and a little white frill covering its behind.

'Cook said she's cooked it à la française,' she sniffed, as Mimi bustled in with dishes of vegetables. Eliza looked at her and smiled but the little maid seemed too busy to notice.

Monsieur Farrant made an elaborate show of carving

but luckily left Eliza to help herself. As the meal dragged on, she made a pretence of eating, spreading the food around the plate, wishing her ordeal over. As the room grew hotter, the smell of Monsieur got stronger and she turned towards the tree, inhaling deeply. But the freshness of the pine reminded her of Duncan and his beloved woods. What she wouldn't give to be walking in them now.

'Would you care for dessert?' Charles asked, breaking into her thoughts.

'Goodness me, I couldn't eat another thing. As it is still light, a walk in the garden would be nice,' she ventured.

He glanced out of the window. 'Alas, it is raining,' he said with a shrug.

'I don't mind, in fact it would be quite refreshing,' she said.

'*Non*. However, Charles, he has been thinking. He has been very remiss.'

'He has? I mean you have?'

'Oui. All the time you have been here, you have been cooped up like a chicken, yes?'

'Well I . . .'

'Non, it is true,' he said, 'And tomorrow, we shall ride out in my carriage so I can show off my future wife to all the people of Follytown.' Eliza was stunned into silence. Show her off? Surely he wasn't serious?

'It will be a joy, oui?' he said, rising to his feet. 'Now, I thank you for the pleasure of your company, but alas, being a busy man, even at Christmas I have things to attend to. I will meet you in the hall tomorrow at two o'clock. Sleep well, ma petite.'

Realizing she was being dismissed, Eliza got to her feet.

'Thank you for a lovely meal,' she stammered, remembering her manners as she hurriedly took her leave.

Passing the dining room, she could hear the staff making merry. How she'd love to be in there with them. She would join them now, she thought, reaching for the handle. Then she remembered the housekeeper's glare, Mimi ignoring her, and carried on walking. They wouldn't welcome her for it was obvious they thought she'd chosen to spend the day with Monsieur Farrant.

What a day it had been, she thought, carefully removing the shimmering dress and hanging it in the closet. Although it was still early, the events of this strange day had caught up with her and she climbed into bed. It appeared Monsieur Farrant was serious about her becoming his wife after all. But why? He was heaps older than her, smelled vile and had the table manners of a pig. As for riding out in his carriage, she really didn't want to be seen with him. And it didn't form part of her apprenticeship agreement, did it, so she'd spend the next day in her room. If she ignored his proposal perhaps he would too, she thought, falling into a dreamless asleep.

However, despite her resolve, just after two o'clock, there was a sharp rap on her door.

'Monsieur Farrant is waiting in the main hall,' Bertram sniffed and, as on the previous day, he marched off, leaving her to follow.

Their ride around the town square would have been enjoyable if Monsieur Farrant hadn't insisted on waving to everyone they passed. The little place was thronging with people taking their Boxing Day constitutional. He couldn't have picked a busier time if he'd tried, Eliza thought.

'Wave, Eliza,' he encouraged. She did as he ordered but couldn't help noticing the surprised look on all their faces and the nudging that ensued. Meanwhile, Monsieur beamed and preened, acting as if he were royalty. It was embarrassing and Eliza was glad this was the only time she'd have to witness such behaviour.

Finally, they pulled up outside the house and Eliza gave a sigh of relief that her ordeal was over. Monsieur Farrant smiled as he helped her down from the carriage.

'That was most enjoyable, Eliza, and I shall look forward to our ride out again next Sunday.'

She stared at him in surprise. 'Next Sunday? But I thought we'd be riding out just the once.'

His smile widened. 'We shall make it a date each Sunday afternoon. I want everyone to take a good look at my future wife, Eliza.'

'But, Monsieur Farrant . . .'

'You are wondering at my generosity, non?' he beamed, but before she could say what was bothering her, he'd snapped into tutor mode. 'Right, festivities are over. I will see you in the laboratory first thing tomorrow. I suggest you study your notes to be ready for my little test. Supper will be sent to your room in future as I do not wish you to mingle with the staff in the dining room.'

Her heart sank. Surely he didn't intend keeping her away from everyone else?

'But . . .' she was about to protest, then realized she had no choice in the matter.

26

When Eliza arrived in the laboratory the next morning, she was overjoyed to find Amos already there.

'Why, there's a sight for sore eyes,' he chirped. 'Did you have a good Christmas?'

'Not really, how about you?'

'Got spoiled rotten by Father and fussed over by Mother. Hey, what's up?' he asked, seeing her frown.

'I was just thinking how lucky you are to have such caring parents,' she sighed.

'I know. They are the tops and I shouldn't make light of them. Still, you have the staff here and they're all right, aren't they? Well, aren't they?' he asked when she didn't answer.

'They're not talking to me or, as Mimi informed me, I've been sent to Doventry, wherever that is.'

'I think she means Coventry, but why?'

'Oh, Amos, I've had the most awful time,' she wailed. And like water released from a dam, everything burst out of her as she told him what had gone on whilst he'd been away. 'So you see, the staff ignore me, I have to eat in my room and Monsieur insists he is marrying me.'

Amos stared at her in horror. 'That can't be right. I mean he can't force you to . . .'

'Bonjour, mes enfants,' Monsieur Farrant said, breezing into the room. 'We have all had a good Christmas, non? Now I have exciting news for whilst you have been chitting and chatting the morning away, I have been devising the new perfumes.'

'We're making perfume today?' Eliza asked, brightening at the thought.

'Non, Mademoiselle, I shall be making perfume while you and Amos pack away the Christmas merchandise and prepare the perfumery for the new stock. We are in the lead-up to spring and summer and must prepare, non?'

Seeing Eliza's face, Charles said, 'You think you are not learning that way, but everything you touch, see and smell is a lesson in itself. And,' he paused dramatically, 'when my perfumes are ready, you may assist Amos in measuring them into the amber bottles, oui? Now, have you been studying your notes?' As his green eyes bored into her, she nodded. 'Bon, then you will be ready with your mathematics, non?'

Mathematics? What had sums got to do with anything? But Monsieur was waving them away.

'Amos, you know what needs to be done so you will instruct Eliza. Here are the keys to the perfumery. Make sure it is locked each night before you leave.'

'Yes, Monsieur Farrant,' he said, catching them and snatching up his lunch tin.

'What are you looking so happy about?' she asked as they made their way towards the perfumery.

'A bit of freedom, that's what. We will be able to talk while we work without being overheard.'

Although they worked hard, Amos's cheery banter soon raised Eliza's spirits. He was right, she thought. Nobody could make her marry against her wishes. If Monsieur mentioned it again she'd let him think she was going along with it until she'd completed her apprenticeship.

'He will soon tire of these Sunday jaunts, believe you me,' Amos reassured her. 'Try to get ahead with your studying. The sooner you have absorbed all his notes and passed his tests, the sooner you will be able to assist him making the perfume. In the meantime, sharing my luncheon will be the highlight of your days,' he quipped.

She grinned, thankful for his down-to-earth reasoning.

It took them all week but finally both the stockroom and perfumery met with Monsieur Farrant's approval.

'Amos, enjoy your day off and I will see you in the laboratory on Monday.' He waited until the young apprentice had left, then turned to Eliza. 'And I will see you in the hall at two o'clock tomorrow for our ride around Follytown. Monsieur, he remembers he must not keep you cooped up like a chicken, non?' he grinned.

Although Eliza nodded, her heart sank.

This trip was even more embarrassing than the last, for Monsieur Farrant insisted Dawkins pull over so that they could promenade around the town.

'I remember you say you like the fresh air, non?' he said, taking her arm as they walked by the church, resplendent with its cockerel, and on through the square. Eliza might have enjoyed the outing had he not greeted everyone he saw, raising his hat and introducing Eliza as his future wife. The looks she received were incredulous to say the least, and she was relieved when they returned home and she could escape to the sanctuary of her room.

Although she arrived at the laboratory early the next

morning, Monsieur Farrant was already deep in conversation with Amos. Numerous bottles were laid out on the counter in front of them and Amos was busy taking notes.

'Ah, Mademoiselle, I have been instructing Amos that in my absence he is to take charge. Amos, tell Dawkins to have my carriage waiting in ten minutes, non?'

Amos jumped up, then, pausing in the doorway, grinned and gave Eliza the thumbs-up sign behind Monsieur's back.

'You are going somewhere, Monsieur?' she asked, her heart soaring.

'Exciting new things are happening in the perfume world and Monsieur, he intends to be part of it. Do not worry, ma petite, I will only be gone a matter of weeks,' he shrugged. Her heart soared higher and she tried not to grin. 'Amos is to continue your instruction including the mysterious art of the bottling. Regrettably, I have been too busy to test you on the mathematics so it will fall upon his shoulders to make sure you get the measurements right. Alas, I shall not be able to take you out for our Sunday rides.'

'I'd be happy to escort Eliza into town in your absence,' Amos offered, coming back into the room.

'Indeed you will not!' Monsieur cried. 'Mademoiselle she has her reputation to think of.' He turned to Eliza. 'Do not worry, ma petite. When Monsieur returns, we will have dinner together in the parlour. That will be something to look forward to, non?' She nodded, hoping that would be a long time in the future.

'I wish you a successful trip,' she said. Please don't hurry back, she thought.

During the following weeks Amos diligently showed

her how things were done and Eliza found his enthusiasm for making perfume stimulating. His relaxed approach was more conducive to learning than Monsieur's pernickety ways, although her favourite time of day was when they broke for luncheon. Along with his food, he shared tales about his antics on his days off and before long she found herself opening up a little about her time on the moors with Fay. In return for his generosity, she sewed back the buttons that popped from his shirt with amazing regularity. He insisted it was his landlady's fault for feeding him so well but, in truth, both enjoyed the enforced closeness.

One day she was stitching up the hem of his amber jacket after he'd caught it on the still when their gaze met and held. Energy crackled between them, her pulse quickened. Slowly he leaned towards her and if the little bell in the perfumery hadn't rung, she was certain he would have kissed her.

'Don't go away,' he said huskily as he reluctantly shrugged his jacket back on. Her laugh sounded squeaky even to her own ears. Where would she go even if she wanted to, which she didn't? She wanted to stay in this room with him for ever.

To her disappointment, he didn't return to the laboratory and she didn't see him until the next day.

'Morning, Eliza, I trust you slept well?' he asked, smiling as usual as she entered the laboratory.

Although she'd been awake half the night, she nodded.

'You didn't come back yesterday,' she said, trying to keep her voice light.

'Sorry, the gentleman was one of Monsieur's best clients,

nice but hard to please. He insisted on sampling every perfume before buying the first one I'd suggested,' he grinned ruefully. 'Still, we will work hard this morning to make up the time and then enjoy our luncheon break, non?' he added, looking at her meaningfully.

Her spirits rose. 'So what will you be teaching me today, Oh Master?' she quipped.

'Today, Mademoiselle, we will be discovering how to discern the different constituents in this perfume,' he said, carefully pouring liquid from a flagon. 'This is one of Monsieur's new fragrances,' Amos explained, passing her the glass tube. Inhaling deeply, she raised her brows.

'That's actually nice. Quite strong, but it's kind of green and leafy.'

'And then?'

'A kind of minty undertone.'

'And what do you smell now?'

She frowned. 'It smells like some kind of rose.'

'Well done, Eliza. You're very good. As Monsieur would say, it all comprises the symphony, non?' he grinned, wagging his finger as he did so in a passable impression of their boss.

She laughed, suddenly feeling she could burst into song herself but Amos was continuing.

'Monsieur likes to give his clients something that reflects the seasons, so his fragrances for spring and summer all contain geranium. However, as ever he has worked his magic and by blending other components, has created three quite different perfumes. Remember, it is all in the power of the ingredients, Mademoiselle, non?' he said, waving his hands in the air.

'Blimey, it's just like listening to him,' she grinned. 'Where are the other two you mentioned?'

He pointed to bottles under the counter and she leaned down and took off their lids.

'That's incredible. They really are quite different,' she said, blinking in amazement. She sniffed them again.

'Careful, Mademoiselle, remember to over-smell will confuse the nose,' he remonstrated. 'And please put the caps on so the precious liquid it does not evaporate.'

Eliza laughed. 'You might sound like Monsieur but at least you don't smell like him.'

Amos looked at her in surprise.

'My stomach tells me it is time for luncheon,' he said. 'Let's sit at the other table and you can enlighten me while we eat.'

'So you think Monsieur smells?' Amos asked, having made short work of his bread and cheese.

'Pongs, more like. Surely you must have noticed?'

'Can't say I have,' he frowned. 'Well, that's a good reason for not marrying him.'

'I have no intention of doing so anyway, thank you,' she protested.

'No, seriously, this could be the answer to your dilemma. It's a well-known fact that if you don't like the smell of your partner, you won't get on. It's the chemistry. Have you not been reading my notes, Mademoiselle?' Amos quipped, but Eliza was deep in thought.

'I've really enjoyed learning from you, Amos.' She sighed. 'And I'm dreading Monsieur coming back. I'm not sure I can put up with his fastidious ways again.'

He stared at her, his gaze serious. 'You must complete

your training, Eliza. Monsieur is one of the finest perfumers and a testimonial from him will guarantee a good placement in the future.' He sighed. 'Which reminds me, he is likely to be returning soon and I have important work to complete before then, so why don't you go to your room and study your notes?' he suggested.

'Can't I stay here and help?' she asked, loath to exchange his warm company for her solitary room.

Unusually, however, Amos was emphatic she leave him to get on.

'Sorry, Eliza, I love you being here but your presence is distracting and puts me behind.'

Not wishing to show her disappointment, she got to her feet. He had spent a lot of time teaching her and it wouldn't be fair to get him into trouble.

'Be here first thing in the morning, Mademoiselle, and we will continue your instruction, non?' he quipped, but the look in his eyes promised more. Her spirits soared and, grinning broadly, she nodded.

Over the next week, Amos showed her some of the finer points of perfume making. They worked closely together, the bond between them strengthening.

'Just wait until I show Monsieur what I can do now,' she said, jubilantly holding out her glass for him to smell.

'That is indeed very good, Eliza,' he cried. 'Well done. We work well together, non?' he quipped.

She flushed with pleasure both at his praise and the look in his eye.

'Now off you go, ma petite,' he said quickly. 'For I have work to do and your delightful presence it distracts me, non? Tomorrow we will work out how much of that,' he tapped the glass, 'will go into that,' he said, picking up the perfume bottle. She pulled a face but hurried to her room, knowing she should really look at the notes Monsieur had left for her. Still, at least she felt she was really learning more about the actual art of perfume making.

As ever, Amos greeted her enthusiastically the next morning. There was an array of jars and tubes set out on the table.

'First we need to know the quantity of each essence that Monsieur has used in his blend. We make a careful note in this,' he said, pointing to the notepad alongside.

'Can't we just remember?' she asked, eager to get on with the actual task.

He shook his head. 'It's easy to forget and sometimes you can get distracted by other things,' he said, gazing at her so intently her heart leaped. He cleared his throat and pointed to the bottles.

'Now it is vital we count out the exact number of drops or the end result will not match Monsieur's sample here.' Amos tapped the bottle containing the new scent. 'Pencil at the ready,' he quipped, filling his pipette from one of the tubes. As he counted out drops from each one she diligently wrote down the numbers. 'Right, now we need to study the formula I have written down here.'

Heads bent close, they competed to see who could work out the answer first.

'Twenty,' laughed Eliza.

'Ah, but you forgot to divide as well and the answer's 8.51,' Amos pointed out jubilantly, writing it down.

'Clever clogs,' she giggled, nudging his arm so that his writing shot across the page.

'Why, you little minx,' he cried, grabbing her arm and pulling her closer.

'So this is how you spend your time in my absence?' Monsieur Farrant's icy tones cut the air, freezing them into silence.

'Sorry, Monsieur, we were just working out the calculation for . . .' Amos began.

'I have been observing for some moments so I know what you have been doing. Eliza, go to your room and spend the rest of the day studying your notes. We will have the big test first thing tomorrow and I trust you will know all the answers or . . .' He left his words hanging in the air.

'Please, Monsieur Far—' she began, but he held up his hand and glared until she left the room.

'Welcome home,' she muttered under her breath.

Crossing the courtyard from the main house to her room, she noticed a weak February sun breaking through the clouds and had a sudden yen to walk round the perfume garden. After that encounter, she needed some fresh air and she was keen to see what flowers were emerging. Then she remembered Monsieur's glassy glare, his veiled threat and thought better of it. She hoped Amos wasn't in trouble. Still, she'd find out what Monsieur had said tomorrow. Knowing her friend, though, he'd be sure to turn it into a joke.

However, when she entered the laboratory next morning, there was no sign of Amos. Monsieur Farrant was waiting and she braced herself ready for him to fire his questions at her. She'd been studying until her candle guttered and hoped her memory wouldn't fail her.

'Ah, Mademoiselle Eliza, you are looking très élégant this morning. How have you been in my absence?'

Eliza blinked, in surprise. 'I've been fine, Monsieur, thank you. Studying and working hard. Amos has taught me so much,' she said, looking around the room in case he was hidden by one of the stills. 'Is he not here yet?'

'Alas, he has gone,' Monsieur Farrant cried, throwing up his hands in despair.

'Gone? But he was here yesterday.'

'Oui, I come home and he tell me he has got himself another position. He has left me completely in the lurch. After all I taught him. You will not leave me, will you?' he beseeched.

'Er, no, of course not,' she replied. 'But Amos has been working so hard teaching me how to bottle your new perfumes and many other things. I can't believe he has just walked out,' she cried, hating the thought that her dear friend was no longer here.

'Probably he steal my receipts too,' Monsieur cried. 'Dear Eliza, I shall need you more than ever now.'

Her heart sank like a pebble in a pond. How could she stay here without Amos? The staff ignored her and Monsieur Farrant's mood changes were impossible. Why, he still hadn't showed her how to make perfume.

'Monsieur Farrant, I have learned how to source ingredients, about smell, the origins of perfume and chemistry. Now, Amos has taught me about blending and the calculations required for bottling perfume, but when can I make some from scratch?'

'My dear Eliza, over the next few weeks we will be working very closely together.' He gave his charming smile. 'Without Amos you will become my number two, non?'

'So we can make some today, then?' she persisted.

He sighed. 'Amos leaving has thrown me into turmoil. To think he has been plotting and planning to leave behind my back. It is more than I can bear.'

'That really doesn't sound like Amos, Monsieur. He diligently worked on your perfumes whilst you were away.' She was about to say more but remembered how Amos had insisted she leave him alone in the laboratory. Surely he hadn't really been planning anything?

Suddenly Monsieur gave a growl, stormed over to the counter where Amos had worked and tore his notebooks into shreds. Then he yanked open the drawer and rifled through it. Holding up a little green bottle, he frowned, undid the lid and inhaled.

'Traitor,' he cried, marching over to the sink and pouring out the contents. As the fragrance of heather and sweet peas wafted her way, Eliza could have wept. So, that was why Amos had wanted her out of the way. The dear man had been creating that fragrance especially for her, for hadn't he asked what smells she liked? And hadn't he promised they would celebrate their special days together? Tears welled, for today was 19 February, her sixteenth birthday, and Amos had gone.

'To make perfume one must be in the creative state, not an emotional one,' Monsieur Farrant stated, giving her an unfathomable look. 'I have things I must attend to so you will please occupy yourself for the day.'

'May I take a walk in the garden?' she suggested.

He nodded and waved her away.

'Thank you, Monsieur,' she said, snatching up the little green bottle and secreting it in her pocket.

Although the garden was her favourite place, Eliza hardly noticed the perfume wafting from the daffodils, narcissus and grape hyacinths, their vibrant colours a stark contrast to her dark thoughts.

She couldn't believe Amos would have left without telling her. It didn't make sense. He'd been so excited about Monsieur Farrant's new perfumes and happy to share all he'd learned with her. Surely if he'd found a new position, he would have said something? And, if he knew he wasn't going to be here today why hadn't he given her that perfume before he left?

Eliza knew she couldn't leave things hanging in the air like this. She'd go to his lodgings and find out what had really happened. Although she didn't know the address, Mimi did. But the maid was forbidden to speak to her. It was hopeless, she thought, stamping her feet so that red-hot pain shot through her twisted one.

'Happy birthday, Eliza,' she muttered, thinking back to last year when Fay had given her the little picture she'd painted and Duncan had repaired her grampy's box. Even Rose had iced her name in wobbly letters on her cake. Well, there wouldn't be one this year for, along with the other staff, Cook ignored her completely.

Preoccupied by her thoughts, she'd paid little attention to where she was going and found herself standing beside the hothouse where Dawkins was working. She waved, but he studiously bent over his plants. Sighing, she continued her walk and after a while the outline of the other outhouse loomed before her. Remembering Monsieur

Farrant's orders, she turned to retrace her steps. A man's raucous laughter stopped her in her tracks. Then, Monsieur's gleeful voice carried clearly on the breeze.

'Don't worry, nobody ever comes down here and if they did they'd be dead meat.'

A muffled reply was followed by more guttural laughter.

Eliza shivered and fled to her room.

27

'Good morning, Mademoiselle,' Monsieur Farrant greeted Eliza the next day. She'd spent a sleepless night mulling things over, eventually coming to the conclusion that she could no longer stay.

'Monsieur Farrant . . .' she began but he held up his hand.

'I have the most wonderful surprise for you, Eliza,' he said, smiling effusively. 'Monsieur Farrant, he think it is high time he teach his star pupil how to make the perfume, non?'

'Oh,' she said, all thought of leaving evaporating like scent in an open bottle.

'As you know, I have already made my perfumes for this season. That is good for the people who wish to call into the perfumery and buy from the shelf, as it were. Monsieur Farrant, he has such a good reputation they trust his judgement, non?'

Eliza stared at the smirking man all plumped up with his own importance, and nearly laughed out loud.

'However, the real satisfaction comes from creating a fragrance to a client's specific requirements. Before you can begin, though, you need to ask some questions, non?'

'Indeed, Monsieur,' she replied, thinking of the little green bottle she'd hidden in her grampy's box. Having asked what she liked, Amos had cleverly created a smell that encapsulated the very essence of the moors.

'Your thoughts are elsewhere, Mademoiselle?' Farrant asked, frowning. She shook her head. 'Well in that case, perhaps you can tell me what questions you would ask the client?'

'First I'd ask them what things they like. Then, how they want the perfume to smell, whether it is to be worn for daytime or evening and, probably more importantly, what they don't like,' she said.

'What they don't like?' he asked, arching an immaculate eyebrow.

'Yes, that's really important, isn't it? I mean, if you don't like the smell of someone you could never mar . . .' Realizing what she was about to say, she stumbled to a halt. Monsieur Farrant grinned and leaned closer, his own peculiar scent wafting her way.

'Luckily, we will not have that trouble, non?' Before she had time to answer, he pointed to one of the stills. 'In there I have already placed the geraniums, or cranesbills as they are sometimes known.'

'Why cranesbills?' she asked, fascinated despite his close proximity.

He picked up a flower and held it out to her. 'See, these little black seed heads here, they resemble the bill of the crane, non?' Never having seen a crane, Eliza had to take his word for it, but she nodded anyway. Monsieur Farrant lined up a collection of bottles on the counter in front of them.

'Before we begin blending we take this geranium oil and smell deeply of its aroma.' Eliza looked over at the still. Following her glance, Monsieur Farrant frowned. 'Time, it is money, Mademoiselle, and we cannot just sit here like the tailor's dummies while the apparatus does its work. We will be using that distillation another time, non?'

Eliza stared at him in surprise. How many flowers did he have?

'Although it will be reminiscent of its originating material, the extraction process may have captured a different layer of its scent. No two distillations will ever be the same, Eliza, you need to remember that. Now, tell me, what do we mean by blending?'

Eliza frowned, trying to recall his notes precisely. 'Blending is the building-up of a scent drop by drop. You choose what you wish to use for the notes, top, middle and base, and harmonize until they become a symphony,' she said.

'That is very good,' Monsieur Farrant grinned. 'The perfumer, however, he uses his experience and passion too. He listens to his heart, smells with his nose then mixes the ingredients and sees how they react together, non?'

'Yes, that is it exactly,' she agreed.

Monsieur wagged his finger. 'But the Master Perfumer, he adds another thing. He sprinkles in the je ne sais quoi, non?'

Eliza stared at the bottles in front of them. 'Which one is that?' she asked.

To her surprise he rocked with mirth, laughing so much he nearly fell off his stool. 'Oh, Eliza, you are very sweet and innocent. We will make a good couple, non?'

'We will make good perfume together,' she said, quickly changing the subject.

'Ah, ma petite, you are so keen to please me, non?'

She smiled as sweetly as she could manage. 'So what are you going to use with the geranium?'

'The client in question, she is wishing a perfume for the evening so it needs to be enticing and long-lasting. First we will try this.' Eliza watched as he took his pipette and counted drops of bergamot into a tube-shaped container, jotting down the figure on his notepad beside him. 'Always write down what you use as you go along. You think you will remember but it is easy to get absorbed in the process. To find you have created a fine fragrance but cannot recreate it because you don't know the exact proportions of each component you used would be frustrating, non? It is no good composing the symphony if you cannot perform the encore, oui?' She bit down a sigh, remembering Amos telling her the selfsame thing.

Unaware of her turmoil, Monsieur showed her how to blend the different oils he'd selected for his fragrance then lined up more bottles in front of her.

'Now you have a go,' he said.

Her spirits lifted but it wasn't nearly as easy as he'd made it look. Time after time she tried mixing the oils in varying proportions, only for him inhale, grimace and shake his head.

Eliza worked hard and it was only the blossoming flowers that made her realize spring had turned to early summer. As Monsieur continued to impart his wisdom, Eliza concentrated, trying to absorb all the information as well as meeting his meticulous standards. Although she missed Amos terribly, she couldn't deny she was benefiting from the undivided attention. As her nose became attuned to which smells worked well together and in what quantities, her art of blending improved.

She was fascinated by the use of fixatives such as ambergris from the sperm whale, civet from the cat, castoreum from the beaver and musk from the male deer. All of these added their own particular fragrant element as well as making the scent last.

Encouraged by Monsieur Farrant to clear her nose, she took to taking a stroll around the perfume garden at lunch time and in the late afternoons. Always hidden in her pocket was the little black bottle and whenever she could, she would compare its evocative smell to that of the flowers.

'Remember not to go further than the hothouse, Eliza,' Farrant repeatedly warned, green eyes boring into her so that she wondered if he knew of her earlier visit to the forbidden building at the bottom of the garden.

'Of course, Monsieur. Now that I have learned how to make perfume, may I have Fay's address?' she asked, for her conscience had been pricking her.

'Ah, ma petite, always you worry. As your tutor and intended, I have taken it upon myself to keep your guardian up to date on our progress.'

'You mean you've told her you intend to mar . . .' She stuttered to a halt, unwilling to voice the word.

'Marry? Non. It would be incorrect to do so without formally asking her permission. I tell her you have the makings of the fine perfumer, with a little more tuition from the Master, of course.' As he puffed out his chest, she shook her head at his own sense of importance. Still, if he'd already written to Fay letting her know how she was doing then that was good, for even after all this time the fact the woman had wanted her gone from the hobble still hurt and she would find it hard to put pen to paper.

If it hadn't been for Monsieur's insistence that they promenade around the town each Sunday, Eliza would have been almost happy. Whilst he maintained strict professionalism in the laboratory, as soon as she climbed into his carriage he snapped into solicitous-follower mode, which made her cringe. Finally, she could bear it no longer.

'I know you are a busy man, Monsieur, so if you didn't wish to waste your valuable time on these outings, I would understand,' she said. There was a pause whilst he smiled and waved grandly to a little group gathered on the corner. Once he was sure they'd seen him, he leaned forward, almost overpowering her with his scent.

'We are not in the laboratory now so it is Charles, non? Eliza, you have the makings of a fine wife.'

She gulped. 'I do?'

'Oui. Alas, though, you will have to be patient for tomorrow I leave for France,' he announced.

Mistaking her sigh of relief, he smiled and took her hand. 'I know you will miss me, ma petite. Remember I told you exciting things were happing in the perfume world? Well, a French parfumier has now perfected the use of a synthetic substance that will revolutionize the way we make perfume. Can you imagine every batch smelling the same? I simply have to go and find out more about this, for Monsieur Farrant cannot afford to get behind the times, non?'

But Eliza hardly heard. Her heart was soaring at the news that he was going away.

'How long will you be in France?' she asked.

'Ah, you are upset we part, non? Although I lock the perfumery, you can access the laboratory and perfume garden.'

'Does that mean I can pick any of the flowers and try the still myself?' she asked, thinking of the little black bottle.

'Mais oui. You can gather the flowers from wherever you wish. Just remember what I said about not going past the hothouse, yes?' She nodded. 'Monsieur has more notes for you to study so you will not have time to pine for him.'

She smiled sweetly. Freedom beckoned and she intended to make the most of it.

'Now your appearance, it needs updating. I will have Mrs Buttons call and measure you for some new outfits. Those are . . .' He wrinkled his nose and she smiled.

It was true her dresses had become tighter as she'd filled out. She'd also grown taller and more of her boots were on show, which, from the way he was frowning down at her feet, evidently displeased him intensely.

'You are a fine-looking woman, Eliza, but if you are to be my wife you need to have more class, more finesse. I shall add in my note to the sewing lady that you also require hats and trimmings, oui?'

More finesse indeed. Just the notion made Eliza cringe, but the thought of seeing that motherly lady again outweighed his petty niggles.

'That would be most kind, Mons— Charles,' she amended. 'I wonder if she'll be able to have them ready for when you return,' she said, trying another ploy to discover how long he'd be away.

'There will be plenty of time for that, ma petite. Alas, this mission may necessitate my being away for some time.' Her heart soared even higher only to plummet when he added, 'However, do not distress yourself. As soon as I return, we will begin making plans for our future, non?'

'Look, I really feel it's time we . . .' she began, but he was already striding away. As soon as he returned from France, she'd have it out with him, for this charade had gone on for too long and he must be made to realize she had no intention of marrying him.

That evening, beside herself with excitement, she felt too restless to stay in her room. Having eaten the supper that had been left for her, she took herself out to the perfume garden. It was a beautiful evening and the scent from the flowers was intoxicating, though she still couldn't match any of them to the black bottle. She decided to widen her search using Monsieur's absence to explore the nearby fields. The chiming from the church clock roused her from her reverie, reminding her it was time she was in her room. Running back across the courtyard, she heard the sound of men's laughter drifting down from an open window. Looking up, she saw Monsieur Farrant making merry with a group of lads. Obviously he was having a party before he left.

Next morning, Eliza woke with a sense of anticipation. This turned to delight when she heard the crunch of carriage wheels on the drive and knew Monsieur Farrant was leaving. Looking out of the window, she saw the sun was cracking the flags, as her grampy used to say, and hurriedly dressed in her work clothes. She would have preferred to wear her cotton skirt and top but was worried the staff might report back to Monsieur when he returned. Although they didn't bother her these days, she'd heard them gossiping about her having come here to snare the boss and make a good marriage. Then they'd lowered their voices and she'd been unable to make out what else they were saying. She just heard the loud guffaws that ensued shortly afterwards.

Still, it wasn't a day for worrying, she thought, placing her bottle in a basket. Letting herself out of the side gate she'd seen the staff using, she headed for the fields. Luxuriating in her unaccustomed freedom, she ambled leisurely, picking a plant here, plucking a bloom there. It was only when her foot began to ache that she realized she'd wandered further than she intended. She was about to go back when her attention was caught by a bright blue flower beside the river. Turning to take a better look, she didn't notice the old tree stump sticking out of the bank, and caught her foot in its root. She went sprawling, hitting the earth with a thud. Stunned, she lay there, her breath coming in little gasps. As she struggled to get up an agonizing pain shot through her good foot.

Ominous clouds were gathering in the previously clear sky and, knowing she couldn't stay in the open field, she began crawling towards the nearest building. It took an age, the sharp stones and thistles making her cry out in pain. Eyes fixed determinedly on the sprawl of outbuildings ahead, she was inching slowly forward when, seemingly from nowhere, a shadow hovered above. As it towered over her, blocking out the light, she froze in fright.

28

'You all right?' a male voice asked.

Hearing the concern in his voice, she looked up and found herself staring into the worried face of a young man. He had eyes the bright blue of cornflowers and his strong jaw spoke of determination.

'Yes, I'm just dandy,' she gasped, not sure if she was breathless from the fall or the way he was looking at her.

'Sorry, that was a stupid question. I'm James Cary and I work in the tannery over there,' he said, pointing to the buildings she'd been making for. 'You can probably smell it,' he added with a grin.

'Not half,' she grimaced.

'Let's get you to the workshop before it rains, then we can see what damage you've done,' he said, putting out his hand and helping her to her feet. She wobbled woozily for a moment and for the first time since she'd left the moors wished she had a stick with her. But, as if she weighed little more than thistledown, James swept her up and hurried across the field. The warmth of his strong arms penetrated the material of her dress. It was a pleasant sensation and made her feel safe, but she had no time to dwell on the thought, for no sooner had they reached shelter than the heavens opened.

'Just made it,' he said, setting her onto a chair. 'Now let's have a look at that ankle. I'll need to remove your boot before your ankle swells, otherwise you'll never get it off.' He gave a sharp tug and she gripped the chair arms, trying not to cry out as a sharp pain shot right up her leg. Although his hands were calloused, they were surprisingly gentle as he felt along her foot. 'No bones broken, just a wrench, I think.'

'I'd hate to think how much it'd be hurting if I had broken it,' she muttered.

He patted her shoulder, making her skin tingle so that she felt bereft when he took his hand away and went over to the fire. She watched as he poured something into a mug.

'Here, drink this. It's good for shock,' he said, handing it to her then perching on an upturned box. As the sweet tea revived her, she became more aware of the way he was staring at her than the pain in her foot.

'Gosh, I must look a sight,' she gabbled, grimacing down at her torn dress and pushing her straggling hair back into its net.

'Well, apart from a few smudges of earth, you look fine to me,' he grinned. 'Here, use this to wipe your cheeks and hands.' He untied the red and white scarf from around his neck and held it out to her. She rubbed her face and hands, frowning when she saw the dirty marks left on the cloth.

'I'm sorry, I'll wash it, then bring it back,' she offered.

He stared at her with those cornflower-blue eyes, then smiled. 'I was going to say there's no need, then realized it'd be a good excuse to see you again . . .?'

'Eliza,' she said, smiling back. As their gaze held she felt her face growing warm and looked quickly away.

In the ensuing silence, she sipped the rest of her tea and stared out over the yard beyond. The rain had stopped but the wind was freshening, blowing that unpleasant smell their way. She wrinkled her nose.

''Tis the finest oak bark tannery around and that be the hides you can smell. I'm apprenticed here and hope to be a trained currier one day.'

'What's that?' she asked, curious to know more about this attractive man, who, unlike Monsieur Farrant, seemed interested in her and not the least bit concerned she wasn't looking immaculate.

''Tis someone who dresses and finishes the leather after it's been tanned. Of course they give me all the menial tasks to do at the moment, but I'm a fast learner,' he said, flashing his easy grin. 'What about you?'

'I'm apprenticed to the perfumer, Monsieur Farrant.' His eyes widened in amazement but she was too concerned to notice. 'Which reminds me, I must be making tracks,' she said, getting to her feet then wincing as a sharp pain shot up her leg. 'How will I get back? I'll never be able to walk all that way,' she cried.

'Don't worry, Eliza. I've an idea,' James said. He went over to the nearby shed, then returned trundling a little wooden cart. 'Hop on,' he grinned.

'You couldn't possibly push me all the way back,' she gasped.

'Doth the lady dare to challenge the strength of James Cary?' he quipped, flexing his arms so that she could see the muscles rippling through the coarse material of his shirt. 'Besides, do you have any choice?'

'I guess not.'

'Wait a moment,' James said, running outside and talking to a burly man with a ginger beard. He returned directly.

'Right, that's cleared. Guv says I can borrow the cart and take you back as long as I make up the time this evening.'

'Are you sure you don't mind?' Eliza asked.

'Do I mind taking the prettiest girl I've ever met for a ride on the cart? Hmm, hard question,' he grinned, helping her up.

To the whistles and shouts of 'Go, Jimmy, go,' from his workmates who'd gathered to watch, he pushed her out of the yard. Steam was rising from the rapidly drying ground and the river chuckled as they made their way back towards the fields. When they came to the spot where she'd tripped, Eliza remembered her basket and gave a groan.

'Something wrong?' James asked, grinning at her over the handles.

'I was gathering flowers and dropped my basket when I fell. Oh, there it is.' She pointed to where it still lay beside the stump. He bent and retrieved it, then shrugged.

'No flowers, though,' he said, handing it to her.

As their fingers touched she felt a tingle up her arm and looked away. Must be the effect of the shock, she thought. However, James's gaze was still upon her but thoughts of Duncan flashed through her mind and she turned slightly away.

As if he sensed her mood, James began singing a song, adding silly words here and there until they became so ridiculous, she had to laugh. He grinned and let go of the cart. To her surprise she saw they'd already arrived back at the house.

'My lady,' he said, holding out his hand to help her down. She hesitated then took hold of it, trying to ignore the funny sensation that again tingled through her.

'Thank you, my good man,' she quipped.

'Will you be all right?' he asked, holding out her boot and staring down at her ankle.

'Yes, and thank you for bringing me home.'

'Erm, I, er . . . that is, I finish work around seven most evenings and wondered if you'd care to go for a walk? We could pick more flowers for your basket,' he added, the words coming out in a rush.

'I'd like that. Better give it a few days for my ankle to recover.'

'Right, Saturday evening it is, then. I'll meet you here?'

She frowned. 'Can we make it by that big oak?'

He followed the direction she was pointing and nodded.

'Till Saturday then, Eliza,' he said, doffing his cap, then snatching up the handles of the cart and running back the way they'd come.

Although she was limping as she made her way towards the little gate, she couldn't help smiling. What a nice, easy-going man he was, and such a contrast to Monsieur Farrant with his pernickety ways. Catching sight of herself in the glass in the closet, she gasped at her bedraggled state yet, curiously, her eyes were shining like the little stoppers on Monsieur's perfume bottles.

Next morning she answered the knock at her door to find Mrs Buttons, tape around her neck, material under her arm and sewing box in hand, hovering on the step.

'Morning, ducks. Oh, what you done to your foot?' she asked, staring at Eliza's bare feet.

'Wrenched my ankle,' she grimaced. 'Are you coming in?'

'Better had, ducks, Monsieur Farrant sent me a note detailing what he wants me to make. Right posh costumes, they are, and a toque, no less.'

'A what?'

'One of them hats that stand right up in the air.' Mrs Buttons sniffed. 'Surprised you'd want to wear something like that, but then you've done well for yourself, haven't you?'

'Sorry?' Eliza frowned.

'Getting hitched to the boss,' Mrs Buttons said, spreading out a length of rich-coloured material across the bed. It reminded Eliza of raspberries. Then she realized what the woman had said.

'Look, Mrs Buttons, when Monsieur made his proposal in the perfumery before Christmas I was too stunned to say anything, let alone refuse. Why, even the constable looked shocked.'

'The constable, you say?' the dressmaker's eyes flashed with interest. 'Well, 'tis none of my business, I'm sure,' she sniffed, snatching her tape from her neck. 'My, my, we have grown, ducks,' she commented, jotting down measurements in her little book. Then she stood back appraisingly. 'You know, you look much prettier in that little blouse and skirt. More natural, like.'

Eliza stared down at her green cotton skirt, which was looking the worse for wear, and sighed.

'I prefer wearing clothes like this but the skirt's really too tight now. Anyway, Monsieur insists I wear all that fitted stuff,' she pouted.

'Well, I guess that's the price you pay for elevating your status, as they say.'

'Look, Mrs Buttons, I have no intention of marrying him. It's in my interest to finish my apprenticeship, then I'll disappear.'

'I guess you know what you're doing. Just be careful, eh? Can you sew, ducks?'

Eliza nodded.

'Well, happen we might have a little of this left over here.' She winked and tapped the side of her nose with her finger. Then noticing the torn work dress hanging on the door, she added, 'I've still got a bit of that material so I'll take it away and mend it.'

They were interrupted by Mimi coming into the room, tray in hand. When she saw Eliza, the little maid gasped.

'Sorry, miss, I thought you'd be in the laboratory. I just came to take your breakfast tray and leave this,' she said, putting down the lunch tray and snatching up the remains of Eliza's breakfast.

'That's all right, Mimi,' she said, but the girl hurried out without responding.

'What was all that about?' Mrs Buttons asked, lifting the cloth, sniffing, then wrinkling her nose. 'Blimey, what's that stuff when it's at home?'

Eliza laughed. 'Hazelette. Cook makes it for Monsieur and is probably trying to use up what's left.'

'Yes, but why are you having trays sent to your room?' the woman persisted.

'Monsieur doesn't want me mixing with the staff. Mind you, they don't want to mix with me either,' she muttered.

'Don't tell me you eats all your meals in here?' Mrs Buttons asked, raising her eyebrows in disbelief.

'I don't mind,' Eliza answered. 'Besides, I have Monsieur's notes to study.'

'Well, it don't seem right to me,' the woman sniffed, gathering up her things. 'I'll drop your dress in later then be back when these are finished, ducks.' And with another frown, she left.

Eliza spent the rest of the day resting her foot and reading her notes. Then she got out Fay's receipt book and flicked through the pages. The flower illustrations were beautiful and so lifelike Eliza could almost smell their fragrance. She took out the little black bottle and inhaled its lingering scent, but even now she couldn't identify what it was. It certainly was something she'd never encountered before. By contrast, no sooner had she taken the top off the little green bottle than she was transported back to the moors. Compared to Monsieur Farrant's complex perfumes, the smell in both bottles was more natural. As she sat reflecting, the sun glinted on the jewel stopper of the black bottle, reminding her of James's bright blue eyes. She sighed, thinking how good it would be to see him again.

On Saturday, James was waiting by the oak and smiled warmly as she approached.

'How's the ankle?' he asked.

'A bit weak but it doesn't hurt half as much. As you can see, I was able to get my boots on.'

'Want to walk or would you rather sit?'

'Let's do both. I'd love to search for flowers, if you don't mind.'

'Whatever the lady wishes,' he quipped. 'Is this collecting a hobby or does it have something to do with your perfume making?'

'A bit of both,' she answered, not ready to share her secret with him.

'You like your work?' he asked.

'Oh, yes, I love all the different smells, and Monsieur Farrant has taught me how to blend them to make the most beautiful fragrances. Although I still prefer the simple ones. Monsieur's in France at the moment learning about some synthetic stuff they've discovered.'

James grimaced. 'Don't know much about that kind of thing, working with leather and oak bark. Still, I guess we have the creative side of things in common.' He turned and smiled at her. 'You're looking really nice this evening. Not as formal as the other day, or as dirty,' he teased.

'I don't know what you must have thought of me. I couldn't believe it when I got back to my room and saw how dishevelled I was. Oh, I nearly forgot,' Eliza said, delving into her basket and drawing out his kerchief. 'All the dirty marks have come out.'

'Thank you,' he said, taking it and staring at it solemnly.

'Is something wrong?' she asked.

'I guess I'll just have to rely on my natural charm to entice you to walk out with me in future.' Looking at his serious expression her heart soared.

The next few weeks were the happiest she had ever spent. Mrs Buttons appeared with her new 'walking out' dress and the formidable hat, which Eliza vowed she'd never wear. She did manage to persuade her to remove the flamboyant gold bow, which she hid in her box in case

Monsieur should ask any questions. Then the woman handed her a length of leftover material.

'Make yourself another skirt, ducks. Best not tell Monsieur, though,' she said, tapping the side of her nose with her finger, as was her way. 'What he don't know won't hurt him, and I'm sure your young follower will appreciate you looking all natural and pretty, like. Besides, it's healthier you walking out with someone like him, rather than . . . well, you know,' she said, giving a wink, then disappearing before Eliza could ask her how she knew about James.

The staff began speaking to her again and Eliza had a feeling Mrs Buttons was behind that for soon after the woman had left Mimi had been sent to invite her to join them for her meals in the dining room. After the initial embarrassment, it wasn't long before their former friendliness was restored. Only Bertram remained aloof.

'I don't know what Monsieur will say when he finds out,' he muttered.

'Well, he won't know if you don't tell him, will he?' Mrs Symms snapped.

'But it is my duty to inform him what goes on in his absence.'

'What, like you having hands like a blinking octopus,' Mimi piped up.

Bertram glowered, then rose to his feet and walked stiff-backed out of the room, their laughter following after him.

As the heat of summer cooled and the leaves on the trees turned glorious gold and russet, Eliza continued walking out with James. Although she enjoyed his company immensely, whenever he tried to turn the conversation to the future, she changed the subject, saying they both had their apprenticeships to think of. After Duncan's abandonment and Amos disappearing without telling her, she wasn't about to trust another man again anytime soon.

One evening she was humming happily as she let herself in through the little gate before curfew when Bertram appeared.

'Monsieur Farrant has returned and wishes to see you in the parlour,' he announced.

Her previous good mood vanished like the morning mist. She looked down at her new cotton skirt and grimaced. There was no time to change into her formal work wear or put her hair up.

'Good evening, Monsieur Farrant,' she said, entering the room.

He was stood staring out of the window but turned on hearing her voice.

'Is it?' he hissed, green eyes glittering.

29

Clearly Monsieur Farrant was in a foul temper. Perhaps his trip to France hadn't gone well, Eliza thought, as he threw the letter opener he'd been toying with down on the table with a clatter.

'Before I left, I gave strict instructions on how you were to spend your time, Mademoiselle. Yet now I return to find out you have been mixing with all sorts. What do you have to say for yourself?' he demanded, his shiny moustache quivering as he enunciated every syllable.

'Is it so bad that I joined the others in the dining room?' she asked, assuming Bertram had carried out his threat.

'You mixed with the staff as well?' he exclaimed, his eyes narrowing. 'This is too much.'

'Really, Monsieur, I can't believe that eating with the . . .' she began, but he moved closer until he was inches from her face, his peculiar smell wafting literally up her nose.

'That is bad enough, certainement, but to hear I have been cuckolded is more than Monsieur's pride can bear,' he hissed.

'Cuckolded?' she laughed. 'Surely a man can only be cuckolded if he's married?' Silence hung heavy in the air as Monsieur Farrant reflected on her words. Then a gleam sparked in his eye.

'That is the literal meaning, of course. However, we have an understanding, do we not?'

'As I was trying to tell you before you left, I never agreed . . .'

'Oh, but you did, Mademoiselle,' he insisted, his voice ominously low. 'And on Saturday we will see the jeweller and choose the largest betrothal ring he has.'

'There really is no need,' she cried, but he held up his hand to silence her.

'Oh, but there is, and then we shall hold a big party to celebrate. We will invite the whole of Follytown and everyone will see that you belong to me.'

'Belong?' she started, but he was in full flood.

'I have even set the date for our wedding. We are to be married on the 19th of February next year.'

'But that will be my birthday,' she cried.

Monsieur Farrant grinned. 'Exactement. You will be seventeen so it will be appropriate, non?'

Stunned into silence, Eliza could only stand there gaping at him.

'You cannot believe your luck? I understand, for it would be a lesser man than Charles Farrant who would take on a . . .' He pointed to her foot. 'No other man would risk the siring of another crip—'

'That is a despicable thing to say,' she cried, her voice returning at last.

'Non, Monsieur, he speak the truth. He also knows that when we marry he can expect the rest of the Beaumont woman's receipts.'

'But . . .' she began, but he held up his hand to silence her.

'Which, despite your denial, I know you have. Monsieur Farrant is far from stupid, Mademoiselle. Now I have things to do. You will go to your room and reflect upon your good fortune. My proposal is a generous one, but in return I expect you to act and dress like a lady.' He waved his hand at her dress, curling his lip in disgust. Then a gleam appeared in his eyes. 'Ah, I do believe Saturday is tomorrow, non?'

Her heart sank to her boots. 'I'm sure you will be busy after your time away,' she ventured. He shook his head.

'I will see you in the main hall at ten of the clock. You will wear the new outfit I ordered. It is one befitting the betrothed of Monsieur Farrant, Master Perfumer – and the toque will add the finishing touch, non?' he said, giving a mocking bow.

Back in her room, Eliza paced the floor. What should she do? The very idea of marrying the man made her stomach churn. He was old – why, he must well into his thirties – and had that peculiar smell. And frighteningly, there had been something quite cruel in his demeanour tonight. Things were moving too fast, she thought, snatching up the toque from the dresser and glaring at its ostentatious points. Never would she wear such a ridiculous thing on her head, she thought, scrunching it in half then and twisting it round and round in her hands.

She looked down at the misshapen mess and sighed, for that was the least of her problems, wasn't it? By this time tomorrow, if Monsieur Farrant had his way, it would be a ring on her finger she'd be wearing. She could not, *would not* contemplate such a thing. Married women had to . . . With her insides heaving, she ran outside to the privy.

Feeling better and clearer headed, she made her way back across the courtyard. She would leave this wretched place. The sound of ribald laughter nearby clarified her thoughts. If Monsieur Farrant was having one of his house parties this would be the time to make her escape. Back in her room, she quickly gathered her precious things into a bundle. Throwing her cloak around her shoulders she made her way back outside and was heading towards the staff gate when she saw the glow of a lantern flickering its way down the garden. A light didn't move by itself did it, she thought, dodging back into the shadows. Squinting into the dark, she could just make out the shape of two figures heading towards the forbidden building. As others joined them, more laughter ensued. What was going on, Eliza wondered. All went quiet, but her curiosity was piqued. Using the bushes as cover, she made her way to the perfume garden, past the hothouse and onto the building that rose ominously out of the shadows.

She could hear men making merry, see lights flickering as strange sounds like she'd never heard before wafted out on the stiff breeze. Noticing the door slightly ajar, she inched her way nervously towards it and peered inside. The room was filled with smoke and the sickly, sweet smell filtering out reminded her of Monsieur Farrant's pungent odour. Peering through the hazy light, she stood transfixed at the scene before her. If he was like that then . . . She shook her head as realization hit her full in the solar plexus. So he intended marrying her in order to use her as a cover, she thought, hurrying back up the path as fast as her twisted foot would allow. Well he could think again.

Stealing out through the staff gate, she ran until her breath was coming in gasps. Then her foot gave way, folding under her so that she collapsed on the ground. She closed her eyes but could still picture the scene she'd witnessed. The wind rose higher, moaning and shaking the branches so they showered her with the last of their leaves.

Forcing herself to her feet she stumbled on. Where could she go? Would James help her? The heavens opened and, with icy rain stabbing her face like needles, she peered ahead. She could hear the river and could just make out the outline of the tannery looming in the distance. Summoning the last of her strength, she dragged herself towards it. Despite the late hour, a light was shining in the workshop and she hammered on the window, desperate to make him hear above the roar of the wind.

'Eliza? What on earth . . .?' James cried, pulling open the door.

'Monsieur Farrant, he . . .' she muttered, collapsing onto a chair and closing her eyes. As she sat shivering, she heard him rake the fire, then seemingly moments later a mug was placed in her hands.

'Drink this,' James ordered. She nodded, then saw concern puckering his brow. 'Deja vu,' she began. 'Don't try to speak,' he said, placing a hand reassuringly on her shoulder. ''Tis lucky for you I was working late. Got a bit behind, what with all our meetings under the oak, and Guv said if I didn't catch up he'd put a stop to my gallivanting, as he put it. Well, I couldn't risk not meeting my favourite girl, could I?' he grinned ruefully.

Hardly aware of what he was saying, she bent her head over her tea, sipping the hot liquid and listening to the comforting crackle of the fire until gradually her body stopped trembling.

'I'm sorry to turn up at this time but . . .'

'Something bad happened?' he guessed.

She nodded. 'Something so terrible you wouldn't imagine.'

'I might,' he muttered. There was a noise from outside and he frowned. 'Look, I don't mean to be rude but I'm guessing from your bundle you've left your employment?'

'I had to. Monsieur Farrant insists we buy a ring tomorrow and make the betrothal official. I can't, won't marry him so I decided to leave.'

'Look, Eliza, you can't stay the night here. It'd be more than my job's worth. My conditions of apprenticeship don't allow visitors. Lights have to be out at ten thirty and it's past that now.'

'Sorry,' she said, getting to her feet. 'I'll leave right away.'

'Where will you go?' he asked, concern clouding his eyes.

'I'll find somewhere,' she whispered, shuddering. He frowned. 'You're shaking still. Did anything else happen?'

'As I was leaving I saw these boys going down the path and followed them. I saw . . .' she stuttered to a halt.

'I can imagine, Eliza. Talk about what happens there is rife. Come on, there's an old shepherd's hut behind the tan yard. It's not used this time of year so you can bide there. I'll bring a blanket and you can bunk down and get some rest.' He snuffed out the candle and they crept outside.

The hut smelled of sheep but provided shelter from the elements. To her surprise, no sooner had Eliza slumped down on the straw than exhaustion overtook her and she fell asleep.

She was rudely awoken by the sound of shouting and doors slamming, followed by a carriage being driven away at speed. Daylight was filtering in through the grimy window and she couldn't believe she'd slept so long. Getting to her feet, she was just brushing herself down when the door creaked open and James slipped in, shutting it quickly behind him.

'All right?' he whispered, handing her a mug of hot tea then producing a hunk of bread from inside his jerkin. 'Thought you could do with this.' She smiled gratefully, cupping her hands around the steaming warmth. 'There was a right old hoo-ha outside just now. Monsieur Farrant's out searching for you. Seems to think you might have come here. Like I said to the guv, I was busy catching up on my work all last evening but he was welcome to search my room. Farrant was about to, but the guv said that if he couldn't trust his apprentice then it was a pretty poor show, so the man stormed off. Guv thinks he'll be back, though, so you'd best lie low.'

'I don't want to get you into trouble,' she said, handing him back his mug and gathering up her bundle.

'Don't be daft. Farrant could be watching the place and God knows what he might do to you. Anyway, where would you go?' he asked.

She shrugged.

'Look, I must get back before I'm missed. Eat your bread and we'll discuss what you're going to do later.' He patted her shoulder, peeked through the window, then slipped out of the door.

So Monsieur was looking for her, she thought, shivering and pulling the blanket around her shoulders. Knowing she needed to keep up her strength, she nibbled at the bread, then settled down to ponder her next move. Clearly she couldn't remain here. It had been kind of James to help her but she couldn't risk him losing his job. What should she do? Where could she go? Back to Fay? She could vaguely remember the route the carriage had taken but they'd been travelling for two days so it was clearly some distance. Perhaps she should revert to her original plan, make for a large town and seek employment there. Round and round her thoughts went until she was exhausted.

She must have slept for the next thing she knew, James was standing over her.

'Cor, it's all right for those who can idle the day away,' he quipped. 'Here.' He handed her a piece of pie and another mug of tea.

'Thank you,' she said, biting into the crust. 'Lovely, good old English pie,' she added, remembering all the hazelette she'd eaten.

''Tis my noon break so when you've eaten, happen you can tell me what's gone on?' he said, those cornflower eyes boring into her as he settled himself on the straw beside her.

Briefly she ran through everything that had happened, but when she got to the bit about the men in the forbidden building her voice faltered.

'It was weird . . .' she muttered, shaking her head.

James reached out and squeezed her hand. 'At least you've been spared having to wear his ring. Of course, most sensible girls would be thrilled at the prospect of being taken to the jewellers,' he smiled.

'Huh, he only wanted me to choose one so that people could see I belonged to him. I mean, what kind of man would do that?'

'Probably one with an ulterior motive, like needing a

cover for these activities of his,' he muttered. She stared at him, amazed by his perception.

'I'm not going back, that's for sure,' she said, shuddering. 'I was thinking maybe I could make my way back to Exmoor and Fay. See if she'd take me back. Apart from anything else, it would give me a chance to thank her for all she did for me.'

James sat silently mulling this over.

''Tis a long way, Eliza, and your foot has taken a hammering these past few days,' he said eventually.

'Well, I've no money for fancy travelling. Perhaps a passing carter will take pity.'

'Or you could come to Salting Regis with me.' She stared at him in surprise. 'On me day off, I usually pay a visit to Father and then have lunch with Grandfa Sam and Nan Doll. They're kind people and you'll like them. I was thinking they might even let you bide a night or two until you've recovered your strength.'

'Oh, I couldn't impose,' Eliza protested. 'Besides, I'm scared Monsieur will return soon so I think I'd better make tracks first thing.'

'Tomorrow just happens to be my Sunday off, so isn't that convenient?' he grinned. He took hold of her hand and her heart flipped with happiness. Could she just up and go with him, though?

'I thinks the world of thee, Eliza, and hopes you will come to think of me . . .' His declaration was interrupted by the sound of a carriage screaming to a halt and Monsieur Farrant's shouts.

'I'd better scuttle and find out what's going on,' James whispered. 'Stay here.'

Eliza didn't know whether to laugh or cry. As if she could go anywhere, with Monsieur Farrant on the warpath.

'Blimey, he don't give up,' James said, creeping back into the hut sometime later. 'He insisted he had a right to look over the premises to find out if his betrothed was hiding here. The guv told him there must be something wrong if a woman needed to run away from him. Monsieur went berserk, insisting he would return with the constable and a warrant to have the premises searched.'

Eliza gasped. 'I don't want to get you into trouble, James.'

'In view of what you said, Farrant's hardly likely to involve the police. However, if you comes to Salting Regis with me, we won't be here if he does,' he grinned. 'Guv lets me borrow the cart on me day off.'

'Well, put like that, how can I refuse?' she replied, a feeling of relief washing over her. The sooner she could put some distance between her and Monsieur Farrant the better.

'Get some sleep and we'll leave at first light.'

No sooner had they trotted out of the yard first thing the next morning than there was movement from the bushes opposite.

'Quick, get down,' James hissed.

Awkwardly, Eliza slid onto the floor of the cart and he just had time to cover her with a blanket before Monsieur Farrant stepped out on the track in front of the cart.

30

'Going somewhere, Cary?' Monsieur Farrant demanded.

'Yup, as you will see from the saddle in the back, I have a delivery to make and then I'm off to see my grandfather. He's ailing, sir, so I'd be grateful if you would move out of the way.'

'You're travelling alone?'

'Unless you can see someone sat beside me,' James answered.

Monsieur Farrant cursed and Eliza stifled a giggle.

'Think you're being funny, do you, boy? Well, let me tell you, nobody makes a fool of Monsieur Farrant. Eliza is mine and I intend to find her and return her whence she belongs, Cary. Do I make myself clear?'

'Yup, but it seems strange to me. I mean, nobody owns another person, do they? Surely the girl should be free to go where she wants? I'd only want someone with me who wished to stay out of choice. Still, I'll bid you good day, sir,' he said, calling to the pony to walk on. As the cart began to move, James whispered, 'Keep down in case he follows, Eliza.'

Although she did as he instructed, it wasn't long before her foot protested and she got cramp in her legs. Just when she thought she couldn't stay still a moment longer, the blanket was pulled back and she saw his cheeky face grinning down at her. Easing herself into an upright position she rubbed her legs, then looked nervously over her shoulder.

'Don't worry, the road here's straight so there's no way he can follow without being seen. Good job we hid your bundle under the saddle, though.'

'James, if your grandfather's ill he won't want me descending on him, will he?' she asked.

''Tis true Grandfa suffers badly with rheumatics but he soldiers on. I only mentioned that to Farrant so as to get him out of our way. Don't worry, both Grandfa and Nan will be overjoyed to meet you.'

Finally she relaxed in her seat and looked around. They were travelling eastward and the sky before them was bathed in rosy reds, pearly pinks and glowing gold.

'The sea's over there, through those trees and down the cliffs,' he said, pointing to their right.

'Really?' she exclaimed, peering over his shoulder. 'I've never seen the sea before.' He laughed and shook his head.

'Then you've never lived. Don't worry you'll get a proper view when we've climbed the hill. Mind you, Minty here takes her time, don't you, old girl?' he said, leaning forward and slapping the pony's rump.

'Minty? What kind of name's that?'

He laughed. 'Apt, as you'll see when we stop.'

Eliza smiled, thinking how nice he was. His easy-going nature was a tonic after Monsieur's fiery temper and pernickety ways. Lost in thought, she hardly noticed they'd crested the hill and turned south so that the breeze hitting her full in the face took her by surprise. She pulled her cloak tighter round her, then noticed the wide expanse of blue shimmering in the distance.

'Oh, look,' she pointed.

'That's the sweep of Lyme Bay and the buildings you can see in front are where we're headed,' he said. She sniffed the air. 'What's that smell?'

''Tis called ozone, the fresh, pure air you get by the sea.'

She inhaled again. 'Well I've never seen the sea before but that scent reminds me of something.'

'Some flower perhaps?' he asked. She thought for a moment then shook her head. 'I don't think so, but it will come to me.'

As the fields gave way to buildings, she looked around. The broad street was bustling and James had to concentrate on steering the cart around several carriages pulled up beside the church and people dismounting for morning service. Then he turned right onto a cobbled road, where the pony automatically came to a stop before a shop fronted with latticed windows. Jumping down, James secured the reins to an iron ring then helped Eliza down from the cart. As the pony nuzzled his pocket, James laughed.

'Here you go, old girl,' he said giving her a mint. The pony crunched, swallowed then opened its mouth for more. 'Now you see why she's called Minty,' he said, placing another sweet on the animal's tongue. 'I'll just get the saddle for father. You go on down the entry.'

However, Eliza's attention had been caught by the display of boots and shoes in the window.

'These are beautiful, James,' she said when he joined her.

'Father's the finest cobbler in Salting Regis. Course, he used to be a fulltime cordwainer before Mother went,' he said frowning from behind the saddle.

'Oh, I'm sorry, James,' she said.

'It was a long time ago but best you don't mention it in front of Father. Come on, I'll introduce you,' he said, leading the way down the side passage, then nudging a door open with his shoulder. 'It's me, Father,' he called. ''Tis your lucky day for I've brought the saddle you wanted – and a visitor.'

An older man, dark hair greying at the temples, appeared, wiping his brow on his kerchief. He assessed Eliza with eyes that were the same colour as his son's but without the glow, then nodded.

'How do, I'm sure.'

'Delighted to meet you, Mr Cary,' she smiled.

He grunted then turned to his son. 'Been a fine bit of tanning done there,' he said, running his hand over the shiny saddle James had placed on the workbench. While they discussed its various merits, Eliza stole a look around the room, which seemed filled to bursting with tools, lasts, spools of coloured threads and beautiful-smelling leather.

'Well, better get down to Grandfa's,' James said a few minutes later. 'Mustn't be late for Nan's roast,' he grinned, rubbing his stomach. 'Why don't you come, Father? You know you'd be welcome.'

The man gave another grunt and shook his head.

'See you soon, then.' James patted his father's shoulder and opened the door.

'Goodbye, Mr Cary,' Eliza said.

The man nodded and grunted before turning back to the saddle.

'Don't mind Father,' James said, once they were seated in the cart. 'That's the way he is these days.'

The reception they got from his grandparents was completely different. Eliza followed James to the stairs that led up from behind the apothecary's shop into the living quarters above. As the succulent smell of roasting meat drifted towards them, he turned to her.

'Beef, my favourite,' he whispered.

'James, how lovely,' a voice cried, as a tiny woman with cherry-red cheeks darted out of the kitchen and threw her arms around him.

'Nan, I'd like you to meet Eliza,' he said, when she finally released him. The woman turned dark beady eyes towards Eliza, gave her a long appraising look, then smiled. 'Welcome, Eliza. Let me take your things,' she said. As Eliza handed her the cloak, she stroked the soft material before hanging it on the coat stand. 'That's lovely, dear. Come away into the parlour. Your grandfa's reading the paper. Samuel, look who's here to see us,' she cried, ushering them into a large airy room where a man sat in his easy chair before a blazing fire.

'Still planning on putting the world to rights, Grandfa?' James asked as the man folded his paper and got stiffly to his feet.

'Someone needs to,' he replied, shaking James by the hand. 'Who's this pretty young lady, then?' he asked, smiling at Eliza.

'This is Eliza, Grandfa,' James said. The man held out his hand and as Eliza took it, she was struck by the family resemblance, for he too had blue eyes that twinkled with mischief like James's, although his hair was snowy white.

'Welcome, Eliza,' he said, repeating his wife's earlier greeting. 'Now, do come and warm yourselves beside the fire. Shall we treat ourselves to a spot of elderflower cordial as it's a special occasion, Doll?' he asked, turning to his wife.

She smiled at him indulgently. 'Why not? You set out the glasses and I'll bring in a bottle,' she ordered, bustling out of the room.

'I'll do that, Grandfa,' James said, hurrying over to the highly polished sideboard. As he set them on the table, the old man winked at Eliza.

'Don't think you've ever brought a maid visiting before, young James. Be it a special occasion?'

'Actually, Grandfa, I was going to ask a favour. Eliza here needs a bed for a couple of nights and I was wondering if she might stay here.'

There was silence save for the ticking of the clock on the mantle over the fire as the old man scrutinized her. Eliza steadily met his gaze and he smiled. 'You'll do,' he nodded. 'Doll will be pleased to have some company. Likes a bit of a natter, she does, so you'd better watch your ears.'

James grinned at Eliza and nodded. 'That's fixed then.'

'And what's that you've fixed, young James?' Doll said, bustling back into the room with a bottle in her hands.

'Young Eliza here is to be our guest for the next few days, my dear,' replied Grandfa Sam. 'Now who's going to pour that cordial?' Eliza gazed at James's grandparents, hardly daring to believe they'd agreed to her staying so readily.

After finishing their drinks, they sat down to the most splendid meal of roast beef with all the trimmings. Grandfa Sam and Nan, as they insisted Eliza call them, went out of their way to make her feel welcome and conversation flowed easily. Grandfa Sam was particularly interested in Eliza's work at the perfumery, likening it to his work in the apothecary downstairs.

'Once you've learned what ingredients to use, 'tis all in the mixing and blending,' he said, and Eliza nodded.

'I'd love to see what you do.'

'Then you shall. It'll be nice to have someone show an interest,' he said, looking pointedly at James.

'You know I'm all fingers and thumbs and end up breaking those glass tubes of yours, Grandfa,' he laughed, holding up his large hands. 'He's chased me out of his shop more times than I care to remember, Eliza.'

'Happen that was 'cos you was playing around, my boy,' he chided.

Grinning, James got to his feet. 'That was delicious, as always, Nan. Now you sit by the fire while Eliza and I do the dishes.'

'Oh, but I couldn't,' she began.

'No arguing now. Then, if it's all right with you, I'll bring in Eliza's things and put them in the spare room.'

'Are you sure you don't mind?' Eliza asked, looking anxiously at Doll.

'Why bless you, no. It'll be good to have another woman to chatter to. Samuel isn't one for conversation, are you, my dear?' The old man winked at Eliza. 'I'll warm a brick for your bed later,' Nan added.

'Are you sure I won't be imposing,' Eliza asked James later, as he prepared to make his way back to the tannery.

'They love you already, Eliza, as do . . . Well, let's just say I shall rest easy knowing you're away from Farrant.

Besides, Grandfa's keen to show you around his domain. Nobody's ever shown that much interest in his work before. I've cleared it with them that you can stay until my next day off, so I'll be back Sunday to see how you're getting on,' he said, touching her cheek gently with his hand as he left.

'Thank you for everything,' she whispered.

That night, tucked up in the little bed in the spare room, she thought back over the past few days. How kind it was of Grandfa Sam and Nan to take her in. She couldn't take advantage of their kind hospitality, though. Tomorrow she would look around the town and see if she could find a job with board and lodging. It was time she stood on her own two feet.

Next morning, after breakfasting on porridge with creamy milk, Eliza followed Sam and Nan down to the apothecary's shop. Inside, she was met with the most wonderful fragrance and, inhaling deeply, she detected the sweet smell of lily of the valley, along with violet, rose and lavender. While Sam went round lighting the glass globes and Nan donned a snowy-white apron, Eliza stared around the room in amazement.

It was like an Aladdin's cave. Rich mahogany and glass display cases lined the walls, all housing a collection of little glass bottles, dishes and curious items she'd never seen before. Alongside each bow window was a glass counter, one set with dishes of petals and bottles of powders, the other dominated by a large empty dish, a pestle and brass measuring scales. Towards the back of the room was a large workbench methodically lined with glass tubes, spoons, droppers, cutters, crushers and cups of varying sizes. The shelves above were stocked with numerous green and blue bottles all filled with mysterious liquids. Eliza felt excitement bubbling and hoped Sam would show her what at least some of them were for.

Nan smiled. 'That's Sam's domain and this is mine,' she explained, pointing to the pots of salves, dishes of scented soaps, bath salts and jars of embrocation. 'Sam attends to the customers' ailments while I supply their more personal requirements.'

'And finds out all their gossip,' Sam added with a broad wink.

'Well, if you know what's going on in their lives you can sell them something to help,' Nan chuckled, picking up her broom. 'I'm off to sweep the pavement.'

'Here, let me,' Eliza said.

'You can't do that, you're our guest,' the woman protested, but Eliza smiled and gently took the broom from her.

'It's very kind of you to let me stay when you don't even know me, but I must at least earn my keep.'

Outside the air was cold with a stiff breeze blowing in from the sea. Eliza inhaled deeply. That smell definitely reminded her of something, she thought, sweeping the dust into the road then stepping swiftly back as a carriage and pair swept past. Industrious shopkeepers were pulling down awnings and setting out their wares on tables in front of their windows. Everywhere people were hurrying about their business and she'd never seen so many carts and carriages in her life.

This Salting Regis place was all hustle and bustle compared to the solitude of the moors, she thought, wondering how Fay and Duncan were. She'd have to write and let Fay know her new address now she'd moved on – when she had a permanent one, that was. Spying a smudge on one of the little square windows, she leaned over and gave it a quick wipe. Then she noticed the pestle and mortar on the sign above the shop and underneath in bold script 'Samuel Cary, Apothecary'. She smiled: if ever someone was aptly named it was Grandfa Sam. One window was scripted with 'Dispenser to Physicians and Patrons', the other, 'Purest Powders, Soothing Salves; Scented Salts & Soaps'. Salting Regis was obviously a thriving place that catered for everyone, including the wealthy, Eliza thought.

As another gust of wind blew in from the sea, she shook her head. She wished she could remember where she'd smelled that salty, tangy odour before. Somehow, she knew it was important.

31

Despite Sam's protests that Eliza was a guest, she insisted on helping in the little shop. Seeing her determination, Nan provided her with a voluminous white apron and soft duster, then set her to work polishing the counters and display cabinets. Eliza was fascinated by their contents but found herself jumping each time the shop bell tinkled. Nan soon noticed.

'He won't think to look here, dear,' she whispered. Eliza stared at her in surprise. 'James explained why you'd left your post and asked us to look out for you. Don't you worry, if that man dares to enter our shop, I'll chase him straight out again with the poker.'

'Thank you, Nan. That's very kind,' she answered, trying not to smile at the thought of this diminutive woman chasing Monsieur Farrant down the street.

The shop proved to be a busy place. While Nan dealt with the steady stream of her customers seeking soaps, salts and salves in her cheery, chatty way, Sam took his clients behind the screen where they were able to discuss their ailments in private. He would then study the flagons, take down his selection and measure doses into the glass bowl. Eliza watched as he stirred vigorously then dispensed the restoratives into little medicine bottles, carefully labelling them in his copperplate writing.

Often he ground ingredients together with his pestle and mortar and wrapped the powder in little twists of paper. Occasionally, he would melt lumps of waxy substances, mix with the powders and squeeze in a press to make lozenges. These he stored in little round cardboard tubs, meticulously penning the names on the lids. He took his job seriously, ensuring each customer left with strict instructions on how their restorative should be taken.

The morning passed by in a flash and, come noon, to Eliza's delight, Nan left her in charge of her precious soaps and salves whilst she went upstairs to prepare luncheon and have a rest. When she reappeared, declaring she'd left bread, ham and a fresh pot of tea ready for them, Sam and Eliza took their break.

'You seem to be taking a great interest in my work, Eliza,' Sam commented as they tucked into their food.

'It's fascinating and I'd love to learn more,' she cried, staring at him hopefully. He nodded but didn't say anything else, just wrapped his hands around his cup and stared into the fire. Later, as they made their way back downstairs, Eliza wondered if he'd just been making polite conversation. After all, she was only here for a week.

Customers came and went all through the afternoon but as time wore on Eliza noticed Sam wincing as he stretched up for jars he'd had no trouble reaching earlier in the day. Although he didn't complain, she made sure she was nearby and could hand him what was required. Surprisingly he accepted her assistance, even seeming grateful for it.

By Saturday Eliza had come to know the ways of the

little shop. The customers were friendly and she enjoyed wrapping their purchases and replenishing Nan's little dishes. She was almost sorry when, at the end of the week, Sam locked the shop door and turned the little sign round to show they were closed.

'Well, day of rest tomorrow, Nan, eh?' he said, rubbing his back.

'For some maybe, but no doubt you'll be expecting your roast luncheon, and it doesn't put itself on the table,' she said, wagging her finger at him.

'You must let me help,' Eliza offered, as they made their way up the stairs.

'Thank you, dear. Mind you, I expect Master James will be on the doorstep first thing, if I know him,' she said, turning and giving Eliza a wink.

At the mention of his name, Eliza's heart soared. She couldn't wait to see him again and tell him all about her week. Then her spirits sank. Tomorrow she'd have to leave Sam and Nan and this cosy home. They'd been so kind and she'd already become fond of them. Of course, she'd known her stay here was temporary and hadn't unpacked all her bundle, but she loved her room, its linen fragranced with Nan's lavender, and didn't want to go.

The little shop, with its perfumed products, healing powders and coloured bottles, was a delight, while Sam's dispensary was fascinating. How she'd love to learn more, she thought as the three of them sank into easy chairs beside the hearth. Nan poked and prodded until the tamped-down fire burst into life, then held her hands out to the flames.

'There's nothing like your own fireplace at the end of a busy day,' she smiled.

Eliza sighed, thinking how wonderful it would be to have a home like this, filled with happiness and love.

Just then the kettle on the fender began to sing and Eliza hopped up to pour hot water over the leaves in the ever-waiting brown teapot. As they sipped their tea in companionable silence, Eliza felt she was being watched and she looked up to see Sam eyeing her thoughtfully.

'You've been a real help this week, Eliza. Still interested in learning more about formulating and dispensing, or have we managed to put you off life in an apothecary's?' Although he spoke lightly, Eliza could tell her answer mattered to him.

'I've loved every minute and would welcome the chance to learn more,' she cried.

'The shop doesn't have the glamour of the perfumery, though, does it?' he persisted.

Eliza thought for a moment. Monsieur Farrant had taught her a lot and for that she was grateful. She couldn't deny she'd have liked to have finished her training, but now she was away from his possessive, overbearing ways she felt nothing but relief.

'It's fascinating but in a different way. Monsieur said I had a good nose so I'm sure what I learned before could be put to good use in the shop,' she finally answered.

Nan laughed. 'There, Sam, you can see the girl's keen, so put her out of her misery.'

He nodded, that twinkle in his eye. 'I had detected a certain amount of enthusiasm,' he teased. 'The fact is, Eliza, I'm not getting any younger and your assistance this week has made me realize that. If you are agreeable, Nan and I would like to offer you a permanent position with board and lodging.'

Her eyes widened in amazement.

'Regrettably we can't pay much in the way of salary, but you would be guaranteed something at the end of every month.'

How kind these dear people were, Eliza thought, for in all the time she'd worked for Monsieur Farrant she hadn't received one brass farthing. He'd furnished her with fancy clothes, but that was so she'd look the part in the perfumery or out in his fancy carriage. Although he'd agreed to taking her on, Fay had paid him handsomely for the privilege. Now Sam and Nan were offering her a job and board. What was it Grampy had said about when one door closes another opens? Perhaps, like a guardian angel, he was watching over her.

She was jolted back to the present by Nan talking.

'And Sam is the best apothecary there is, so you would be trained well. I can teach you how to make the soaps and fragrance the salts, if you wish to pursue the perfumery side of things. Why you could even . . .' She trailed to a halt as Sam held up his hands.

'Don't overwhelm the girl, Nan. Mull it over, Eliza, and you can give us your decision in the morning before that scallywag James arrives.'

'Please, I'd love to accept your kind offer. I'll work hard and learn everything you care to teach me,' she cried, eager to accept in case the opportunity should be snatched away overnight.

Sam smiled and held out his hand. 'That's a deal, then.

The only condition being that nothing dispensed here leaves the shop without my approval.'

'Of course, Sam,' Eliza agreed.

Although James arrived early the next morning, Eliza had already unpacked her things and set out her treasured box, the portrait Fay had painted, the flower book, the two scent bottles and Fay's receipt book on the dressing table. She had just taken the stopper off the little black bottle and inhaled the lingering hint of fragrance, when she heard her name being called. Hastily replacing it, she ran her fingers through her hair and, remembering Fay's words, promised she'd make a concentrated effort to find out where the elusive aroma originated.

James was waiting in the parlour and her heart did a funny flip when he turned and gave his cheeky grin.

'Think I must have come to the wrong place,' he teased. 'Grandfa's just been telling me about some angel who's been working in his shop. I don't see you sporting a halo or wings, so I reckon he must have been talking about someone else.'

'Eliza's been more help than you ever have, my lad,' Sam snorted.

'Now, you two, there's a bit of a breeze blowing but the sun's trying to shine. Why don't you take yourselves out for a walk?' Nan suggested.

'But I must help you prepare luncheon,' Eliza protested.

The woman shook her head. 'I need to do some baking first and can't if James is under my feet. He'll pick at this and peck at that till I've hardly anything left to take to his father,' Nan clucked.

'We'll wash up afterwards, Nan,' James assured her.

James helped Eliza into her cloak and they made their way down the stairs and outside, where the stiff breeze carried the tang of salt towards them. She inhaled deeply then sneezed.

James laughed. 'Ozone beats those country smells any day – if you can take it, that is,' he ribbed. 'Come on.' He held out his arm for her to take and they set off at a brisk pace. Before long James turned right and she could see the waves bouncing off a high, curved wall, sending spray everywhere.

'What's that?' she asked.

''Tis the breakwater, built to protect the boats. Those stones sticking out for steps are known as Granny's Teeth.'

'You're joking,' she laughed, but he shook his head.

'Straight up; and that building's the lifeboat station. Those things with sails are fishing boats,' he teased, then groaned when she dug him in the side with her elbow. 'We'll stroll around the harbour and you can tell me all about your week.'

Excitedly she told him all her news, ending with her offer of a job with Sam and Nan.

'I can't believe how kind they've been, especially as they hardly know me.'

'Ah, but you come with the recommendation of their grandson.' She turned to face him.

'You mean you knew this would happen?' she asked, staring at him in amazement.

'I hoped it might,' he admitted. 'However, make no mistake, Grandfa's astute and can suss anyone out in seconds. If he hadn't taken to you he wouldn't have agreed to you staying one night, let alone for the week. His brain is still sharp but, as I'm sure you've seen, he needs assistance with fetching and carrying. Nan's still as nimble as ever, but the truth is neither of them is getting any younger and although they work hard, they seldom turn much of a profit. Here we are, nearly into December and whereas other stores are already displaying Christmas stock nothing has changed in their shop.'

'Perhaps I can help,' Eliza offered, thinking back to last year in the perfumery.

He gave her that smile that made her insides melt. 'I'm sure you will. We're extremely busy at the tannery ourselves with orders for new saddles and equipment for the hunts. I've told Guv I'll work on in the evenings but my Sundays off is sacrosanct,' he assured her. Her insides rippled with happiness but she wasn't sure how to reply, so she kept quiet. While he seemed nice and trustworthy, there was no guarantee he wouldn't disappear, like Duncan or Amos had, was there?

The next morning, whilst Nan and Sam were busy serving customers, Eliza scrutinized the stock. Bright ribbons tied around the tablets of soaps and jars of salts would lend a more celebratory air to the displays and encourage people to buy them for presents. Although the little shop smelled fragrant, it really did need to look more festive in the run-up to Christmas. She remembered Monsieur Farrant saying one had to tempt folk to buy. She was just jotting down some notes when Sam called for her assistance.

They were so busy for the rest of the week that it was

Friday before she thought any more about Christmas preparations. Nan was upstairs taking her break when a lady dressed in a sapphire jacket with long, close-fitting sleeves edged with lace came into the shop. Her overskirt was drawn up at the sides and bunched up at the back with a matching ribbon, while her hat also had a matching ribbon tied around the brim and under her chin. To Eliza, her whole appearance looked a trifle overdone. As Sam was busy behind his screen, she moved forward to attend to her.

'May I be of assistance?' she asked politely.

The woman smiled stiffly. 'I'm merely gleaning ideas for Christmas purchases. This year I particularly need to impress my future daughter-in-law.' The woman lowered her voice. 'She comes from gentry, you know.'

'Here at Cary's we have so much to offer the discerning young woman,' Eliza said, pointing to the display of soaps and salts, lotions and salves. The woman nodded. Then remembering her training at the perfumery, Eliza added, 'What fragrance does she like?'

'Well, that hardly matters, does it? It's the look of the present that counts,' the woman said, lifting a bar of soap to her nose. 'This smells nice but one tablet would hardly impress, would it? I called in here to gain inspiration before going to the renowned departmental store in Exeter. There, one can select a box elaborately decorated and filled with products guaranteed to draw admiration and cries of delight when opened,' the woman expanded, waving her arms theatrically around.

'I'm sure that must cost you, madam.' The woman stared at Eliza in surprise.

'Of course, but that is hardly the point. One wouldn't wish to appear mean by giving anything that looked less than generous.'

'Actually, madam, we offer a similar yet more personal service right here in Salting Regis,' Eliza declared, determined that if this woman was going to spend a lot of money then it would be here in the apothecary's shop. She saw Nan watching from the doorway, her eyes wide with shock.

'Then where are your displays?' the woman asked, looking around.

'Actually, madam, this is where we beat the other stores hands down. Here at Cary's we guarantee that no two boxes will ever look the same.'

'Really?' the woman cried, her eyes gleaming with interest. 'And how, may I ask, is that possible?'

'By allowing the customer to select the products they wish to purchase, tell us the colour they wish the box to be lined in, and whether the decorative bow should be large and flamboyant or small and tasteful. Should you care to use our services, your gift box will be ready within twenty-four hours. And, of course, we wouldn't even think of invoicing until you call to inspect the finished box.'

'Really, that all sounds quite splendid. The idea of somebody else purchasing the same gift always fills one with horror, don't you find?' Eliza nodded, thinking Grampy was right when he'd said that a fool and his money were soon parted.

'Well, madam, I'm sure your son will have had the good taste to choose someone similar to his mother, so perhaps you would like to sample the fragrance first. Then we can select how many items you would like the box to contain,' Eliza said, holding out the various soaps.

'I rather think Daphne would like this,' the woman said, pointing to the lily of the valley.

'A wise choice indeed, madam, so sweet and innocent yet sophisticated somehow, don't you think?'

'That's why I chose it, young lady. Now I wish you to select one of simply every product, and have them displayed in a box lined with green velvet and tied with a large, golden bow. I shall call at noon tomorrow to collect.' And with that the woman nodded and swept from the shop.

Eliza turned triumphantly to Nan, but the old lady shook her head.

'What have you done, Eliza?' she muttered.

32

'But that's the way to increase your sales, surely?' Eliza protested. 'Present the customer with a something tailored to their requirements and they'll buy more products.' She was sure that's what Monsieur Farrant had said.

'The principle is good, Eliza, but we have no fancy cloth for lining the box.'

'Then I'll get some from the haberdasher's or the market,' she said.

'But we've no money to buy any,' Nan explained. 'The ingredients I purchased for making extra soaps and things for Christmas took the last of our reserves.'

'I'm sure we can find something,' Eliza said, gazing hopefully round the shop.

'I wish we could because that idea you had was a sound one, and I could just picture the window adorned with pretty boxes. Never mind, you meant well, and I'll explain to the customer when she returns tomorrow,' Nan said, patting Eliza's shoulder reassuringly. 'You go and have your luncheon. I'll send Sam up when he's finished with his customer.'

Determined not to be thwarted, Eliza racked her brains. There must be something she could use, she thought, munching on her cheese. Having promised the woman she could have the box lined in the colour of her choice it was up to her to come up with the goods. It wouldn't be fair to leave Nan to face the woman's wrath. Oh, why hadn't she kept her mouth shut? But she knew the answer. It was because she'd promised James she'd try to help them increase their sales. Well, sitting here fretting wouldn't help.

On her way back downstairs, she passed the coat stand and stopped in her tracks. There before her hung the answer. It would make the perfect lining, but could she cut it up? Should she? Dare she?

All afternoon she pondered, then realized she had little choice. It had been her suggestion and therefore it was her responsibility to fulfil the order.

'May I select one of each lily of the valley product, Nan?' she asked later as Sam was locking the shop door.

Nan gave her a shrewd look. 'Don't tell me you've thought of something?' she asked, gathering together the items herself and handing them to Eliza.

'I hope so. Can you tally the cost for me?'

As Nan jotted the sum down in her cash book, Eliza hurried up to her room. An hour later, she surveyed her handiwork and smiled.

'What do you think?' she asked, throwing open the parlour door and holding the box aloft.

'Well, I never, that's quite a work of art,' Nan exclaimed. Then her eyes narrowed. 'Oh, Eliza, you've never cut up your beautiful cloak?'

'Needs must when the devil drives, as my grampy used to say,' she quoted.

'But where did that beautiful ribbon come from?' Nan asked, fingering the gold-edged gauze.

Eliza grinned. 'Monsieur Farrant insisted the dressmaker make me a toque and it was so flamboyant I asked her to remove the bow. I'd quite forgotten I'd hidden it in my treasure box. It's a shame I didn't bring all the other posh outfits he had made. The fine material would have come in useful,' she sighed.

'You did right to leave them behind, young lady,' Grandfa admonished from his armchair. 'A clear conscience means more than fancy fripperies.'

'You're right, of course,' she said quickly, then turned back to Nan. 'Add something for the cost of the box, velvet and ribbon to that of your products, plus a bit for time and effort and you should make a good profit.'

'She's got something there, Nan,' said Sam, looking up from his paper again.

'I've got plenty of velvet left to line more boxes. If we use some of the money that customer pays to buy ribbons in different colours, we'll be able to offer a service to rival anyone in the city. Your products are the best you can buy, Nan, and if you display prettied-up boxes in varying sizes and prices in the window, they would catch people's attention as they walk by,' she cried, excitement rising as she visualized them.

'Let's see how we get on tomorrow first,' Nan cautioned.

The customer was delighted at the beautifully presented gift box. 'I shall have no hesitation in recommending the service I have found to my friends,' she announced grandly. As the bell tinkled behind her, Eliza and Nan collapsed on the counter and burst out laughing.

'How kind, I'm sure,' Eliza announced in a fair imitation of the woman.

Sam frowned over the top of his spectacles, but when

he saw the little pile of coins in Nan's hand, his eyes widened.

'Well done, Eliza. I reckon you should go and purchase those ribbons you were talking about,' he said.

Although James was delighted with Eliza's scheme, he wasn't too happy that she had only her old shawl to wear out walking the next day.

'Are you ashamed of me, James Cary?' she asked, glaring at him.

'I could never be ashamed of you, Eliza. I'm just worried you'll catch your death in that,' he said, putting his finger through one of its many holes.

'Oh, James, don't nag so,' she giggled. 'I'll save up and buy another cloak. The main thing is that with Sam and Nan agreeing to my idea, they should turn over a profit and that's what you wanted, wasn't it?'

He nodded. 'Quite the little business woman, aren't you?'

'Not really, it's only what I learned at the perfumery.'

'Beauty and brains, I'm a lucky guy and no mistake,' James smiled lovingly at her, making her feel warm all over.

Then she stared down at her built-up boot and sighed. Beauty, indeed! But James was speaking again.

'Talking of the perfumery reminds me, Farrant came snooping around again yesterday. Seems to think you've gone off with a receipt book of his. More worried about that than you, to be honest. Anyhow, I told him I'd never seen one and sent him packing.'

Eliza shivered but it had nothing to do with the cold.

'Look, this wind's bitter,' he said as another gust blew in from the sea. 'Let's go into the café over there. Carla does a mean chocolatina,' he said, gripping her arm and leading her across the street.

As they sat sipping the delicious concoction of coffee, chocolate and cream, James grinned at Eliza across the table.

'Thought I'd stay with Father over the holiday so we can spend the time together,' he said.

Her heart soared. For the first time ever, she'd have a Christmas to look forward to.

'He said you could even come over for a drink if you wish. Now believe you me, that's a first.'

'Won't he be spending Christmas with Sam and Nan?' she asked.

James shook his head. 'Truth is, he's become a bit of a recluse. If it wasn't for Nan's baking, goodness knows how he'd survive.' He then fell silent and Eliza had the sense not to say any more. He took another sip of his drink.

'I'm afraid I'll only be able to get you a little something for your gift, Eliza. My wages at the tannery are pitiful, to say the least. In the New Year, when I finish my apprenticeship, things will improve and I'll be able to treat you to something special.'

'Oh, James, you really don't need to buy me anything. Just spending Christmas with you and your family will be special enough.'

'Don't you have anyone to . . .' he began, but stopped when he saw her face.

'It was different when my sisters were at home. Now they have their own lives and seldom return, not that I blame them.' She shuddered. 'The only person I wish to contact is Fay, the woman who took me in. You remember me telling you how, unbeknown to me, she undertook to be my guardian.'

He nodded. 'Haven't you been in touch at all?' he asked.

'I started to write to her but gave up,' Eliza confessed. 'She wanted me gone, after all. Anyway, Monsieur Farrant said he'd penned a letter advising Fay of my progress.'

'So you've had no contact with her since you left?'

'No. Probably thought she'd done her duty by me,' she sighed.

James reached across the table and squeezed her hand. Their eyes locked and, seeing the love reflected in his, joy flooded through her. Then she remembered other eyes, the colour of chestnuts, gazing lovingly at her and pulled her hand away.

'We'd better get back and see if Nan needs any help,' she said, jumping to her feet.

'You remind me of a little sparrow, Eliza. You edge tentatively closer, then, just when I think I've gained your trust, you hop away again.'

She stared down at the floor, knowing what he said was true.

'Don't underestimate me, though. James Cary might be patient but he is also persistent,' he said. Then with his winning smile, he took her arm and they made their way back to the shop.

As word of their gift boxes spread throughout the town, Eliza and Nan worked flat out satisfying demand. Nan found remnants of different-coloured material in her closet and Eliza spent her time lining the various sized boxes that Sam used for the delivery of his orders, decorating them with elaborate bows. Although she still helped Sam when necessary, he and Nan agreed she would begin her training in the New Year.

Before they knew it, the last Sunday before Christmas dawned. James arrived early and Nan shooed him and Eliza out of the way, saying she wanted to spend the day baking. Sam grumbled good-naturedly at having to make do with a late 'pot luck' luncheon instead of his beloved roast, but he was looking tired and Eliza knew he would welcome a bit of peace and quiet.

There was a bitter breeze blowing, whipping up waves on the slate-grey sea, and as they hurried towards the café, Eliza tripped. It was only James grabbing her that saved her from falling.

'Steady,' he said.

'Sorry, my foot goes numb in the cold and although these boots are better than my old ones, I still have to think before I step,' she explained. 'Bet you think I'm a right clumsy clod.'

'Actually, I think you are the loveliest, sweetest, prettiest girl I've ever met,' he declared.

'If you think that, then you must be blind,' she muttered. 'Pretty I am not.'

He frowned and shook his head but said nothing.

They hurried into the café, welcoming the warmth from the little fire as they settled at their favourite table and ordered large mugs of Carla's speciality drink.

'Well, here's to you, Eliza,' James said, raising his mug

to hers. 'Grandfa reckons takings are up, thanks to you and your boxes.'

'I'm just pleased everything worked out,' she smiled. 'Grandfa Sam and Nan have made me really welcome. They're a lovely couple, and so close, aren't they?'

'Just the way a marriage should be, I've always thought,' he replied, staring at her intently.

'Anyway, I've really enjoyed the hustle and bustle in the lead-up to Christmas,' Eliza said quickly. 'The customers are especially friendly at this time of year. It is satisfying helping them make their selections and decorating the boxes as they want. Mind you, Nan reckons Christmas Eve will be the busiest day yet, with husbands hurrying in to buy something at the last minute. It was the same at the perfumery. That's the only thing I've missed, actually, making perfume.'

'That's quite a speech, Eliza. You are enjoying your job, though, aren't you?' James asked, stirring his drink thoughtfully.

'Yes, I am. Why, don't you enjoy yours?' she asked. He shrugged then grinned. 'Did I tell you I'll be finishing my apprenticeship come the New Year?'

She rolled her eyes. 'Only about a thousand times, James Cary. I think I should be getting back now,' she added, draining her mug. 'Nan was looking tired and, pot luck or not, I'd like to help prepare luncheon. No doubt you're hungry?' she teased.

He stared out of the window and frowned. 'The weather's closing in and, with Minty taking longer than ever to make the journey, I think I should be heading back. I need to speak with Father before I leave anyway, so I'm afraid my visit today is short,' he said.

Her heart plummeted. She'd really been looking forward to their time together and knew Grandfa Sam and Nan enjoyed sharing luncheon and listening to his tales about the tannery.

'Never mind, Guv said that as I've been working late each evening I can finish at noon on Christmas Eve,' James smiled. 'I should be here by mid-afternoon and we'll be able to spend the festivities together.' He reached out and took her hand. As he stared into her eyes, her heart flipped and this time, she didn't look away.

All that week the weather worsened, with snow blowing in from the hills. By Christmas Eve the pavements were coated white and although there was a steady stream of customers anxious to make last-minute purchases, they didn't dally. By noon all the boxes had been sold, and the window on Nan's side of the shop was bare. Grandfa Sam, looking ashen, began to cough and Nan insisted he close the shop.

'If it continues snowing like this, we'll have a white-out and there'll be no customers on the street anyway. Go and rest beside the fire, I'll tidy up here and then be up to make you a brew. Good job I took a basket of baking down to Jim earlier,' she muttered.

At the mention of James's father, Eliza ran over to the window and stared out. The sky was dark, with lowering cloud ominously threatening more snow, and everywhere was deserted.

'I do hope James gets here soon,' she cried.

Nan looked at her with wise old eyes. 'I rather fear he'll be lucky to get here at all, Eliza. Those hills up from Musby are steep and get blocked by snowdrifts.'

'But I've made him a cake,' she muttered, then realized how stupid she sounded. 'I hope he's all right,' she added, recognizing how much he had come to mean to her.

'Don't worry, he's a sensible lad. He'll only attempt the journey if he thinks he's a fair chance of getting through. Come away upstairs and we'll have a cup of tea. That'll make you feel better,' Nan said, covering the counter with a cloth.

The family Christmas Eliza had so been looking forward to didn't materialize. In fact, they didn't celebrate at all. Grandfa Sam took to his bed, coughing and spluttering. While Nan fussed over him, doling out liberal doses of linctus and rubbing his chest with liniment, Eliza found herself staring out of the window, willing James to appear. Surely if he'd really wanted to see her he would have found some way to get here, the gremlin in her head demanded. The day that should have been filled with joy and celebration crawled past and it was with relief they tamped down the fire and went to bed.

Although weak and still coughing, Grandfa Sam insisted on opening the shop the day after Boxing Day.

'Someone might be ill,' he said when Nan complained he should be resting. Nan raised her eyebrows but knew better than to argue.

The morning dragged, with hardly a soul venturing out in the abysmal weather. Nan spent the time showing Eliza how to make up new stock for the shop. Then they replenished the depleted shelves, setting out dishes of scented soaps and salts where the boxes had been. At noon, with not a customer to be seen, Nan persuaded the spluttering Sam to take his luncheon break first.

'I wonder if I should go and visit Jim. He might be running low on bread,' Nan muttered.

Eliza looked out at the snow-filled sky. 'I'll go, if you like,' she offered, suddenly wanting to be outside.

'I'm not sure, dear. This is a bad time of year for him, what with his wife going then.'

'Oh, how terrible to die at Christmas,' Eliza cried. 'Had she been ill for long?'

'Die? Ill? Why no, dear, I think you must have gotten the wrong end of things. His wife ran off with James's uncle Wilf, that's our younger son . . .'

'Hush thy mouth, woman.' Grandfa Sam's icy voice sliced the air, cutting Nan's explanation short as he hobbled back into the shop. 'We have no other son.'

33

The atmosphere in the rooms above the apothecary's was as frosty as the weather outside. The arguments between Grandfa Sam and Nan became increasingly bitter, reminding Eliza of life back home. She began to wonder if there was any point in ever getting married. Perhaps she'd stay single, like Fay, for the woman had always seemed happy with her own company. *Yes, so happy she couldn't wait to get rid of you*, a voice inside her head reminded her. Even James hadn't bothered to come to see her, she thought. Surely if he really cared he'd have found some way to brave the elements.

Grandfa Sam's cough showed no sign of improving, which didn't help his temper, and unless a customer braved the snow, he spent most of his time sitting beside the fire in the parlour staring into the flames. Although they were alone in the little shop for most of the time, Nan didn't say any more about James's uncle and Eliza didn't like to ask. It seemed to her that families meant trouble. She'd harden her heart from now on and concentrate on her work.

It was the middle of January before the weather began to improve. Eliza was in the kitchen helping Nan to prepare their luncheon from the meagre supplies left.

'I'll be glad when the fishing fleet can go out again and the butcher can get his supplies from the abattoir. Then perhaps we can have something other than soup,' Nan grumbled.

'Your wish is my command,' said a voice from the doorway.

'James! You did give me a fright creeping up on me like that,' Nan scolded, but she looked pleased to see him anyway.

Despite her resolve, as soon as she saw his dear face, Eliza's heart began thumping in her chest.

'Well, what kind of greeting is that, when a man travels through snowdrifts and scales icebergs to bring his favourite ladies some decent meat?' he laughed, placing a sack on the kitchen counter. 'There, a brace of pheasant, no less, plucked and ready for the pot.'

As Nan clapped her hands in delight and began inspecting his spoils, James turned to Eliza.

'I've missed you something terrible these past few weeks. You wouldn't believe the number of times I set out to see you, only to have to turn back,' he declared, gazing at her with those cornflower eyes.

Eliza cursed herself as she felt her cheeks flush. 'Well, it has been cold,' she conceded. He looked so crestfallen at her response she wished she'd held her tongue. Despite everything, she really had missed him more than she could ever have imagined.

A rasping cough cut through the silence.

'Is Grandfa unwell, Nan?' he asked.

'He's been real poorly since before Christmas. Nothing I try will ease that coughing for more than an hour.'

'Has he seen the quack?'

Nan sighed. 'You know your grandfa; he insists there's

nothing a doctor can give him he can't make up himself in his dispensary.'

'Thinks the apothecary can heal himself, eh? I'll go and see him,' James said, going through to the parlour without looking again at Eliza.

'Poor James, I think he was expecting a bit more of a welcome than that, Eliza,' Nan chided.

Eliza sighed. 'Well, he didn't hurry himself, did he?'

Nan stared at her in surprise. 'We've just had the biggest freeze in history, Eliza,' she reminded her.

'Besides, it seems to me relationships just mean hurt,' Eliza muttered.

'Whatever do you mean?' Nan frowned.

'Father bullied Mother, James's father got hurt, you and Grandfa Sam have been arguing so much I bet you wish you lived by yourself,' she burst out.

Nan stared at Eliza in amazement and the room was heavy with silence.

'Oh, Eliza,' she said sadly, 'I know Grandfa Sam and I have exchanged some pretty harsh words but underneath it all we love each other dearly. I was that worried when he was ill and couldn't bear to think of life without him.'

'Oh,' Eliza muttered, realizing at last that the woman's short temper had probably been masking her anxiety.

'To live without love must surely be a sad state of affairs.' Nan gave her one of her knowing looks. 'Now maybe I've misread the signs but you can't tell me you haven't missed James these past weeks.'

'Yes, but . . .'

'No buts. You can't wrap yourself in cotton wool in

case you get hurt. You're worth more than that and so is James.'

'I've been stupid, haven't I?' Eliza admitted.

'Not stupid, just a bit confused, maybe. Now a man needs a bit of encouragement – that's if the woman wants his attentions, of course,' Nan said, winking at Eliza then turning back to the pot. 'Relationships are a bit like a good meal: you take good ingredients, sprinkle them with seasoning to add interest, then stir regularly with love so that the flavours combine and develop harmoniously. Of course, you can have all the good constituents, but if they are thrown together any old how, left to get on with it, or ignored even, well, you can't be surprised if they separate, can you?'

Eliza stared at the woman as she took all this in, then nodded. 'Yes, I can see what you're saying.'

'So that's the end of your staying-by yourself malarky?' Nan asked, eyeing Eliza shrewdly.

'Yes,' she grinned.

'Thank the Lord for that. Now go and make the boy tea, then let him see some of that love I know is bubbling away inside you. I'll be in when I've given this meal some attention,' she said, looking meaningfully at Eliza.

James looked up warily as she entered the parlour, but she gave him her brightest smile.

'Tea, anyone?' she asked, going over to lift the kettle from the fire.

'Not for me, girl,' Grandfa Sam said. 'Happen I'd like a bit of a nap.' He turned away so she didn't see the wink he gave James.

'Perhaps we could go for a walk, if you wouldn't be too

cold?' James asked lightly, but the irony wasn't lost on her.

'I'd love to. I'll get my shawl. I've lined it with a piece of material left over from my cloak but it will be better if we can keep warm together.'

Beaming at the significance of her words, James jumped to his feet.

The wind was rising again as they hurried along by the harbour where the fishing boats had taken shelter once more. By tacit consent, they turned into Carla's café where the proprietress greeted them effusively.

'Ah, my *bambini* come in from the chill. I will get you my speciality chocolatina on the house, yes?'

Settled at their favourite seats beside the fire, James grinned at Eliza across the table. 'Better late than never,' he said, handing her a small package. 'It was meant to be for Christmas of course, but . . .' He shrugged. Carefully she folded back the paper and drew out a small purse.

'It's beautiful, thank you,' she whispered, stroking the soft leather.

'Made it myself from an off-cut at the tannery. Cleared it with Guv, of course. Thought with you making all that profit at the shop you'd need something to put your wages in.'

She smiled, wondering how she could ever have contemplated not seeing him again.

'That's thoughtful, but we'll need more customers if we're to break even this month. The weather's kept most people indoors.'

'I know. It's been driving me mad not being able to visit you. It wasn't the happy family Christmas we'd been planning, was it?'

She shook her head. 'Poor Grandfa's been really poorly and then he and Nan had a terrible spat and . . .' Her voice tailed off.

'That doesn't sound like them. What was it about?'

'It was about your uncle, but I didn't understand.'

'They didn't tell you?'

'Not really. Grandfa told Nan to be quiet,' she said, moderating the truth.

'It's a sorry tale. Grandfa and Nan had two sons: my father, James, known as Jim, and Wilfred. Father fell in love with my mother, Annie, they married and had me, but apparently she'd always had a thing for Wilf. Anyhow, they ended up running off together.'

'And she left you behind?' she asked, wide-eyed.

'Father made her choose.'

'Oh, James, that's terrible.'

'Well, I was too young to know much about it. Grandfa and Nan pitched in to help bring me up, but Father became bitter and turned in on himself. Don't get me wrong, he's a good chap, just wary of women – apart from Nan, of course. You can see why my mother's and uncle's names are never mentioned, though.'

Eliza nodded, suddenly understanding more about James as well.

'That's why you are so close to your grandparents.'

'Yes, they've been my steadying influence, I guess. And that's why I value their opinion,' he said, staring at her intently. 'Vowed never to get involved with a woman, but Nan soon put me right on that score,' he grinned ruefully, and Eliza couldn't help silently sending up thanks for the shrewd woman's advice. It would appear she'd been instrumental in sorting them both out. 'Well, water under the bridge as they say, except . . .' He paused and took a sip of his drink, then stared out of the window as if weighing up his next words.

'Go on,' she encouraged.

'Well, lots of things really. I'm fond of you, Eliza, and would like us to spend more time together. I went spare as a spindle not being able to reach you over the holiday, and it made me realize that long-distance relationships aren't a good idea. Obviously, you weren't as bothered.'

'I'm sorry for earlier. I was confused until Nan put me straight,' she explained. 'I really did miss you.' She paused, deciding it would be futile to say any more but the words poured out nonetheless. 'Why, I even made you a cake,' she cried.

His eyes lit up. 'You did?'

'Yes, it was full of currants and spice. Nan helped me and . . .'

'No, you clod,' he interrupted. 'Much as I love cake, I love you more.' There was silence while he sat there looking as shocked as she felt. 'I hadn't meant to blurt it out like that but I was pleased to hear you say you'd missed me. When I arrived earlier, I thought perhaps you hadn't.'

'I'm sorry, James. I'm not very good at displaying my emotions. I guess . . .' She was interrupted by Carla placing fresh drinks in front of them.

'For my two love birds. You sit there staring into each other's eyes and let your chocolatini go cold,' she admonished.

'Sorry, Carla,' James said. 'We haven't seen each other since before Christmas and have so much to catch up on.'

'Ah, well, I forgive you then and leave you to more lovey-doveys, yes?' she laughed, clearing away their old mugs.

'Perhaps you do show your emotions after all,' James laughed. 'Anyway, I've been thinking for some time now that I'd like to move back to Salting Regis. We could spend more time together, get to know each other better.'

Eliza's heart started thumping so loudly, she picked up her spoon and stirred her drink vigorously in case he should hear it.

'But what about your job?' she asked.

'I've finished my apprenticeship but my heart's not in tanning hides. Truth to tell, I only left here at Father's insistence. He thought I should spread my wings and get a qualification. Grandfa Sam thought it best, too, but I have found out I prefer making shoes and boots for local people, rather than saddles and stirrup butts for the farming community. Not that there's anything wrong with them, of course; I just like the more personal touch and besides . . .' He shook his head. 'That's quite enough of me. You must be bored rigid. Tell me, have you made any perfume recently? Grandfa said he offered you the use of his equipment.'

'Yes, that was kind, but with him being ill and Nan rushing round after him . . .'

'You've been the one looking after the shop,' he guessed.

She nodded. 'Not that many people have ventured out these past weeks. Still, come the better weather, when the flowers are in bloom again, I shall certainly take up his offer. I also intend seeking out flowers to try and match the fragrance in my black bottle. I told you about that, didn't I?'

'Numerous times,' he laughed. 'You believe it's important to follow your passion, don't you?' he asked, staring at her intently.

'Yes, I do,' she whispered, wondering what he was leading up to. He opened his mouth and she thought he was about to say something else, but he smiled and said it was time they were getting back. Feeling relieved yet disappointed, and not really knowing why, Eliza got to her feet.

As they made their way back to the shop, they heard the maroon being fired, followed by the pounding of feet on the cobbles. James stopped dead so that Eliza cannoned into him.

'Hey, careful,' she muttered, but James was staring transfixed as the rescue boat was launched. 'Come along,' she urged. 'It's time we were getting back.'

Reluctantly he nodded and followed her.

Next morning, the weather was brighter, bringing customers and all their news to the shop once more. A fisherman, desperate to feed his family, had set sail only to be caught up in a storm the previous day. The lifeboat had been launched and, much to the community's relief, the man and his boat had been rescued.

'Such brave men risking their lives, else poor Mrs Hook would have been a widow this morning, and her with thirteen mouths to feed,' one woman whispered to Nan. 'Waves washing right over the harbour wall, they were, then this morning sea's calm as a millpond. Beggars belief, doesn't it?'

'It does indeed, Mrs Cutler. Now what can I get you?' Nan enquired.

While Nan attended to the customer and Grandfa took her husband behind his screen for a consultation, Eliza tidied the shelves and thought about James. It was a shame he'd had to leave just as they were getting comfortable with each other. It had made her aware of two things, though. Although they'd spent many evenings walking around Follytown collecting flowers and chatting, they hadn't really found out much about each other. More importantly, she really wanted to get to know him better.

As if her thoughts had conjured him up, the little bell over the door tinkled and there he was.

'James, what are you doing here?' she cried, hurrying over to greet him. 'Did you not get back to Follytown last evening?'

'I did, but I've been busy since. Oh, Eliza, I have so much to tell you,' he said, his eyes bright with excitement.

An equally surprised Nan looked up from serving her customer and smiled. 'It's almost noon, Eliza. Take James upstairs and make a brew. I've left a plate of sandwiches ready, but kindly leave some for our luncheon too,' she said, wagging her finger at them.

'So what brings you here on a workday?' Eliza asked, once they were settled in the easy chairs with their mugs of tea.

'After I left you yesterday, I went back and watched the lifeboat. Those men were so capable and calm, even though the waves were breaking right over their boat. They're doing something worthwhile with their lives, Eliza, and it got me thinking.'

Eliza's heart nearly stopped. 'You don't mean . . .?' she whispered, hardly daring to go on.

'Well, it's early days. Before I can volunteer I need to be living in Salting Regis. You have to be on the spot when the maroon's fired, you see. Anyhow, I've spoken to Father and he's agreed I can work alongside him in his shop and have my old room back. The guv wasn't happy when I said I was leaving, but I've finished my apprenticeship so there was nothing he could do. He was more understanding when I explained I intended training for the lifeboats, though, and wished me well.'

'But isn't it dangerous?' she asked.

'Not if you do what you're told. They have very strict rules about safety and such. Anyhow, I've to speak to the coxswain this afternoon. Oh, Eliza, I'm so excited. If I'm accepted for training, I shall be doing something rewarding with my life. Plus . . .' He got up and pulled her to her feet, nearly spilling her tea over the rug.

'Careful,' she said, but he was too excited to pay any attention and, taking the mug from her, whirled her round the room.

'Don't you see? It means we shall be able to see each other every day after work,' he cried, grinning from ear to ear. His enthusiasm was so infectious, she couldn't help but smile back, even though a little knot of worry was coiling itself like a snake in the pit of her stomach. Could she really bear the thought of losing him now she'd finally found love? Didn't everyone she loved disappear from her life one way or another?

34

Sitting at 'their' table, chocolatini in front of them, Eliza listened as James told her he was to report to the lifeboat station for training the next day. He was so excited he could hardly sit still, and it was some moments before he noticed her lack of enthusiasm.

'I thought you'd be pleased for me,' he said.

'I am,' she answered carefully, staring down at her drink.

'But . . .?' he persisted.

'It sounds so dangerous, going out in heavy seas to rescue sailors who've themselves fallen victim of the same weather.' And everyone I get close to disappears, one way or another, she thought. He smiled and took her hand. *And I can't face losing you,* the voice in her head screamed.

'So you do care a little for me, then?' he teased. She swallowed down the lump in her throat and nodded. 'Well, that's good to know. And you needn't worry about safety. Most of the crew are seasoned fishermen used to sailing in all conditions, and there are cork lifebelts to wear. Besides, the lifeboats are now purpose built and self-righting since that tragedy when some of the boatmen perished. They were on service to a barque carrying emigrants bound for Australia and . . .'

'But what happens if you're out when it gets dark?' she interrupted.

'Oh, Eliza, you are a worry pot,' he laughed. 'The

lighthouses display leading lights to guide vessels into port. Now come along, drink up or Carla will be after us and we'll be up the creek without a paddle,' he laughed. 'Get it? Boats and up the creek . . .'

'If that was meant to be a joke, it was the worst one I've ever heard,' she admonished.

'I love it when you're angry,' he grinned. 'Those pretty hazel eyes of yours spark with gold and the way you're pouting those rosebud lips makes me want to kiss you right this minute.'

'James Cary!' she cried, peering around in case anyone had heard.

'Well, if a chap can't tell his girl how attractive she looks, then it's a rum deal. Rum deal, get it?' he chortled. 'Sailors' grog; rum . . .'

'James Cary, this boating lark's gone to your head.'

'Sorry, Eliza. I meant what I said about you being pretty, though.'

She snorted and lifted her heavy boot. 'With this? Hardly.'

He frowned. 'I think you make too much of that. Oh, I know you limp sometimes when the weather's cold or you're tired, but you really are an attractive young lady.'

'I wish you wouldn't tease me so,' she muttered, looking down at her drink.

'Seems to me someone's done their best to knock the confidence out of you,' he said. 'One day, I will make you see you are the most desirable woman in Salting Regis. Now, as Nan's given you the rest of the afternoon off, let's go and see Father and tell him my good news.'

She stared at him in surprise, remembering her last

visit. 'Apparently all I've been doing is talking about you and he said he'd like to see you again.'

This time James's father greeted Eliza with more warmth and was overjoyed to hear his son's news.

'That's grand, lad. You must be proud of him, Eliza,' he said, turning his gaze on her. She nodded but his eyes narrowed. 'You are pleased, I take it?'

'As long as he doesn't take any risks, though how I'll feel when I hear the maroon go up . . .'

''Tis your place to support him, my girl,' Mr Cary cut in.

'Hey, they haven't taken me on for definite yet,' James pointed out.

'They will, strapping lad like you. Why, you were practically born sailing and rowing. Eliza, why don't you make us some tea while James tells me more about his training?' he suggested, nodding towards the scullery.

Feeling she'd been dismissed, Eliza did as he'd suggested. The kitchen area was tiny, every surface littered with dirty dishes. She was really going to have to keep her fears to herself in future, she thought, automatically clearing away and giving the grimy surfaces a wipe before setting out the tea things. Carefully, balancing three full mugs, she made way back to the workroom. The men were deep in conversation but stopped abruptly.

'Have I interrupted something?' she asked. The two men exchanged glances then James shook his head.

'Father was just saying that now I'm working with him he might introduce a new line he's been thinking of making. Seems before he can start, though, he needs a small foot to measure. Unfortunately, mine's too big,' he said, laughing down at his size elevens. Eliza stared down at her built-up boots and grimaced.

'I'd offer but, as you can see, my feet wouldn't be much use.'

Mr Cary looked at her foot. 'Happen they'd do just fine, but to make sure, would you mind me taking off them boots so I can take a look?' Eager to do something right, Eliza placed her mug on the bench and perched on his stool.

'Nice bit of craftsmanship,' he said, studying them. 'How do you find they fit?'

'They're much better than the ones I had before, though I still walk like a clumsy clod, especially when it's cold.'

The man frowned then bent and placed her foot on his knee. He twisted it this way and that, then shook his head.

'Seen worse,' he finally muttered, handing her back her boots.

'Oh,' she said, slightly put out by his off-hand manner. Then she saw James watching her. 'Well, I hope that's been of help,' she added politely.

'Yes, ta,' the cobbler answered. Then he turned to his son. 'Well, you'd best let me get on if I'm to make a start on that new line.'

'Right, see you later then. Come on, Eliza, I'll walk you home,' James said.

''Bye, Mr Cary,' Eliza said. The man grunted, having already turned back to his workbench.

'Well, that went well, didn't it?' James said, as they made their way through the streets where the shopkeepers were closing up for the night.

'Do you think so?' she asked, recalling the way Mr Cary had rebuked her.

'Oh, yes, very well indeed,' James said, taking her hand.

Eliza saw little of James over the next few weeks and when they did meet, he looked tired and preoccupied. He blamed it on the new line his father was introducing and the extra hours he was putting in training now that the Lifeboat Institution had accepted him, but she wondered if she'd done something wrong.

Although business picked up in the shop, Nan seemed to be spending more time upstairs, leaving Eliza to deal with the customers. Whenever she asked Grandfa Sam if everything was all right, her questioning seemed to bring on a fit of coughing, making her wonder if she'd out-stayed her welcome.

One morning she decided she'd ask if they wanted her to move on but as she opened the parlour door to offer her prepared speech she was met with a chorus of

'Happy birthday!'

'Oh,' she gasped, staring at the smiling faces of James, Grandfa Sam and Nan. 'Is it my birthday?'

They burst out laughing.

'Indeed it is,' James said, kissing her cheek.

'But shouldn't you be at work?' she asked.

'No, today is a special day. Now sit down so we can tuck into Nan's special birthday breakfast. Then, if you eat up nicely, we might have a few surprises for you,' he said.

'Happy birthday, my dear,' Nan said, placing a plate of bacon, eggs and fried bread in front of her.

'And may you have many more, if it means we get fed

like this,' Grandfa Sam added, raising his mug. They all laughed and began eating.

'That was delicious, Nan, thank you so much. You have been so kind the least I can do is our dishes,' Eliza said, when they'd finished eating.

'You'll do no such thing on your special day, my girl,' Nan chided. 'You and Sam go and sit beside the fire while James and I clear the table.'

'But . . .' she began.

'I wouldn't argue, Eliza. I never do,' Sam said, sinking thankfully into his chair.

'How true,' Nan laughed, collecting up their plates and bustling from the room.

'Happy birthday, Eliza,' Nan said, reappearing moments later and handing her a neatly wrapped parcel.

'Why, thank you,' she cried, tearing at the string, then unfolding the paper. 'Oh, they're beautiful,' she whispered, holding up a sprigged cotton dress in peaches and cream along with a russet cape.

'I hope you like them, dear. That's what I've been making whilst you've been serving in the shop.'

'But this material must have cost you a pretty penny,' she murmured.

'You've earned it and, besides, we've not forgotten you donated that cloak of yours for the boxes. Think of it as a combined birthday and Christmas present, for we never did get round to celebrating, did we?' Grandfa Sam said.

'Thank you,' she whispered, stroking the soft material. 'This stitching is so neat it must have taken you ages to do. I really appreciate all your hard work, Nan,' she cried, jumping up and giving the woman a big hug.

'Hope I get the same treatment,' James teased, handing her a large box. Inside was the most beautiful pair of leather shoes Eliza had ever seen. They were a similar russet colour to the cape, fastened with the daintiest peach buttons. Her heart jumped, then flopped.

'These are gorgeous . . . but shoes?' Wordlessly she lifted her twisted foot.

'No buts,' James said. 'Take off your boots.'

She stared at him. He couldn't be teasing her, surely?

'Go on, girl,' Sam encouraged. James kneeled in front of her and gently eased the shoes onto her feet. They fitted perfectly.

'Right, now take a walk across the room so we can all see,' he urged. Hesitantly she got to her feet and took a few steps. It felt as if she was stepping on air.

'I'm walking properly,' she cried, but her words were lost amongst their cheers. 'I can't believe it.' She turned to stare at the grinning James. 'But how . . .?'

'Remember that new line Father was talking about? Well, that was for you. I explained the trouble you had walking sometimes and asked if there was anything we could do. That's why he wanted to inspect your foot,' he grinned.

'Why, you cunning . . .' she began, realization dawning.

'I was thinking more along the lines of clever, handsome young man,' he quipped, and Nan snorted. 'Anyway, Father said if we carefully crafted the leather, taking your shape into account, there was no reason why we shouldn't be able to make you a lighter pair of shoes. We burned many a candle till we got them right, I can tell you. Now go and put on your new finery. Today, Eliza, you are to be treated like a beautiful princess,' he declared.

'Oh, thank you,' she cried, throwing herself into his arms.

'Well, that sure was worth all those sleepless nights,' he laughed.

'But what if I get them dirty?' she asked, staring down at her shiny new shoes.

James rolled his eyes. 'Then we'll clean them.'

A weak winter sun was breaking through the cloud, casting yellow rays over the calm waters as they strolled around the harbour.

'This is the life,' Eliza exclaimed, revelling in their unexpected time together. What a contrast it was to the moor, she thought, thinking back to her birthday before last. Fay and Duncan had been so kind making a fuss of her special day. It had been the first time since Grampy died that her birthday had even been acknowledged, let alone celebrated. Last year had been horrible, with Amos suddenly disappearing from the perfumery, but now James was making a fuss of her. As if picking up on her thoughts, he turned to her and grinned.

'Happy?'

'More than I can say,' she said, nodding to a customer out walking her dog.

'And you're getting to know people too, which is good,' he commented.

He began telling her about the men he now worked with on the lifeboat and how friendly they were. Then he pointed to a large vessel below the boat station, explaining how it was being checked over in case it should be needed for a rescue. She could hear the enthusiasm in his voice, see the gleam in his eyes and realized just how much his confidence had increased since he'd begun training. He looked so handsome in his navy jacket and light blue shirt, his dark hair now neatly cut, just hitting the back of his collar, that her heart gave a flutter. She stared down at her new outfit and beautiful shoes and for the first time truly felt she was worthy of being seen with him. If only she didn't have this anxiety about his job hanging over her, everything would be perfect.

'Hungry?' he asked.

She shook her head. 'We've only just had that enormous breakfast.'

'That was hours ago. Come on, Carla's got a treat for you,' he said, his grip tightening on her arm as he led her carefully past all the fishing nets that were spread out to dry over the harbour wall, across the road and up into the lower town.

'Happy birthday, Eleesa,' Carla cried as they entered her little café. 'You look like ze handsome prince and princess today! Go and sit down and I will bring you the biggest ice cream sundaes you have ever seen, on the house, of course.'

'Thank you, Carla,' James said, leading Eliza to 'their' table. 'You do look lovely,' he added, holding out her chair for her. Her eyes widened in surprise. His manners were always good but now he was treating her like a lady.

'And how old is ze pretty girl today?' Carla asked, bustling back with tall glasses heaped high with swirls of different-coloured ice cream, topped with grated chocolate, nuts and a single, shiny cherry.

'Amazing,' said James, licking his lips.

'You no get any down your jacket or your Nana will be very cross with me,' Carla said, wagging her finger at him. Then she turned to Eliza and raised her eyebrows expectantly.

'Seventeen,' Eliza answered.

'Ah, that is the perfect age for ze lovey-dovey, yes? But not before you eat my special sundaes or they melt.' She winked suggestively before wiggling back behind the counter.

At the word 'seventeen' something niggled at the back of her mind, but not being able to remember what it was she giggled and picked up the long-handled spoon. She'd expected James to start eating straight away but instead he was looking at her in a way that set her body tingling.

'Penny for them?' she asked, to cover her confusion.

'Actually, I was just thinking how adorable you look and that I shall have to keep my eye on you or all the local swains will be after you, the swines,' he joked.

'Well, it's good you recognize that fact, James Cary,' she replied. Golly, had she really said that? It must be her new clothes and shoes, for in truth she was feeling quite grown up today, and the way James was staring at her made her sit taller in her seat. Smiling at him, she dug her spoon into her sundae and began to eat.

They were halfway through their ice cream when they heard the maroon go off. James was on his feet in an instant.

'Where are you going?' she asked, fear making her voice sound shrill.

'Answering the call,' he said, already heading for the door.

'But it's my birthday,' she cried.

'Sorry. I'll be back as soon as I can,' he called over his shoulder, and before she could answer, he'd gone.

'Ah, 'tis shame,' Carla sighed as Eliza rose to go. 'But he is brave man, yes?'

Eliza blinked back her tears and nodded. Surely they wouldn't expect him to go out on a rescue on her birthday, she thought, making her way back to the shop.

'I heard the maroon,' Nan said, looking up as the little bell tinkled.

'I was having a lovely time,' she cried. 'And after all the trouble everyone has gone to.'

'Now, young lady, don't take on so,' Grandfa Sam said, looking up from his weighing scales. 'James is risking his life to help poor souls in danger and needs you to be supportive.'

35

'Go upstairs and change out of your new clothes, Eliza. Then put the kettle on. I could do with a brew,' Nan said. With a last look at Grandfa Sam's set face, Eliza went upstairs. So much for her birthday and feeling grown up, she thought, prodding the fire until the flames blazed. She put the kettle to boil and had just donned her usual work dress and boots when Nan appeared.

'Don't mind Grandfa. Although he's proud young James has been taken on by the lifeboats, it rankles a bit. Sam set his heart on joining but even as a young man his health . . .' She shrugged.

'Wouldn't you have minded? Would you have let him?' Eliza asked.

'The answer's yes to both questions,' Nan declared. Eliza stared at her in surprise. 'When you are with someone, married or walking out, you don't own them. They are still their own person and you have to let them do what they want; show support, or resentment will build.'

'Even if you risk losing them?' she whispered.

Nan nodded. 'Nothing in life is guaranteed. If you don't mind my saying, Eliza, for someone with a good business head on her shoulders, you seem emotionally immature. Of course, I don't know anything about your upbringing. Perhaps you haven't had a woman's nurturing.' She gave Eliza a penetrating look.

'Mum always seemed to be pregnant, looking after babies or recovering, so my sisters Hester and Izzie brought me up, really. Then after many miscarriages Mother had two more children, by which time my sisters had gone into service and I was left to help with the little uns. Fay was more of a mother to me.'

'The woman on the moors, who took you in? Yes, James mentioned her. So you were a middle child, eh?' Nan observed. Eliza nodded, feeling forlorn, for in truth she'd never felt she belonged either with her older sisters or her much younger siblings.

'I've been so happy here but if you want me to leave then . . .'

'Love a duck, why ever would we? You do have some weird notions in that noddle of yours,' Nan cut in, shaking her head.

'You've both been so kind but I feel it's time I stood on my own two feet. Besides, I get the feeling Grandfa Sam is disappointed in me.'

'He's a strongly principled man. When Wilf ran off with . . . Sorry, I promised Sam I wouldn't mention this again. All I'll say is that since you came here our home is bursting with life again, especially as we've seen how happy you make young James.'

'You mean I can stay?' Eliza whispered, her heart lifting.

'Of course you can. Mind what I said about supporting your man, and we'll all get along fine. Now, go downstairs and help Sam tidy away for the night. He relies on your assistance now his legs are so bad, and with that cough . . . well, I don't know how much longer he can carry on, I really don't. I'm going to enjoy a cuppa then make some soup for when James comes ashore. He'll need something warm and nourishing.'

Eliza went down the stairs, pondering on all Nan had said. The bit about owning someone had finally jogged her memory, for hadn't Monsieur Farrant declared she was his and they would marry on her seventeenth birthday?

As she entered the shop, Sam looked up from his bench and gave her a level look.

'Sorry, Grandfa Sam,' she whispered. 'It's just that I love James and can't bear the thought of losing him. I will try and be more supportive.'

'Good,' he grunted. 'Now let's get cleared away. I'm dying for a cuppa.'

Eliza smiled inwardly. What was it about a cup of tea that made everything all right?

'So what do you think?'

Eliza blinked at Sam. Lost in thought, she hadn't realized he'd been speaking.

He sighed. 'I was saying that when I was looking through the back cupboard, I found some equipment that might be useful for perfume making. You're always poring over that receipt book you brought with you, and I thought it would be good for you to concentrate your thoughts on something productive.'

'That would be marvellous, Grandfa Sam. I do love helping here, but my passion really is for making scent.'

'I'd never have guessed,' he quipped, looking so like his grandson, her breath caught in her throat. 'Well, don't tell Nan I said this, but she's not getting any younger and, between you and me, I think she'd welcome more time to put her feet up. Bring that black bottle down tomorrow when you come. Happen we'll see if we can work out what that smell is you're always on about. It'll keep you occupied when the maroon next goes up.'

'Thank you,' she said, touched that he'd obviously been planning this whilst she'd been upstairs. 'I really will try not to nag James.'

Grandfa nodded.

They'd just finished clearing away when there was a hammering on the door. Eliza ran to open it and found James, water dripping from his sou'wester and oilskin coat, shivering on the step.

'Oh, you're all wet,' she cried.

'Sea gets a bit that way sometimes,' he teased. 'Just wanted to say we're back. We threw a line to a vessel that had gone aground and managed to tow her in. Sorry about your birthday, Eliza. I'll get Carla to make us another sundae on Sunday,' he grinned. 'Get it?' She shook her head in mock exasperation, but he was yawning. 'I'm away to my bed.' And with a quick peck on her cheek, he was gone.

Eliza tried not to get upset whenever she heard the maroon fired, turning her attention to her perfume making, but the sick feeling in the pit of her stomach would persist until she knew James was back on dry land. Queasiness and perfume making did not go together, she thought, ditching yet another failure.

Nan began spending more time upstairs leaving Eliza to deal with the customers who came and went, as well as helping Sam. Finally the weather improved and so did Sam's cough. However, his movements were becoming increasingly clumsy and he was finding it harder to reach the jars on the higher shelves. Eliza's offer to rearrange everything was met with a grunt, and she knew he was finding it difficult coming to terms with the fact he could no longer do what he had previously.

James helped her set up her own worktable with an old copper alembic Grandfa Sam had unearthed, and each evening she'd pore over Fay's receipts. In the quiet times between customers, she began distilling flowers she gathered from the little garden behind the shop. With daylight hours lengthening, she was able to widen her search, spending time after work walking the cliffs and nearby fields, searching for materials that might hold the answer to that elusive scent.

Both Nan and Sam had been unable to recognize the lingering trace in the black bottle. Sam's sense of smell had been impaired by his bad cold but he promised that, as soon as it improved, he would focus his attention on trying to match it to something in his little bottles.

'Never smelled a flower like that before, but it does seem familiar somehow,' Nan had declared, furrowing her brow. 'Blowed if I can put my finger on it, though.'

James was no help, wrinkling his nose and saying he preferred the smell of Nan's stew and dumplings. Eliza pretended to clout him over the head but, later, the savoury aroma of braising meat drifted down the stairs, making them smile.

'Right, you two, it's a lovely afternoon so take yourselves out for a walk whilst Sam and I snatch eighty winks,' Nan ordered after they'd eaten.

'Forty, you mean,' James laughed.

'Not when there's two of us,' Nan retorted, sharp as a butcher's blade.

Although there was a breeze, the sun was shining brightly from a clear blue sky and the birdsong from the trees was louder than the cry of the gulls as they made their way up the cliff track.

'I don't know why you insist on wearing those old boots,' James commented when Eliza stumbled on the rough terrain.

'Because I don't want to ruin my beautiful shoes,' she said, swooping down to pick some pink sea thrift, then placing them carefully in her basket. 'Haven't tried these yet, or those,' she cried, spotting yellow flowers and trying to avoid the thorny leaves as she picked some.

'Hmm,' James muttered, distractedly. 'I was talking to Father and he said it'll do your foot no good you walking properly in your shoes one day, only to change into those the next,' he said, pointing down at her boots. 'He says you're undoing all his good work and if you come up to the shop when you've got time, he'll see about making a pair of boots to the same design.'

'Oh, that is kind. I'll pay, of course.'

'And offend him! I think not. Golly, that's a large vessel out there,' he said, squinting out to sea. 'Cox was saying the other day that they're getting bigger and bigger.'

Not wanting to waste their precious time together talking about boats, Eliza linked her arm through his and led him back towards the fields.

'I love this time of year,' she cried. 'Everything's blossoming.'

'Yes, isn't it?' he agreed, staring at her with unfathomable eyes until she felt her cheeks growing hot and looked away. 'Ever the country girl,' he teased. 'And there was me thinking you'd become a siren.'

347

'A siren?' Eliza asked, shivering at the unwelcome reminder of a distress signal.

'All right, sea nymph then. With your long hair waving in the wind and those gold flecks glinting in your hazel eyes, all you need to do is sing beguilingly and you'll tempt the sailors to their doom.'

She shivered once again. 'Come on, let's get back. I'm dying to check Fay's receipt book to see if these flowers prove to be the answer,' she cried, eager to change the subject.

'Thwarted again, James Cary. There I was going to ask the girl of my dreams to spend her life with me, and she's more concerned about her blooming flowers,' he moaned, looking up at Eliza hopefully, but she did not appear to have registered what he'd said. Puzzled, he swallowed his pride. 'Never mind, tomorrow's Sunday and I've told Carla to have our sundaes ready.'

She smiled, relieved he'd changed the subject because she had been listening but was shocked and really didn't know how to react. Now Sam shut the shop on Saturday afternoons, she and James had more time to spend together, and although she was really getting to know him, she wasn't sure she was ready to take things further. Knowing his commitment to the rescue boat, she had to be sure she was strong enough to cope.

That night the wind rose, rattling the windows in her bedroom, screeching down the chimney. Then the rain came, hitting the glass like pebbles, and Eliza huddled under her covers, praying the lifeboat wouldn't be called out. For two hours the storm raged and then came the sound she'd been dreading.

Throwing her shawl over her nightdress, she ran downstairs and opened the front door just as another bang rent the air. She could hardly see through the driving rain but could hear the pounding of feet on the cobbles, men shouting, then the unmistakable sound of the lifeboat being launched down the slipway and into the harbour.

'Shut the door, Eliza,' Nan said from behind her. 'It won't do you or young James any good standing there letting in the wet. I'm going to make some tea, want some?' Eliza shook her head, feeling sick to the stomach. 'I find it helps to keep busy till they return so after I've taken a drink into Sam I'll set to and make a pan of hot broth. Why don't you light the globes and try out those?'

Eliza stared at the pink and yellow flowers she'd collected earlier and nodded. There was no way she'd be able to sleep.

All night long, as the seas heaved, so did her stomach. She began making her first distillation, but it was as though her curdled insides tainted the liquid. All the while her thoughts were running round her head like a hare on heat as she mulled over what James had said earlier.

Almost without realizing it, she'd come to love him dearly, but in her experience people she loved either went away or wanted her to go. She'd already lost her family, Fay and Duncan, hadn't she? Even Amos had gone away. Dare she risk losing James to the sea? Finally she came to the conclusion that, much as she loved him, she wouldn't be able to live with all this uncertainty. Pouring the unfinished concoction down the sink, she watched as the liquid drained away, taking her hopes for the future with it.

Come the morning, as was often the way, the wind had dropped and the water was as flat as a millpond. Eliza saw the rescue boat tied up in the harbour and knew what she had to do.

James was eating a bowl of porridge and talking to his father when she arrived at the cobbler's shop. His eyes lit up, when he saw her. Then, noticing her expression, he frowned and looked down at his dish. Mr Cary just grunted, then excused himself.

'I want to explain how I feel . . .' she began.

'It were a scary night, Eliza, but so rewarding to be able to help those poor souls,' he said ignoring her. 'Their vessel foundered on rocks and they would have perished if we hadn't reached them.' He shook his head, then yawned. 'Sorry, it was nice of you to come and make sure I was safely back, but I'll have to hit the hay before I fall asleep at the table. I'll get Father to wake me in time for us to go for our sundaes,' he added. The thought set her insides heaving again, but she knew she had to say what she'd come for.

'James, it's a brave calling you've answered and I really admire you for what you are doing . . .'

'But?' he asked, eyeing her in the same shrewd way Nan had the previous day.

She took a deep breath. 'But I can't stand the uncertainty. Every time the maroon's fired, my insides go crazy. I feel sick, can't eat . . .' Her voice tailed off as she saw him stiffen.

'You mean you're putting your feelings before my wishes?' he said so quietly she could hardly make out his words.

'It's not like that,' she protested.

'Looks like it from where I'm sitting.'

'Oh, you don't understand,' she cried, making for the door.

'Typical blooming female, taking off as soon as the going gets a bit tough,' Mr Cary spat, coming back into the room.

'I'm sorry,' Eliza began.

'We don't need your platitudes, girl. My James here is a fine fellow and you should be proud to support him. Had my doubts about you the first time I set eyes on you. Now get out of my house and don't ever set foot in it again,' he ordered.

She turned to James but he shook his head, and turned away.

Feeling sicker than ever, she headed back through the town, where church bells were pealing joyously. Dodging the Sunday worshippers alighting from their carriages, she wiped her tears and tried to harden her heart, but the memory of the despairing look James had given her wouldn't go away. Perhaps it was she who should get away. Grandfa Sam and Nan were James's family, after all, and it couldn't be easy for them having her living in their property, knowing she was unable to give him her full support.

With her thoughts whirling she found herself back at the shop before she realized it. To her surprise, although it was Sunday, the shop door was ajar. Thinking Nan must have decided to do some cleaning she pushed it open then came to an abrupt halt. Standing beside Grandfa Sam and Nan was a figure she hoped she'd never see again.

'Well, don't just stand there gawping, girl. Aren't you going to say hello?'

'Father? What the heck are you doing here?' she cried.

36

'That's a fine greeting and no mistake, and after I've brought Luke all this way to see his big sister,' he said, pointing to the lad by his side. Eliza turned helplessly to Grandfa and Nan, but they were looking bemused.

'How did you find me?' she muttered.

'Ah well, a bit of luck, that. We was on our way . . . well, somewhere. Anyhow, when the staging post stopped at Follytown I got chatting to a pleasant woman who was delivering something to the hostelry. When she heard my tragic story, she was only too happy to tell me where you'd gone. Apparently a Mr Farrant had found out you was here but decided you weren't worth pursuing,' he smirked. 'Mrs Buttons, this woman was called, said to be remembered to you. After that it was easy to find where you were working. ' He grinned, his yellowing teeth and triumphant sneer giving him the appearance of an ogre she'd once seen in a picture book.

'We'll be upstairs if you want us,' Grandfa Sam said.

Eliza nodded, hardly taking in what he'd said.

'What tragic story?' she asked, only too aware how her father could spin a yarn when it suited.

He sighed and clutched his chest. 'Your mother died in childbirth. Course, I always said she shouldn't have any more,' he moaned, and Eliza remembered then why she'd never liked him. Her poor mother never stood a chance with his constant demands, she thought with a pang. 'Then Timmy went and got that influ . . . in . . . well, that sickness thing, and was gone just like that.' He snapped his fingers.

'Oh, no, that's terrible. What about Hester and Izzie? Haven't they been back to help?'

Her father snorted. 'Selfish, callow cows. Couldn't care a cuss for their father or young brother. Left me to carry on by meself after the funeral. Said I was mean 'cos I wouldn't fork out for a decent burial, but like I told them, when you're dead you don't know, do you?'

Eliza shuddered. He was still as selfish and self-centred as she remembered. She crouched down beside her little brother, who was watching wide-eyed. 'Hello, Luke, do you remember me?'

'Course I do. I members yous smell. Sides, I'm a big boy now,' he said puffing out his bony little chest.

Eliza smiled and ruffled his short spiky hair, then got to her feet.

'Well, he seems . . .' But she was talking to thin air. Her father was nowhere to be seen. Running to the door, she peered up and down the street but he'd been swallowed up by the sea fret that was sweeping in. Frowning, she closed the shop door. It was then she noticed the bundle beside the counter.

'Father said I'm staying with you,' Luke grinned as she picked it up. So her father had it planned all along, Eliza thought, staring down at the scrawny little boy with his cheeky face. She didn't have the heart to disillusion him. It might be hard to manage, but rather nice having a member of her family with her at last. Sensing Luke was waiting for her to say something, she smiled.

'Are you indeed?'

'Of course he is,' Nan said, coming back into the shop. 'And I'm betting this young man would like some of my meat stew with dumplings,' she added, smiling down at Luke. His eyes widened and he nodded vigorously. 'Well, come upstairs and wash those grimy paws and we'll see what we can find.'

'I'm sorry, Nan,' Eliza muttered.

'It's hardly your fault, is it? I was looking out of the parlour window when I spotted that man hurrying down the street and guessed what had happened.'

'How will we manage?' Eliza asked.

Nan shrugged. 'The boy can share your room for the moment. I've got spare blankets and we can make him up a bed on the floor. I'm sure if we tell him it's an adventure, he won't complain. I seem to remember little boys love adventures.'

'Oh, Nan,' she said, throwing her arms around the big-hearted woman. 'Whatever would we do without you?'

Nan smiled then asked: 'And how was James?'

Eliza swallowed hard. 'I'm really sorry, Nan. Although I love him, I had to tell him I couldn't live with the worry and uncertainty every time the maroon goes up. Of course we will leave if you no longer want us here.'

'Oh, Eliza, that's a crying shame. It's admirable work he's undertaken and he's right fond of you.' She let out a loud sigh. 'But then we all are. Stay for the moment and we'll see how things work out.'

'Thank you, Nan. I feel dreadful about hurting James but every time the maroon is fired my stomach heaves at the thought of losing him.' She swallowed hard, seeing again the hurt in his eyes and vowed to seek other lodgings. Grandfa Sam would be sure to ask her to leave when he heard.

'Well, if that's how you feel, then there's nothing more to be said. At least you've played fair with him, but I guess he'll not be calling in so often now,' she sighed.

'Oh, Nan, I've really made a mess of everything. I'll find somewhere else for Luke and me to live.'

The woman shook her head. 'James will be all right. He has Jimmy and a roof over his head. Luke's lost his mother and been abandoned by his father. Poor lad's so thin he needs a few square meals and looking after. You've had a shock yourself, so it's best you both stay with us, at least for the time being. Who knows, a young boy around the place could be just what Sam needs to perk him up?'

Eliza smiled, feeling love for this big-hearted woman tinged with sadness for the loss of her mother. If only her father had more restraint she might not have died, she thought.

Later they watched Luke gobble down his food as if he hadn't eaten for weeks.

'Cor, that were tasty,' he said, running his fingers around the side of the dish and licking off the gravy.

'Well, if you promise to use your spoon instead of those fingers, I might be able to find some of my fruit crumble and custard,' Nan offered.

Luke's eyes nearly popped out of his head. 'Coo, we don't even get that at Christmas, missus.'

'Well, this is a special occasion having you come to stay,' Nan smiled. 'You can't go round calling me "missus", though. I'm Nan and that is Grandfa Sam,' she said, smiling at her husband as she got up to get their pudding.

'It must have been fun riding on the staging coach,' Grandfa Sam said.

'Yeah, we was on it for weeks and weeks. When we got to the hostelry, Father asked why we'd stopped. The driver said the horses was tired and needed a rest but Father said he hadn't time to waste and he should whip them and show them who was boss.'

Sam frowned, but Nan came bustling in with a large pudding bowl and Luke's attention was distracted.

'Goodness me, I don't know where you put it all,' Nan said, when Luke held his empty dish out for more. 'There's nothing of you. I've seen more meat on a butcher's pencil.'

'Pencils don't have any meat on them,' Luke scoffed.

'So they don't,' Nan smiled.

'You knew that really, didn't you?' he grinned at her, looking so innocent and appealing Eliza couldn't help but ruffle his hair.

'Gerr off,' he protested, but she could see he liked it really.

'Did you have anything nice to eat in the hostelry?'

Luke shook his head. 'Father was chatting to that Mrs Buttons. She said she was having a quick snifter whilst waiting to be paid and what her boss didn't know wouldn't hurt him. Father got all smiley then and said he wouldn't tell, so why didn't she have another? They was talking for ages. By the time we left all Father's money was gone so I never got no pie,' he sighed.

Eliza saw Grandfa Sam's mouth tighten and quickly got to her feet.

'That was a lovely meal, Nan, thank you. Come on, Luke, you can help me with the dishes while Nan and Sam put their feet up.'

Luke chattered away as they cleaned and stacked the dishes, but by the time they'd finished he was yawning.

'Early night for you, young man,' Eliza said, spreading out the blankets Nan had left in her room. He was asleep almost before she'd covered him over and, leaving the door ajar in case he should wake, Eliza went back to the parlour.

'Nan and I have been discussing things, Eliza,' Grandfa Sam said. 'Naturally you and the boy are welcome to stay, that goes without saying. Luke's a lovely but lively little chap and will need a firm hand, so we propose that you take over all Nan's duties in the shop while she looks after things up here.'

'I can't thank you enough,' she whispered. 'I'll make a success of downstairs and look after Luke when the shop's quiet. I can help you too, and work on my perfume.'

Grandfa Sam smiled. 'I can't deny your help would be appreciated.' Then his expression turned serious and he stared at her with his wise old eyes. 'Nan's told me you no longer feel able to walk out with James. I can't pretend I'm not disappointed because I am, particularly after all he's done for you. However, you're a great help around here, so we will respect your decision and see how things work out.'

'Thank you. I'm really sorry but . . .'

Grandfa Sam held up his hand. 'It's been an eventful afternoon so I suggest we turn in.'

Exhausted from her troubled day, Eliza fell into a disturbed sleep, only to be woken by the sound of sobbing.

'Luke?' she whispered.

'I'm lonely and can hear bears roaring. Can I come into bed with you?'

'Of course,' she said, putting out her hand to help him in. 'That's the sound of the waves you can hear.'

'What are waves?'

Eliza smiled into the darkness, remembering how the vast expanse of ocean had been new to her, too. 'It's the sound of the sea talking to the mermaids,' she said, stroking his hair. 'They are pretty ladies who live in the sea and sing songs to the sailors.'

'Like Mother used to afore she died?' he yawned.

'Yes, just like that, Luke. Would you like me to sing to you?' she asked, but he had already fallen back to sleep.

Eliza lay staring into the darkness, listening to the seas breaking against the harbour wall. Her heart gave a pang as she remembered her mother and little brother Timmy. She closed her eyes and prayed they were in a happier place, along with the new baby who'd never drawn breath.

Then, as the images of them faded and were replaced by one of James's handsome face, the tears she'd been holding back all day poured down her cheeks. Stuffing her fist into her mouth so she didn't wake Luke, she sobbed until she was spent. She truly loved James, of that she had no doubt, but in her experience loving meant losing, and there was no way she could bear the hurt again.

The following days fell into a pattern. Nan bustled around, happily taking charge of her household while Eliza took over the running of her side of the shop, using the lull between customers to make some more of Nan's fragrant soaps and salves. In any spare time, she experimented with her own perfumes and found to her delight that the one with the yellow flowers smelled quite uplifting.

It was helpful that Luke was kept busy. He adored Grandfa Sam and took to following him about like a shadow, passing him whatever he needed. Despite his rheumatics getting worse, Sam patiently showed Luke around the dispensary, even permitting him to measure out tablets on his weighing scales. Nan let him have scraps of leftover pastry or dough so he could cut out his own. When Sam was there, Luke was perfectly behaved, but whenever the old man went upstairs for a rest, the lad became bored and fidgety.

During her luncheon breaks, Eliza would take him out for a walk. He was fascinated by the sea.

'Cor, what's that smell?' he asked.

'That's what they call ozone,' she explained, remembering with a pang the time James had explained the same thing to her.

Then Luke's attention was caught by the boats moored in the harbour.

'What's them big flapping things?' he asked.

'Sails. When the wind fills them it carries them far out to sea.'

'Can we go on one?' he asked, his eyes sparkling.

'Perhaps, one day,' she said. 'Now, though, we'd better get back to the shop or Grandfa will use our guts for his garters.'

He giggled and her heart lifted. Even in the short time

he'd been here his little cheeks had begun to fill out and he was looking healthier.

As they wended their way back through the shops, Eliza's attention was caught by a figure unloading a bundle from a cart. She stopped abruptly, making Luke cry out.

'Oi, you just trod on me foot.'

But Eliza's attention was fixed on the young man and Luke's protest didn't register. There was something familiar about his movements, the shape of his head. It couldn't be? Then he looked up and she gasped. It was.

'Amos!' she shouted in surprise. Hearing his name, he stared at her, then grinned.

'Eliza! What are you doing here?' he asked.

'I was about to ask you the same,' she said, her smile turning to a frown as she took in his ragged clothes, thin frame and the sandy hair hanging around his shoulders. 'I thought you'd be at your new place of employment.'

'I am,' Amos said. 'Easy boy,' he added, turning to Luke who was reaching up and vigorously patting the horse's nose.

'Gently with him, Luke,' she admonished.

'Horse is all right, it's the lad's fingers I was worried about,' Amos said, giving Luke a smile.

'This is Luke, my younger brother. We're biding at the apothecary's over there,' she explained.

'You're not with Farrant, then?' he asked.

'He really wanted to marry me, can you believe?' she spluttered, shuddering at the memory.

'Thought as much,' he muttered. 'He flew into a jealous rage, accused me of becoming too familiar with you whilst he was away and sent me packing.'

360

'But he said you left to take up a new position.'

Amos snorted. 'What position? Without a testimonial I couldn't get another job, hence . . .' He gestured towards his horse and cart.

'But that's such a waste,' Eliza cried. 'Oh, Amos, that's terrible.'

'What about you? Couldn't you have finished your training before you left?'

'Not when he insisted I wear his ring. As I was leaving I found out what went on in that building in the garden. It was clear then he only wanted to marry me to cover his own activities.'

'Hey, driver, I pay you to deliver my victuals, not stand there gossiping,' bellowed a sharp voice from the shop doorway.

'Just coming, guv,' Amos called. 'Sorry, Eliza. I'd love to hear more but I must go,' he said, hefting a sack onto his shoulder.

'Why don't you come for supper? Nan always cooks masses,' she invited impulsively.

'Yeah, go on, mister. If you come it'll be a special ocas . . . occi . . . a special time and we has pudding then,' Luke piped up.

Amos grinned at him. 'How can I refuse such a tempting offer? Are you sure it'll be all right?' he asked Eliza.

'Of course, I'll go and tell Nan right now,' she said, taking Luke's hand and leading him away.

'Is he your fella, Eliza?' Luke asked as they made their way into the shop.

She shook her head and laughed. 'No, Amos is someone I used to work with.'

'I reckons he likes you 'cos his eyes went all funny when he saw you,' he grinned.

Amos hit it off with Grandfa Sam and Nan immediately, and the atmosphere around the table that evening was convivial. He showered Nan with praise, saying he'd never tasted such delicious apple pie in his life before.

'Get on with you, lad,' Nan chided, her cheeks growing warm at the compliment. 'Now come along, young Luke, it's time you were in bed. No, you stay here, I'll see to him,' Nan added as Eliza got to her feet.

'Are you sure?' Eliza asked.

'Sounds like you and Amos here have lots to catch up on. If you'll excuse me, I'll say goodnight, Amos. It's been lovely meeting you and you're welcome to call in whenever you're passing.'

'Thank you, Mrs Cary, and thanks again for such a delicious meal,' Amos said, standing politely and shaking her hand. 'Goodnight, Luke.'

'Night night, and do come again so we can have more pudding,' he grinned, and they all laughed.

'I was so touched when I found the perfume you made for me,' Eliza said as the door shut behind them.

'Did you like it? I remembered what you said and tried to make it smell like the fresh moors, woody heather and floral sweet peas,' he said, eyes shining as he stared across the table at her.

'It was better than I could ever have imagined, although I only got to smell it when Monsieur Farrant emptied it down the sink in a fit of temper. I managed to keep the little bottle, though, and have kept it safe along with Fay's black one.'

'Did you enjoy making perfume, Amos?' Grandfa Sam asked.

'Oh, yes, it was fascinating. Monsieur Farrant's a fine teacher but . . .' Amos shrugged.

'It's a shame both you and Eliza had your training cut short. Come and sit by the fire and tell me more about the distilling process,' Sam invited. Much as she would have loved to join them, Eliza knew she should clear away the dishes. It wouldn't be fair to leave everything to Nan.

By the time she rejoined them, Amos was on the point of leaving.

'Oh, must you go?' she cried.

'Regrettably, I have to be up before dawn to make my deliveries.' He turned to Sam. 'Thank you for your hospitality and kind advice, sir.'

Sam held out his hand and, as Amos took it, Eliza saw him pass over an envelope. Knowing how generous the older man was even with the little they had, she assumed he was giving Amos the price of a bed for the night.

37

Eliza was woken the next morning by a strange scrabbling sound. Prising her eyes open, she saw Luke looking through her flower book. She watched through half-closed eyes as he eagerly turned the pages. Wouldn't it be lovely if he shared her passion? But when he turned his attention to her treasure box she had to intervene.

'Hey, minx, leave that alone,' she admonished, getting out of bed and taking her pressed flowers and leaves from him.

'Why do you keep funny things?' he asked, wrinkling his nose as he took the top off the black bottle and sniffed. 'That's like that sea stuff,' he muttered.

'Pardon?'

'It smells like that ooh zone you was talking about.'

Then Nan called through that their food was waiting and Eliza's attention was diverted.

'Hurry up and get dressed or you won't have time for breakfast,' she said, knowing he wouldn't risk missing a meal. Much as she loved him, she knew he was proving a handful for both Nan and her to look after. After a long discussion they'd decided he should be enrolled at the local school and, after yesterday's escapade, she was hoping they'd agree to take him straight away.

Nan had developed a headache and gone upstairs to lie down. Knowing the smell of bluebells would help her,

Eliza had taken Luke up to the wood to gather some. Being early summer, there was a profusion of different blooms and she'd intended picking some to distil.

While she'd been busy selecting her flowers, Luke had run off. Worried he'd get lost she'd gone in search, only to find him happily scrabbling around in the rock pools on the beach. When they went home, Grandfa had read him the riot act, pointing out the dangers of the sea and forbidding him to play on the beach unaccompanied until he could swim. Luke had stuck out his jaw, looked mutinous, and played up for the rest of the day. He certainly needed the discipline and routine that school life would bring.

After breakfast, having made sure Luke was looking clean and smart, Eliza ushered the protesting boy along the busy streets towards the distinctive red-brick almshouses with their adjoining charity school.

'This lovely place is close to the sea, so if you're good we can spend some time there after classes,' she said, trying to placate him. But he just stared at the school and grimaced.

Sister Maria listened sympathetically and then agreed, as they had a place, he could be enrolled immediately.

'Thank you, Sister,' Eliza cried with relief. 'Behave yourself, Luke, and I'll be back when school has finished,' she instructed, trying to ignore the way he was glowering at her.

Reminding herself it was for the best and that she had shopping to do, she made her way to the market. It was a beautiful day and as she scanned the stalls, selecting the vegetables Nan had asked for, she felt as if a weight had been lifted from her shoulders. Although she was fond of her little brother, he was proving to be a wilful and unruly child. She hoped school would occupy his mind and the Sisters would be able to instil some of the discipline he needed.

Lost in thought, it was some moments before she became aware someone was watching her.

'Hello, Eliza.' The familiar voice sent shivers down her spine. She stared up at the gentle giant with his halo of curls and shook her head in disbelief.

'Duncan, what are you doing here?'

'I've been searching for you,' he told her.

She eyed him sceptically. Even though it was a hot day, he was wearing his old greatcoat and Fay's satchel was slung over his shoulder. He looked as out of place amongst the loud traders as a goldfish in a rock pool.

'Hey, you making a study of 'em 'ere veggies or are you buying 'em afore 'ey wilt?' the stall holder shouted, jolting Eliza back to the present. Quickly, she paid for the carrots, put them with the potatoes in her basket and turned away.

'How have you been?' Duncan asked, falling into step alongside her.

'As if you care,' she burst out.

'But I do,' he said. 'As I said . . .'

Eyes blazing, she spun round. 'If you cared for me you wouldn't have disappeared when Fay made arrangements to send me away,' she cried, the frustrations of the past months bursting out of her.

'Eliza, I really need to speak to you about that, and other things as well,' he said quietly, ignoring her outburst. 'Is there somewhere quiet we can go and talk?' He stared at her with those penetrating eyes the colour of darkest chestnuts and she felt some of her anger evaporate.

'I must get back to the shop. Nan will be wondering where I am. Come with me and we'll talk there,' she said, leading the way down the broad street.

Mr Cary, who was coming the other way, glared at her in disgust. 'Didn't take you long to find a replacement. Heard you had another one on the go. Women: can't trust any of them,' he muttered, shaking his fist at her.

'But . . .' she began. It was too late, though, the man was already stomping away. Duncan raised his eyebrows but she didn't feel like explaining.

As she showed him into the shop, Nan stared in surprise.

'This is Duncan, Nan. He's a friend of Fay. You remember I told you about her?'

'Indeed I do. Welcome, Duncan. It's good to meet you,' Nan said, seemingly unaffected by his strange appearance.

'You too, ma'am,' Duncan said, bowing deferentially. He looked so incongruous that despite herself, Eliza almost giggled.

'Duncan has something he wishes to explain to me,' she said.

'Go up to the parlour, then. The kettle's on the fender if you want a hot drink. Go on,' she urged, as Eliza hesitated. 'The shop's quiet this morning.'

Not sure if she was upset with Duncan or Mr Cary's outburst, she led the way up the stairs.

'Well?' she asked, as soon as he'd closed the door behind them. 'This had better be good.'

'Can we sit at the table?' he asked mildly. 'I have some

things I wish to show you.' She nodded and he took off the satchel and sank into the nearest chair, which looked ridiculously small under his large frame. He gestured to the seat beside him. Eliza remained standing and he shook his head. 'It might help if you sit too, Eliza. What I have to tell you is going to come as a shock.'

The look in his eyes sent a prickle of fear down her back and she perched primly on the edge of the chair furthest from him.

'I can't think I'll be interested in anything you have to show me,' she muttered. To her surprise, he reached across the table and caught hold of her hand.

'Fay is dead, Eliza,' he whispered.

'What? But she can't be. She was standing in the doorway when I left. She looked fine,' she cried.

'I'm afraid she knew she was dying even then,' he said gently. 'That was why she made arrangements for you to be apprenticed to Monsieur Farrant. She was very fond of you and wanted to secure your future.'

'But all this time I thought she didn't want me. I wrote a letter but tore it up, thinking she wouldn't be interested. I would have stayed and looked after her if I'd known,' she said, tears welling at the thought of the old lady, ill and alone.

Duncan smiled sadly. 'That's exactly why she didn't want you to know. She realized, you being kind-hearted, you'd insist on staying until she went. Not knowing how long she had, she didn't want you watching her waste away. Don't worry, I stayed until the end. It was all very peaceful, and afterwards I saw her buried on her beloved moor. I'm sure her spirit is skipping over them as we speak.'

'Oh, Duncan,' Eliza cried, gripping his hand tightly as hot tears rolled down her cheeks. He reached across the table and gently wiped them away with his kerchief. 'But why did you leave me?'

'I had to. I'd promised Fay I'd keep her secret and was worried I wouldn't be able to hide the truth from you.'

'But I thought you didn't care about me,' she burst out. He shook his head sadly.

'Oh, I did. I still do, I just didn't think it appropriate at the time to be too affectionate, little un,' he said quietly. Then he became brisk, drawing out papers from the satchel and handing Eliza a thick envelope. 'Go on, open it.'

She did as he urged, then gasped.

'But there's a wodge of bank notes in here,' she exclaimed, staring at him in amazement.

He nodded, then handed her a roll of illustrations all signed by Fay. She looked from the pictures to him and shook her head. 'They're exquisite.'

'Far from being a penniless recluse, Fay was born into a rich family who owned a mansion in Sussex by the sea. She proved to be a talented artist and was sent to train at the finest academies in London and Florence. During her travels she met and fell in love with a naval captain. Sadly, she'd just returned from the first exhibition of her paintings when she received word his ship had foundered in a violent storm.'

'Oh, poor Fay. That's a terrible thing to have happened,' Eliza whispered, dabbing at her tears.

'She was dreadfully hurt and completely went inside herself, shunned society and took off to live on the moors.

To ensure her wellbeing, her father deposited an annuity at the local bank but she only ever used sufficient for her needs. The rest she hid, along with her prized pictures, in the antlered head on the wall of her hovel.'

Eliza gasped. 'That old stag's head hid her treasures? Well, I never. But why me . . .?' She pointed to the envelope and pictures.

'She thought of you as the daughter she never had and wanted you to have them.' Eliza stared at the detailed illustrations of wild flowers. How had she got things so wrong? Clearly Fay had cared for her and hadn't just packed her off to Monsieur Farrant's, as she'd thought. If only she'd sent that letter then Fay would have known she appreciated all she'd done for her.

'But you were her closest friend so surely these should be yours?'

'Fay left me her hovel and everything else in it. She talked of you often and was only sad she never heard how you were progressing.'

'I started writing to her but thought she didn't care. Oh, if only I'd known,' Eliza cried. 'Monsieur Farrant said he sent her notification of how I was doing,' she added, remembering his promise.

Duncan shrugged. 'Perhaps his letter got lost. He never mentioned it when I visited the perfumery, asking to see you. In fact, he seemed upset about your disappearance and told me he couldn't understand why you'd run off.'

Eliza snorted. 'More like he was upset I'd spoiled his plans. He wanted me to marry him, you know.' Duncan raised his eyebrows but she shook her head. 'It might sound ridiculous but I know his reasons weren't honour able,' she added, remembering what she'd seen the night she left.

'Whatever do you mean?' Duncan asked.

'Don't worry about it. I'm settled here now and, with Grandfa Sam's help, am carrying on my perfume making. Luckily I learned enough from Monsieur Farrant to be able to work on the receipts Fay gave me.' Then, as a memory struck, she burst out laughing. 'She was canny and knew Farrant wasn't to be trusted 'cos she gave him only half of the book she promised him.'

'She must have been suspicious for it wasn't like Fay to break her word.'

'And how are Ben and Rose?' she asked, remembering her dear friends.

'Ah,' he murmured, shaking his head. 'Don't see much of them now. Mother Evangaline in her wisdom insisted on having her own cottage built on the farm so she could see more of young Joshua. She also hired a full-time hand to help out on the farm. Still, Ben and I meet at Dulvester market each month, which gives him a chance to get things off his chest,' he grinned.

'Oh, poor Rose. Do give them my best wishes,' Eliza said.

Duncan nodded. 'Look, I hate to leave you so soon after imparting the sad news about Fay but I must go. If you need me at any time, you'll find the address of the hovel inside the envelope. Be happy, my little Dryad,' he said getting to his feet.

'But you can't go. I love you,' she cried, panic rising in her breast.

371

He smiled sadly. 'And I love you, Eliza, but you're no longer the country bumpkin who lived on the moors. You've grown into a beautiful young woman who suits this way of living. My home is the woods and I only ventured on that noisy staging coach because Fay made me promise to carry out her wishes. Although I wanted to see you again, of course.' He shrugged. 'But I can't stay. All these buildings and hundreds of people milling around make me feel hemmed in.'

'But I will see you again?' she asked.

'Be happy, Eliza Dryad,' he whispered, bending down and kissing her cheek. Then he put the old satchel over his shoulder and quietly left the room.

It was only as the door shut behind him that she realized he hadn't answered her question. She put her hand to her cheek. His kiss had left her feeling warm and cherished, but not tingling and on fire. In that instant, she realized the love and emotion she felt for Duncan was deep and gentle. She looked up to him as a daughter should her father. It was different to the overwhelming passion she felt for James.

As tears welled again, she buried her head in the cushion, seeing his smiling face and bright blue eyes. How she wanted to be with him, needed to be by his side. The only way she could ever win him back was by convincing him she'd try to overcome her fear of the summons of the maroon. But could she?

'Are you all right?' Nan said, bustling into the room. 'Only I saw your friend leave and when you didn't reappear . . . oh,' she gasped, staring at the pile of bank notes.

'I think this is what they call a legacy,' Eliza whispered, scrubbing her face with her hands.

'Blimey O'Riley, no wonder you're shocked,' exclaimed the usually mild Nan, glancing at the little clock on the mantel. 'It's nearly noon and the shop was empty when I came up, so I'll get Sam to lock the door and you can tell us all about it over luncheon. I'm sure you'll feel better for a cup of tea.'

As Eliza outlined the reason for Duncan's visit, Grandfa Sam listened carefully.

'Well, well,' he chuckled. 'We have our very own heiress under our roof, Nan.' Then he became serious. 'I'm sad for your loss. It sounds as though this Fay was a lovely woman who didn't let her bitterness stand in the way of helping others. Have you counted that money?'

'Well, no,' Eliza admitted.

He clicked his teeth. 'First rule of business, Eliza, is know your assets, otherwise how can you plan effectively?'

'Pardon?'

'You've been talking about getting your perfume business off the ground and now you have the chance. That money will pay for rental of suitable premises and the equipment required in setting it up. I took the liberty of smelling your latest creation and it's quite good, but if you want to go into production, you'll need to make more than a pot. You'll have to buy a decent-sized still.'

Eliza looked at the dear man with his sensible business brain, her heart sinking. 'You want me to leave?' she whispered.

'Not necessarily,' he said. 'As you know my old body's

not up to the demands of running an apothecary's any more and I've been thinking of retiring. Happen I need to do a bit of rethinking about my plans,' he said enigmatically. 'Now, first things first, count those notes then I'll enter the amount on the first page of a new ledger and lock the money in the safe.'

'These pictures are beautiful, Eliza,' Nan said. 'That Fae was a talented lady and she's signed every one too. It's an unusual way of spelling her name – F. A. E. – don't you think?'

'Oh, I hadn't realized,' Eliza said, her mind still spinning with shock from the woman's death and the amount of money she'd been left.

'While Sam locks that envelope safely away, you'd best go and collect the young rascal up from school.'

'Goodness, is that the time?' Eliza gasped, jumping to her feet.

As she sped through the town, the salty tang of the ocean wafted her way. She inhaled again. Although it wasn't quite the same as the lingering fragrance in her black bottle, she could see what Luke had been getting at. The sea breeze cleared her head and lifted her spirits but when she reached the school, Luke greeted her glumly.

'Had a good day?' Eliza asked.

He scowled and shook his head. 'Not going back again,' he declared.

'Look, the tide's out, why don't we go over to the beach and you can tell me about your day?' she suggested. Immediately he brightened and moments later was haring along the sand, kicking at the piles of seaweed.

Her thoughts returned to James. She would go and see

him, for after much thought she knew her love for him was greater than her fears, and in future she would make more effort to control her feelings.

'Hey, Eliza,' Luke called, breaking into her thoughts. She looked over and saw he was holding up some seaweed to his nose.

'This smells even more like that stuff in your bottle,' he cried, presenting her with the string of shiny weed.

She leaned forward and inhaled deeply. Then she smelled it again. Maybe Luke had something after all, she thought, gathering some to take home. She hadn't been getting anywhere with her flowers so it was worth a try, wasn't it?

'Luke, I could kiss you,' she cried.

'Yuk, I'd sooner be back in school,' he muttered, taking off along the beach.

38

It wasn't until Luke fell asleep that Eliza had time to reflect on the strange events of the day. Then she lay back against her pillow and let the tears come. She'd been fond of Fae and would always be grateful for the kindness she'd shown in taking her in and encouraging her to believe in herself. If only the woman had confided in her so that she could have looked after her during her illness. She'd never even had the opportunity to thank her for her incredible generosity in funding her apprenticeship. And now she'd left Eliza a sizeable legacy along with her beautiful pictures.

It had been wonderful to see Duncan. Dear, sweet Duncan, who'd made sure he kept Fae's secret, then ventured all this way from his beloved woods to find her as he'd promised. She would always remember him with affection, and be grateful for all he had taught her. He was right, she had grown up and now she understood the feelings she had for James were the grown-up love of a woman for a man.

James! She sat bolt upright in bed and stared out at the moonlit night. In the excitement of discussing her future plans with Grandfa Sam, and then her discovery on the beach, she'd forgotten to go and see him. As soon as she'd dropped Luke off at school tomorrow, she would visit him and explain everything. She just hoped she hadn't left it too late.

Next morning, as if he was sensing her impatience to be away, Luke took his time over breakfast, moaning about having to go to school until Grandfa Sam looked at him sternly.

'So you don't want to be an apothecary, like me?'

'Course I do, which is why it's a waste of time going to school,' he declared.

'Right, so know your sums, do you?'

'No, but . . .'

'And you can read and write?' Grandfa continued on relentlessly.

'Not yet, but I can roll out and cut tablets,' he said, puffing out his little chest.

'Indeed you can, lad, and that's a great start. However, in order to become an apothecary, you need to be able to count so you can make up medicine and measure out the correct doses. You'll need to be able to read so you know what ingredients to use and you need to write so you can pen the instructions for the patients, many of whom are unable to do it themselves.'

Luke thought for a few moments then grinned. 'All right, if I go to school today and learn all this stuff, can I work in your dispensary tomorrow?'

'When you can read, write and do your sums then you may join me,' Sam agreed, winking at Eliza.

'Come on, Eliza, hurry up,' Luke cried, suddenly eager to be away.

No sooner had they reached the school than Luke dashed inside. Shaking her head, yet relieved he had listened to Grandfa Sam, Eliza hurried to the beach. Although the sea was on its way in this morning there was still weed

377

strewn along the tide line. Quickly she filled her basket, inhaling the distinctive briny scent. She couldn't believe she hadn't made the connection that Luke had. Excitement tingled at the thought of trying her hand at this new perfume, for surely it would match the one in the black bottle? As soon as she'd finished here, she would go and visit James, apologize for her behaviour and promise to try to overcome her fear.

Her heart singing at the thought of seeing him, she set to filling her basket with the shiny weed. She was just stamping the sand from her boots when, as if her thoughts had conjured him up, James came striding down the other side of the street. Her heart gave a jolt.

'James,' she called, hastily dodging horse-drawn carts and carriages as she tried to cross the busy thoroughfare. In her haste, her foot twisted and she tripped just before reaching him. His hand shot out and drew her safely onto the pavement.

'If you wore those shoes we made you wouldn't stumble,' he said gruffly.

'But they're much too nice to wear on the beach. Oh, James, I've missed you so much. I was coming to see you later.'

There was a momentary spark in his eye, then his expression became stiff as a mask. 'To tell me your glad tidings?' he scoffed. 'You needn't bother. Father has already told me about curly-haired Duncan.'

She stared at him in surprise. 'Duncan?'

'He heard you call his name,' he said, glowering.

'But you don't understand . . .' she began.

'That you found a replacement so soon? No, I don't.

But you needn't worry about me, if you ever did.' He gave a harsh laugh. 'Anyhow, no time to waste, I'm on my way to join the others for training with the breeches buoy. They, at least, know what loyalty is,' he spat over his shoulder.

'But you've got it all wrong . . .' she called, but he lengthened his stride.

Stunned by his antagonism, she watched his retreating back. After a moment she made to follow him, then stopped. Nan would be waiting for her to take over in the shop. Sighing, she crossed back over the road. She'd call and see him at the cobbler's after collecting Luke from school. The misunderstanding needed sorting out before she could tell him about her decision.

When Eliza got back to the shop, Nan insisted she get on with making her perfume while she served the customers.

'To tell the truth, I'm finding it a bit lonely upstairs without young Luke to mind. A good chinwag will do me the world of good,' she declared. 'I can keep an eye on Sam at the same time. He's getting clumsier by the day and I'm beginning to think he should retire sooner rather than later.'

'Well, let me know if you need me,' Eliza said, wrapping a clean white apron around her, then eagerly beginning her preparation. Her thoughts still on James, she chopped the seaweed and made a distillation. It produced a curious aroma and she tried blending it with a few drops of the one she'd made from the pink flowers. Inhaling deeply, she shook her head: that didn't work well at all. Just like her attempt to talk to James, she thought. Then she tried mixing the seaweed distillation with some from the yellow flowers. That was better but still not the result she'd hoped for.

Disappointed, she was about to throw the liquid away

when the doorbell tinkled and Amos appeared. He was smartly dressed in a grey high-buttoned frock coat, stiff choker collar and knotted tie, and his hair had been cut.

'Amos, you're looking very smart. What are you doing here?' she asked, her mood lifting at the sight of her friend.

'I have an appointment with Mr Cary,' he answered.

'He has a customer with him.' She pointed to the partition.

'I'm early so I'll wait, if I may?' Eliza nodded and was about to ask him what had brought about the change in him, when he came over to where she was working.

'Something smells, er, interesting,' he said, sniffing the air. Then he pointed to her alembic. 'Cripes, that's old-fashioned, isn't it?' he laughed.

'I know, but I'm hoping I'll be getting a new one soon.'

'Lucky you! What are you brewing?' he asked, bending over her jar of liquid and inhaling deeply.

'I'm trying something new. What do you think?' she asked.

He wrinkled his brow. 'Erm, it's quite nice, but a bit bland and one dimensional, don't you think? A bit Schubert,' he proclaimed.

'Pardon?'

'Unfinished. Remember, Mademoiselle, the perfume, it should have all the notes of a symphony, non?' he intoned in a perfect imitation of Monsieur Farrant.

'Of course,' she said, shaking her head. How could she have forgotten? Amos dipped a paper into the jar and waved it in the air between them.

'Non, Mademoiselle, this will not pass the test,' he imitated, wagging his finger at her.

As they dissolved into hysterics, the little bell tinkled. Looking up, she saw James had entered the shop and was staring at her in disgust.

'I thought I might have been hasty earlier, but now I see even Father underestimated your appetite for men,' he said, his voice so cold it sent shivers spiralling down her back.

'Hey, that's not fair . . .' Amos replied.

'James, it's not what . . .' Eliza began. But James had gone, slamming door behind him, setting the little bell jingling and jangling.

'James,' Eliza shouted, hurrying after him, but he'd been swallowed up in the crowd and she couldn't see any sign of him.

Upset by his accusation, she took herself back inside just as Nan came scurrying in to see what the fuss was about.

'What's going on? Oh, Amos, how lovely to see you, though you could have been gentler with my poor bell,' she said.

He laughed. 'Sorry, Mrs Cary. May I thank you again for that delicious meal the other evening?'

'It was my pleasure, Amos. Sam won't be long, so you go on up and pour yourself a cuppa.'

'Thank you. You all right?' he asked.

Seeing the concern in his eyes Eliza forced a smile and nodded.

'Next time, try drying that weed before you use it; it might help,' he suggested, making his way towards the stairs.

Her upset at James's outburst turned to anger and Eliza

slammed the jar down on the table. How dare he say such nasty things? She wasn't sure she wanted to walk out with someone who jumped to conclusions all the time. Mr Cary's bitterness had obviously rubbed off on him. Well, she wasn't going to waste her precious perfume-making time fretting, she thought, pushing his harsh words to the back of her mind and turning her attention back to her creation.

Inhaling her mix again, she had to agree it wasn't right and was definitely lacking something. But the question was, what? She referred to Fae's book but couldn't find anything relevant to the plants she'd been using. Perhaps she should try drying the seaweed, as Amos had suggested. As she sat mulling over what he'd said about blending and notes, Grandfa Sam emerged with his customer.

'Two twice a day should cure that, Mr Jackson,' he instructed, handing over a bottle. As the little man scurried from the shop, Grandfa Sam turned to Nan, who was dusting the shelves. 'Did I hear young Amos?'

'He's waiting for you in the parlour, Sam.'

'I'd better go on up then. How's it going with you and that seaweed, Eliza? There's certainly been some unusual aromas wafting around in here this morning,' he grimaced.

'I'm sure I'm on the right track but it's not quite there yet,' she sighed.

'Oh, well, don't be disheartened. Even mighty oaks come from little acorns, don't they?'

'Grandfa Sam, you're a genius,' she cried, jumping to her feet and snatching up her basket. 'Nan, can you manage without me for a little while?'

The woman looked around the empty shop. 'Think I can handle this rush,' she quipped.

Eliza hurried up to the big oak tree in the woods behind the little town, her mind going into overdrive as she gathered up the bright green velvety plants growing to the north of its base. Only when her basket was filled did she pause for breath.

A cuckoo calling from somewhere nearby reminded her of Grampy, and how he'd told her about the parent laying its egg in another bird's nest, expecting it to feed and look after its chick when it hatched. She sighed. Wasn't that what she was: an interloper in Grandfa and Nan's home? They'd become like grandparents to her, looking after her and guiding her. But they weren't getting any younger and, with Grandfa's health failing, Nan wanted him to give up work. Then there was Luke, a lovable but strong-willed child who tested them all to the limits. Now she had Fae's money, surely it was only fair to move out and give them the peace and quiet they deserved? Perhaps she could treat them to a holiday, offer to look after things whilst they went away? Goodness knows, she should do something for these dear people who had shown her so much kindness.

She wandered back through the fields where the bluebells were already wilting. One minute they were waving about in all their beauty, the next they faded and disappeared. Just like everyone she cared about, she thought, the crash of the waves pounding the beach below reminding her of the last time she'd been here with James. He'd been so loving then, and nothing like the tight-lipped man who'd stormed out of the shop today, she thought, hurrying back towards the apothecary's.

To her surprise Grandfa Sam and Amos were bent over the worktop in the dispensary.

'Nan's gone to collect young Luke from school so put that basket down and come over here. I've things I wish to discuss,' Sam said.

Pulling up a chair, Eliza glanced at Amos, who winked back.

'Right,' Grandfa Sam said. 'As you both know, my health is not what it was. Nan has been nagging me for ages to retire, but of course there is the running of the shop, the income from which keeps us in food and pays our rent.'

'I was thinking about that, Grandfa. Now I have that legacy I feel Luke and I should do more to help. Perhaps I could invest in your shop? Or we can move out and rent somewhere to live?'

'I agree you should pay rent, Eliza,' he said. 'That's what business people do.'

Although she smiled, her heart sank. Before she could ponder where she could go, Grandfa Sam was talking again.

'Now, young Amos here is a clever lad, eager to put his training to good use.' He paused as Amos beamed and nodded her way. 'And you're a bright girl with a very good nose, so combine the two and what do we have?'

'Two bright, eager people, ready to run your shop and dispensary,' Amos supplied.

'Exactly, and once you have learned the trade, that is exactly what I see,' Sam agreed.

Eliza stared from one to the other, certain she was miss-ing something. 'You mean I can stay here?' she asked.

'Of course,' he replied. 'My proposal is to rent one half of the shop to you, initially for making and selling Nan's soaps then, later, your perfumes. Meanwhile, I shall train

Amos up as an apothecary with a view to him taking over the dispensary side.'

Eliza stared from Grandfa Sam to Amos in disbelief. 'Really? You hatched all this up this afternoon?'

Sam laughed. 'Not exactly. When I saw how interested young Amos here was in my work, I invited him over for a discussion. He is keen to learn and take over from me, and his previous training will give him a good foundation on which to build.'

'And I can help you find the missing notes to your symphony,' Amos added.

'Well, I don't know what to say,' Eliza said, her heart swelling with happiness.

'Of course, a good businesswoman would have asked by now how much rent she would have to pay,' Grandfa Sam pointed out, his eyes twinkling with amusement. 'I'm going to leave you two to discuss how you propose working together in the future,' he said, then turned to Eliza. 'Talking of which, have you spoken with young James yet?'

She shook her head, her heart sinking. 'I've got to sort things out in my mind now and then I need to go and see him,' she replied.

He stared at her with wise old eyes. 'Don't leave it too long,' he advised, then made his way laboriously up the stairs.

'This James, I take it that's the chap who glared at me earlier?' Amos said.

'Yes, we were walking out and everything was fine until he volunteered for the rescue boats. Hearing that maroon go off makes me feel sick to the core and I called things off.'

'Well, it's a fine institution and he must be a brave man. Even if he has dashed my dreams to smithereens,' he said, putting his hand on his heart.

'Oh, Amos, I'm sorry, I do like you but . . .'

He smiled gently, stopping her from saying more. 'Come on, let's talk about our fantastic opportunity then. Aren't you excited?'

'Very, although it hasn't really sunk in yet,' she replied, shaking her head. 'Grandfa Sam is so generous.'

'He is. I couldn't believe it when he slipped me that envelope the other night. The note suggested I use the money to buy new clothes and then come back for an interview. He didn't know me from Adam and yet he offered me the opportunity to make my way in life again. He's truly a good man.'

'Yes, he is,' she agreed, thinking the man's generosity knew no bounds. 'I'm still having difficulty grasping all he's done for us,' she whispered, staring around the little shop.

With its two bay windows and the door in the middle, it afforded them space to run their businesses independently yet together.

'It's absolutely perfect,' she enthused. 'And running Nan's business whilst I build up my own perfume side of things will give me the opportunity to earn as I learn. Grandfa Sam has thought it all out.'

'I'm pretty pleased with my deal, too. What's in the basket?' Amos asked, going over to her work table. 'Ah, Mademoiselle, you have been listening to what I say about the extra notes. Soon you will have the symphony, non?'

'I hope so,' she said. 'I'm going to start straight away.'

Amos frowned. 'You'd be better off letting those dry

out first, too. They'll be more potent then and you'll get a better result.'

'Oh, Amos, what would I do without you?' she cried, tipping out the leaves and spreading them out to dry.

'That's what I was trying to point out earlier,' he said, sighing and looking so serious Eliza's chest tightened. Then he gave a wink.

'Amos, you do tease so. Are you joining us for supper?'

'No, thanks. Nan's given me the name and address of a woman who runs a boarding house near here. Sam's written out a testimonial as my prospective boss, so fingers crossed, eh?'

'Good luck, and I'll see you tomorrow then. It's going to be fun working together again, isn't it?'

'Bet you're only saying that so that you can avail yourself of my superior knowledge,' he grinned.

As the bell tinkled behind him, Eliza looked around the space that until now had been Nan's domain, and sighed with pleasure. Her own business – she could hardly believe it. Life was on the up and no mistake.

How she longed to share her news with James. The only cloud on the horizon was her falling-out with him. Tomorrow she would go and see him and tell him she'd really try to overcome her fear of the call of the maroon. She just hoped he'd listen to what she had to say and realize she meant it.

Next morning, whilst Sam was busy in the apothecary with Amos, Eliza replenished her dishes with the soaps, salts and salves Nan had let her buy. The woman hadn't wanted to take anything for them, but Sam had insisted, explaining Eliza needed to learn about the costs of setting up and running a business. He'd also offered to help manage her legacy and was going to make an appointment for them to see the manager of his bank. In the meantime, he'd suggested Eliza make a list of the equipment and materials she needed.

After dealing with a couple of customers, she settled at her work table behind the counter and began sorting the partly dried plants, impatient to get distilling. She became so absorbed in her task, the sudden bang from the maroon made her jump so that she nearly toppled from her stool. Stomach churning, she walked over to the door. She couldn't see the water, of course, but she could hear the familiar pounding of feet on the cobbles and knew James would be amongst the men racing towards the lifeboat. Heart heavy, she returned to her work but couldn't settle. Even the encouraging scent coming from the alembic didn't help. She got up and prowled around, rearranging the soaps and changing the displays around.

Then the shop door flew open and Nan stood there, white with shock and shaking her head.

'It's Luke,' she gasped. 'He absconded from school when the Sisters weren't looking and he's taken one of them little boats out.'

39

Eliza ran over and put her arm around the trembling woman.

'Come and sit down, Nan,' she urged, leading her towards a chair.

'What's going on?' Amos asked, thundering down the stairs, followed more slowly by Sam.

'It's Luke,' Eliza cried. 'The little fool's taken one of the boats and he can't swim.'

'That's not all,' Nan said, having regained her breath. 'The lifeboat's gone out after him, but the wind's now gusting to gale force and the waves are sweeping Luke towards the rocks.'

'Oh, no, I must go down to the harbour; make sure they're safe,' Eliza cried, making for the door.

'I'll come with you,' Grandfa Sam said.

'No, let me, sir,' Amos insisted.

The harbour wall was crowded with people, all silently peering out to sea and waiting. Amos elbowed their way through until they reached the lifeboat station.

'Any news?' he asked. The watch-master frowned and lowered his telescope. 'The boy in the rowing boat is Eliza's brother,' Amos explained.

The man's frowned deepened. 'Silly little fool should have been in school,' he muttered.

'He was,' Eliza cried. The man raised his bushy brows. 'I mean, he ran out of class.'

The man's expression softened slightly and he raised his telescope to his eye. 'Rescue boat's nearly alongside but that little craft's almost onto the rocks. Hang on.' There was a pause. 'One of my men's tying a rope round his waist. Yep, he's gone over the side. He's swimming towards the boat.'

There was another pause and Eliza felt Amos grip her hand.

'He's got the boy and the crew's dragging them back to the lifeboat. Now the men have hauled the boy over the lee side.'

'Thank heavens,' Eliza whispered.

'Oh, no,' the man gasped. 'Rope's snapped. Christ, that were a huge swell. Where's my man, where's my man . . .' he muttered. 'My man's been swept away,' he cried, turning an ashen face towards them.

'Oh, dear Lord, no. They've got to save him!' Eliza cried, wringing her hands.

They're doing their bloody best!'

'Easy, mate,' Amos said, patting the man's shoulder.

The watch-master nodded and raised his telescope again. There was a murmur amongst the crowd.

'Lifeboat's trying to row between the breakers, circling; surfing towards the rocks. Look-out is signalling they have to head back out to sea. Nothing! Damn.' The man fell silent.

'Can you see who's in the water?' asked Eliza, almost fainting with fear.

'This is only a blinking telescope,' the man muttered.

'Best be quiet,' Amos whispered in her ear. 'He won't tell us anything if you upset him.'

Eliza nodded but the wave of sickness was growing stronger, her insides heaving and churning like the sea before them. It was James in the water, she just knew it. *Please God let him be saved*, she mouthed silently. How could she have been so selfish, worrying about her own petty fears when he was risking his life to save others?

'Ah, something's bobbing up now. Yes, it's my man,' the watch-master cried, pointing towards the sea, some yards from the rocks. ''Tis that cork lifebelt what done it. Good job he had one on. Come on, boys, heave, heave,' the watch-master cried.

Peering into the distance, they could just make out the white-topped foam where the oars were hitting the water as the lifeboat circled again.

Dear God, please let them rescue him. I'll never question his volunteering again, I promise, Eliza prayed, peering out over the crashing waves.

'You're shivering, do you want to go back to the shop and wait?' Amos asked.

Too numb to speak, she shook her head.

'They've got him,' the watch-master muttered. 'By Jove, they've got him,' he shouted.

A cheer went up from the crowd and Eliza reeled with relief.

The lifeboat slowly made its way back towards them, sometimes disappearing out of sight between the swells, to the gasps of the onlookers. The wait seemed to last for ever. Finally, as they neared the shelter of the harbour, the shore crew rushed down ready to haul the boat onto the beach. As they assisted the exhausted men from the boat,

Eliza could wait no longer and sped down the beach towards them.

'James,' she cried.

He had Luke in his arms and wordlessly handed her the drowsy boy.

'Oh, James, I was so worried about you both. I'm so sorry for being difficult. If you can find it in your heart to forgive me, I promise I'll never make another fuss when the maroon goes up.'

He looked at her for a long moment, then smiled wearily before a man from the other crew led him away.

'Come on, let's get this fellow home,' Amos said gently, taking Luke from her. 'Didn't know you could run so fast, Eliza. That James sure must have something,' he teased. With a final look at the bedraggled group making its way towards the lifeboat station, she followed after him.

Nan and Grandfa Sam were waiting with warm water, towels and the ever-boiling kettle ready for tea. While Nan fussed over the still half-asleep Luke, Grandfa Sam took Eliza and Amos into the parlour.

'Now sit down beside the fire and tell me what happened,' he instructed, handing them their hot drinks. Briefly Amos gave him an outline of the rescue.

'You should be very proud of your grandson, sir,' he finished up.

'I am, of that you can be certain. Did you make your peace with James?' he asked, turning to Eliza.

'I just had time to apologize before he was led away.'

'Had to get out of those wet things, have something hot to drink and then a debrief, I guess. Poor chaps, bet all any of them wanted was to go home and get their heads down.'

'Would you mind if I turn in early?' Eliza asked, suddenly wanting to be alone.

'It's the best thing for shock. See you in the morning,' Grandfa Sam said.

'Night, Eliza,' Amos murmured. 'Tomorrow you will find the missing notes to that symphony, non?' Knowing he was trying to cheer her up, she smiled.

Nan was sitting on the edge of her bed watching Luke. 'He's asleep, the young wretch. What a scare he gave us,' she murmured. 'Are you all right?'

Eliza yawned. 'Just bone weary so I'm going to turn in.'

Nan got to her feet and, reaching up, gave Eliza a kiss on the cheek. 'Sleep tight. I'm just so thankful you're all safe.'

'Me too. I'm sorry we always seem to cause trouble, Nan,' she whispered.

''Tis life, my dear,' she murmured as she left the room.

Although Nan had pulled the curtains, it was still light outside and Eliza lay staring up at the ceiling, the events of the day going round and round her head. Supposing James hadn't been saved and she'd never had the chance to apologize? How could she have lived with herself? Had she even thanked him for saving Luke? And as for that scallywag, she'd have to be firmer with him; get someone to teach him to swim. Supposing the boat had capsized and he'd been thrown into the sea? It didn't bear thinking about. Whatever would she have done without Amos's steadying influence this afternoon? And what about poor Nan and Grandfa Sam? They didn't deserve all this upheaval and worry at their time of life. It was time she took charge of things, made sure they rested more.

Finally, her eyelids grew heavy and the last picture she had before she slept was that of James smiling at her. Tomorrow she would go and see him, thank him for rescuing Luke and try to make her peace properly.

40

Next morning over breakfast, Grandfa Sam lectured Luke about the previous day's escapade.

'Your thoughtlessness affected many people, young man. Firstly, those poor Sisters at the school were going frantic in case you'd had an accident. Then there was the anxiety you put poor Eliza, Nan and Amos through, not to mention the person whose boat you stole.'

'I never stealed nothing, I only borrowed it,' Luke argued.

'Without permission, so that is stealing. Then there's the question of the lifeboat crew and that man who risked his life jumping into the sea to save you. He could have drowned, had you thought of that?' Luke shook his head. 'And whilst the boat was out rescuing you, another vessel might have been in distress and what would have happened then?' Grandfa Sam asked, looking sternly at Luke.

'I never thought. Guess I'd better be getting off to school,' he said, anxious to get away.

'There'll be no school for you today, young man.'

'But you said I had to learn my sums and fings,' Luke protested.

'Indeed, that is the reason for going to school. However, you put the Sisters to a lot of trouble yesterday and I'm not sure they'll want you back.' Eliza stared at Grandfa

Sam in dismay but he shook his head. 'Amos needs help in the dispensary unloading and arranging new stock. Go downstairs and tell him I said you are to sweep the floors, dust and polish the shelves and then do anything he asks of you.'

'Yes, Grandfa Sam,' Luke muttered.

'And I shall be arranging for you to learn to swim in the very near future. Now be off with you,' Sam said, waving the boy away.

'The Sisters haven't really said they won't have him back, have they?' Eliza asked in dismay.

'No, of course not, but it'll do no harm to let him ponder on the effects of his misdemeanour. Now, are you all right this morning?'

'Yes, thank you, but I would like to go and see James during my noon break.'

'Well, as it's Saturday and our half day, you will be free to, won't you?' Grandfa said, his lips twitching.

'Oh, Grandfa, there's no school today anyway,' she laughed.

'Don't let on, and with any luck he'll be bursting to go to school in future. There's nothing like the threat of having something taken away for you to realize you want it after all.'

How right he was, Eliza thought, thinking of James.

'Now to business. Tomorrow we must go through your finances. Have you made a list of your requirements?'

Eliza nodded.

'Well, we can go through that tomorrow as well. Now, I'm sure you're anxious to get back to that concoction you began brewing yesterday,' he smiled.

'Thank you again for your generous offer of letting me rent half your shop. I'm still overwhelmed.'

'You do realize I'm looking to you and Amos to keep Nan and me in our dotage?' he laughed.

As she made her way downstairs, an idea popped into her head and she decided she'd discuss that with Grandfa Sam the next day as well.

Down in the shop, Eliza donned her apron and began breaking up the partly dried moss. She could hear Luke chatting away to Amos as he carried boxes back and forth and, relieved he was occupied, she settled down to her work.

All morning, between serving her customers, she distilled, inhaled, added, blended and inhaled again. Her glance kept going to the clock, though, as she could hardly contain her impatience to see James. But just before noon, she tested her final blend and let out a jubilant yell.

'What's up?' Amos asked, hurrying over to her work table.

'Smell this, I'm sure I'm on the right track now,' she cried, her eyes shining as she held out her mixing glass. He dipped in the paper, wafted it under his nose, inhaled then repeated the process.

'Well, well, well, that is almost a symphony,' he proclaimed.

'Almost?' she cried.

He grinned. 'Very almost.'

'It's still not quite right, though, is it?' she asked.

He shook his head. 'Look, where's that bottle you're always on about?'

Eliza scrabbled in her drawer and handed it to him. Taking off the top, he inhaled then went back to the testing paper and wafted it around first under one nostril and then the other to compare. 'Hmm, yours is close but heavier. The balance is wrong. That freshness needs to be more dominant. Your symphony, it needs to sing with the fresh notes, Mademoiselle,' he said, throwing his arms in the air as he imitated their old tutor.

'Come on, Amos, I've been waiting ages,' Luke called.

'Leave it for today and return to it fresh on Monday,' Amos grinned. 'Fresh, get it?'

'Yes, very funny,' she smiled.

'The plants will have completely dried out by then and your nose will have cleared. Oh well, better get back to the urchin before he finds more mischief to get up to. I shall be staying on this afternoon to get things sorted so you can leave him with me if you want to go and see James.'

'Thank you,' she said gratefully.

Hearing the clock chime the hour, Eliza cleared away her things. Then, after checking her appearance in the little glass on the wall, she went to the bottom of the stairs.

'I'm just going out,' she called. 'Luke is with Amos.'

Making her way through the busy town towards the cobbler's, she nervously rehearsed what she was going to say. Then, when she arrived, she stood dithering outside. Should she go in through the shop door or down the entry to the side one? Thinking the latter would be too personal, she stepped into the cool interior of the shop with its rich smell of leather, only to be confronted by old Mr Cary.

'Come to thank him for saving the boy's life, have ee? Well, he's out the back, but if you upset him you'll have me to answer to, got that?' he snarled, rubbing his cheek.

He turned back to his work and began hanging in a nail with unnecessary force.

Nervously, she pushed open the door to find James finishing his meal. As he looked up she saw his eyes were red with tiredness. The breath caught in her throat and she couldn't speak. Finally he broke the tension.

'Late breakfast,' he said, pointing to his empty plate. 'Slept the clock round,' he said ruefully.

'I'm not surprised after yesterday. I can't begin to thank you for what you did. If it wasn't for you, Luke could have been . . .'

'Well, he's not. Luckily I had the lifebelt on. They're vital in keeping us afloat yet they don't have enough to go round. Crazy, isn't it?' he shrugged. 'Anyhow, it was all part of the service, Eliza.'

'But you could have drowned and if that had happened and I hadn't apologized . . . Oh, this is coming out all wrong. I meant what I said yesterday. My behaviour has been selfish and unforgivable but if you can find it in your heart to forgive me, I really will try.'

He gave her a level look. 'You'd best be sure, for I'll not give up the boats,' he warned.

She nodded. 'If you can just give me another chance . . .' The rest of her sentence was muffled as James jumped up and threw his arms around her. Breathing in his familiar scent, she felt her senses race. It felt so right.

'Oh, Eliza, I've been so unhappy without you, especially when Father said you had other . . .'

'Now let's get one thing clear, James. I have not walked out with anyone else and I never will.'

He chuckled. 'No, Nan put me clear on that the other

afternoon. I should never have doubted you on that score,' he admitted, staring at her so tenderly her heart flipped. 'But with you working with that Amos . . . I mean, he's a handsome fellow and . . .' He shrugged.

'Amos is a fine fellow,' Eliza agreed. 'He makes me laugh but doesn't make my heart beat fast.'

James grinned. 'Eliza Dryad, will you do me the honour of walking out with me again?'

'I would be delighted to, James Cary,' she answered.

He beamed and, leaning forward, kissed her gently on her lips.

'Oh, James, I have so much to tell you,' she said, when the room finally stopped spinning.

'Let's go to Carla's and catch up on all our news,' he suggested. 'We'd better say goodbye to Father first, though,' he grinned, and held out his hand.

'You'll be pleased to know that Eliza and I have sorted out our differences and are walking out again, Father. We have a lot to catch up on so if you can spare me this afternoon, I'd be obliged. Of course, I'll make up the time tomorrow,' he added quickly as Mr Cary grunted.

'Go on, then. Nan told me off good and proper for jumping to conclusions, but just you make sure you treat him right, girl.'

'I will, Mr Cary, I promise,' Eliza assured him.

'Pleased to see you're walking better in them shoes.'

'Thank you so much, Mr Cary. They've truly made a tremendous difference. They're a fine piece of workmanship and I'm very grateful.'

Mr Cary nodded, then winced and put his hand to his face.

'Is something wrong, Mr Cary? Only I notice you keep rubbing your cheek,' Eliza asked.

'Bit of neuralgia, since you ask. Pains me something terrible,' he admitted.

'My grampy had that too. He used to grate horseradish and hold it to his temple. Swore it worked every time,' she offered.

'Bloomin' old wives' tale,' the man grunted, and turned back to his last.

Eliza looked at James but he shrugged and made his way outside.

The walk down back through the town was such a contrast to her earlier journey. Now she was aware of everything: James close by her side, the waves and tang of salt carried by the gentle onshore breeze. He grinned down at her and she felt her heart do that funny little skip again.

'Ah, my *bambini*,' Carla cried, as they stepped inside the little café. 'At last you have seen the sense. I so glad. True love, it does not run smooth.' She clutched her chest dramatically.

'We've missed you, Carla,' James declared. 'And your chocolatinas.'

'Two of Carla's specialities coming up. The making up is fun,' she said, giving them such a saucy wink, that Eliza felt her cheeks grow warm.

James laughed. 'Now tell me all your news. I know about young Luke, of course, and Nan made sure I understood Amos has been taken on to train as an apothecary,' he grinned, shamefaced.

'So much has happened, I don't know where to start,'

she said, nodding her thanks as Carla placed their drinks in front of them.

'Now I leave you for the lovey-dovey,' she giggled, wiggling her way back behind the counter.

'How about starting at the beginning,' James quipped.

Eliza nodded and told him about Duncan's visit, Fae's bequest and Grandfa Sam's offer to rent her Nan's part of the shop.

'So you're rich?'

'Hardly. What Fae left me was generous in the extreme, and will enable me to set up my perfumery in the shop and give something back to everyone as well. But I shall need to have an income. Nan kindly offered to give me her products but I insisted on paying her a fair price. I will still make a profit on sales and can use this whilst developing my perfume. And guess what? You remember that black bottle?'

James rolled his eyes. 'As if I could ever forget those evenings spent looking for flowers to match the scent in it.'

'James Cary, I thought you enjoyed our time together.'

He immediately became serious. 'Of course I did. Now what were you going to tell me about that bottle?'

'I think I've found the ingredients to recreate that fresh scent. When I've finally perfected it, I intend to call it Fae's Fragrance and sell it in little black bottles just like hers, with blue labels to match the stopper. It will be my way of honouring her and thanking her for all she taught me. Or does that sound stupid?'

'I think it sounds amazing, and so are you,' he said, his eyes lighting up.

'I'm so pleased you're happy,' she said, feeling her face growing hot once more.

'Oh, I am. Now we can spend our time together doing sensible things rather than collecting blooming plants,' he replied.

Next morning, Eliza sat at the table in the parlour with Grandfa Sam, watching as he showed her how to enter things in the ledger. He explained about business practices and asked to see the list of equipment she'd made out.

'Doesn't seem too unreasonable,' he commented, running his finger down all the items. 'By my reckoning you should be able to buy these, pay your first month's rent and still have some put by. I take it black bottles are essential?'

'Most definitely. I want them to be a tribute to Fae, you see.'

'Commendable, and it could also be a good trade symbol to distinguish you from your competitors. That's important, too. However, I would recommend you buy the smaller size ones first to see how that perfume sells. Is that agreeable to you?'

'Yes, that makes good sense, Grandfa Sam. Thank goodness I have you to advise me.'

The old man smiled. 'Well, we'll see Mr Sharp at the bank on Tuesday and get his professional advice,' he said, snapping the ledger shut.

Eliza opened her mouth then shut it again.

'Got something on your mind?' Grandfa Sam asked, shrewd as ever.

'I'd like to make a donation to the lifeboats,' she

answered. 'James mentioned they desperately need more cork lifebelts and I would like to use some of my legacy to buy some.'

'I think that's an admirable idea, Eliza,' Nan said, coming into the room.

'It is, but your legacy, while generous, is not a huge amount, and you will need a fair bit of it to set up your perfumery,' Grandfa Sam pointed out. 'When you first start a business your outgoings exceed your income, and you will need to have some put by to live on.'

'I know, but I would like to give them something. Grampy always said if you had three pennies then you should spend one, share one and save the remaining one.'

'Quite right too,' Nan applauded.

'You're not doing this to curry favour with James?' Grandfa asked, staring directly at her with wise eyes.

'Of course I'm not. I don't even want him to know. Donations are anonymous, aren't they? Besides, if you give it to them, nobody will be any the wiser,' she said.

Sam was silent for a few moments. 'In that case, I will make the appropriate arrangements and get them to issue a receipt so that you have an audit trail. That's another thing you need to understand. Everything you spend, purchase or sell must be accounted for in the ledger.'

Exhausted from recent events, yet excited by the future, Eliza curled up on her bed and flicked through the notes she'd brought with her from Monsieur Farrant.

A light, fresh, delicate fragrance can be centred round the top note . . . may contain less base notes than a heavier one. Consider . . . citrus for freshness The character of the finished fragrance will be determined by the proportions of each . . . Blend can be what you choose . . . Experiment until your nose tells you it is right. Remember the *je ne sais quoi*! Once you have learned the rules, you can then begin breaking them.

Of course! She'd been concentrating on the base and blindly adhering to the rules. As she mentally sniffed her way through the different plants and flowers she'd tried, something Nan had said clicked in her mind. Hurrying downstairs, she snatched up her basket and made her way to the undercliff where she'd picked the yellow flowering plants earlier in the year. Now they'd deepened to orange and were bearing berries. Sea berries, Nan had called them. Splitting one open, she inhaled, then smiled. It just might work!

Her first attempts came close to the smell in the bottle, but were still not perfect. Knowing she was on the right track, she continued experimenting until she was boggy-eyed from concentrating.

Determined not to give up, she spent the next week refining the proportions of her *je ne sais quoi*, until, finally, she managed to recreate the fresh, invigorating aroma she'd been seeking. James was busy with his training and she was feeling so much better now they'd made up she could concentrate fully again.

Thank heavens Grandfa Sam had advised buying small bottles otherwise she'd never manage to make enough, Eliza thought, as she lined them up ready for filling. In her mind, it had already become the Fae Sea Breeze Fragrance and eagerly she began scripting the blue labels. One day she might be able to afford jewel-blue stoppers too, she daydreamed. Only when the perfume was bottled and labelled, did she let the others test the fragrance.

'Well done, Eliza, you have finally found the last note to finish your symphony,' Amos beamed.

With Nan's help, she added the Sea Breeze fragrance to the soaps, salts and salves for sale in her shop. Her artistic window display of little black bottles nestling in beds of shiny green moss surrounded by bright orange sea berries aroused great interest. She continually had to replenish the tester flagons depleted by ladies eager to sample the new scent. Even customers visiting the dispensary were intrigued, many leaving with little bottles of the perfume or soaps alongside their tablets or embrocation.

As word of the new fragrance spread, ladies visiting Salting Regis or staying on holiday were drawn into the fragrant little shop, often leaving with gifts for friends as well as purchases for themselves.

'Suppose I'll have to book an appointment to see you now?' James moaned good-naturedly, after he'd had to wait whilst Eliza wrapped yet another customer's purchases.

'Oh, James, I'm sorry. I had no idea these summer months would be so busy. I'm sure it will quieten down in the autumn and then we'll have more time to ourselves.'

'Don't knock it, Eliza. You make the most of it. Grandfa Sam was saying only yesterday that with you turning over a good profit and Amos doing well in his training, it won't be long before he can put his feet up in style. By the way, we had a surprise of our own today. Six new lifebelts were delivered to the lifeboat station. Six! That's going to make such a difference to the men's safety.'

'Oh, I am pleased,' Eliza said, clapping her hands. James looked at her with eyes of the same shrewd blue as his grandfather's.

'Don't suppose you have any idea where they came from?' he asked.

'Me?' she asked, feigning surprise. 'It's good to know the men will have some protection, though, isn't it?'

'It is,' he agreed, his lips twitching. 'I guess you're so busy these days you would hardly notice when the maroon's fired.'

Eliza kept quiet, for hadn't she promised she wouldn't stand in his way or make a fuss? The trouble was, the stronger her feelings for him became, the worse she felt.

41

One morning Eliza had just turned the sign to open when the shop door burst open.

'So, Mademoiselle, you think you can rival Monsieur Farrant's sublime perfume-making skills?'

As his weird smell pervaded her space, Eliza took a step back. If only he could do something about his own particular brand, she thought, forcing her lips into a smile.

'Good morning, Monsieur Farrant, how may I be of help?' she asked.

But he ignored her, lifted the stopper from the tester flagon and wafted it round in front of him. Inhaling deeply, he stared at her over the glass tube, his eyes narrowing. 'You never made this?' he barked, all pretence of his French persona disappearing.

'Indeed I did,' Eliza protested, her voice rising. He stared at Fae's pictures that Grandfa Sam had framed and hung on the walls behind the counter.

'Those are Miss Beaumont's pictures. I recognize her style from the receipt book. So, you did keep some of her receipts and used one to make this fragrance,' he accused, leaning over the counter and waving the tube in front of her, nearly sending a dish of soaps flying in the process.

'No, my perfume is my own receipt,' she cried.

'Is everything all right, Eliza?' Amos asked, hurrying over from the dispensary.

Monsieur Farrant stared at him in surprise. 'So, it is a conspiracy,' he hissed. 'You think you can steal my business? Well, let me tell you, Monsieur Farrant, he is the one wanting the warrant from the Queen and he is the one who will get it. Your little business, it will go pouf,' he said, waving his hands in the air.

'I think . . .' Eliza began, but he was already storming out of the shop.

'Remember, there is no smoke without fire,' he warned, pausing on the doorstep and shaking his finger at them.

'Pompous idiot,' Amos said. 'Take no notice. He's obviously jealous.'

'But how did he know about my perfume and why has he sought me out after all this time?' she asked, clutching the counter for support. 'He gave up before.'

'Ah, but now you are hitting him where it hurts most, Eliza – in his pocket. Everyone is talking about your perfume, saying it smells like an energizing sea breeze. My landlady was telling me only the other night that her daughter, who lives in Bath, has asked her to take two bottles of your uplifting scent when she visits at Christmas.'

'Energizing perfume? Great heavens, I'd never thought of it like that,' she replied, automatically rearranging the soaps in her dish on the counter. Then the little bell tinkled and, snapping into business mode, she turned to greet the customer.

'Good morning, my dear, I'm sure you will remember me. ' Eliza stared at the well-dressed woman, something about her overdone appearance chiming in the recesses of her mind.

'Of course, madam, how lovely to see you again,' Eliza

gushed, deeming deference the reaction someone of her stature would expect.

'Last year, when I was looking for a Christmas present for my future daughter-in-law, Daphne, you were particularly helpful.' At the mention of the name, a chord struck.

'Of course, madam, and I seem to remember you were most generous in your choice. I trust she liked her green velvet-lined box tied with that gorgeous gold bow?'

The woman's face lit up. 'You do remember, clever girl. Daphne was indeed impressed. In fact, her gift was the talk of the town. Therefore, I would like you to make up boxes of the new perfume I have heard so much about, along with all the matching products. I take it you are still offering the same service?'

'Indeed, madam,' Eliza assured, her spirits soaring. This year she would be able to buy quality material and ribbons, and really go to town with her wrappings.

'Good. I know it's early to be thinking of Christmas, but we shall be over-wintering *en famille* in warmer climes, so if you could have ten boxes made up in varying coloured materials, all with elaborate bows, I'll have Jenson call to collect them in a week's time. I shall, of course, give him the means by which to settle my account. Present buying *en masse* can be such a headache and I can't tell you what a relief it is to have everything sorted in one go. Good day to you.' She swept from the shop, leaving Eliza staring after her. An order for ten boxes might be remarkable but it had made Eliza realize she was nowhere near ready for the lead-in to Christmas, as Monsieur Farrant had called it.

Hearing a chuckle behind her, she turned to see Nan grinning.

'Well, you've started something there, Eliza. I reckon you're going to be busier than ever once people see your pretty boxes displayed in the window.'

Eliza gulped. 'But I haven't even begun to organize things,' she said, grimacing as she stared round at her rapidly diminishing stock.

'Want a hand?' Nan asked.

Eliza brightened then frowned. 'But you're meant to be retired, Nan.'

'Pah, I'm bored stiff idling my time away upstairs alone. Decide what materials you want and I'll go to the market later this morning.' She glanced over at the grandmother clock in the hallway. 'It's almost ten o'clock, let's go upstairs and draw a plan of action over a pot of tea. We will hear the bell jangle if someone comes in,' she said, bustling towards the stairs.

Heads together, they discussed which colours would best complement the little black bottles of perfume, jars of salts and tablets of soaps. Eliza wanted something festive yet reminiscent of the sea, and they settled on turquoise with coral for the different lining materials then silver and gold ribbons for contrasting bows. Over a second cup of tea, they decided what sizes of boxes they would use and the pricing of them. Then Nan snatched up her basket and happily took herself off, leaving Eliza to work out how much extra stock they'd need. As she worked, she couldn't help thinking about Farrant's threats. He blew hot and cold so she just hoped they'd been empty ones.

With her plan worked out, she discussed it with Grandfa Sam over supper. Although she'd taken delivery of her new equipment some weeks before and could distil in larger quantities, she now required more plant material. With the promise of extra pocket money provided he behaved, Luke was dispatched at the weekend, under the watchful eye of Sam, to gather as much as he could.

Meanwhile, Nan undertook the lining and making up of the boxes. Mindful of people's differing means, these ranged from small ones containing a couple of soaps, to the largest which included every product in the Fae Fragrance range. Then they set to, stocking shelves and arranging the window. Keen to keep to the seaside theme, Eliza set the festive boxes around a mirror to depict water then sat little mermaid figurines on pebbles and shells in the middle. Finally she draped an old fisherman's net, entwined with the sea berries Nan had crystallized, around the sides.

The artistic display soon drew attention from people walking by and the shop bell tinkled constantly. The uplifting fragrance of sea breezes wafting around the shop was pleasing to the customers, enticing them to linger longer and to buy. At times it was hard keeping up with the demand.

Sam joked it was turning into a family affair, for even Amos found himself serving more in the shop than the dispensary, while James helped replenish the shelves in his spare time.

'I think Mr Sharp is going to be very pleased with your takings this month, young lady,' Grandfa Sam chuckled one evening. He'd just finished entering the figures in the ledger and stood there rubbing his hands together with glee.

'Yes, but I must pay you all a wage after all that hard work,' Eliza pointed out.

'Stuff and nonsense,' Nan scoffed. 'That's what families are for.'

'Oh, Grandfa Sam, you don't know how much that means to me. To hear you referring to me as family is like a dream come true.' A lump filled her throat as she stared at them all.

'Yes, well, let's go upstairs and have supper,' Grandfa Sam said gruffly. 'You joining us, Amos?'

'No, thanks, Mrs Nell's got a nice pie waiting for me. Couldn't ask for a better landlady,' he winked.

Although they were tired, the meal was convivial as they relaxed and discussed the events of the day.

'Who would have thought our little shop would be so busy?' Nan commented, stifling a yawn.

'You go and sit by the fire, Nan, while I clear away,' Eliza said, collecting their dishes together.

She carried them through to the little scullery, poured water into the bowl and added flakes. Too tired to do any more, she left the dishes to drain. It had been a long day and she was looking forward to putting her feet up and relaxing.

Making her way down the hall, she stopped in her tracks. What was that smell? She sniffed, went to the top of the stairs and sniffed again. Smoke! Without stopping to think, she hurried down the stairs and gasped. Flames were licking at the door.

'Fire!' she screamed, snatching up a rug from the floor.

'Here, give that to me,' James ordered, bursting in

through the shop door and taking her by surprise. 'Saw the smoke from the street,' he gasped, throwing the rug over the fire. 'Quick, get that other one.'

When both rugs had been thrown on top of the flames, they stamped on them and then stood back and watched. After a few minutes, when nothing happened, Eliza went to lift the rugs to have a look.

'Leave those there,' James instructed. 'Lifting them might cause a draught and fan the flames back into life. Luckily, I don't think the fire had time to do much damage. Are you all right?' he asked, placing his arm around her trembling shoulders.

'Yes . . . Monsieur Farrant came here threatening to set fire to our business. You don't think this was his work, do you?' she whispered.

'I shall make it my business to find out,' James assured her.

'What's going on?' Grandfa Sam asked, shuffling into the room. 'I heard shouting but it took me so long to get down those dratted stairs.'

'Been a bit of a fire, Grandfa,' James said, pointing to the charred rugs. 'It's out now but I'll keep an eye on it just in case. You go back upstairs and tell Nan there's nothing to worry about. Make sure young Luke doesn't come down, though. Go on, before Eliza has us restocking her shelves,' he teased, when the older man hesitated.

'No chance of that tonight. What a good job you were passing, James. It could have been so much worse,' she muttered, staring around the shop filled with their precious Christmas stock.

'You look all in. Go upstairs to bed. I'll stay here and

make sure everything's safe,' he said, putting his arm around her and gently kissing her cheek.

'I can't just leave you here,' she argued, stifling a yawn.

'You'll be no use tomorrow if you don't get some rest,' he pointed out, pushing her towards the stairs. 'Sleep tight and I'll see you in the morning. Don't worry, I'll snatch some sleep on Grandfa's consultation couch,' he grinned.

It was only after she'd climbed into bed that she remembered there wasn't any couch in the dispensary. Too exhausted to get up again, she closed her eyes and fell into a heavy sleep. She dreamed of huge balls of fire rolling around the shop, bouncing over the counter, until the whole place was a mass of blazing red and orange.

Unsurprisingly, she was late rising the next morning so that by the time she went downstairs James had gone home and Grandfa Sam was deep in conversation with Amos.

'Seems like someone had it in for us,' Grandfa Sam said, holding up two strips of burned rag. 'James reckoned these were doused in paraffin and thrown in through the door. Of course, it would normally have been locked by that time, but we've all been working late and . . .' He shrugged but he was obviously anxious.

As Eliza looked at his ashen face, anger rose up inside her like a roaring dragon.

She'd make that fiend pay if it was the last thing she did. Her thoughts were so vivid she was sure she'd spoken them aloud but Amos was still staring around the shop.

'There doesn't appear to be too much damage,' he said. 'Only the rugs that were used to contain the flames and

James took those out to the yard. He also cleaned up the floor while keeping an eye out for anything suspicious. You haven't noticed anybody loitering outside, have you?' Grandfa Sam asked. Amos shook his head. 'Well, keep a lookout, we don't want any repetition.'

'Do you think it'll happen again?' Eliza asked, vowing to keep watch for any sign of Farrant.

'It might,' Grandfa Sam sighed. 'The best thing is not to mention this to anyone and carry on as usual. Waft some of that perfume of yours around to disguise any lingering smell of smoke. Amos, you keep an eye on the dispensary and help Eliza in the shop if things get busy. I'm going up for a rest.' Eliza watched as Sam shuffled up the stairs and felt a pang. He looked exhausted and really didn't need this extra worry.

'Don't worry, I'll keep an eye out for Farrant,' Amos assured her. 'Let's get cleared up so we can open for business.'

While Amos attended to the dispensary, Eliza quickly washed the sills of the windows and the doorframe with scented soap, then sprinkled a few drops of perfume on the displays. As the aroma of sea breezes wafted around the little shop, she felt her spirits begin to lift. Taking a good look about, she was surprised that, apart from the bare floors, there was nothing to show there had even been a fire.

Then, as the little bell tinkled and the morning rush of customers hunting for Christmas gifts began, she became too busy to reflect on the previous evening's events. Half-way through the morning, she was reaching up to get one of the boxes from the shelf when a shadow blocking the light caused her to look up. Monsieur Farrant was staring in through the window, his lips curled in annoyance. Fire flared up inside her again and, calling to Amos to take over, she ran outside. Seeing her, Monsieur Farrant gave her a sneer and began walking away.

'Stop right there, Farrant,' she ordered, oblivious to the curious stares of people passing by.

Surprised by her strident tones, he paused. 'You wish something from me, Mademoiselle?' he smirked, sending his shiny moustache quivering like a beetle's antennae.

'I know you were responsible for last night's fire . . .'

'That is preposterous. The fire in your shop, why it could have been caused by anyone,' he said, shrugging.

'Ah, so you admit there was a fire?'

'Well, yes, you just said so, did you not?'

'I never said where it was,' she pointed out.

'You think you are clever but you have no proof,' he hissed, moving closer. The smell of his peculiar odour wafting her way galvanized her into action.

'I think the police would be interested to hear . . .'

'As I said, you have no proof of your outrageous allegation,' he said, moving away.

'But I am sure they would be very interested to hear about your night-time visitors to the perfumery and what goes on in that building at the bottom of the garden.' He stopped dead. 'I saw it all with my own eyes the night I left.'

'You wouldn't dare,' he blustered, fear sparking in his eyes.

'Try me,' she challenged, staring him straight in the face. 'There are enough people here to witness what I've just said.'

He stared around in horror, suddenly aware of the attention they were attracting. Cursing her to hell and damnation, he turned and hurried away.

'If you ever show your face round here again I shall make sure everyone hears about your nightly activities,' she called after him for good measure. He broke into a run, his coat-tails flapping like sails in his wake.

'What's going on?' James asked, appearing by her side. 'I was just leaving the lifeboat station and heard you shouting. Then I saw Farrant haring up the street like the devil was after him.'

At his choice of words Eliza couldn't help but burst out laughing.

42

Sensing they were being watched, Eliza looked up to find Nan beckoning from the upstairs window.

'Come on, Nan's itching to know what's been going on,' she said, pulling James back into the shop. 'I'll put you both out of your misery over one of her cure-all cuppas.'

'Are you all right, Eliza?' Amos asked, looking up. 'That customer I was with dithered so long I couldn't come and help.'

'All sorted,' she said, rubbing her hands together. 'From now on, Monsieur Farrant will be nothing but an annoying fly on some distant turd.' As Amos and James exchanged shocked looks, she chuckled. 'Don't worry about it, boys. That was the most satisfying experience of my life. Come on, James, let's go and have that tea. You all right to watch the shop?' she asked Amos, who smiled and nodded.

'Take as long as you like. I've got to make sure the medicine ledger tallies before I can go home for Christmas. It's a dog's life,' he moaned good-naturedly.

'Better than being a fly on a turd, though, eh?' James grinned, slapping him on the back.

'Well, you certainly told that pompous-looking little man,' Nan chuckled, as they entered into the parlour.

'How do you know?' Eliza asked in surprise.

'I just happened to be shaking my duster out of the window,' she shrugged.

Grandfa Sam snorted. 'You had your face half out of the window, woman. I tell you, Eliza, if that man had put a step wrong she'd have been out there with her poker.' Eliza smiled at Nan, for hadn't she said the self-same thing on her first day in the shop when Eliza had been worried Monsieur Farrant might come looking for her?

'I told you Nan and Grandfa would look after you, didn't I?' James said.

'Yes, and you've all been so kind to me,' she said, relaxing back in her seat and staring around the cosy room. 'And one day I intend making it all up to you. I shall pay . . .' She broke off as Nan shook her head.

'There's really no need. As I keep saying, that's what families are about,' Grandfa Sam smiled. 'Now, what was that all about outside, eh?'

Briefly Eliza told him, adding, 'That perverted little creep will never bother us again, of that I am certain.'

'Remind me never to get on the wrong side of you, Eliza,' James laughed. 'You scared the living daylights out of me, the way you were shaking your fists and looking so ferocious.'

'Happen you'll have to behave yourself then, our James,' Nan chortled, pouring more tea into their cups.

'Talking of behaving oneself, where's young Luke?' Grandfa Sam asked.

'He's tidying his side of the bedroom,' Nan said.

'Now I've heard everything. How did you manage that?' Eliza gasped.

'Bribery, I would imagine,' Grandfa Sam said, grinning as Luke bounded into the room.

'I've finished, so what's my surprise?' he asked.

'Sit down beside me, boy, and I'll tell you.' Grandfa Sam waited until Luke had settled at his feet then he leaned forward. 'As you know it's nearly Christmas,' he began, 'and that man with the sleigh, what's his name now . . .?' He stroked his chin, pretending he'd forgotten.

'You mean Father Christmas,' Luke said.

'That's right. Well, at the moment he is loading his sleigh with presents and . . .'

'That ain't no good, he never comes to us,' Luke cut in. 'Father said he only visits rich houses where they leave him things to eat and drink.'

Grandfa Sam looked taken aback.

'Well, I've news for you, young man,' Nan said. 'Here in Salting Regis, Father Christmas visits all girls and boys who have been good.'

Luke eyed her warily. 'You kiddin' me, missus?'

'Luke,' Eliza warned, but Nan smiled.

'No, I'm not. So have you been good?'

'Blimey, I've bin an angel,' he assured her. Eliza smiled. With his spiky hair, grimy face and ripped shirt anything less like an angel she'd yet to see. 'Why, I've bin collecting that seaweed and stuff for ever and ever.'

'Indeed you have, so you'll have to think what you'd like that man in red to bring you,' Grandfa Sam agreed.

As Eliza sat watching them, her heart filled with warmth. Did she dare to think she'd be spending this Christmas with the people she loved and that it might be filled with happiness?

'What about you, Eliza? Do you know what you want?' Sam asked.

Eliza smiled and nodded. There was only one thing she'd ever wanted but it hadn't come true yet and she wasn't about to put a jinx on it by voicing her wish aloud. She turned to look at James and as he smiled back she thought she should amend her list to two wishes.

'Well, I know what I want,' James said, staring into her eyes until she felt her cheeks grow warm.

Eliza woke early on Christmas morning, a sense of anticipation and excitement bubbling up inside her. Luke was already up and she could hear him chatting excitedly to Nan in the scullery. She loved having her little brother around and now things had settled down she was going to try to contact her sisters. Dear Nan and Grandfa Sam had showed her the real value of family life and she was determined to follow their example.

Sitting up in bed, she reached for her treasures, which lined the table beside her. What a year it had been, she thought, stroking the smooth wood of her box then lifting the lid and peering at her mementoes stored safely inside. Silently, she sent up a prayer for her dear departed grampy, mother and brother, and for Duncan, who had so carefully restored the box. Nan had said she could invite him to spend Christmas with them, but Eliza knew in her heart he'd have felt like a caged tiger cooped up in their small home. To think she'd once believed herself in love with him. How patiently he'd tolerated her infatuation, she thought, shaking her head at her childish notions.

Next she picked up Fae's receipt book and thumbed through it until she came to the last page, which was blank. Carefully she penned in the ingredients for Sea Breeze.

'There, your book is complete now, Fae. Merry Christmas, and be happy, wherever you are,' she whispered. 'If only you'd told me you used to live by the sea, it would have saved me hours of searching.'

Undoing the top of the little black bottle, she inhaled its lingering smell. 'I hope you are able to see how I've used your legacy and that you approve.' It might have been her imagination, but the scent seemed to grow stronger, the room warmer, bathing her in a rosy glow of contentment.

Shaking herself back to the present, she replaced her treasures, then put on the lovely dress Nan had made for her birthday, along with the shoes James and Mr Cary had crafted for her. Then, tying her hair up in a peach ribbon she'd bought in the market, she went through to the scullery.

'Merry Christmas, Nan,' she said, kissing the woman's cheek. 'What can I do to help?'

'Merry Christmas, Eliza dear. Everything's done. This young scamp woke me in the small hours to see if Father Christmas had been. I told him before we could find out he had to help me prepare the vegetables.'

Luke grinned at Eliza, through chocolate-coated lips.

'And he's been well rewarded for his efforts, I see,' she laughed.

'We're just waiting for Grandfa Sam and then we can go through to the parlour. Ah, here he is now.'

'Merry Christmas, Grandfa Sam,' Eliza said.

'And season's greetings to you,' he responded. 'Right, if everyone's ready, shall we go through and see if Father Christmas has been?'

'Yes,' shouted Luke, just as James appeared, followed by Mr Cary.

'I'm so glad you came, Jimmy,' Nan cried, holding out her arms in welcome.

James grinned at Eliza and kissed her cheek.

'Merry Christmas,' he whispered. 'I made it this year.'

'I should hope so, seeing as you only live on the other side of town now,' she replied.

'We still had to battle through the snow, though,' he teased, brushing white flakes from his sleeve.

'Hurry up, we need to see if he's been,' Luke cried, jumping up and down as he tugged at Grandfa Sam's arm.

'Come on then,' he said, theatrically throwing open the parlour door.

'Oh,' Eliza gasped, shaking her head in disbelief. A beautiful tree adorned with myriad twinkling candles stood on a table in the window. Holly and ivy festooned the picture rails and the dining table, covered in a snowy cloth, was beautifully set with silver cutlery and sparkling glasses. The logs crackling in the grate sounded homely, its warmth contrasting against the snow falling outside. 'That all looks quite beautiful.'

'As do you,' James whispered in her ear, sending tingles down her spine.

'Blimey, we never had a tree before,' Luke exclaimed. Then he saw the brightly wrapped presents nestling beneath it. 'Father Christmas has been,' he cried, beside himself with excitement.

Eliza smiled at his animated face, then at James, who smiled knowingly in return.

'There's just one thing missing,' he said, handing Eliza

a little parcel. 'Go on, open it.' Folding back the paper, she saw a little fairy doll, complete with halo and silver wings. 'Every Christmas tree needs a fairy on the top to bring good luck. Fae means fairy in folklore, so I thought it appropriate,' he explained.

'Oh, James, she's wonderful,' Eliza whispered.

Only James could have chosen this perfect gift, she thought, carefully placing it on the highest branch. Breathing in the scent of Christmas, she blinked back tears of happiness and smiled at the people who meant so much to her. Never before had she experienced such feelings of warmth and contentment. Then, as James leaned forward and kissed her lightly on the lips, she felt her insides fizzing like bubbles in champagne.

Surrounded by love, joy and good cheer, her wish for a happy family Christmas had finally come true.

Acknowledgements

To Teresa Chris, with grateful thanks for her continued encouragement and pearls of wisdom. All at Penguin for their support and guidance. John Stephens at Cotswold Perfumery for a fascinating insight into the world of fragrance. I am so grateful for his advice and guidance and any mistakes are totally mine.